ARCTIC
FLOOR

ARCTIC
FLOOR

ARCTIC FLOOR

MARK AITKEN

This edition published in 2012
First published in 2011

Arena Books, an imprint of
Allen & Unwin
Sydney, Melbourne, Auckland, London

83 Alexander Street
Crows Nest NSW 2065
Australia
Phone: (61 2) 8425 0100
Fax: (61 2) 9906 2218
Email: info@allenandunwin.com
Web: www.allenandunwin.com

Cataloguing-in-Publication details are available
from the National Library of Australia
www.trove.nla.gov.au

ISBN 978 1 74331 068 7

Typeset in Joanna MT by Midland Typesetters, Australia
Printed and bound in Australia by the SOS Print & Media Group

10 9 8 7 6 5

For Sally and Euan

CHAPTER 1

Gallen switched to whisky when the band started its second set. The drink burned down behind the beer, warming him against the cold seeping through the concrete floor. From his corner of the ballroom he watched soldiers trying to boogie around Tyler Richards, who was moving his wheelchair to a version of 'Start Me Up'.

'Still say he gotta get hisself a better lawyer,' said Bren Dale, pushing himself back with a big cowboy boot on the edge of the table. 'Shit, Washington always sends a rejection first up. Daddy knew that from back in the Nam.'

Looking around at the streamers and balloons, Gallen shrugged. Brendan Dale had been a first-rate sergeant when they served together in Afghanistan but the booze made him repeat himself. What no one at this shindig wanted to say was that former specialist first-class Tyler Richards had finished his tour and was on leave when he polished off two quarts of rye and drove his '68 Impala off a bridge out of Torrington, near the Nebraska state line.

'He'd be happy for the benefits and the pension,' said Gallen, sipping the whisky and nodding at Richards. 'Wasn't like he was in line for a disability, 'less you count that bridge on eighty-five as an enemy position.'

1

'Shit, cap'n,' said Dale, feet thumping on concrete as he sat upright. 'The man got a new wife and a little baby. He weren't discharged, still with the Corps.'

'So was Nyles,' said Gallen, throwing back the drink and standing. 'And most of his leg's still in Marjah.'

'Still, it's no use being such a hard-ass to Richards. Not now.'

'I wrote to the appeals board,' said Gallen, irritated that his field image had followed him into civvie life. 'But there wasn't much to say.'

'What about that he served his country? That he went the extra yard for his crew? That he saved our asses on that highway ambush in oh-seven? That worth saying?'

'I wrote that, Bren,' said Gallen, trying to avoid Dale's eyes. Bren Dale was strictly loyal to Gallen in front of the men but, like most sergeants in the Marines, he reserved the right to speak his mind in private.

'You write that we all drunks now, after that shit?' Dale threw a thumb over his shoulder. 'That it takes a quart just to get through the day?'

'No,' said Gallen, moving away. 'I didn't write that.'

Feeling Dale's eyes on his back as he crossed the dark dance floor, Gallen saw the women bunched around a table. Flabby middle-aged Mae Richards, telling the story of her son to anyone who would listen, and Phoebe Richards, holding a baby across her lap, staring at her husband who was now trying to make his wheelchair wiggle to 'Band on the Run'.

'Early start tomorrow.' Gallen leaned over Phoebe. 'I'm cuttin' out.'

The woman didn't take her eyes off the dance floor, just nodded at the seat beside her.

Gallen pulled an envelope from the inside pocket of his windbreaker and handed it over, wondering if the IRS staked out events like this. The envelope disappeared without a thank you.

'You spoken with him lately, Captain Gallen?' said the woman, a skinny redneck girl with a piercing in her lip and an Aries glyph tattooed on her neck.

'Please, call me Gerry.'

'Well, have you?' She turned to him. 'Gerry?'

'Seen him a couple times at Elkhorn,' said Gallen, meaning the rehab hospital in Casper. 'Not lately though.'

Phoebe sucked on her cigarette too hard. Gallen looked at his watch—11.06 pm. He wanted to time his exit before Richards' mom started in on him. For many people in rural America, a former captain in the US Marines was as close to Washington DC's officialdom as they'd ever get, and Gallen could sense a sermon in Mae Richards.

'Well,' he said, rising to go.

'I want you to talk to him, Gerry.'

'He looks happy to me,' said Gallen.

'Oh, really,' she said. 'So why'd he try killing hisself?'

The cold came up through Gallen's boots as he crossed the tarmac of the East Side Motel, a salesmen's stopover on the outskirts of Red Butte, south of Casper.

Walking past his truck he was reminded of tomorrow morning's drive north, where he was picking up two horses and taking them back to the ranch to condition them for a season of showjumping. His father hated jumpers but no one paid quite like the showjumping crowd.

Marijuana smoke drifted in the stillness as Gallen hit the stairs to his room on the upper deck. In the cast of the motel neon he could see a man partying with a woman in the back of a red Cutlass; it was former corporal Donny McCann, a man the rest of Gallen's Force Recon team once relied on in the hills and mountain passes of northern Afghanistan. In their typical vehicle patrols—two Humvees, eight men—McCann operated a .50-cal turret gun on the second Humvee, the vehicle that was usually targeted by sniper fire and rocket attacks. Under the incoming, McCann would lay down enough fire to allow Gallen's men to take cover and counter the attack. He was a hound with the ladies but totally stand-up in a fight.

Easing into his room, Gallen went to the bathroom and washed his face with cold water. He wasn't drunk but his hands were shaking slightly. Wiping off with the towel, he looked himself in the eye: a full freaking six months out of the Corps and these people still called him Captain, still sought his leadership. The fundraiser for Tyler

3

Richards followed the one he'd attended in February down in Mobile for Joe Nyles: Joe had the full disability and compensation package because of his combat injuries but his wife said there was only one way the two kids could get to college and that was to bank twenty grand in a fund and let it mature. Gallen had driven down, stayed in a motel slightly better than the East Side, and got hammered with his old crew before passing the wife his envelope and wandering out of their lives. Military service was like that—it gave you a family you knew better than the one you grew up with. And once you knew what a scared, cold man said in his sleep, you knew him too well to ever turn your back.

Wandering back into the living area, Gallen turned off the bedside lamp and edged to the side of the window. Finding a chink where the curtain didn't quite meet the window frame, he positioned himself and looked down on the car park.

The red Cutlass emitted wafts of smoke from the slightly cracked front passenger window. Gallen couldn't see the cars directly beneath his room—they were blocked by the balcony—but he could see the car that had caught his attention on the far side of the parking lot. It wasn't just that it faced Gallen's room while the rest of the line were nose-in. It was also the make and model: a dark Crown Vic with car-pool tyres and a lack of detail. Gallen didn't like it.

Grabbing a set of binoculars from his overnight bag Gallen let the auto focus clarify the interior of the vehicle. It wasn't the best picture because the glasses wanted to focus on the curtains, but he could see two men sitting in the front of the car; no cigarettes, no movement. Nondescript white guys, perhaps middle-aged, looking straight at him.

Gallen focused on the Colorado plate and made a note of the numbers.

Were they really looking at him? Reaching sideways as he kept his binoculars on the car, he turned the handle on the door and pulled it open slightly. Before the door was more than four inches ajar, the passenger in the Crown Vic slapped the driver's chest and the driver's posture changed.

Pulling a pack of Marlboros from his pocket, Gallen threw the field-glasses on the bed and stepped onto the balcony. Lighting

4

the smoke, he avoided looking straight at the car. If the surveillance was innocent, someone could step out of the car, call out *Hey, Gerry* or *Excuse me, are you Gerry Gallen?*

By the time he was halfway through the smoke, Gallen's pulse beat at his temples. The approach was clandestine, the men in the car were shrinking further into the shadows. Plunging his smoke into the sand box beside the door, he returned to the room, just a motel guest having a cigarette before bed.

Turning on the TV and the bedside lamp, Gallen got to his knees and crawled to his overnight bag on the bed, found his farrier's penknife complete with hoof picks and a Phillips screwdriver.

Crawling to the bathroom, he stood and set to work on the screws that held the security screen in place over the lavatory. Standing on the toilet seat, he removed the security screen, slid back the six frosted-glass slats and placed them on the security screen now sitting on the basin's counter top.

It was a twenty-foot drop to the concrete path below. Making sure he had his room key, Gallen shimmied through the narrow space, grabbed at the plumbing sticking out of the wall, and twisted himself upright as he emerged into the night. Panting from the exertion as the pipes took his weight, he pulled his legs out, scraping his new Wranglers across the cinder blocks, and let himself drop to the concrete path. Pausing, he could hear Tyler Richards' fundraiser hitting another gear as the band covered 'Friends in Low Places', the singalong drowning out the band's vocalist.

Padding along the path, Gallen watched the plumes of steam shooting from his mouth as the still Wyoming night plunged to freezing. Feeling the frost crystals crunch under his feet as he passed through the maids' passageway, he paused where the dark tunnel opened to the neon-flooded car park. To the left sat his truck, a white F-350, where Gallen knew a Ruger .38 handgun was taped beneath the driver's seat. Opposite the truck, the Crown Vic sat in silence.

Moving under cover of the shadows that surrounded the court-yard, Gallen stealthed around the motel until he found a hide—the service alley on the other side of the courtyard, which was positioned almost behind the Crown Vic.

In the darkness, Gallen squinted into the car, looking for two shapes. Beside him was a sand box, and he had an idea. A door opened on the upstairs balcony where a drunk yelled into a cell phone. Using the distraction, Gallen grabbed the sand box off its wooden legs and moved through the dark blind spot behind the Crown Vic. Closing on it quickly, he threw the sand box over the car and watched it land on the hood of the vehicle. As the driver emerged to investigate, Gallen leapt from the shadows, punching the tallish man in the side of the throat with a fast right hand. Throwing a forearm around the man's neck as his legs gave way, Gallen reached for the exposed shoulder holster as he slammed the man's head into the doorframe.

The holster was empty.

'Shit,' he said, seeing a black Beretta 9mm lying in the front seat console.

Dropping the driver, Gallen reached for the firearm in the car. As his fingers closed on the gun, another hand slapped down on it and Gallen, kneeling on the driver's seat, froze as he stared into the eyes of the passenger.

'Hello, Gerry,' said the dark-haired man, who was dressed like an accountant but held a handgun steady at Gallen's heart.

'Paul,' said Gallen, his eyes fixed on a face he hadn't seen for two years.

'Long time—' started the man, then there was a blur of movement and a thudding sound, and Paul Mulligan's eyes rolled back before his head lolled sideways into Gallen's chest.

Grabbing the Beretta off the unconscious man, Gallen looked up and saw a dark face peering in the passenger side of the Crown Vic.

'You okay, boss?' said the man, tyre iron held down by his Lakers boxer shorts.

'Am now,' said Gallen, pushing Paul Mulligan off his chest. 'Thanks, Donny—I owe you, man.'

6

CHAPTER 2

The eggs weren't to Gallen's liking but the coffee and biscuit at the motel restaurant worked fine. Raising a finger for a refill he took note of the clock, which showed 7.08 am. Around him sales people and businessmen were reading their comped *Star-Tribs*, hair wet, tiny nicks betraying rushed shaving. Outside, the interstate rigs roared by on Highway 220, heading south for Rawlins and Colorado.

'No cream, right?' said the waitress, a brown-eyed thirty-year-old with biker rings.

'You got it,' said Gallen, scrolling through the contacts on his cell phone and double-tapping the listing that said *Kenny*.

The phone rang twice as drizzle descended on 220.

'Yep,' said the croaky voice.

'Kenny—Gerry.'

'Hey, boss.'

'How those horses?' said Gallen, as a Crown Vic pulled up in a parking space outside.

'Easy,' said Kenny. 'That limp on the sorrel weren't nothing but an abscess.'

'Can we do anything with 'em?'

'Sure. Had that mare over some rails yesterday, after you left.'

7

Gallen watched Paul Mulligan stalk to the restaurant door, white plaster fastened behind his ear.

'These people want the nags ready for the No More Snow, come May,' said Gallen into the phone. 'Can we do this in five weeks?'

'Sure,' said Kenny. 'They're good ponies.'

'I'll see you for lunch.' Gallen disconnected as Mulligan threw his *Star-Trib* on the table and eased sideways onto the vinyl.

'Ace. How's the eggs?' said the former spook, his dark hair having receded further since Gallen knew him in Kandahar and Marjah.

'They're edible. The biscuit's good,' said Gallen.

Mulligan ordered the Red Butte Special Breakfast. 'Steve's feeling okay. Thanks for asking.'

'Steve got out of the car,' said Gallen, sipping the coffee. 'Never get out of the vehicle, right, Paul?'

'Yeah, well,' said Mulligan. 'I stayed in the vehicle and got a headache the size of Montana for my trouble.'

Mulligan's coffee arrived and they sat in silence, Mulligan checking emails on his BlackBerry. When his basket of biscuit was slapped on the table, he pushed it across to Gallen. For people like Paul Mulligan, biscuit was redneck food.

'So?' said Mulligan.

'So, what?' said Gallen, wanting to stand out in the drizzle and smoke a cigarette.

'So,' said Mulligan. 'Told me to meet you at seven for breakfast. Here I am, Ace.'

'No, Paul,' said Gallen. 'I told you I'd be in the restaurant first thing, should you want to talk like a normal human being.'

'Normal's a relative term with us, don't ya think?'

'By normal I mean talk to me, don't stalk me.'

Mulligan leaned back, rubbed his eyes. He was four or five years older than Gallen, a DIA operative who'd worked in the Special Intelligence Unit. The SIU had done the homework on so-called High-Value Targets in Afghanistan, and sent teams of SEALs, Green Berets and Force Recon soldiers to either find out more or snatch an HVT. The relationship between the intel guys and special forces soldiers was, at best, coldly professional and at worst, totally dysfunctional. From the perspective of the operational leaders in Afghanistan—

the special forces captains—the problems started with incomplete briefings, continued with amended orders mid-mission and was capped by a constant sense of hidden motivations in just about every word uttered by an SIU spook.

Gallen had history with Paul Mulligan, a mission in north-east Afghanistan in 2006. It had started with a need for detailed surveillance of a Taliban HVT—a trucking operator named Al Meni—with apparent ties to Pakistani intelligence. The spooks had wanted photographic evidence of Al Meni and his secret associates to clarify what they'd intercepted in the cell phone traffic. But as Gallen's team had prepared to wind up, the recon gig had suddenly been amended to a snatch of Al Meni and his family. It was a disaster: a newbie fresh in from Camp Pendleton had been killed by Taliban sniper fire and Joe Nyles had lost his leg from a lobbed IED. The ambush had been located on a route Gallen had never intended to use and had therefore not recce'd.

The snafu was written up as an unforeseen combat accident, but Gallen heard another story. Apparently, once the digital photographs had started arriving at the Pentagon, certain levels of brass were embarrassed by who was secretly associating with whom and they'd panicked, tried to protect Al Meni.

'You been out, what, a year?' said Mulligan, leaning back as his plate of eggs and sausage arrived.

'Six months,' said Gallen.

'Back working on the farm with old Roy, huh?'

'You know where I am,' said Gallen. 'That's your job.'

'How's the cattle business?' Mulligan smirked slightly.

'You know how cattle's going in northern Wyoming, or you wouldn't be here.'

'Hey,' said Mulligan, raising his hands.

'The fuck you want, Paul?'

Mulligan recoiled slightly and then made a slow scan of the restaurant before bringing his eyes back to the eggs over-easy. 'I want to hire you, Gerry.'

'Hire me?'

Reaching inside his windbreaker, Mulligan removed a small leather clasp and gave Gallen a business card from it. The card announced

Paul Mulligan MBA—Vice-President, Security under a coloured banner for Oasis Energy, a massive oil and gas company based in Calgary.

'MBA?' said Gallen, having to smile. 'Annapolis boys think wearing their ring is enough to run the world.'

'Just staying current.'

'I know nothing 'bout gas, except how to pump it into a truck,' said Gallen, thinking about making it north to a town called Shell, hopefully with the transmission healthy enough to tow a horse trailer.

'Not oil and gas,' said Mulligan, chewing on sausage. 'Security.'

Gallen sipped on his coffee and looked out the window. The sun was fighting through the cloud.

'Heard of Harry Durville?' asked Mulligan.

'Owns Oasis Energy,' said Gallen. 'Real rich guy. What about him?'

'I need a detail on him. Bodyguard, PSD—you know the score.'

'What happened to the old one?'

Mulligan laughed. 'Shit, Ace. You soldiers always ask the same questions.'

'Well?'

'They were British guys, ex-Paras and Royal Marines. Got an offer from a big contractor in Iraq and they were gone.'

'Who were they?' asked Gallen.

'Can't say,' said Mulligan. 'Code of silence, omerta—all that shit.'

'Doesn't sound like my line,' said Gallen. 'What's wrong with using the cops?'

'Durville's a billionaire but he's hands-on,' said Mulligan. 'One day you're escorting him onto an Arab's super yacht, next thing you know he's drinking fermented goat piss with peasants in Turkmenistan.'

'Man gets around.'

'Grew up in Alberta logging camps. He gets drunk and wants to fight—he can be trouble. I need a special crew on him.'

They swapped stares. Gallen wanted to be on the road, collecting those horses and banking the thousand dollars a month he was going to charge to prepare them for the first showjumping competition of the season. Mulligan was an annoyance, a hand reaching out from his past, trying to pull him backwards.

'Thanks for thinking of me, Paul,' said Gallen, searching for cash in his breast pocket.

'I'll get this,' said Mulligan. 'Keep my card.'

Gallen looked at him. 'I'm not interested, Paul.'

'Sure, Gerry. But for the record: you can run a team of four, they get two thousand a week. You get four. Full Oasis health and disability. The whole nine.'

Grabbing his keys and phone, Gallen stood.

'You know, I didn't have a say in the Al Meni snatch,' said Mulligan as they shook hands. 'Wasn't my call.'

'You made the call, Paul.'

Mulligan rolled his eyes. 'It came from above, Gerry. Shit, you know how that works.'

'Sure do, Paul,' said Gallen, turning to go. 'You were my above.'

CHAPTER 3

The transmission started slipping about ten minutes after Gallen took the road east out of Greybull for Shell. It didn't happen on every change but you could feel it on the change up from second to third—a transmission that wasn't handling the diesel's torque as the truck climbed along 15 into the Bighorn range.

Smoking one cigarette every half-hour, Gallen sipped on take-out coffee and willed on the transmission, deciding the truck would get them home if he had to drive at thirty mph across the whole damn state. It might have to rise up the to-do list he'd been writing since leaving the Marines and getting back to the farm; the list started with getting Roy to stop his drinking and went on through re-posting the horse yards, gravelling the driveway, getting the main load bearing fixed on the snow blower and replacing the boundary fencing on the bottom forty acres. The barn foundation had cracked and collapsed at the north end, the loading gates for the cattle were bent and broken, and the sump pump wasn't working properly in the cellar. With spring starting, the cows were about to drop and Roy's stock management system was in his head. There were animals all over the Gallen family's three hundred and eighty acres and he only knew where two-thirds of them were hiding.

It all came back to money and the fact that Roy Gallen didn't have any. After a lifetime of raising cattle and rough stock for the rodeo circuit, Roy was hiding away from decisions in a fug of drinking and hangovers.

Showjumpers weren't his people, said Roy, and Gallen would say, 'So the bankers are your people? You want them shutting you down?'

Taking it slow through Shell, the tawny-white Bighorns rising in the background, Gallen took a side road out of town and drove it till he pulled left into a large iron gate with the legend *Tally-Ho Ranch* across the arch. The Robinson property, the details of which Roy had begrudgingly passed on to Gallen.

Taking it slow up the tree-lined driveway, he noted the white post-and-rail fencing and the warmblood horses in their paddocks, a few patches of snow still visible in the fence lines. There was more invested in each of those jumpers than Gallen used to make in a year in the military and he had a sudden blast of self-consciousness about the Arvada-Clearmont High School Panthers sticker on his rear screen. Did showjumping folks trust hockey players?

The stock trailer Gallen had left at Tally-Ho was parked up against the barn on its struts and Gallen swung the F-350 in an arc, reversing the dually rear axle under the gooseneck hitch.

'Kenny,' he yelled, slamming the truck door and throwing on a heavy Tough Duck jacket against the cold of altitude. 'You around?'

'Here, boss,' came a low voice, and Gallen walked around the barn to the yard where one horse was tethered to a rail. Beyond was a sand riding arena where Kenny Winter sat on a stationary horse.

'This them?' Gallen let himself into the yard, dodging the puddles as he closed on the tethered sorrel gelding. Running his hand along the animal's withers and across his back to his rump, Gallen liked what he saw.

'This the abscessed one?'

'Easiest fix I done for a long time,' said Winter, spitting into the sand. 'Vet been coming out charging the lady four hunert a time for X-rays in the shoulder.'

'You poulticed it?' Gallen lowered his voice lest the owner overheard the redneck horse doctoring.

13

'Sure. It burst this morning. Got half a bottle of peroxide up that hoof and he was purring like a cat inside an hour.'

'Beats surgery,' said Gallen, climbing onto the top rail and looking down on Winter, who sat on a black mare almost sixteen hands.

'This one's Peaches,' said Winter. 'She's going over basic rails. I can have her over five-footers inside two weeks.'

'The other?'

'Name's Dandy. Haven't rode him yet, but Peaches is the money.'

After walking the horses to the stock trailer where Winter had spent the night in the living quarters, Gallen approached the house, wanting to handle this right. He'd driven down on a look-see basis and now he wanted those horses back at the farm, bringing in real cash. If it meant making horse-promises, he'd become a horse-bullshitter and promise them the world.

Knocking on the door of the two-storey Territory-status house, Gallen tried to scrape the mud from his boots and wondered if he reeked of cigarettes.

The door opened and a child of nine or ten stood there. 'Yes?' she said, friendly.

'Howdy, ma'am. Name's Gerry Gallen. I'm here to see Mr Robinson about the horses? Peaches and—'

The girl turned away. 'Mom!'

Gallen shifted his weight as the girl walked away, waving without looking at him. A woman came into the hallway and Gallen smelled baking, felt hungry.

'Hi—Yvonne Robinson,' said the woman, brown eyes and spilling dark hair which she pushed aside with her wrist as she put out her hand. 'And you're . . . ?'

Feeling his jaw drop, Gallen flushed red. Before he could speak, the woman was beaming.

'Gerry Gallen!' she said, chuckling. 'How you doin', Gerry?'

'Yvonne McKenzie,' said Gallen, now realising which Robinsons this farm belonged to.

'Robinson for twelve years,' she said, rolling her eyes.

'Oh, well, congratulations,' said Gerry, not seeing a ring.

'I was expecting Roy. I'm sorry,' she said, as if remembering her manners. 'Lunch is on. You want to grab that Mr Kenny and eat with us?'

'Sure,' said Gallen, his face flushing again as surely as it was senior prom night 1992, when Gallen was in the back of a car with Yvonne McKenzie while Tessa White and Butch Droman tried to get beer from a Clearmont liquor store. Both of them dating someone else, a little tipsy on sly whisky and the smell of that Opium perfume, all coming together in one long kiss. Nothing ever said about it, and then Yvonne was gone to the University of Nebraska and Gallen was joining the US Marine Corps, hoping for a shot at officer candidate school.

And then there was now. And Yvonne still looked like she did in the early nineties—only now she wasn't a pretty cheerleader with athlete's legs. Now she had some curves.

Gallen spent the next hour worrying that his socks stank, that Winter would hawk or light up a smoke. He told himself it was because he didn't want to lose Yvonne Robinson as a client, but he was looking at her far too much for it to be just that.

'Dad says Dandy is lame; plain and simple, lame,' said Lyndall— the child—as Yvonne cleared the plates from a formal dining table and offered coffee. 'And he don't like Peaches neither—says Mom is wasting her time with that glue-bag.'

'Well Dandy ain't lame now,' said Winter, his drawl so slow that it sounded like a slur. 'Just a hoof abscess. He'll be jumping in a couple of weeks.'

'I asked the vet to check that,' said Yvonne, making a face. 'He kept doing X-rays of the shoulder.'

'Gotta pay those student loans somehow,' laughed Winter, grabbing at a biscuit as the plate was removed.

Lyndall asked Winter to play Wii and he obliged, following her into the next room.

'What's your friend's story?' said Yvonne, pouring coffee.

'Used to play pro hockey in Alberta,' said Gallen, catching a flash of her slender neck. 'After Afghanistan, he was approached by a bunch of Clearmont businessmen to bolster our team.'

'And?' said Yvonne, with the smirk of a woman who'd grown up hearing hockey stories.

'He went into the car park to settle a dispute with another player. Turned out the guy was a deputy sheriff from Gillette, and Kenny was expelled from the league. Roy gave him a job with the horses.'

''Cos he's good at it?'

'The best I've seen,' said Gallen. 'If Kenny says that Peaches is the money, then tell those folks in Douglas County to start engraving your name on that cup.'

'How's a thousand a month, all in?' said Yvonne. 'That gives me feed, shoes and meds—and it gives me a jumper. Kenny can decide which one.'

'You got it.' Gallen took her outstretched hand. 'But it don't include no fancy vet from Shell.'

A door slammed and boots stomped down the wooden boards of the hallway. Gallen noticed Yvonne wince and realised this was a shoe-free household for all but one person.

A man appeared in the dining room, ash-grey hat, turquoise rodeo buckle in his Wranglers and a set of Texan dress boots. There was a cold greeting between the man and Yvonne and then Gallen was being introduced to Brandon Robinson.

Gallen knew the name; Brandon Robinson was a one-time quarterback for the University of Nebraska Huskers. Then he'd gone on to law school at UCLA and become a developer of strip malls in Wyoming and Montana. It stood to reason that he'd marry someone like Yvonne.

Brandon Robinson puffed out his footballer's chest, his blond moustache twitching. 'So. Gerry Gallen, huh?'

'That's me,' said Gallen.

'Hockey star and war hero, right?' Brandon swung back to Yvonne as if sharing a joke.

'No,' said Gallen, as Winter silently appeared in the doorway behind Yvonne's husband. 'Wasn't like that.'

'You sure?' said Brandon, like he was teasing a child. 'Way Yvonne told it, you were black missions, special ops. All that spooky shit.'

'I drove a truck,' said Gallen. 'It was nice meeting you.'

CHAPTER 4

The engine pinged as it cooled and Gallen gave their location for the third time: County Road 42, the extension of 195 along from the old Fenton place. Roy grumbled and growled and Gallen still wasn't sure if he was coming to get them when his father hung up the phone.

They were west of Clearmont, in the boonies of northern Wyoming, the transmission having quit and the horses getting moody in the trailer as the sun dipped behind the Bighorns, bringing the temperature down in a hurry.

'Thought Roy was fixing that thing.' Winter nodded at the hood as he lit a cigarette.

'I was,' said Gallen, leaning back in the driver's seat and sighing. 'Had the money and all.'

Gallen liked that Winter didn't ask him what happened. When Gallen had arrived back on the farm three weeks earlier, Winter had been there working for Roy, and they'd avoided one another. Gallen liked that Winter didn't push and pick about the tranny like Marcia would have when they were married. Truth was, Gallen had had a reconditioned tranny on order with the local Ford mechanics, but the fundraiser for Richards had come along and by the time he'd made the drive south he'd put more into that envelope than he could afford.

'Give the tranny money to that boy in the chair?' asked Winter, staring out the windscreen.

'Something like that,' said Gallen.

'Least it went to a good place.'

'Hope you're right, Kenny.' Gallen exhaled smoke out the cracked window. 'Richards was a good soldier once.'

'Can't always be a good soldier in civvie life,' said Winter.

'No. But you don't have to get drunk and drive off a bridge when your wife's expectin'.'

They sat smoking, the truck cab cooling in the silence.

'So, you been away?' said Winter.

Gallen exhaled. He'd come out of the Marines, taken his cheque and drifted around for almost six months: saw people who served with him in the Ghan and Mindanao; met relatives of young men who'd lost their lives; saw other lives, other ways of living, and he liked them. But not enough to stop him drifting back to Wyoming and to Sweet Clover. The farm wasn't much, as far as lives go. But it was his.

'Wasn't away.' Gallen looked through the side window. 'Just taking my time coming home, is all.'

'You mind?' said Winter, reaching for the glove compartment and coming out with a fifth of Jim Beam.

'What's the occasion?' Gallen offered his coffee traveller.

'We talking about the shit?'

'No,' said Gallen. 'Thought we'd done a good job of not doin' that.'

Winter swigged at the bottle. 'Roy told me not to bring it up.'

'He taught you good.'

Winter showed a busted incisor as he smirked. 'Said when it came to war, Gerry weren't much of a talker.'

'Not much talk from you neither, Kenny.'

'What's to say? Got cold, got shot at. Got out still able to fog up a mirror.'

'What I call a good war.' Gallen smiled and touched his traveller to the bottle of Beam.

'Amen,' said Winter.

'You Canadians. In the south, right? Fighting out of Kandy?'

'Yeah. But I worked in the north, with Americans and Aussies.'

'Special forces?'

'In the Canadian forces they called us Assaulters.'

'Kind of sums it up,' said Gallen, relaxing as the bourbon warmed his stomach. Headlights shone as a truck rounded a bend in the road—Roy, coming to pick them up.

'You were Marines Recon, right?' said Winter. 'Made captain.'

'You been in Roy's office.' Gallen knew that his Marines plaque and his Silver Star were mounted where his father could see them while he drank.

'Yeah, he's proud,' said Winter.

'I know,' said Gallen. 'He rescued that crap out of the trash. I don't have the heart to take it down.'

Before they reached the house yard, Gallen felt something was wrong. There were no lights on in the house and the big floodlight that hung over the main sliding door of the barn wasn't working.

'What's up, Dad?' said Gallen. His father's whisky-fuelled snores rasped from the back seat where he was lying.

'Lights out,' said Winter as Gallen stopped the truck. 'Power?'

Winter walked to the front door and tried the switches. Gallen could see him shrugging by the light of the truck's headlamps.

'Power's off,' said Winter.

The two of them carried Roy to his bed.

'You know about this?' Gallen asked as they stood in the kitchen.

'No,' said Winter. 'You think he was ducking the bills?'

'Dunno.'

Winter took a kerosene lamp and headed for the bunkhouse, a hundred-year-old wooden shack that had once housed the farm labourers of Sweet Clover, the Gallen family spread.

Watching the mysterious Canadian pad across the house yard, Gallen noticed a sense of containment and caution in his stride. Like many soldiers, when the war was over some habits couldn't be erased.

Grabbing a lamp, Gallen went to Roy's study and sat down at the desk. A pile of papers, envelopes, bank files and ledger books rose and spread like a mountain range in front of him. Sorting through them in the dim light, Gallen cursed quietly as he assembled a pile of the bills that seemed to have been paid, judging either by the '*paid*' scrawled in Roy's hand or because Gallen could find the clearances in the bank files. Roy'd paid the cattle haulage and the cattle feed and the hay man. And he'd repeatedly paid his bill at the liquor store and a company called La Paree Beautee.

Then Gallen made another pile of the final demands and disconnection warnings. There was a bill from Clearmont Fuels— diesel, propane and gasoline totalling $3817, account in arrears, payment due three months ago, credit no longer being extended on the Sweet Clover account; the co-op had a final demand for the $892 owed for Roundup, electric fencing wire, fence transformers, nails and cattle wormer; Alpine Ford wanted the $1600 it quoted and charged to fix the axle bearings and four-by-four hubs in Roy's own F-250, a bill rendered in the fall of the year before; and sitting in Gallen's hand was the power company's bill: three billing cycles in arrears, and a disconnection for 20 March—the official first day of spring.

'Damn,' said Gallen, rubbing his face. Roy had ignored a power bill for more than three months and the power company had cut them off.

Lying awake, Gallen listened to the coyotes howl in the still night air. He remembered life in this farmhouse before his mother left, before Roy gave his life to the drink and before his older brother and sister took off for the big cities and their big careers. He remembered being driven home from high-school hockey, his father giving him the run-down on what he did right and what he had to learn; he'd limp into the house and his mom would have a hot bath ready for him, salts and all, mumbling her insults about the game, telling him that he didn't have to play hockey if he didn't want to. One morning, his mom had walked out of the bathroom and screamed at Roy when she discovered Gallen's split eyebrow, an injury Roy saw no reason to bother the doctor with.

Gallen was always going to be Roy's boy. As close as he was to his mother, he was drawn to hockey, to the code of never backing down, never abandoning a team-mate, never staying down on the ice, no matter who had landed you there. His coach from his midget-league days, Pat Murphy, had once gone crazy after one of the team had stayed on the ice, writhing in agony, after being checked into the boards by the biggest boy on the opposing team. At their next training, Murphy had told the group of ten-year-olds: 'No one stays down in this team. This ain't no soccer game and you ain't no fucking Mexicans.'

And that was about as philosophical as it got in Wyoming hockey. His mom had managed to influence his older siblings and they were both lawyers, Patricia in San Francisco and Tom at a bank in Denver. But Gallen had toed the line, played hockey, taken a few bronc rides at the rodeo and then joined the Marines after high school. Back then it seemed enough: the other kids didn't want the farm so it fell to the youngest. And the youngest had bought the whole redneck dream.

When Gallen had just turned fifteen, his mother left and Roy started drinking. Roy had a succession of girlfriends and there was a sudden lack of discipline in the life of the youngest Gallen. His mother would call from California and then Hawaii, but she'd never called him to her. Then, in his final year of school, the hay paddock—a hundred-and-forty-acre segment of the Gallen family's cattle empire—had been sold. Gallen hadn't seen it coming and hadn't even thought about it until one day he was sitting in the barber's chair in Clearmont and a real estate broker called Frank Holst started mouthing off.

'Seen old Roy sold the hay paddock over on East Fork?' said Holst, and before the barber could point out that Roy's son was sitting in the next chair, the broker had offered it up: 'Old Roy's drinking the farm away.'

Gallen had spent many summers wet-backing in that hay paddock, making the hay for the winter with Tom and Roy, a third of it sold to other farmers.

Lying awake now, Gallen thought about his mother and her new life and new husband and new friends. He thought about the split, about his mother's desire for something bigger and Roy's love of cattle, horses and hockey.

He thought about Roy losing it all and he knew what he had to do.

Never stay on the ice.

CHAPTER 5

Gallen put a piece of wood in the stove's fire box and placed the coffee perc on the hot plate. Through the kitchen window he could see long plumes of steam shooting from the horse yards built off the back of the old ramp barn—a hundred-and-thirty-year-old wooden cathedral on a high foundation of river rocks. Sometime while Gallen was in the Marines, the earthen ramp structure had collapsed through the stone foundation wall and now Roy was loading in hay with a belt through one of the side doors.

The only remnant of the old days was the huge white lettering painted on the red boards: Sweet Clover, and beneath it, Gallen Family Farms. For the millionth time in his life he wondered why an Irish farmer would paint a three-leaf clover. Gallen's grandfather must have been the one and only Irish-American not to paint a four-leaf clover on his barn.

Taking his mug of coffee to the boot room, he dressed in a red blanket-coat and workboots and headed for Winter in the yards. It was 6.52 am; a line of blue and yellow had formed on the eastern horizon and frozen dirt clattered under his cold feet. 'Nice morning,' said Gallen, taking a seat on the platform beside the main gate to the round pen, where Winter was working with Peaches.

'Nice enough,' said Winter, vapour escaping his mouth.

Sipping at his coffee, Gallen smoked and watched the Canadian do his thing with the horse, leading her in simple circles around the pen. After a few minutes Winter walked back to the centre of the fifty-foot pen and kept the horse walking on the end of long lunging line. Using voice commands, he made the horse lope—off either leg—and then trot, before backing her off again. The horse was obviously well worked but good trainers built them up from the basics, asserting their dominance and making the animal confident about commands.

'She's a good mare, this one,' said Winter. 'Nice 'n' easy.'

Gallen ducked into the barn and carried the saddle to the sand arena for Winter, who'd already constructed some basic rail jumps. Gallen leaned on the fence, threw out the cold coffee and lit another smoke.

'We were going to talk about the shit, weren't we?' said Gallen.

'Got one of them for me?' asked Winter, bringing Peaches around and reaching down for a cigarette.

'Ever thought about going back?'

'To Maple Creek?' said Winter, sticking the smoke in his teeth and stripping off his gloves, which he shoved in his jacket pocket.

'No, to soldiering.' Gallen squinted as the sun came over the trees.

'Just as well,' said Winter. 'Saskatchewan's a big place, but maybe not big enough for me.'

'Well?' said Gallen, after they'd spent a few moments smoking and looking into the distance.

'Think about it every day,' said Winter. 'Don't know how you wouldn't.'

The mare snorted and shook herself, the tack ringing like a box of nails.

'Could be something for us,' said Gallen.

'What?' said Winter, eyes focused.

'Bodyguard. PSD. Protecting an oil executive.'

'Protecting from what?'

Gallen sucked on the smoke. 'From hisself.'

'Sounds easy.'

'Easier than an intel briefing,' said Gallen.

24

'Ha!' Winter shook his head with genuine amusement. 'All looks easy on a board.'

They chuckled in the morning light. Anyone who'd seen action in special forces knew how brave an intel staffer could be when he was scribbling his lines and crossing his targets on a whiteboard in a briefing room.

'Well?'

'Well, what?' said Winter.

'Would you go back?'

'Depends.'

'On what?'

'Who for, and why,' said Winter.

'For me, Kenny.' Gallen eyeballed him. 'You work for me and you do it for two thousand a week, full medical, death and disability.'

'I see.'

They smoked in silence until Gallen mashed his cigarette in the sand of the arena. 'Guess the first step is knowing if you can work for me.'

'Am right now, ain't I?'

'Roy hired you,' said Gallen. 'This is different—this is back to the life, chain of command.'

Winter exhaled smoke and flicked his butt end over end into the sand. 'I can work for you, Gerry.'

'Big dog say, little dog do?'

Winter spat, looked away. 'You say two thou?'

'That's what I can pay.'

'The fuck we doing here then?'

Arnell Boniface smiled as the administration woman carried in the Sweet Clover file and handed it to him.

'Okay, so what have we here?' said Boniface, a chrome-dome bank manager who hid his distaste for farmers with a chirpy tone.

'I should be on there,' said Gallen, his hair still wet, his left foot pinching in the brogues he wore three times a year. 'Dad had me signed onto the trust when I was twenty-one.'

'Here it is,' said Boniface. 'Gerard Roy Gallen, Sweet Clover farm on the Line Draw road. There's your signature, you're authorised.'

'How're we placed?' said Gallen. 'What does the bank need?'

Boniface said 'Well . . .' like a man who was about to lie. 'There's three months' mortgage in arrears, so we'd like to have that settled. Then there's another payment due on the fourteenth.'

'Let's call it four,' said Gallen. 'And then?'

'We could discuss the line of credit.'

'Can we shut it down? It's just eating away at that property.'

'I've suggested that to Mr Gallen—Roy, that is,' said the banker, 'and he doesn't like the idea.'

'Can we take the cheque book away from him?'

Boniface laughed. 'You try that. Tell me how you go.'

'What about you dishonour every Sweet Clover cheque?'

'It'll work for a while, then Roy'll be in here yelling at my staff.' Boniface leaned forward. 'And if it's after lunch he'll be excitable, if you see what I mean.'

'I want to bring the mortgage back to square,' said Gallen. 'But there's no point if the money keeps leaking out.'

'You could start with these payments to the beauty shop,' said Boniface, his finger tapping on the latest statement. 'I know Roy and Leanne have a friendship, but that's the main cash flow problem I can see.'

'Can we freeze that chequing account? Just for a month?'

Boniface spoke into the intercom, asked for the assistant to come through with a bank form. 'We'll try it your way, Gerard, but when Roy comes in here I want your John Hancock all over this.'

'That's fair. By the way, that letter of foreclosure I seen in Roy's study,' said Gallen, closing his eyes slowly, 'that's not the first, right?'

'He's had warning letters, but that's the first foreclosure document.'

'Gimme two days,' said Gallen, as the forms arrived for Boniface to fill in and Gallen to sign. 'I'll see what I can do.'

The beauty parlour smelled of hairspray and bad perfume—the ones that said *If you like Joy, you'll love Glory.* The disco phase of Tom Jones played on the sound system and Gallen pushed back his thin dark hair with his fingers as he waited at the desk.

'Hi, Leanne,' he said, as the woman walked around a Chinese silk screen to the counter. 'Long time.'

'Well, well,' said Leanne Tindall, wrong side of fifty and still wearing a Wonderbra. 'If it's not our war hero. What can I do you for, Gerry?'

'Could we talk?'

'Sure,' Leanne gestured around her, 'but I'm busy. Got a bridal party in right now.'

'Need to talk about these payments,' said Gallen.

'Payments?' Leanne averted her eyes, big acrylic nails resting on her hip, accentuating the swell of her ass in the black leggings.

'Yeah, the cheques Roy's been sending.'

'Well,' she said. 'I'm sure there's been a couple.'

'There's been twenty-three, Leanne,' said Gallen, staying calm, just like they taught him in the Marines. Before you can control a situation, you must first control yourself.

'Now look, Gerry—'

'The cheque-book stubs say renovations and services and investment,' said Gallen. 'I'm a trustee of Sweet Clover. Thought I'd come down, see what we're getting for our money.'

'That ain't none of your concern, young man,' said the woman, a darkness building behind the makeup and peroxide bangs. 'That's private. You don't come in here—'

'I'm a trustee of the farm and a signatory to the bank accounts,' said Gallen. 'It's not private.'

'That's between Roy and me.'

'There's just under eighty thousand of the farm's cash invested in this place. That's between you and me.'

'How dare you,' she said. Employees looked up from their foils and hair-dryers. 'You're as bad as your mother.'

'Not quite, Leanne,' said Gallen. 'I ain't walked out on Roy just 'cos he's a drunken cheat.'

'That's it! Get out, you damn redneck.' Leanne bustled around the counter, hugging her tiger-stripe shirt like armour. 'I don't need no Gallen money, never did. Now git.'

Gallen walked into the sun on Water Street, one road back from Clearmont's main street. Leanne Tindall had been toying with Roy Gallen since long before the divorce, keeping her own husband on ice while leeching money out of the lust-struck cattle farmer. Roy's accountant had tried to intervene and he'd been fired; the solicitor was banned from seeing the cheque book. Now Leanne was divorced too and pulling money out of Roy like he was a walking teller machine.

Sitting in the diner, Gallen ordered coffee and pie and played with his cell phone. Beside him, a man stood and cleared his voice.

'That Gerry? Roy's boy?'

Gallen looked up into a fleshy face with dead eyes. Frank Holst, still talking the talk, still wearing his real estate brokerage blazer like it was something to be proud of.

'Frank,' said Gallen. 'How's business?'

'Fantastic, Gerry,' Holst said, flecks of dandruff on his shoulder catching the sun.

'Glad to hear it.'

'Something might interest you,' said Holst, his voice switching to the same small-town gossip tone that he'd once used in the barber chair as he accused Roy of drinking away the farm.

'I see.'

'Just closed on a farm, up on the forty-two.'

'Nice for you,' said Gallen.

'Maybe nice for you, eh Gerry? A new class of neighbour?'

'I'm sorry . . . ?'

Holst's eyebrows rose and fell and he licked his lips. 'Sold the Fenton place to guess who?'

'Have no idea, Frank.'

'Yvonne McKenzie. Remember her?'

Gallen's ears roared. 'Yvonne?'

'Yep. Didn't you hear?'

'I guess not.'

'Divorced that football player. She's coming home.'

'Shit,' said Gallen.

'Oh yeah,' leered Frank Holst. 'Y-vonne!'

28

CHAPTER 6

Gallen moved off the United flight with the foot traffic, towards the arrivals concourse at T3. Fifty feet ahead of him he could see Kenny Winter's short blond hair moving past the shopping malls and cell phone kiosks of LAX.

'Move to your four and wait for contact,' said Gallen into his cell phone earpiece. 'I just want to know about the cavalry.'

'Got it, boss.' Winter's head moved through the crowds to the right of the milling area. Gallen remained on the upper level, looking down on the concourse as Winter moved into it.

'See the big bald guy near the doors?' asked Gallen, hiding behind a flag-like marketing installation for Verizon.

'Got him,' said Winter. 'Sign says "Clearmont".'

'On the other side of the entry doors, check the Anglo male reading the magazine. I've got him as a spook.'

'Copy that,' said Winter, and Gallen watched his employee slip behind a group of Koreans.

'I think that's all we have in the concourse,' said Gallen, scanning the vast hall, his old instincts coming back to him fast. Special forces wasn't anything like it was in the movies. Ninety-five per cent of the gigs were pure recon missions: get in, mind someone else's business, and then get out. And do it clean.

'If we assume they're fixed, I might look on the apron,' said Winter.

'Assume they're fixed for now,' said Gallen, getting cover from a businessman on his BlackBerry. 'Move down to the south entry and have a look for nondescript Crown Vics with UPIs.'

'That's a broad description, boss,' said Winter, his head moving south.

'You'll know it if you see it. Like every blank Crown Vic you ever saw in the Army.'

'Filled with clipboards, you mean?' Winter was referring to the military managers who usually rode in such cars.

Gallen had bought a ticket for Winter and flown him down on the same flight that Paul Mulligan had booked him on. Gallen wanted to do basic surveillance on Mulligan before trusting him.

'I'm getting our parcel,' said Gallen. 'RV here ten minutes, can do?'

'Can do, boss,' said Winter, disappearing behind the Hertz office.

The woman behind the counter didn't ask too many questions, just wanted his driver's licence and a signature.

Taking the FedEx box that he'd sent the previous afternoon, Gallen made for the men's washroom on the ground level of T3, took a booth and slowed his breathing as he waited for noises out of pattern.

After forty seconds of waiting—listening to the consequences of bad food, stress and flying—Gallen ran his thumbnail down the end of the purple and white box, and opened it. Putting his hand inside, he pulled out the Ruger automatic that usually lived under the seat of the Ford, and checked the full spare clip that was held to it by a rubber band. The second weapon was smaller but with bigger firepower: a chromed Colt Defender that shot .45 ACP loads. It looked like a pop-gun but it could put a hole in a man if you knew what you were doing.

Standing, he shoved the guns into his jeans waistband and pulled the hem of the plain black hoodie low over his hips. Whoever had invented the hooded sweatshirt probably never factored in how useful it would be for people like Gerry Gallen.

Pulling his off-white cap down to hide his eyes, Gallen flushed the toilet and walked to the hand basin, keeping his face down to dodge the security camera. He kept his eyes on the ground as he dried off at the paper-towel dispenser, then exited and moved back to the concourse.

Assuming his position on the upper level, he looked down, saw Winter moving back from the south entry.

'How we looking?' said Gallen, liking that Bald and Magazine had held their positions.

'Dark blue Crown Vic, parked in the VIP set-down,' said Winter. 'Security asked the driver something—my guess is, driver told him to fuck himself.'

'Driver?' said Gallen.

'Late twenties, Anglo, dark hair. Has a suture plaster over his left eye—no one in back.'

'Okay,' said Gallen. 'Seats at your six. Take the middle one and I'll leave something for you. Then find a cab, wait for me to get in that Crown Vic, and follow us. Can do?'

'Can do, boss.'

Gallen seated himself one chair away from Winter and put a motorcycle magazine on the seat between them. Winter's hand dropped on the magazine and he was gone, now armed with a Ruger .38 and a spare clip.

The bald greeter with the sign called himself Toby and was pleasant enough for someone who might wish Gallen harm. The sun was warm as they walked to the VIP set-down and Gallen knew he'd overdressed with the hooded sweatshirt.

As he reached the Crown Vic, Gallen saw the driver—the same one he'd hit at the motel in Red Butte. Gallen gave him a quick nod of recognition and received a sneer in response.

'This is Aaron,' said Toby, indicating Magazine.

'Hi, Aaron,' said Gallen, smiling at the anonymous face beneath accountant's hair. Over Aaron's shoulder, Winter's cab was waiting sixty yards down the apron.

31

'Don't mind, do ya?' said Aaron, moving for a pat-down without Gallen's consent.

Grabbing the outstretched right hand, Gallen moved his body at Aaron's, twisting the wrist behind the man's back as he wrapped his right hand around the back of Aaron's neck, slamming his unguarded face on the Crown Vic's hood. Pulling the head back with a handful of hair just before Aaron's nose made contact, Gallen threw his arm around the man from behind and whipped the handgun from his hip rig.

Pulling back in shock, Aaron slapped at his empty holster.

'This what you looking for?' Gallen held the Beretta down at his groin, unclipping the magazine and flipping the loads onto the concrete apron.

'The fuck?!' said Aaron.

'Your question,' said Gallen, returning the Beretta, stock first.

'My what?' said Aaron, mouth hanging open.

'Answer's yes—I do mind.'

They moved through the LA traffic, headed north along Sepulveda and then Lincoln. Gallen remembered LA well enough to know that if you avoided the freeways when leaving LAX northbound, then you were probably headed for the beach suburbs of Venice and Santa Monica.

'You always attack your employers?' said Aaron, blowing on the rescued 9mm cartridges and reinserting them into the clip.

'You always touch a man you just met?'

Aaron gave the driver a sideways look, like *Who the fuck is this guy?*

'Didn't touch you, Gallen,' said Aaron, speaking over his shoulder.

'Rather my good management than my bad luck.'

Beside him, Toby laughed softly. 'Five minutes, guys. Hold off five minutes.'

Passing Marina Del Rey Hospital, the driver took a left across traffic and they were wending their way along the canal systems behind Venice Beach.

Pulling into a palm tree-shaded parking lot behind a large

apartment complex, the car stopped and Gallen got out, keeping his eyes off the street where he knew Winter would soon be pulling up.

Emerging from an elevator at the third floor, Gallen followed the trio through air-conditioned stucco corridors and into apartment 312. The dark hallway opened into a huge living room that looked over a swimming pool and barbecue area, then over a canal to the white flash of Venice Beach and out to the glistening Pacific. Gallen gaped momentarily: he'd seen this sight on his honeymoon, long ago when his Marines crew had chipped in to buy him a package to Peurto Vallarta; he and Marcia had been hot and tired after delayed flights, and then he'd walked through the condo to the balcony and looked over the Pacific Ocean in the brilliance of early afternoon and he'd been floored. He remembered just standing there, not wanting to speak, amazed that such a sight existed—finally understanding that when people said the Pacific, it was beyond simply a thing.

'Need a drink, Gerry?' Toby moved into a large kitchen. 'Juice? Soda?'

'Sprite, thanks,' said Gallen.

Aaron walked onto the sun-bleached balcony where Paul Mulligan sat beneath a Miller beer sun umbrella. Mulligan put his cordless phone to his chest for a second while Aaron spoke, then Aaron came back into the room.

'You're up,' he said, flicking his head.

Moving past him into the heat, Gallen smiled as he patted his pockets. 'I'd tip you if I had some change.'

Taking a seat in the shade, Gallen drank the Sprite. Mulligan put a hand up to apologise for the phone call and started yelling into his handset. 'Sevi, I don't care if your crew's afraid of the dark, honest to God—that section along the canal has to be recce'd by clearance divers at least once every twenty-four hours and any tampering advised to me immediately, understand?'

Mulligan lit a smoke as the excuses poured in from wherever Sevi was at. Gallen guessed southern Thailand.

'No, no, no. Listen to me, buddy, and write this down,' said Mulligan. 'Pipelines that cost half a billion real US dollars are not assets that we allow to take care of themselves, okay?'

Sevi must have interrupted, because Mulligan sucked on his smoke like he was going to have a heart attack. 'Are you kidding me, Sevi? Is that it?'

Gallen could hear the other man's voice pouring out of the cordless.

'Listen, okay,' said Mulligan. 'Look at your contract, Sevi. It stipulates total pipeline coverage for a fifty-mile segment, and that includes the canal section. If you were a bad guy who wanted to destroy Oasis oil flows, you'd probably hit the pipe where it goes underwater, right?'

Mulligan stood, nodding and trying to smile. 'Okay, Sevi. Good talking as always. I'm transferring you to Aaron and you two can find a couple clearance divers, okay?' He fiddled with the handset and a phone rang inside the apartment. Mulligan yelled, 'Aaron! Sevi needs some divers. Just deal with it.'

Sitting again, Mulligan reached over and shook Gallen's hand. 'Chrissakes. Sorry, Gerry.'

'Got a security crew doesn't like the water?'

'What is it with soldiers? They see a bit of action, take a bit of shit, and then as soon as they go civvie there's this list of things they won't do.'

Gallen smiled. 'Nothing like taking shit to swear you'll never do it again.'

Mulligan drank European water from a bottle and eased back in his chair, the dark sunglasses concealing his expression. 'Got your wish list, Gerry. Looks okay.'

'They're all proven.'

'This Dale,' said Mulligan. 'Your gunnie in Afghanistan, right?'

Gallen nodded.

'Ern Dale's boy?'

'Yep,' said Gallen. Ern Dale was a Vietnam veteran who'd come back to the States, started selling used cars and transformed himself into a multimillionaire with Dale Auto City car lots all over Colorado, Wyoming and Nebraska. Ern Dale called himself the King of Chevrolet and he'd done everything he could to keep his son in college and out of the military.

Mulligan pushed. 'Those special forces gunnery sergeants are pretty hard boys.'

'Bren's a good 2IC. He picks up where I let down.'

Nodding, Mulligan looked out to sea. 'There's never the perfect profile for protecting a man.'

Gallen lit a smoke, hunching from habit into a wind that didn't exist. 'No?'

Mulligan shook his head. 'Tried cops, tried ex-SWAT, tried MPs and special forces guys. None of them cover it perfectly.'

'I see.'

'Sometimes it's the bodyguard who needs to be the first to draw and the last to shoot. See what I mean?'

'I don't like being touched, Paul,' said Gallen, a little defensive about the airport scuffle. 'Tell Aaron to keep his paws to himself.'

'Aaron pat you down?' laughed Mulligan. 'Can he eat solids?'

Gallen looked away, not enjoying the teasing; not ready to laugh at himself so close to the end of his last tour. 'Just disarmed him . . .'

'Hey, Gerry,' said Mulligan, friendly. 'I wasn't talking about you.'

'No?'

'No, buddy. It's this Kenny Winter.'

'What about him?'

'You really want him in your crew?'

Gallen was confused.

'Take a look.' Mulligan pushed the manila folder at Gallen as he stood and took a note from Aaron. 'Gotta go, Gerry. There's an apartment on the next floor for you. Let's talk tomorrow and get you on the job?'

'What about Kenny?' Gallen squinted into the sun.

'If you're happy, then I'm happy,' said Mulligan. 'But you know about the DD, right?'

'No.' Gallen looked at the folder like it was poison ivy. 'For what?'

'It's all in there and I'm not having a hernia about it.' Mulligan threw a linen sports coat over his arm. 'It's not unusual to end your career with a court martial when you do what Kenny did.'

'What did Kenny do?'

'You don't know?' said Mulligan as he got to the sliding doors. 'Sergeant Kenny Winter was an assassin. Damn good one, too.'

CHAPTER 7

The sunset lingered over the Pacific in a long blaze of orange as the waitress delivered two more Buds off the handle. Easing back from his surf 'n' turf, a specialty of the Pacific Mariners Yacht Club, Gallen wished he could light a smoke.

He and Winter had spoken about life on the farm and how different things could have been if they'd been raised in southern California: no hockey fights, no rodeo hangovers, no hauling water in an ice-bound barn at six in the morning, getting tired before school even started.

'Must be some drawback to living in this place,' said Winter, wiping his fingers before grabbing his beer. 'Just ain't seen it yet.'

Gallen knew the Canadian wanted to know about the gig so he got straight to the point. 'Kenny, they raised something in your file.'

'The DD?' said Winter, expressionless.

'Gave me a NATO-ISAF file,' said Gallen, meaning the International Security Assistance Force fielded by NATO in Afghanistan. 'You seconded from the Canadian Forces?'

Winter gulped at the beer and looked out at the marina. 'I'm not at liberty, Gerry. I stayed out of the stockade because I signed their goddamn NDA.'

'ND what?'

'Non-disclosure agreement,' said Winter. 'Said if I wrote a book about their fricking court martial they'd cut my benefits. Couldn't do that to my kids, right? Ryan got teeth needing braces.'

'Shit,' said Gallen. 'Could've told me this.'

'Told you what?' said Winter, ligaments straining in his bull neck. 'That I got a dishonourable discharge but it was all horse shit? That those cocksuckers were passing the buck all the way down to the trigger-man earning sixty-eight grand?' Throwing his napkin on the table, he stood.

'Sit down,' said Gallen, avoiding eye contact. 'Please.'

The Canadian stood over him, a classic hockey player from the prairies: six-two and built like a refrigerator; big farm-boy hands and arms like slabs of rock against the side of his chest. In a street fight, Gallen would have two, maybe three seconds to immobilise someone like Kenny Winter before the sheer power overwhelmed him.

Winter's jaw muscles tensed and then relaxed. 'Sorry 'bout that, boss,' he said, sitting and reaching for his beer.

Drinking in silence, they watched the sunset fade to purple and yellow.

Winter cleared his throat. 'Can we just say I was a supplies corporal who screwed up?'

'Sent toilet-blue when they wanted diesel?'

'Something like that. Don't wanna lie to you, Gerry, but I can't share the details.'

'Okay, you're in,' said Gallen. 'But my number two is Bren Dale. Worked with him in the Ghan.'

'Happy to be a soldier.' Winter shrugged. 'So, three of us?'

'Four,' said Gallen. 'Donny McCann said yes.'

'Recon?'

'Yep. We were a good crew, but never any babysitting for oil executives.'

'What about these people we're working for?' asked Winter. 'The dude you disarmed? Or the one with the sign? Didn't look like no office boys to me.'

'They're ex-intel, ex-military,' said Gallen. 'But I think they're the good guys.'

'You know this Mulligan?'

Gallen nodded. 'Paul Mulligan, ex-DIA.'

'He looks corporate.'

'Annapolis boy, rose to captain in the ONI,' said Gallen. 'He's out of the spooking game now.'

'Okay,' said Winter. 'So why was I being followed in the cab?'

Gallen paused. 'Today?'

'Late-model Impala, California plates,' said Winter.

Gallen held his gaze. 'They show 'emselves?'

'No,' said Winter. 'Peeled off a mile short of the apartment building.'

'Knew where you were going?'

'Seems like it.'

Gallen tried to relax. This wasn't Afghanistan, wasn't a Taliban stronghold. He had to detune from that old shit or he'd go crazy. 'Okay, let's keep an eye on that.'

'We can get eyes now,' said Winter, a smile creasing his long face.

'Now?'

'Other side of the road, in that Spanish cafe,' said Winter. 'Back in the shadows, at the bar. I make an Anglo male, early thirties, glassing us. Been there since we arrived.'

Without looking in the direction Winter had indicated, Gallen excused himself to take a pee. Along the hallway to the washrooms, he found a credenza sitting in front of a window. Peering through the leaves of a lily, careful not to make a silhouette, he stood still and let his eyes adjust to the change in light across eighty yards, from shade to light to shade.

After ten seconds he picked up what Winter had seen: a lone man, behind the brass tap bollards, with a set of field-glasses to his eyes. The trajectory suggested surveillance of the Pacific Mariners Yacht Club restaurant.

Leaning back, Gallen held up three fingers at Winter: three minutes then come get me.

Charging down the stairs, Gallen passed the girl at the club desk and bought a white PMYC polo shirt and a club cap, putting them on as he pushed out into the heat of early evening. Walking fast through the foot traffic he crossed the road with other walkers and kept his eyes on the tarmac, his mind running over the possibilities: Mulligan had left a dinner comp for the yacht club restaurant, and Gallen had decided to use it—now they were being followed. What were the chances of that being a coincidence?

The rules of engagement in recon units changed with the target and the gig: you were either pure reconnaissance or direct action and very rarely both. But one rule overrode all the rest: if a shadow attached itself to your party, you got to the bottom of who that fucker was and you did it real fast. Whether you scared him off, killed him or dragged him into a basement for a conversation, that was up to people like Gallen. But no special forces commanding officer ever let an undeclared snoop conduct counter-surveillance without there being some consequences. It wasn't the reputation you wanted in the field, that you'd let that go.

Gallen decided to flush the watcher, see what he'd do, where he'd run. The Colt was back in the apartment, but the surprise factor would balance it out.

Rounding the sidewalk area of the restaurant, Gallen glanced up and saw Winter at the table in the yacht club: they'd been seated perfectly for surveillance.

Pushing into the shade, Gallen walked to the bar and kept his eyes on the tanned girl in the black tank top. Moving to his left, he could see the watcher from the corner of his eye, the pocket-sized Pentax binoculars held up to his face. Gallen ordered a beer and watched the field-glasses drop. Winter had obviously left the table at three minutes and the watcher was wondering where his target had gone.

Turning his head slowly, Gallen came eye to eye with the watcher: a sallow Anglo with goldfish eyes, which turned to saucers as Gallen gave him a wink.

'Nice night for a perv?'

Falling sideways off the stool as he recognised Gallen, the watcher scrambled to leave by the rear door of the restaurant. Gallen saw worked shoulders under the light windbreaker, suggesting a professional, and this was verified as the watcher shouted something into his cuff as he headed for the door.

Following at a walk, Gallen had to allow the waitress with the full drinks tray to move along before he could go after the panicking field-glasses guy.

Watching the man's ankle disappear as the rear door flapped back on the spring, Gallen moved along the toilet hallway and paused at the door: who was on the other side? A man exited the washroom beside him and Gallen held up his arm.

'Sorry, buddy,' he said, smiling. 'Just got my cast off and I can't shift that door. Would you——'

The youngster didn't even reply, just threw his shoulder into the swing door and held it open for Gallen.

'There you go,' said the Samaritan, and Gallen saw a black handgun reaching from across the doorway into the side of the man's face.

The watcher's face came into view, his face dropping as he realised he had a stranger. 'Shit,' he said, and turned for the car park.

The rear of the restaurant opened into a service and deliveries area, a black Escalade parked with a door open. The watcher leapt into the rear door and Gallen paused, seeing three shapes through the tinted windows. Panting in the stand-off, Gallen realised the Escalade was going nowhere. As he approached it slowly, a commotion on the other side of the vehicle made the four-by-four rock on its shocks.

The rear door flew open and the watcher dropped to the tarmac, handgun pointed at Gallen. Slowly raising his hands, Gallen eyeballed the watcher as two other men walked around the front of the Escalade, arms raised, a tall blond man following with an automatic handgun in each hand.

'Hey, boss,' said Winter, the guns trained between the shoulder blades of his captives. 'Looks like we're popular.'

'That's far enough, tough guy,' said the watcher, getting to Gallen and standing behind him, gun jammed in his kidneys. 'Drop the guns.'

'Like watching a man eat?' said Winter, slow as the sun. 'Take you down McDonald's, see plenty of it.'

Behind Gallen, the friendly Samaritan squawked, the fear getting too much. The watcher twisted as the restaurant door banged shut and Gallen pirouetted into the watcher's chest, taking the gun hand away with a wrist slap and immediately changing to a Korean wrist-lock. Open-handing the watcher under the chin, Gallen brought the gun wrist back on itself and pushed it down hard with his body weight, snapping the ligaments and making the gun bounce free on the delivery apron.

The man opened his mouth to scream but nothing came out as he collapsed, unconscious, to the ground.

Picking up the gun—a SIG 9mm—Gallen turned back to Winter, whose captives gulped with fear but maintained their composure. A sandy-haired yuppie dressed like a lawyer muttered something like, *Okay*.

'That civvie's calling the cops,' said Gallen. 'Why don't you pick up your buddy and leave?'

Gallen winked at the lawyer guy and stepped back as the two men retrieved the watcher with the busted wrist and dragged him to the Escalade.

Winter collected the handguns, threw them in a dumpster as they jogged through the service lanes, looking for a way out that the cops wouldn't be using as a way in. They found a cab and took it to Santa Monica, silence enveloping them as they dealt with the adrenaline come-down. Crossing the road beside the pier, they cased the ground and found another cab, took it south to Venice Beach. Grabbing a booth at the back of a bar located three blocks from the sand, Gallen bought the beers and they finally looked at each other.

'Any ideas?' said Winter.

'The dude with the glasses spoke into his cuff once I made him,' said Gallen.

'See the tyres on that Escalade?' Winter scanned the bar over Gallen's shoulders. 'Self-sealers. Looked military, or—'

'Those weren't standard door pillars, neither,' said Gallen.

'Built for armour and one-inch glass.'

They looked at one another, the question hanging: what the hell did the US Government want with Gerry Gallen and Kenny Winter?

CHAPTER 8

Aaron didn't give away much about himself but Gallen noticed that he liked his toast cold and his coffee black.

'So, Mulligan not around?' said Gallen, as they finished eating breakfast and Toby cleared the balcony table.

'I run the Durville detail,' said Aaron. 'You're dealing with me now.'

Gallen's new boss had an oval face that twisted when he was pissed. His thin hair was cut in a side parting and he had reached forty with no busted facial features or missing teeth.

Gallen lit his first smoke of the day. 'You okay with that?'

'I'm okay with doing my job. I'm okay with others doing their jobs.'

Aaron took a manila envelope from the seat beside him, placed it on the glass-topped table and pushed it across. Gallen looked at it, felt the sun's heat and wondered if Aaron was ex-Agency.

'Employment documents, life insurance and the health packages,' said Aaron. 'I have you starting Monday week, gives you eleven days to get those signed and your crew on board. That a problem?'

'Should be fine,' said Gallen, glad he'd refused the seat opposite Aaron and taken one at his side. He wanted eyes on the other condos and on the street. Winter was still in the upstairs apartment, watching the environment with field-glasses, but Gallen didn't want his back to the street—not now.

'You got the measurements for your team?' said Aaron. 'Like Paul told you?'

Gallen patted the piece of paper in his jeans pocket.

'Then let's get the kit,' said Aaron, looking at his watch. 'Told my man we'd be in Longbeach before ten.'

Gallen shrugged, sucked on the smoke. 'Let's go.'

'Wanna bring that gorilla you hiding upstairs?' said Aaron.

Gallen wasn't too concerned about Aaron making Kenny Winter— the Canadian wasn't a long-term secret, just short-term insurance. 'He wouldn't miss it for the world.'

Toby took the Crown Vic off the San Diego Freeway at 9.48 and wove through the light industrial zone surrounding the port district, the part tourists don't see.

Trying to keep his bearings, Gallen caught a glimpse of the Naval Weapons Station across a canal and figured they were in the south end of Longbeach. At the end of a trucker's road into a distribution depot, they veered right, avoiding the loading bays, and drove into the dimness of a large warehouse with no signage.

The suspension squeaked as they emerged from the car, the four of them removing sunglasses as they looked around. It was a tin-sided facility the size of a hardware Supa Store, with six aisles between racking that extended to the ceiling. The front of the aisles contained boots and fatigues, tents and field shovels, some of them in sale bins and others modelled on military mannequins. Gallen knew what would be down the back.

'This way,' said Toby, leading them towards a metal scanner of the type used at the bag search area of airports. A tall security guy took the team through the scanner one by one, issuing white plastic bar-coded security numbers that they pinned to their shirts. The scanner beeped and they turned, watching Aaron remove a handgun from his hip and a bitch-gun from his ankle rig.

The security guy took the weapons and secured them in a lock-box under his desk. 'This way,' he said, walking them towards an office where a thickset black man in his fifties stood, lighting a cheroot.

'Chase,' said Aaron.

Gallen noticed that Chase shook the offered hand but kept his eyes on the people unknown to him.

'These the boys?' Chase asked, walking around Aaron.

Gallen stepped forward, offered his hand. 'Gerry Gallen.'

'Chase Lang,' said the big man. 'Corps, right?'

'Ex.' Gallen noticed a SEALs ring on Lang's heavy right hand, and recognised the name. Chase Lang was a military services provider, what in the old days was known as a middleman for mercenaries.

'The man say you got a budget of twenty-five grand,' said Lang. 'Let's go shopping.'

The golf cart hissed around the aisles, Chase Lang giving a running commentary as they passed the bins of everything a small army would need for life in the field. Starting with the fatigues, Gallen read from his piece of paper the dimensions and boot size of a crew that were accustomed to ordering precisely the fit they wanted. He ordered sets of blacks, jungle camos and arctic camos, and then sifted through the racks of civvie fatigues, military gear designed for use by special forces and intel teams when they wanted to pass for mining assayers or geology analysts.

The security guy beside Lang input the orders into a handheld device and Gallen noticed that a John Deere Gator was following them, the items being dumped in the tray on the back.

They threw in socks, underwear, undershirts, thermals and field toilet bags with the good razors that lasted for at least twenty shaves. He ordered caps, hats, gloves, travel pouches that were really handgun holsters and sunglasses that held boom mics and earpieces. Winter pointed out a selection of tiny cameras that transmitted wirelessly to a screen. The whole set-up seemed to run on lithium batteries and Gallen ordered one screen and four cameras.

There was a bin of boots on sale—JB Goodhues, known to soldiers as Canadian fire-fighter boots. They were ten-hole lace-ups with steel shanks and a sole rated for walking across burning coals without melting. They were lined with fire-retarding insulation and because they usually cost two hundred and fifty per pair, the military didn't stock them in the PX and didn't have them on general issue. Winter seized on them when he realised what they were and Gallen ordered two pairs each at the sale price of forty dollars a throw.

'Make a man happy with good leather, boss,' said Winter, lighting a smoke and pleased with the boots.

Gallen smiled; at officer training there had been an old-school instructor who used to tell the young candidates that if you looked after a soldier's feet and stomach—and gave him fair warning of what was expected each day—then you were basically a good officer.

They took six Kevlar vests—all in taupe—before driving through the internal security fence at the rear of the complex, Chase Lang holding forth on why his teenage kids sat twenty yards from one another and communicated via text messages.

'I think this generation are the smartest young people ever,' he said, shaking his head. 'So what are they so afraid of?'

The golf cart stopped in front of a weapons cache as large as any Gallen had seen outside of Camp Pendleton, the home of the US Marines 1st Recon Battalion. Following Lang along the display racks, Gallen and Winter noted the handguns, the assault rifles, the grenades and marksman rifles. There was a special section for the assault rifles with grenade launchers under the barrel and night sights on the top.

They'd agreed on 9mm handguns and 7.62mm assault rifles, so Gallen ordered five SIG Sauer handguns in matt black, ten spare mags and two large boxes of Winchester loads, each containing thirty-two smaller boxes. Gallen was about to get a set of Colt M4 assault rifles loaded in the Gator when Winter cleared his throat.

'Problem?' said Gallen, playing with the breech and cocking the action of a weapon he'd come to know very well during his time in Mindanao and Afghanistan.

'You ever seen the NATO-issue?' Winter pointed down the display racks to the Heckler & Koch section.

Following Winter to the German weapons, Gallen was out of his comfort zone. US-made firearms may not have been the most advanced, but they worked in all environments and all weather. He watched as the Canadian picked up a futuristic assault rifle labelled 'G36'.

'Looks fancy,' said Gallen, as Lang joined them. 'But I don't bet my crew's life on fancy.'

Lang and Winter chuckled at each other and Gallen felt the flush of anger in his face. 'Something funny?'

'Boss,' said Winter, handing the G36 to Gallen, who immediately felt its lightness and balance, 'when I first joined ISAF and realised I'd be using the Heckler, I didn't like the idea. Next morning, my captain tells me to go into the galley, get the rifle from the deep freeze and go shoot some targets.'

'What happened?' said Gallen, reaching for his smokes.

'Took this G36 out of the deep freeze—one just like that—walked out to the range and put a whole magazine into the big spot from eighty yards.'

Looking down at the rifle, with its weird handle over the top of the breech, Gallen didn't know how to respond. 'How long had it been in the deep freeze?'

'Overnight, boss,' said Winter. 'Mag too. It was so cold my hands stuck to it, and there I am putting eyes and smile in a black circle from eighty yards.'

'On auto?' said Gallen, getting annoyed.

'Sure—singles, full auto. Learned to love that rifle.'

'Well.' Gallen rotated the weapon in his hands. 'Looks like a prop from *Star Wars*.'

'It's the latest and the best—Heckler & Koch,' said Lang, like a philosopher.

'I got one answer to the latest and the best.' Gallen handed the Heckler back to Winter.

'What's that?' said Lang, as Gallen turned to go.

'Winchester .30-30,' said Gallen as he walked back to the Colts, laughter banging around the warehouse.

CHAPTER 9

Winter did the driving, north from Natrona County airport on I-25, the northbound interstate into Montana. Sitting in the passenger seat Gallen scrolled through his cell phone, picking up texts and voicemail. He'd said yes to the Heckler & Koch rifles; the quip about the .30-30 had been a joke at his own expense. Most North American farmers kept a Winchester .30-30—the 'lever-action' rifles from western movies—even though the weapon was invented more than a century ago. The .30-30 was easy to use, didn't fail and any gunsmith could work on one. What he really wanted was more control over the kit he'd bought. He'd have preferred to dump it in a lock-up until it was needed but Aaron had it bundled into a bunch of black holdall bags and said he'd store it, like it was his property. Gallen's time in the field had taught him valuable lessons about the crew's kit and who gets to touch it. Too many hands on the bags was a doomed recipe. Only one approach got personal gear where it had to go, and that was signing it over to each man and making him responsible.

'So Donny said yes?' said Winter as he got Roy's truck settled at sixty-five mph and found a country music station based in Casper.

'Said yes on the phone. Last night was just catching up.' Gallen grimaced at a series of voicemail alerts from his father. 'About to take a job on the armoured cars, so this gig's what he's looking for.'

47

'He's not married is my guess.'

'Hah!' Gallen smiled at the idea. 'Donny McCann likes being single. Can't imagine him taking crap from a wife.'

'Roy said you was married.'

'Divorced. Two years ago. Two and a half.'

'While you're in that shit?' said Winter, cracking the window and flicking his ash at the gap.

'Technically,' said Gallen. 'But it was failing before then.'

Winter paused like he was trying to establish something. 'So she divorced you while you're dodging bullets from Towelie?'

Gallen put down the phone, looked at Winter. 'Got one for me?' Taking a smoke, he lit it.

'Didn't mean to pry,' said the Canadian. 'Just that a woman can break a man like no Talibani ever could.'

'Marcia didn't break me.' Gallen cracked his window as 'Louisiana Saturday Night' started on the radio.

They drove after that without talking, Gallen thinking back to that morning at the US forward base in Marjah. Spring was taking forever, the rare patches of warmth suddenly whipped away by the vicious alpine winds that swooped down from the Kush, making grown men stand still in shock.

In special forces, the enlisted men and officers messed together, and as Gallen had passed into the chow tent for breakfast he'd seen Marcia on the Wall of Shame, a public noticeboard where dishonourable wives and girlfriends were displayed. He'd taken down the photo, embarrassed, as he prepared himself for the morning briefing.

The picture was on the board again by lunch and Gallen had let it be known that he didn't want his disintegrating personal life played out on a wall of shame in Afghanistan. He was too private for that.

By the second day of the Marcia episode, he'd shared a coffee with the commanding officer of the forward base, Major Andrew Dumfries—a veteran of Desert Shield/Storm. Dumfries was a no-bullshit Texan who came straight to it, telling Gallen that the Wall of Shame wasn't about a single individual.

'You put my ex-wife up there,' said Gallen, 'and that's about an individual.'

'No.' Dumfries pointed at his chest. 'It's about all of us. We're a corps, a single body. Your men want to put shame on your wife, it's their way of taking the pain for you. So let 'em!'

Gallen had let it go, just as he'd let Marcia go off with her dentist boyfriend.

'It's okay to be beaten by a lady,' said Winter as they hammered along in the overtaking lane, the V8 purring. 'You can go AWOL for a while, shake her out of the system.'

Gallen picked up on what Winter was talking about. He'd drifted around the country after discharge before arriving back at the farm, but it wasn't something he wanted to go into.

'I shook her out,' said Gallen. 'She's gone.'

The lawyer's office advertised *McRae Doon Partners—Attorneys at Law* on the wall behind the receptionist, but Messrs Doon and McRae hadn't been around for fifty years. The only practising lawyers in the office were Rob Stansfield and Wes Carty, the dead-eyed lawyer who emerged in front of Gallen.

'We're inside,' said Carty, thumb over his shoulder.

Carty's room was large and sun-filled, an 1890s tribute to what the founding fathers once thought Clearmont could be.

'Well, lookie here,' said the red-faced man in the armchair, sneering as Gallen sat down.

'Dad,' said Gallen. 'How you doin'?'

'You little fucker,' said Roy Gallen, standing.

Carty threw himself between the armchairs. 'Roy! We spoke about this.'

Gallen eased into the armchair that faced Carty's desk. There wasn't much Roy Gallen could do to him these days, 'less he was carrying a gun, but Gallen flinched all the same, felt the ice in his stomach as his father eyeballed him. Too many hockey games, too many broncs broken, too many winter mornings being thrown out the door to do barn chores. They had left their mark. Gallen was no longer scared of his old man, but he wasn't immune to his anger.

'Gallen Family Farms Sweet Clover Trust,' said Carty, sitting behind the desk and reading straight from the filing tag of the manila folder on the desk. 'We're all present: trustees Roy Gallen and Gerard Gallen, and the designated trustee, Wesley Carty. Agreed?'

Gallen swapped a look with Roy and the lawyer continued.

'There is a dispute around the finances of the Sweet Clover Trust and given that we are all here, does anyone object to the motion that the designated trustee be the arbiter of the dispute?'

Roy sighed, Scope mouthwash coming off him in waves. 'Depends where you come down, Wes.'

'I come down in the best interests of the trust, Roy,' said Carty, a scratch golfer whose daughter was a champion barrel racer thanks to the horses he kept buying her.

'I accept your decision, Wes.' Gallen raised his hand like he was at an intel briefing. 'Let's get it done.'

Carty scribbled a note in his minutes. 'Roy?'

Roy sighed, like someone had pulled the plug on an airbed. 'Shit.'

'That a yes, Roy?'

'Sounds like I need my own lawyer.'

Carty noted it in the minutes but Gallen wasn't going to ignore it. 'Dad, Wes is the trust lawyer. This is his job.'

Roy Gallen waved his hand like he was swatting a fly at the sale yards. 'Yeah, yeah, yeah. Like the colt said. Let's get it done.'

Gallen found him at the diner's window table, Roy wearing his uniform of Carhartt canvas jacket, white western shirt and an old pair of Wranglers. Hair pulled back in a Brylcreemed wave that hadn't changed since Gallen was a boy.

'Can I join you?' said Gallen, pausing before he touched the chair.

Roy looked out the window. 'No law against it.'

Gallen removed his cap and signalled the waitress for one coffee. 'We'll clear the debts and then let's start again, okay?'

'Didn't know it was that bad,' said Roy. 'Been drinking too hard, I guess.'

'The creditors just want an arrangement, Dad,' said Gallen, not wanting to talk down to his father or lecture him about the booze.

'Wes will control the creditors and the cheque book for the next month and then we review it, okay? It's not forever.'

Roy nodded. 'We still need cash. Those steers don't ship for another ten weeks at least.'

'I'm putting in two thousand a week,' said Gallen, treading carefully. 'Wes takes care of the creditors and pays you a wage.'

'I ain't being paid by that sissy little Protestant sonofabitch,' spat the old man, sitting up straight. 'No Gallen was ever on no Carty payroll.'

'He's the trust lawyer,' said Gallen. 'And besides, the money comes from me.'

Roy shook his head slowly.

'Look, Dad, the power will go on today. That's something.'

'Yeah,' said Roy. 'That's something. So where's this money of yours coming from? Marines ain't givin' it away.'

'Got a gig,' said Gallen. 'Corporate security.'

'Who for?'

'Doesn't matter,' said Gallen. 'Kenny's signed on too.'

'Take my farm labourer?' Roy tapped a big forefinger on the tabletop. 'Know we got some jumpers to work up? For real cash?'

'We start in ten days. Kenny can start 'em, and you can finish.'

Roy sipped at the coffee. He was as good a horse trainer as you could find in Sheridan County but he didn't like jumpers and he'd obviously been planning to hide behind Kenny's expertise.

'Ain't been over a rail for ten, twelve years,' said Roy. 'Might have to stop the drinkin' for a whiles.'

'If Kenny gets them horses to the point, then we can have Yvonne over to do the rail work.'

'Yvonne?' said Roy, confused. 'McKenzie? She's down Shell.'

'She just bought a place on the forty-second,' said Gallen, feeling his voice squeak. 'She divorced.'

Roy's face flashed concern and then his eyes were warmly focused on his son. 'Yvonne and you.'

'No, Dad. Not—'

'Yeah, son. I remember,' said Roy, his face blossoming into the charmer of old. 'Patricia told me, when you was in high school.'

Gallen blushed. 'Told you what?'

'Yvonne McKenzie was sweet on you, is what.'

'She got it wrong,' said Gallen, wondering where that coffee was.

'I don't think so,' said Roy, dentures lighting up his face. 'Women don't make mistakes with all that.'

CHAPTER 10

Gallen stood in the forecourt of the Logan Super 8 Motel, watched a 767 landing in the grey morning light as he waited for Winter. It was the first day of his employment by Oasis Energy and while he was happy with the corporate MasterCard he'd been mailed, he didn't like his name jumping up wherever Mulligan or Aaron felt like tracking it. Still, it eased a cash-flow problem in the short term and he was feeling more relaxed than he had at any time since resigning his commission.

'Time for breakfast?' said Winter, approaching with his small backpack.

'Coffee and biscuit, at least.' Gallen headed across the car park.

They discussed how they were going to structure the bodyguard and decided that, regardless of the chain of command, they'd rotate the personal aspect so as to keep things professional. Didn't want anyone making friends with the client—that created mistakes.

Gallen glanced at his G-Shock: time to meet McCann's flight from LA.

As they stood, his cell rang.

'Yep,' said Gallen, noting Bren Dale's name on the screen.

'Boss, it's me,' came Dale's voice, not happy.

'Yeah, Bren?'

'I can't make it. Sorry, boss.'

'What?' said Gallen, turning from Winter. 'Can't make it this morning?'

'No, boss,' said Dale. 'Can't make the gig.'

'Not at all? Shit, Bren. The gig's built around you.'

There was a sound of someone hyperventilating. 'I'm sorry, man. Find someone else, okay? Sorry.'

The line went dead and Gallen stared at the phone.

'What's up?' said Winter, zipping his pack.

'Bren's out.' Gallen could barely believe it.

'Why?'

'I don't know,' said Gallen.

Winter got to his feet, slung his bag over one shoulder. 'Cold feet?'

'Not last I checked,' said Gallen.

'Lady got to him?' said Winter.

'Could be.' Gallen dropped change on the table.

Waiting for a cab in the forecourt, he mulled on it. He hadn't just lost his 2IC. He'd started a gig with a bad omen.

Gallen spotted Donny McCann as the crowds spewed out of the domestic arrivals gate of Denver International. McCann was in jeans and a polo shirt under a ski jacket; he had a lean middleweight's body and a set of aviator shades.

'Hey, boss,' said McCann, stopping in front of Gallen and Winter.

'Donny,' said Gallen, shaking his hand. 'This is Kenny Winter, former Canadian Assaulters, served in ISAF.'

McCann shook Winter's hand, gave the slow nod of a veteran recognising another's credentials.

They drank coffee in one of the airport's cafes as they waited for Aaron to arrive from LA with the gear.

'Slight change,' said Gallen, once the middle-aged Anglo male at the adjacent table had moved on. 'Bren can't make it.'

'Why not?' said McCann. 'That's not like Bren, pull out when he say he in.'

'I know,' said Gallen. 'Phoned me an hour ago. Said he can't make it, now all I can get is voicemail when I call back.'

McCann looked around the cafe and the concourse, scanning the crowds. 'So now we're three?'

'Till we get a replacement, yeah.' Gallen cleared his throat. 'But for now, Kenny's my second.'

McCann and Winter eyed one another for several seconds, Gallen hoping nothing would start. Donny McCann was the smaller man but he'd grown up in Compton Beach and Gallen had never seen him take shit from anyone; Winter was the hulking farm boy and—if Mulligan was correct—a NATO assassin.

'You okay with that, Kenny?' said McCann evenly, not taking his eyes off the Canadian.

'I do what the boss says,' said Winter, not even a bob from his larynx. 'I'm okay with that.'

Gallen was about to leap in when McCann broke with a big smile. 'Shit, boss. You hear that? Damn good answer, if he gonna work for you.'

Gallen leaned back. 'It's a perfect answer, Donny.'

McCann shrugged, extended a hand to Winter. 'Let's take the money and not the bullets, okay?'

'My sentiments exactly,' said Winter, his broken incisor showing as he grinned.

The Oasis jet was late but Gallen and his crew were airborne shortly before two pm, heading north for Calgary.

Leaving McCann and Winter in leather seats facing one another at the front of the cabin, Gallen moved down the plane to where Aaron was seated in conversation with a blond man with a military haircut. Gallen had him at late twenties, perhaps thirty.

'Gerry, have a seat,' said Aaron, pointing at the seats across the aisle. 'Need a drink?'

'No thanks,' said Gallen, sitting. 'I work dry.'

'Good,' said Aaron, raising his whisky glass so the ice clicked. 'Meet Mike. Ex-Aussie Navy.'

'G'day,' said the man, leaning over and delivering a dry shake from a large forearm. 'Mike Ford.'

Gallen took the handshake, realised the Aussie was putting nothing into it. 'Gerry Gallen.'

'Know how I was looking for combat divers two weeks ago?' said Aaron. 'Found a crew of Aussies working salvage out of Honolulu. Sent two out to Thailand and offered Mike a job.'

Gallen nodded politely.

'So, Gerry—three of you?'

'Yeah,' said Gallen. 'Last-minute drop-out from my sergeant.'

Aaron slugged at the amber fluid. 'Mulligan wants four.'

Gallen tried to keep it light. He knew the theory behind a bodyguard of four: you could rotate teams of two and always have a strong presence. 'We'll be four soon. I need a couple days.'

'Gig started this morning, at oh-nine-hundred, Gerry. I don't need soon. I need four guys now.'

Returning to the front of the plane, Gallen felt the adrenaline rising. Not just the same old uncertainties and threats from the field, but the trickle-down of bullshit that people in Gallen's position had to accept, whether they were being micro-managed by some spook from the Pentagon or taking shit from a corporate senior manager.

'All okay?' asked McCann, dealing a game of gin rummy with Winter as Gallen scrolled his cell for a name. 'They cool 'bout Bren?'

'Yeah, they're fine,' said Gallen, mentally playing with scenarios. They were meeting Harry Durville tomorrow morning at nine, and Gallen had until then to recruit his fourth man.

CHAPTER 11

The Oasis headquarters was in Calgary's downtown but the minivan dropped Gallen and his crew at the oil company's compound, over the river from the city and a few blocks north of the Calgary Zoo.

The compound had a trucking and gas storage component but also demountable quarters and a mess hall, arranged on little 'streets' with hedges and trees that blocked them from the distribution operation. It wasn't the Marriott, but as far as transit bases for North America's oil and gas workers went it was clean, and the minivan driver promised that the showers ran hot.

'Got that manifest?' said Gallen as the minivan motored away, leaving them outside their barracks.

'Yep, boss.' Winter showed the bill from the PX buy-up in Longbeach.

'Stow that gear and tick everything off, okay?'

'Got it, boss.' Winter turned to the pile of black holdalls on the step of the barracks.

'And, Kenny—check for tampering, right?'

Finding a table on the small veranda that fronted the demountable, Gallen sat with a pen and pad and started calling.

Of the people who were out of the Corps, there were guys doing night security at Sea World in Florida, guys riding shotgun in armoured trucks, and guys wandering the floors of casinos in Las Vegas, ready to show drunks to the door when the booze and losing streaks became too much.

Wendell Favor had taken over his father's sports store in east Texas, Tigger Lawrenson had pursued a lifelong dream and was playing AAA-league baseball for a team in Omaha, and Len Mantrill—the biggest, meanest street fighter Gallen ever saw—was going door to door for Jesus somewhere in the suburbs of Seattle.

Everyone wanted to catch up with Captain Gallen, but no one wanted to join a bodyguard detail at short notice.

Some of Gallen's calls went straight to voicemail; Gallen guessed they were part of the flood of US Marines being immediately re-absorbed into Iraq and Afghanistan under the military contractors.

The afternoon turned into early evening and Gallen re-entered the demountable as the chill descended. On the floor in front of him, McCann stacked and counted while Winter ticked the items on Chase Lang's manifest.

'How we going, boss?' asked McCann, counting out the magazines for the Heckler & Koch assault rifles.

'Striking out,' said Gallen, moving out of the small living area to the kitchen. There was a stash of basic provisions on the counter: bread, coffee, milk and cereal. Opening the refrigerator, he found a six-pack of Sprite and handed them out.

'Can we work a crew of three?' Winter lit a smoke.

'Not ideal,' said Gallen. 'As you told me: two teams of two, rotating. That's how to get it done.'

'You sure Bren's out?' said McCann, slugging at the soda.

'What he told me.'

'He won't return your call?'

'Trying since the AM. You wanna try?'

McCann reached out his hand for the cell, and then thought again. 'Might use my phone, see if he picks up.'

He dialled and reclined back on a stack of fatigues. 'Brenny Dale, my man,' he said, thumb raised at Gallen as he sat upright. ''Sup, dawg?'

Gallen watched as McCann's bonhomie succeeded only so far, right up until he told his old unit-buddy that he was in Calgary with Gerry Gallen, and what's this about not being able to make it?

McCann took the cell from his ear and looked at it. 'Hung up. Bren Dale hung up on me.'

Gallen sighed. 'What'd he say?'

'Said, tell the boys I's sorry. Not my call.'

Gallen's ears pricked up. 'He said that?'

'Just like that. Not my call,' said McCann. 'Think his daddy put down the foot?'

'Don't know,' said Gallen.

'What about his daddy?' asked Winter.

'Seen the TV ads, car salesman calling hisself the King of Chev?' said McCann. 'Seen that scary-ass fucker pointing at the screen, telling you to come down, see the King?'

'Yeah,' said Winter, smiling. 'That Bren's dad?'

'Fuck yeah,' said McCann. 'Come back from Vietnam, makes a fortune selling cars and says ain't no son of his ever gonna fight in no shit overseas, for no fucker.'

'So Bren?'

'So Brenny turn around, joins the Marines when he's supposed to be on a football scholarship to college, and the next thing you know he in the shit in Mindanao, getting chased by Filipino bad-asses through the jungle.'

'Donny's thinking that Bren's dad has told him, *Don't think you can inherit this empire if you go back to that shit,*' said Gallen.

'Yeah, but—' said McCann, then waved it away. 'Who else we got, boss?'

Draining his Sprite, Gallen moved back to the veranda, shrugging into his jacket as the temperature plummeted.

Looking at the phone, he toyed with an idea. In Indonesia it was about eight or nine in the morning, but it wasn't the time that worried him. The number on his phone was for Pete Morton, a former Marines Recon captain who'd leapt to DIA while Gallen was posted in Zamboanga City, Mindanao. Morton had remained in South-East Asia, in an indistinct capacity, although Gallen had heard that he now arranged off-the-books solutions for US intelligence, using local assets and deniable payments. It was the side of the military Gallen hadn't wanted to be associated with while he was commissioned, and even now—though he was privateering himself—he baulked at calling the man.

Gallen waited for the call to connect. It purred for five seconds and clicked into what sounded like a different system.

Just when he was about to give up, someone answered.

'Yep,' said the man's voice.

'Morton? Pete, that you?' said Gallen. 'It's Gerry Gallen, from Recon.'

'Hey, Gerry. How's life in Calgary?'

'I—'

He couldn't finish because of Morton's laughter. 'Enjoying the lions and tigers, are you, Gerry?'

'Shit, Pete,' said Gallen, not in the mood. 'You got one of them boxes?'

'Sure. It says Mountain Bell, roaming, Calgary Zoo.'

Gallen waited for the giggling to subside. 'Okay, Pete, you got me. I'm feeding the monkeys. I need a favour.'

'Try me, sport.'

'You know any military guys, preferably special forces, want to work a corporate bodyguard detail? Starts tomorrow morning, North America. I'm the boss.'

'What's the money?'

'Two grand a week, full health, death and disability.'

'Nice work, if you'd called a year ago,' said Morton. 'Now they're all going back to Iraq and the Ghan. Every time a bomb destroys a souk, the contractors are upping the money, and you know what soldiers are like.'

Gallen knew what soldiers were like: as soon as the bivvie chatter laid off on women, it went straight to money and how to make it so fast that the cold and the bullets wouldn't matter.

'Okay, just thought I'd touch base.'

'Hey, good to talk, Gerry. Heard you kicked on to captain?'

'The only punishment they could think of.'

'Hah!' said Morton. 'I've got your number. I'll call if I think of anyone, okay?'

They found a bar with a good menu in East Village and Gallen bought a round of Buds off the tap.

'Break a leg,' said Winter, raising his glass.

McCann raised his too. 'Mud in your eye.'

They all touched glasses and Gallen relaxed slightly, glad the gig had now been launched without jinxing it with a call to good luck, or any of the other sentiments that troopers could live without.

Gallen still had no answers for Aaron, but for now McCann and Winter were getting along and that mattered more to him than having the full crew. The barbecue ribs arrived with more beers and they unwound with the band playing 1980s covers.

As they walked from their cab to the guard house of the Oasis compound a couple of hours later, Gallen's phone rang. The screen said Pete Morton.

'Pete,' said Gallen.

'Hey, Gerry. The penny dropped, buddy. You're not wiping the ass of a certain oil billionaire who likes getting hammered, getting in fights?'

'That's no comment, Pete.'

'I met the Brits who came before you, Gerry,' said Morton, a slight taunt.

Gallen stopped and waved the others on. 'Oh yeah?'

'Yeah. A Para named Piers, did a lot in western Iraq.'

'Nice for him,' said Gallen, fumbling for a smoke.

'I guess you're not interested.'

Gallen tried to play it cool, but he was hooked. 'Anything I should know?'

'Like, why they were fired?'

Gallen looked at the orange glow of Calgary on a still and cold night. 'Fired?'

'What Piers told me,' said Morton.

'Thought they took a big contract in Iraq.'

'Sumatra ain't exactly Iraq, buddy,' said Morton. 'Shit, they don't even wear towels on their heads.'

'Piers and his crew are in Sumatra?'

'Sure,' said Morton. 'Chasing them separatist Muslims up in Aceh. ExxonMobil got a big push on there right now.'

'So why were they fired?'

'Don't know, buddy,' said Morton. 'This was a social introduction, a week ago.'

61

'Can you find out?'

'I can do a lot of things, Gerry. You know that.'

Gallen felt conned, but he wasn't going to let this go. In the days when he was responsible for up to fifteen men in the field, getting good intelligence was crucial to everyone's survival. And if any of it pointed to increased danger to his men, he'd squeeze that intel until it bled.

'Okay, Pete, what will it take?'

'We can keep it informal,' said Morton, the spy in him creeping out like a shadow. 'I help you and you help me, right?'

'Help?'

'You know how it works, Gerry. You need information and I need information. We meet in the middle.'

'Sounds like a pact with the devil.'

Morton laughed hard. 'You're very dramatic for someone who spent years collecting information and handing it on to people like me.'

'It's what I was trained to do, Pete,' said Gallen, before realising what he'd said.

'Elegantly put,' said Morton. 'Back atcha.'

The line went dead and Gallen trudged up the driveway to his demountable. Somewhere in the back of his mind he heard the voice of a drunken US Army Green Beret, in a USO facility at Chicago O'Hare, telling anyone who would listen that combat veterans don't ever retire, their senses just play switcheroo: what was once a bivvie dream of comfortable civilian life is now their daily reality, while all the shit they ever took in the field visits them every night in their dreams.

Gallen forced a smile as he entered the demountable and found McCann and Winter watching *America's Funniest Home Videos*.

Lying on his bunk, in the dark, Gallen thought about the conversation with Morton. That a couple of soldiers were fired by a difficult boss was not the issue. What worried him was why Paul Mulligan had lied about it.

CHAPTER 12

The atrium of the Oasis Energy high-rise on 7th Street smelled of freshly brewed coffee as Gallen lead McCann through at 8.55 am. Meeting Winter at the espresso stand they observed the large area of sofas and newsstands, trying to find the people who didn't belong, assess the risks. He saw him on the first pass: Aaron, sitting at a sofa with Mike Ford, the Aussie naval combat diver.

'Christ,' said Gallen to himself as he paid the barista and carried the coffees to his crew, noticing that Winter and McCann had both taken the sofa that faced Aaron.

Aaron rose as Gallen approached. 'You don't have a fourth.'

'You can count.'

'Sure I can, Gerry, and I count four thousand clams a week that you won't be getting 'cos you can't get the crew.'

'I can get 'em,' said Gallen, keeping one eye on the Aussie. The previous night Winter had reminded him that the Aussie naval commandos had done a lot of the hard yards in the Gulf, boarding the vessels that British and US special forces were in no hurry to storm. They didn't have a high profile on CNN but they were respected in the special forces world.

'I count three of you, Gerry,' said Aaron, smirking. 'We're not going up to see the big guy with three. Durville's about comfort.'

'I've got calls out.'

'No, you have your ass hanging out.' Aaron looked, ostentatiously at his big Omega watch. 'I have a solution but we're due up there in three minutes so you decide now.'

'What's the deal?' said Gallen, feeling his pulse bang in his head. He didn't know if he was ready for this, so soon after the shit.'

Aaron flicked his chin over his shoulder. 'Ford's your fourth man.'

'No offence, Aaron.' Gallen held up his hand. 'I don't know the Aussie and my guys don't know him either.'

'Let's change that,' said the former spook, turning and walking for his sofa.

Shaking with Mike Ford, Gallen sat, totally pissed. 'I got nothing against you, Mike, but I don't know you.'

'I get it,' said Ford, cool blue eyes above wide cheekbones. 'Don't know your crew, neither. I like to know who's in my bivvie.'

Gallen couldn't hate a guy who talked straight. 'Tell me about yourself.'

'Aussie Navy, clearance diver, combat diver. Spent four years in the Gulf in a unit called Team Three.'

'Team Three? That's like SEALs, right?'

'I guess,' said Ford, shrugging. 'Vessels, rigs, clandestine insertions. Recon and demos mostly. Some take-downs too, and a lot of welding.'

'Welding?' said Gallen.

'You'd be surprised.'

'So, you saw action in the Gulf, but I think you were in the hills too?' said Gallen, meaning Afghanistan.

'Yeah. That was a great secret, wasn't it?'

'Where were you?'

'Can't say,' said Ford, giving Aaron a look. 'But I can tell you that if a movie maker ever finds a hero in all that shit, then he's the one should have the fucking medal.'

'Hah!' said Gallen, standing. 'Okay, Mike, you're in, but there's one rule.'

'Name it,' said Ford.

'I don't wear no fancy suit, but I'm the boss.'

'Sweet,' said the Aussie.

'I mean it, buddy. You got a problem, it comes to me.'

Ford smiled. 'Got it, boss.'

Harry Durville kept his cowboy boots on the desk for the first eight minutes of the meeting. Gallen focused on them after he lost track of the cussing that came from the Canadian's mouth. There was an attractive executive woman called Florita Mendes, seated to the side of Durville's desk, and where Gallen came from you didn't cuss in front of the ladies.

'I'm easy to dislike,' said Durville, finally putting his feet on the carpet and moving to where Gallen stood, uncomfortable, beside the windows that looked north over the river from forty floors up. The oil billionaire stood about five-ten and had a bandy, lean-forward style of walking; he kept the power in his shoulders and had large hands. If Gallen had been in a bar he'd have assumed the fifty-nine-year-old was coming over to throw a punch.

'See that, Gerry?' Durville pointed out the window, ignoring Aaron's attempts to conduct a proper meeting.

'Sure,' said Gallen. 'Calgary. Had an Olympics here.'

'No, not the fucking city,' the oil man said, mouth smiling but eyes like a reptile. 'The north, the great white north.'

'Okay.'

'That's a licence to print fucking money, Gerry. That's what that is.'

'Sure,' said Gallen.

'That's about twenty-five million square miles of cash, should anyone have the balls and the banking facilities to get in there, haul it out, process it and sell it south of the border.'

'That's great,' said Gallen.

'But in order to be in faster than the next fucker, I go to where I have to be; I walk the ground, I smell the air. You see?'

Gallen smelled whisky on Durville's breath, saw a rheumy shade in the eye.

''Cos you see, Gerry, I'm not some business-school faggot sitting in meetings and being wheeled out for appearances on Bloomberg.

I'm not a CEO, Gerry. I'm a managing director, okay? I'm a fucking owner, and there is a difference.'

Gallen had only a vague idea what Harry Durville was talking about.

'But the more I get out and about, the more I upset the Ruskies, the Arabs and the fucking Texans. And the more I do that the more danger I place myself in, you see?'

'Guess that's what I'm doing here, Mr Durville,' said Gallen.

'This isn't a nice business, Gerry, and those of us who succeed are not nice people,' said Durville, biting a cigarette out of a soft pack and offering one to Gallen. 'Aaron here hates me talking this up—hates me putting ideas out there—but it's the truth, and you should hear it: I know seven Ruskies who'd have me assassinated right now if they could get away with it and it didn't cost them too much money.'

'Harry,' interrupted Aaron, 'let's get back to the meeting.'

Durville lit up and offered the flame to Gallen's cigarette. 'Four years ago, I was closing a deal in Siberia, and my car was blown up.'

'Ignore him,' said Aaron, ushering Gallen towards the sofa at the other end of the office.

'He should hear this,' said Durville.

'That was Russia and you were interested in the wrong woman.' Aaron showed Gallen a seat. 'This is now and this is Canada. We don't do deals in strip clubs, we don't assassinate business rivals.'

'Holy shit, Gerry,' said Durville, pulling a big crystal ashtray towards him as he sat on a sofa. 'Those Russians can fucking party.'

'Okay,' said Aaron, handing Gallen a thin file. 'Here's how we work: you're shown the week ahead every Monday morning, either handed to you or emailed.'

Gallen opened the file.

'You brief me on any extraordinary measures, any security sweeps you want done, any advance searches, and then we go from there,' Aaron continued. 'You pick the weak spots, we do the work-up together.'

Gallen sucked on his smoke, put it in the ashtray as he read the first page of the file. It was a computer calendar printout showing a crowded week of travel, meetings, golf games, hockey seats and speeches. In one week Harry Durville was spending time in Calgary,

Houston, Los Angeles and Mexico City. But it was the Friday–Sunday spread that caught Gallen's attention.

'What's Kugaaruk?' he said, looking from Aaron to Durville.

'It's way up north, in Nunavut,' said Aaron.

'That the tribal province?' asked Gallen, envisaging sealskin kayaks and Eskimos with harpoons.

'You know how I said the north's a huge cash-pit?' said Durville.

'Sure,' said Gallen.

'Well, you want a springboard into that pit,' said Durville, 'you go to Kugaaruk and you build yourself the best rig.'

'Rig?'

'Behind you, Gerry,' said Durville. 'Check that out.'

Turning, Gallen saw a trestle table against the far wall of the office, dominated by a large model. It looked like a space station and had the word *Ariadne* painted in black along its curved, pale blue sides.

'Looks like a UFO,' said Gallen.

'A UFO?' said Durville, sucking on his smoke. 'Shit, that's Florita's project, right there. That's how we gonna make billions out of the great white north, Gerry. That UFO is the key to it all.'

Gallen looked at him to get a sense of what he was talking about, but Durville was laughing so hard that he'd brought on a coughing fit.

CHAPTER 13

Gallen sorted his notes as the Escalade motored south from Denver International Airport. The map showed several ways to get into downtown and Gallen wanted to avoid the route that meant too many fly-overs looking down on Durville's silver SUV.

'Take the next off ramp,' said Gallen. 'We'll come in on Colfax, okay?'

Donny McCann eased the vehicle off the freeway into the city and stuck to the main streets. They were heading for the National Cattlemen's Beef Association on East Nichols Avenue, where Harry Durville was hosting a lunch or a meeting, Gallen had lost track. He'd lost track of just about everything to do with the billionaire except that the man was rarely off the phone and that his chief legal counsel—Florita Mendes—had a mind that trapped the smallest details and held them there for Harry to call upon.

From the back seat, Durville bumped one caller and was suddenly yelling into the phone. 'George!'

There was a pause while the sound of a Texan voice snarled out of Durville's handset and then Durville was laughing, yelling, 'Fuck, yeah!'

As Durville rang off, still chuckling, Florita quietly reminded him that technically George still retained the right to be called 'Mr President'.

Settling into the interminable red lights of East Colfax, Gallen keyed the mic dangling in front of his throat and asked Winter what was happening.

'Nothing back here, boss,' said Winter.

Peering into the Escalade's side mirror, Gallen could see the blue Impala two cars behind the Escalade.

'You look clear,' said Winter.

Closing on the National Cattlemen's headquarters, they passed a large, modern mirror-glass building that looked like a tribute or a statement. Looking up, Gallen saw the golden crown on the top of the building, over a blue cross.

Durville leaned forward to Gallen as they reached their destination block. 'You take note, Gerry,' he said, eyes like an old rail network map. 'You wanna get certain things done in North America, you gotta go to the ranchers. Forget your lobbyists and PR people and crooked congressmen: you have lunch with the people who own most of the land. Understand?'

Gallen tapped the mic as Florita pulled Durville back for his briefing notes and a quick grooming, pulling a hair comb and then a clothes brush from her bag.

'Kenny, you and Mike are on Durville,' said Gallen into the mic. 'I'm covering the entry with Donny. Can do?'

'Can do, boss,' came the reply, and the Impala accelerated in front of the Escalade, taking a park near the front of the Cattlemen's building. When the Escalade pulled up, Winter and Ford were waiting on the sidewalk, scoping the street.

Florita slipped Durville two Tic Tacs and they were gone, ushered into the building by Gallen's men.

Dropping the windows to let in some of Denver's spring warmth, McCann searched for an FM station. 'That Durville can talk harder than my momma.' He shook his head fondly. 'Was that, like, George Bush on the phone? Holy shit.'

'That's Mr President to you, Donny.'

They watched the environment, looking for people or vehicles out of the pattern. Gallen's gut churned and he craved a smoke. It was this kind of gig that defined his time in Afghanistan: hurrying up and waiting. Watching, recording, noting and then delivering back to the

69

spooks at the head shed where, invariably, the questions indicated another agenda had been afoot the entire time.

His time in the field had made him wary—perhaps paranoid—about passive, clandestine engagements. They allowed too much power to the guy eating three squares a day, warm in his bed, surrounded by security. Having to sit still, waiting to observe others, now made him jumpy. It led to an explosion of activity when the soldiers were finally cut loose, and that was deadly. Gallen thought of the guys who'd lost hands because they picked up a laptop in a Taliban safe house or the soldiers with most of their fingers gone because they grabbed a cell phone that was left behind. He remembered what a humourless hard-ass his men thought he was, screaming at them to touch nothing, not allowing them to even use the light switches, open an oven or lift a telephone receiver for a dial tone. Captain Gallen's marching orders: your job is eyes and ears; your job is not to go fucking with the things that mean losing your hands and face.

Most of the special forces units in northern Afghanistan had a pool of ordnance and IED experts to call upon, and the joke on Gallen was that as soon as they turned over a Taliban safe house or supply depot, the first thing he asked the comms guy to do was call in the OED, the bomb-disposal people.

'We clear?' said Gallen now, after they'd scanned the street for five minutes.

'Sure, boss,' said McCann.

Gallen spoke with Winter over the mic.

'I can see nine men, cowboyed-up, sitting around a boardroom table,' said Winter, who was waiting outside the meeting with Ford. 'The food's just arrived. Bunch of dudes dressed like chefs. Might escort them in.'

Gallen signed off. 'Up for a sub and coffee?' He looked around the Escalade.

'Roast beef, mustard and pickles,' said McCann.

'Gimme thirty minutes,' said Gallen, checking his SIG for load and safety before replacing it in the pouch holster over his belt buckle.

Retracing the route by two blocks, Gallen made a pass in front of the building with the crown on top, then passed back and moved into the foyer. He found the name 'Dale Chevrolet Corporate' listed on the eighth floor, and pushed the button for the elevator.

A woman with a cup of coffee and a brown paper sandwich bag rushed for the closing door and Gallen shoved his foot in the gap, made it open.

'Thanks,' she said, pushing a card into a slot and pushing '8'.

Gallen forced a smile. 'My floor.'

'They give you a pass?' said the woman, a secretary type.

Gallen shrugged. 'No. Bren Dale told me to come up to the eighth floor about midday, talk about the fleet lease buy-backs.'

'Okay,' said the woman. 'I'll fix you up.'

Gallen followed her to the reception desk on the eighth floor, an expensively decorated space with art on the walls and cut flowers in vases.

'Mandy, this gentleman has an appointment with Bren. Could you help him, please?'

Gallen smiled his thanks as she left, then turned back to the reception woman. 'David Bashifsky from Charter Stanley Fencing. I've been talking about bringing the fleet over from Ford to Chev. Bren told me to come up about midday.'

'Charter Stanley Fencing,' said the woman to herself, scrolling through a screen. 'Nothing here, sir. It was *David?*'

'Bashifsky, ma'am,' said Gallen. 'Mr Dale said if I have a fleet of more than fifty, I gotta be talking to corporate, gotta come downtown and we'll do the best deal.'

'I'm sorry, Mr Bashifsky,' she said. 'Mr Dale is not in the building. Can I schedule another time, or have him call you?'

'No thanks,' said Gallen, getting a good look at the layout of the floor. 'I'll call him, see what's going on.'

Turning slowly, Gallen heard a fire door slam shut and saw two office workers walk from an alcove into a corridor that didn't route through the reception area.

Waiting for the elevator, he watched men in expensive suits confabbing in another hallway with mahogany doors and frosted-glass panelling: the executive suites.

He was the only one in the elevator, and pushing for '7' he waited until the door opened again, when he made immediately for his right, towards the fire stairs. There was no receptionist—probably accounts or inventory management—but there was a stash of courier drops sitting on the carpet against the hessian-covered walls. Picking up a DHL bag, Gallen kept moving and found the fire door right where he expected it. Pausing in the stairwell, he listened for voices, hearing a few approach and then move past outside the door, his pulse hammering while he controlled his breathing.

Hitting speed dial on the Oasis-provided BlackBerry, Gallen patched to McCann, still sitting in the Escalade outside the Cattlemen's HQ. 'You said mustard. What kind?'

'French's,' said McCann, surprised that someone would ask. 'You know—hotdog mustard.'

Voices approached the eighth-floor fire door and Gallen moved up the stairs, arriving at the door as two young professionals burst through it, laughing about a Broncos player.

'Thanks,' said Gallen, smiling and showing the DHL bag as he slipped through the opened door.

The professionals barely saw him and left him standing in the alcove to the side of the reception area. It was one of the rules of Gallen's world: dress in chinos and a polo shirt, and eyes will gloss over you. Carry a bag belonging to DHL, FedEx or UPS and doors will literally be opened.

Moving down the hallway he passed small offices and administration people, saw Dale Chevrolet mission statements on the wall, and walked through a kitchenette that seemed to link the admin section to the execs. Smiling at a secretary in the kitchen, Gallen kept going till he arrived at a corner section. One door had the name plate Ernest Dale—CEO, alongside another plate identifying the CFO.

Along the plush walkway, Gallen scanned the name plates and passed a meeting room before seeing what he was looking for: Brendan Dale's office.

After looking up and down the walkway, Gallen turned the door knob and peered inside. Empty.

'I help you?' came a deep voice from what felt like his left shoulder. Jumping slightly, Gallen turned, ready to get out of Dodge. He knew that at the end of this corridor was another fire exit.

Coming face to face with a large African-American man, Gallen paused. He'd seen that face and heard that voice many times before, telling him to get down to a Dale showroom and do a deal with the King of Chev.

'I know you?' said Ern Dale, not moving out of the way.

'Don't think so,' said Gallen. 'I was looking for Bren—'

Before Gallen could finish, Ern Dale had taken the DHL satchel in his bear-like paw and was looking at the addressee.

'For Missy D'Angelo,' he said, levelling a stare. 'Downstairs, stock management.'

Taking the satchel back, Gallen tried to avert his eyes and leave but the big man blocked his way.

'Gallen,' said Ern, clicking his fingers. 'Captain Gallen. You're in a photo of Bren's, from that shit in Iraq.'

'Afghanistan—' started Gallen, but it was too late.

Ern Dale's face creased with a big salesman's smile, doing what he did for the TV screen on most nights and all Sunday afternoon during the football. 'Well, well. Got vets delivering the mail. Wanna talk about it?'

They sat in Ern Dale's enormous office, Gallen wondering how he'd talked himself into hunting Bren Dale. What was he after? An explanation?

'You wanted Bren, huh?' said Ern, leaning back in a CEO chair, hands clasped over a wide but not fat belly. Gallen had him as six-four, closing on three hundred pounds.

'Wanted to talk,' said Gallen.

'Coulda called, Gerry,' said Ern, relaxed but with presence.

'He was starting a gig with me this week. He cancelled, I wanted to talk.'

'What's the gig?'

'Corporate bodyguard,' said Gallen. 'He's here, working with you, right?'

'Nope.'

Gallen didn't buy it. 'That's his office.'

'You see him, Gerry?'

Gallen thought about it, going over exactly what Bren had said on the phone. 'Thought you'd talked him into a career in cars, didn't want him hanging round with his old Marines buddies. I wanted him to say that to my face, not make excuses.'

'I hate war and I don't want him in no army,' said Ern. 'But if I knowed it was you, I'da been fine. You taught Brenny good.'

'I did?' said Gallen.

'You told 'im that what happened yesterday happened. Now it's time to make tomorrow happen.'

'I said that?'

'What Bren said. Quotes it like the Bible, and I got no fight with that. When the war is over, man needs a creed.'

'Is he okay?' said Gallen.

'Been a bit touchy,' said Ern. 'And now he hardly here. Can't have it like that. Can't be the boss's son just doing what he wants, right?'

'Can you tell him Gerry Gallen wants to talk?' Gallen pulled a clasp of his Oasis business cards from his windbreaker and handed one to Ern.

'I'll tell 'im,' said Ern, standing and shaking his hand. 'And how're you, Gerry? You okay?'

Gallen paused too long.

'Like that, huh?' Ern smiled as they walked to the office door. 'Same as it ever was.'

Turning, Gallen was thinking about Durville again: his next move, back to the airport, his arrival in LA, the route to his house in Malibu.

'You ever want to talk,' said Ern, 'you know where to find me.'

'Thanks, Mr Dale.'

'Besides, might find you a nice new Chev. What you driving?'

Gallen smiled. 'F-350.'

'I can change that, son,' said Ern Dale with a wink. 'I can surely change that.'

'I don't doubt it,' said Gallen.

CHAPTER 14

Gallen keyed the mic as he looked at the Pacific sunset from the upstairs balcony of Durville's Malibu mansion. It was eight o'clock and he wanted Winter and Ford in the house for the night shift so he could make some calls.

Breathing the ocean air, Gallen worried about Bren Dale and thought back to a time before Afghanistan, to the early years of the War on Terror, when Gallen's unit was posted in Zamboanga City and the enemy was the Moro separatist Abu Sayyaf Group. In those days, Gallen was a reserved but ambitious first lieutenant, looking for his second bar; Bren Dale was a sergeant with the lack of ambition that comes from having a wealthy father. What Dale did have was a hankering to see combat.

Mindanao was a very different experience to Afghanistan or Iraq. It was a war in the islands of the Sulu chain, off the southern end of the Philippines. It was about jungle combat in Moro strongholds like Basilan and Jolo, in rainforest environments which had been closed to the world by the pirate clans for centuries. One of the big problems in Mindanao was the closeness of the collaboration between US special forces and the Philippines military, a coalition formed largely at a cocktail and conference level, but not entirely successful on the ground. Gallen and other Recon Marines had never liked the fact that the Joint Special Operations Task Force between the US and Philippines was housed inside the Navarro base in Zamboanga City. It was a Filipino facility.

After Jolo—a bitterly fought battle lasting three weeks in which a contingent of US Army Green Berets were hammered—the word had passed around Gallen's outfit that some of the intel briefings at Navarro had been leaked to the ASG insurgents in the Sulu islands. Gallen had heard the tittle-tattle on the docks in Zam, before they'd set off for Basilan Island and he'd tried to stop the talk.

Bren Dale had collared Gallen during the submarine insertion to Basilan and tried to add up the coincidences that had seen the Green Berets ambushed on Jolo, almost as if the ASG knew the Americans were arriving.

When Gallen had mentioned it to his boss—Captain James Duncan—Duncan had retold it so it sounded as though Gallen wasn't doing his job. Gallen had backed off and led his team on the flanking run into the village on Basilan. His route called for a northern support-fire approach, through a secondary forest footpad, while Joyce's unit led the primary assault from the south-east.

On their flanking run, Bren Dale had begged him to break with orders and take a western approach.

Sitting in the dark, in that ominous jungle, where even the kids knew how to wire claymore mines to trees and run trip wires attached to frag grenades, Gallen had listened to Bren Dale's plea: 'Tell me you weren't briefed on this northern approach back at Navarro?'

'That's for me to know, Marine,' said Gallen, putting the non-commissioned officer in his place.

'I don't like that northern approach, Lieutenant,' Dale had told him, a pain in the ass when he thought he was right about something.

'You out-thinking the intel boys, are you, Sergeant? That's a lot of thinking.'

'No, sir,' said Dale. 'Just that here we are on the ground, being steered towards a specific footpad by a bunch of intel dudes who right now are watching the Bears play the Packers.'

Gallen had kept his voice low, lest the men hear it. 'So?'

'That sort of detail is something maybe you and Duncan

should've cooked up once we were here. Why's some Filipino dude making that call on us?'

They'd looked into each other's whites, breath shallow, tropical sweat running down their faces in the night.

'You think the Filipinos are leaking? You really think that?'

Dale had shrugged. 'Just saying, I don't like coincidences, especially coincidences that end in ambushes.'

Finally Gallen had let Dale run. 'So what you got, Sergeant?'

Bren Dale had crouched and asked for Gallen's map, a no-no in the conventional forces but not disallowed in special forces.

'This area in here.' Dale pointed to a zone west of the village. 'They tell you what that is?'

'It's their garbage pile and shit dump,' said Gallen. 'It's a gully, and when the monsoon comes it turns into a river and it's washed down to the ocean.'

'Any reason we can't stealth up to the village through that gully, come in from the west?'

'Only that the Blue Team is getting our support from the north,' said Gallen.

'Watts and Zibic just got back from a recon,' said Dale. 'Say there's boogies all along that northern footpad.'

Gallen had made a decision that night about what kind of leader he was. They'd stealthed through the rat-infested gully where months of night bins and tons of rotting garbage had brought vermin from miles around. They'd sat in the stinking darkness, in the choking humidity, waiting for the 3.15 am attack to come from Duncan's men. When the first shots sounded, they watched from their hide as a cadre of black-clad terrorists rose out of the dirt and made straight for the northern footpad where Gallen's team was supposed to be hiding, opening fire as they moved. Gallen's team was able to take out that cadre with surprise flanking fire before moving to get Duncan's team out of trouble.

It had taken the Marines Force Recon teams almost three days to get off Basilan Island as the JSOTF had thrown as many reinforcements as they could onto the terrorist stronghold. An intel debriefer had later referred to the Basilan ambush and botched exfil as 'Dunkirk without the dignity'.

It was a turning point in Gallen's life: he'd learned that simply holding a higher rank didn't make you a better Marine and that the mistakes of the political classes were always paid for by the men in the field.

Gallen took a lingering glance at the Pacific sunset and moved away from Durville's balcony into the security room where Donny McCann was reviewing a bank of security cameras. Winter and Ford joined them.

'He's downstairs, in his office,' said Gallen. 'He's with company, and he's drinking.'

Ford laughed. 'Okay.'

'It's not okay if he wants to go nightclubbing with these ladies, maybe go for a midnight skinny dip,' said McCann.

'If he leaves the perimeter or he wants more company, let me know,' said Gallen, handing over the master keys to Winter. 'When those whores are picked up, you escort the cab into and out of the compound, okay?'

'Got it, boss,' said Winter.

Lying in his bed in the staff quarters, Gallen went through his step-list of all the things that needed doing and whether he'd done them. It had been his ritual in the Marines and it was a habit he couldn't shake.

Before he drifted off he thought back to Bren Dale, Basilan Island and Captain Duncan. Duncan was wounded in that action, three of his men were killed. He left the Marines shortly after, his sponsors no longer interested in mentoring his upward ride. Dale and the men had backed Gallen's actions, giving eyewitness accounts of the boogies on the footpad; Gallen had claimed radio silence as reason for his unilateral action, and in the Marines it was hard to be criticised by a review board if what you did had ensured the welfare of your men. Which Gallen's actions had. The total injury count in his report had been a single shot to Zibic's calf muscle, which had left him able to continue unaided.

Chuckling softly, Gallen remembered how his slightly un-professional conduct had been rewarded: two weeks after the

Basilan snafu he'd earned his second silver bar. Thanks to Bren Dale's rich-boy lack of respect for fools, Gerry Gallen of Clearmont, Wyoming had made captain in the US Marines.

As he fell asleep, he realised that as much as Bren Dale could annoy him, he owed the man. Owed him a career.

CHAPTER 15

The Escalades stopped on the tarmac in front of the Oasis corporate jet, a white Challenger 850 with two large engines mounted on the fuselage below the tail section.

Gallen was the first out, squinting slightly in the brightness of the dawn light poking over the mountains behind Burbank Airport. He keyed the radio. 'Kenny, I want you and Ford searching that luggage hold and supervising every piece loaded into it, okay?'

Winter growled his assent. Gallen could see that the Canadian had already emerged from the rear Escalade and was marching down beside Durville's town car in the centre of the convoy.

Donny McCann joined Winter on the tarmac and then Harry Durville emerged too, his jeans and boots making him look like a paunchy rodeo rider, but one who couldn't stay off the Black-Berry.

Ushering Durville up the stairs into the air-conditioned cabin, Gallen did a quick search of the Challenger and its toilet/shower area, making sure no one was in the plane. As he came back to the front cabin door, Durville was pouring his first whisky of the morning and, facing the oil man, Florita had the satellite phone cradled on her shoulder.

Ducking into the cockpit, Gallen greeted Captain Barry Martin, whom he'd met on the run down from Denver. He didn't know the co-pilot. Asking for the man's ID, Gallen tried to make chit-chat but it was obvious he wasn't joking.

'Okay, Jeff,' he said, handing back the FAA licence and the Oasis Energy employee pass.

The captain gave Gallen a wink as he left. They'd talked about contingencies when they'd met in Denver and Martin had agreed that if he ever had reservations about anything, he'd let Gallen know about it.

On the tarmac, Winter and Ford checked the Durville luggage, looking for listening devices more than bombs. Gallen could see Winter using the wand he'd asked Chase Lang to throw into the pile at the PX. It wasn't a metal detector of the kind found in airport security; instead, it picked up live circuitry, anything that could transmit a signal.

'How we doing?' said Gallen, standing beside Winter as the wand beeped.

'Something in Senorita's bag,' said Winter, unzipping the large Targus business case. Inside was a stack of spare legal pads, cell batteries, pens and what looked like an entire back-up system for the laptop she carried. Pulling out a large Ziploc bag, Winter touched it with the wand and confirmed the signal: inside were two spare BlackBerry handsets with batteries and chargers. The woman was thorough.

Resealing the Ziploc, Winter shrugged. 'We're looking okay.'

'Let's get our gear loaded,' said Gallen, scoping the tarmac, looking for aimless men in coveralls, people looking too interested in a magazine, people talking into a phone but looking at the Challenger.

Gallen took the air stairs two at a time and took a seat at the front of the cabin. He began sorting his notes. The Kugaaruk airport was a tiny strip, closed most of the year due to its location inside the Arctic Circle. A local cab company had contracted to pick up the Oasis team and deliver them to an address where Harry Durville was meeting a local council.

Flipping through the notes provided by Florita, Gallen saw a reference to a group named as the Transarctic Tribal Council, the TTC. Durville was talking with seven of them at a one o'clock meeting.

Florita fetched coffee at the small drinks station and Gallen moved after her.

'Florita, we got any names of these guys?' he asked, holding up the notes.

'Coffee?' said Florita.

'Thanks,' said Gallen. 'I got mention of a "Reggie" but that's it. Who are these TTC people?'

'Eskimos,' said Florita, pouring. 'Reggie's his contact. I don't have last names. I can ask?'

'Thanks,' said Gallen as the earpiece crackled; Winter asking him to look at something.

On the tarmac, Ford, McCann and Winter stood at the loading door for the hold.

'What's up?' Gallen pushed forward to where Winter ran the beeping wand over an opened kit bag.

'Some kind of tracking device,' said McCann, inspecting the remote video set from the PX. 'Lookit.' He held out a tiny stainless-steel capsule on the tip of his index finger.

'Got more, boss,' said Winter, getting a beep from an assault rifle. 'Looks like someone wants to track us.'

'Or hone us,' said the Aussie, which made all eyes turn to him. 'Just saying, fellers. I mean, we've slapped hundreds of those things on building and ships so the fly boys know where to fire their missiles.'

Looking at his G-Shock, Gallen made a decision. 'Kenny, you and the boys find them, but don't destroy them, okay?'

'Can do, boss.'

Slipping back into his seat in the cabin, Gallen made a call. 'Aaron,' he said, cheerful, as the other end picked up.

'Gerry. It's early.'

'Just a question, Aaron. When did you decide to put collars on us?'

'Sorry?' said the American.

'Tracking transmitters, Aaron. They're all through the new stuff from the PX.'

82

'They're not tracking transmitters, Gerry,' said Aaron with a sigh. 'They're RFDs.'

'What?'

'They're small electronic tags like the ones that stop you stealing from a shop, or the ones that mean you can't pass off your company's computer as your own and try to sell it.'

'You think we're gonna sell this stuff?'

'It's standard procedure, puts an ownership stamp on Oasis equipment,' said Aaron. 'It's not even my policy, buddy. That would be the accountants.'

'Maybe,' said Gallen. 'But this kind of technology can be used for other things, and I don't like finding it just before I get on a flight.'

'Where you off to?' said Aaron.

'Hawaii. Where are you?'

'In transit,' said Aaron. 'To somewhere else.'

The plane dipped slightly and Captain Martin's voice told the cabin that they would be landing at Edmonton International for a quick refuelling. Opposite Gallen, Donny McCann inserted a bookmark and closed his novel.

'That's longer than I expected,' he said, stretching.

Gallen smiled. 'We're not even halfway there.'

'How far is this place?'

'Twenty-six hundred miles,' said Gallen. 'It's almost longer than crossing the Atlantic.'

Mike Ford alighted from the seat across the aisle and went forward to use the employees' toilet.

'How's the Aussie?' said Gallen, looking at McCann, but loud enough for Winter to hear.

'Knows his stuff,' said McCann. 'But that accent'll have to go.'

'At least he's funny,' said Winter.

'Them Aussies are all funny, man,' said McCann.

As the Challenger jet stopped at its refuelling berth, a large golf cart rode out to the starboard side of the craft. Standing beside the co-pilot as he opened the cabin door, Gallen felt the blast of cold rush into the cabin and he touched the SIG in his holster.

'It's airport services,' said Florita, standing behind Gallen, pulling on a thick down-filled jacket. 'They're here to take us to the washroom.'

'Go on,' yelled Durville from the rear of the aircraft. 'I'll catch up.'

Gallen issued the order to rug up in the arctic kit and, pulling on his own goose-down windbreaker, followed Florita to the golf cart.

The private lounge was large and filled with natural light and Gallen sat on a sofa, cleared his voicemail as he waited for Florita to return. He wanted a further chat about these Eskimos.

On a kitchenette table there were donuts and coffee and he helped himself as the Canadian Border Services and Customs officers spoke with the maître d'. Gallen pulled out his passport, happy that he'd already put the SIG and its holster under the sofa cushion.

The Customs officer approached him and Gallen stood, offered the passport.

'In from Los Angeles, sir?' said the officer. 'Direct flight was it?'

'Yessir,' said Gallen.

'Carrying any explosives, chemicals, munitions, firearms or prohibited substances, Mr Gallen?'

'No, sir.'

'Any alcohol or tobacco over the permitted quantity?'

'No, sir.'

'You travelling alone, sir?'

'No, my employer, Harry Durville, is in the plane.'

The officer looked out at the Challenger sitting on the tarmac. 'Harry Durville, eh? What do you do for him?'

'Security consultant.'

'Carrying no weapons?'

'In the plane, yes,' said Gallen, wishing Florita would get back to the damn lounge.

'Declared?'

'I'm doing that now.'

The officer looked at him. 'I'm waiting.'

Gallen breathed out. 'Nine-mil handguns and spare clips. We're a personal bodyguard.'

'I see—and you have the permits, I suppose.'

'Sure,' said Gallen, at least confident that Aaron had logged and declared all the firearms under the special security permits between the US and Canada.

The officer slowly pulled a black hand-held scanner from his utility belt and ran it across the information strip of the passport. 'Can you show me your orders?' he asked as he looked at his tiny screen, annoyingly poker-faced.

Gallen was confused. He hadn't carried orders since leaving the Corps.

The officer continued. 'You're in Canada for military purposes?'

'No.'

'So why are you travelling on a no-fee passport?' said the officer.

'Shit.' Gallen slumped. He'd been so focused on this new gig that he'd forgotten to get himself a standard tourist passport. His no-fee version labelled him as an American soldier on active duty, and if he couldn't produce orders, foreign officials could treat him as an unfriendly.

Florita had him out of the lock-up before Durville even made it to the terminal.

'Thanks,' said Gallen, emerging from the small holding room and retrieving his personal effects from the Customs officer. As they moved back to the lounge, he tried to work it out. 'So that was your voice? You were the one telling them off?'

'Wouldn't say I was telling them off,' said Florita, who'd obviously taken a shower in the washroom of the private lounge. 'I said they could stop being so unreasonable or we could wait for Senor Durville to arrive.'

Gallen chuckled. 'Resolve it with an oil billionaire who's been drinking all morning.'

Florita smiled. 'They know him. But you'll still have to have a tourist passport for the next time you enter Canada. You can use the computer at this business centre.'

Through the glass, they watched the golf cart making a return, this time with Durville on board.

'I wanted to talk,' said Gallen.

'We've got two minutes, then I'm the nursemaid again.'

'I'm uncomfortable with this meeting. I like to take away the ifs and the buts, and I can't do that when all I know is that one of the people he's meeting is called Reggie.'

Florita led him to the sofas beside the windows. 'Okay, Gerry, but none of this is in writing. There's no paper trail for these meetings.'

Gallen felt the old nightmares of the intel briefers and their little secrets coming back to him. 'Okay.'

'The TTC is a council of Eskimo or Inuit tribes from the Arctic Circle. They don't recognise national boundaries, so they're from Canada, the US and Russia, mostly, with some belonging to Denmark and Finland.'

'Any names?'

'I think you'll find they're mostly represented by their lawyers, Gerry,' said Florita as the door burst open and Harry Durville marched over to the food like he was looking to kick in someone's teeth.

Rising to fix Durville's coffee, Florita stopped and looked back at Gallen. 'Oh, I suppose the thing I should mention . . .'

'Yep?'

Florita lowered her voice. 'These TTC reps? Their countries and their tribes don't necessarily know that this meeting is happening.'

Gallen tried to get more, but Florita had moved to her boss, who wanted a donut without icing.

CHAPTER 16

The Challenger came in low over the white peninsula on the edge of the Gulf of Boothia after four hours of flying. As they straightened for the runway, Gallen looked down and saw a white wilderness that seemed to blend into the sea with different gradations and shades of ice floe. On both sides of the plane were thousands of miles of ice and snow, contrasting with the darkness of the choppy ocean.

Captain Martin's voice came over the speaker, informing the passengers that the plane would be ready to deboard at 12.50 local time and to rug up because the early spring meant a temperate midday high of minus twenty-five degrees Celsius, or minus thirteen in Fahrenheit.

Gallen watched his men check balaclavas and gloves as they rustled into their arctic jackets and pants, covering two layers of thermal underwear.

'Minus twenty-five,' said McCann, shaking his head. 'Shit, I woke up one morning in Ghor Province and promised myself no more of that shit.'

'Fucking Ghor,' said Winter, pulling his balaclava down so it looked like a neck warmer. 'The only thing I remember about that hellhole is you take a crap, it bounces.'

'Okay, guys,' said Gallen, smiling at the recollections of Afghanistan's coldest regions. 'Let's focus. I want to run a check on the meet site, so I'll go ahead with Donny and Florita, make sure we get the seating organised.'

Winter let the slide go on his SIG and put it on his lap. 'I take Durville, with Mike?'

'That's it,' said Gallen. 'You check the hotel.'

Florita had booked out the Inukshuk Inns North, part of a hotel chain in Canada's far north.

Winter looked at him. 'What are we expecting?'

'Oil people who can't mind their goddamn business,' said Gallen. 'So, if there's any stray vehicles or peeping Toms around the hotel, check 'em out. There's seven or eight people meeting with Durville today, and if I don't like the look of them, I'll be searching them before they enter the building.'

'They gonna buy that?' said McCann.

'Depends who they are,' said Gallen.

He bundled Florita and McCann into the first cab while the Durville party waited in the tiny terminal. The air was cold and still as Gallen made to get in beside the driver, but a gust of wind caught him in the kidneys as he bent to enter the taxi, and the cold whistled into his ribs as though he wasn't wearing a stitch.

He gasped as he shut the door and felt the car's heater. 'Holy Christ. I thought January in Clearmont was cold.'

Holding his breath for a few moments as they set off for the meet, Gallen wondered if the cold-weather gear would be enough. It was the coldest-rated kit available in the US military, the field dress worn by Marines when they did their arctic survival school in Alaska.

The ten-year-old GMC Yukon crackled over the ice and snow as they motored at thirty mph from the airport to a house two blocks behind the hotel.

'That's Jackie's place,' said the driver, nodding sagely in his Edmonton Oilers cap.

Waiting for a resolution to the sentence, Gallen realised there was no more to come. He was rescued by Florita.

'Jackie?' she said from the back seat. 'Who's that?'

'Jackie the elder, but not this people,' said the driver, mouth downturned and hand making a spreading motion.

Jackie's house was a wooden-sided, gable-roofed box of the type favoured in the far north. A tendril of smoke escaped into the air, and Gallen, Florita and McCann got out of the car and walked to the dwelling.

The door was answered quickly by an old man who peered into the sunlight.

'Jackie?' said Florita.

'Yep,' said the old man.

She offered her hand. 'Florita Mendes, Oasis Energy.'

'Yep,' the old man said again.

Gallen kept an eye on him as they were taken through the house and shown the large living room where the meeting was going to take place. There was a long wooden table with ten chairs arranged around it. Gallen looked under the table, searching for listening devices, then up at the ceiling where the bare beams seemed clear. He'd get Winter to sweep it later. Returning to the table, he evaluated the seating.

'I need Harry right there,' he said, pointing to a chair in a corner, away from the window and not within the arc of a shooter who might burst through a door firing.

As they made to leave, Gallen thanked Jackie and took Florita aside. 'Can you ask him to insist on a no-firearms policy for his house?'

They stamped out the cold as the first arrivals pulled up in their cars from the airport; Gallen and McCann were in front of Jackie's, Winter was running a final check inside and Ford was at the rear entry.

A stream of Inuit people greeted Durville at the door. He was almost unrecognisable in his arctic parka with wolverine fur lining the hood. The procession looked tame and Gallen started to relax.

'You looked at those beams?' he said into the mic.

'Yep,' replied Winter over the radio. 'Place seems clean.'

'Mike, how we looking?'

'Clear, boss,' said the Aussie. 'But Christ, is it actually getting *colder*?'

Pushing into the meeting house, Gallen found Florita. 'Which one's Reggie?'

'Not here,' said Florita.

Returning outside, Gallen got a tap on the arm from McCann. 'Lookit.'

Two dark SUVs puttered towards them, steam spewing from the exhausts. The first slid along the snow as it tried to come to a stop, and Durville moved forward, Gallen beside him.

'Reggie,' said the oil man, arms out wide.

The round-faced Inuit smiled big as he hit the snow. 'Harry!'

Embracing, the two men walked towards the door of Jackie's house, each insisting the other go first.

A large man emerged from the rear of Reggie's SUV and another from the driver's side. The second SUV pulled up behind the first, the doors opened and Gallen watched McCann's hand push sideways through the false pocket of his parka, towards the holster.

Gallen reached for Durville, pushed him into the door. Five men with athletic builds and soldiers' eyes edged from the two newly arrived SUVs towards the door. McCann fronted the first as Gallen rejoined him.

'This is a private party, ladies,' said McCann, his LA drawl dulled by the cold.

'We're with Reggie,' said the first of the interlopers, a man with a heavy build and a Russian accent.

'You can be with Reggie out here,' said Gallen, deciding they were all carrying. 'Reggie's busy.'

The Russian's face was obscured by a big hood and sunglasses, but there was something familiar about his mouth. 'And you would be?'

'I'm not confused about my name,' said Gallen. 'But thanks for checking.'

The Russian laughed as he turned to his buddies. 'We have the joker.'

'No,' said the hulking form that appeared from behind the second SUV. 'I'm the funny guy.'

The Russian and his henchmen turned as one, took in Kenny Winter, hand in the false pocket of his arctic parka. The leader turned back to Gallen. 'Okay, so what now?'

'We've been asked by the owner of this place to ensure no one but the delegates come inside,' said Gallen.

'They usually come with me,' came a voice from behind Gallen. He turned towards Reggie.

'Sorry, Mr Reggie,' said Gallen. 'It's easier if none of us are in there, right?'

Reggie broke into a big smile. 'Of course, of course. Can I send out some hot drinks?'

'Four black coffees,' said Gallen.

CHAPTER 17

Sopping up gravy with his biscuit, Gallen wondered if he had been foolish to take this gig. He'd been hardly six months out of uniform, was still a little jumpy at all sorts of things—telephones with weird ring tones, truck reversing beeps, people who didn't say their name when they shook hands. He wasn't totally fit, and now being thrust into a bodyguard detail in the Arctic Circle, unable to get basic answers from his employers, was tuning him for combat. He'd felt the old instincts rising the previous afternoon, when Reggie's convoy had pulled up. It was a mental state that balanced complete relaxation with the most intense awareness; it was unmistakable to anyone with combat experience and he'd entered that zone when Winter had circled behind the henchmen, hand on his gun. If the shit had started, Gallen would have drawn down, finished it. And that scared him.

'Coffee?' said the breakfast waitress, walking past the table.

'Fill 'er up,' said McCann, Ford nodding his agreement.

Winter was stalking the halls of the hotel, looking for trouble, and two tables away Florita made calls and scribbled on her legal pad while Durville cradled his head in his hands, massaging the hangover out of his temples.

Winter appeared in the doorway of the dining room. 'Got some tourist people here, boss. Manager says they're okay.'

An elderly couple walked into the dining room in sealskins and fur boots as Gallen looked up.

'My name's Billy,' said the man slowly. 'This is Sami. You gotta learn how to make the kayak, before you go back to the big city.'

Gallen smiled. 'I do?'

'What's he gonna do with a kayak in Wyoming?' asked McCann.

'Man travels,' said Billy with a shrug. 'Man needs a kayak.'

'It's fucking obvious,' said Harry Durville, overhearing the conversation. 'Shit, Gerry, these people make their living from the guests and you go and book the place out?'

'We're outta here in ninety minutes,' said Gallen, tapping his G-Shock.

'Billy, over here if you would,' said Durville, still slurring slightly.

Pulling out a wad of cash, Durville put several hundred dollars in Billy's hand and pointed at Gallen. 'Billy, would you and Sami please take my ungracious employee and spend an hour showing him your kayaks? Would you do that for me?'

Standing reluctantly, Gallen let Sami grab him by the arm and sweep him off like she wanted to dance. They reached the dining room doors with laughter reverberating behind them.

Billy's workshop was a low-ceilinged shed crowded with wooden frames and skins stretched so tight Gallen could see through them. Lengths of gut rope dried over a wood stove.

Stopping in front of a completed two-person sea kayak—seeming enormous in the enclosed space—Gallen touched the runes and symbols etched into the dried skin of the vessel, painted with dried blood and squashed berries.

'This some kind of tribal thing, for good luck?' said Gallen, amazed at the artwork.

'Nah.' Billy waved him away. 'It's pretty, that all.'

Gallen couldn't help but ask the question. 'You guys have boats, skidoos and jet skis, planes. Who still needs a sea kayak?'

'Don't need it,' said Billy. 'But my people are practical people.'

'Yeah?'

'Yeah, brother. You go on the plane or the jet ski, you don't know how that works, you're not connected with that, so you're apart from your environment, understand?'

'I guess.'

'And when you're on the sea, you want to feel connected to her, not apart.'

They drank tea, Gallen itching to get back to the hotel. The way they cured the wood and used bone and tusk, skin and gut to put the kayak together was fascinating, but he wanted to be on a plane.

Excusing himself, he tried to shake Billy's hand, but the man held it up in the international sign for 'wait'. Bustling out of a back room, Sami came to Gallen, put a loop of gut string around his neck and kissed him in a hug that involved being held by the elbows, a sensation he hated. Gallen grabbed the walrus tusk carving on the end of the gut string. It was the size of a matchbox and by the look of the yellowing bone, it wasn't new. It depicted the head of a polar bear, tiny lumps of anthracite for eyes.

'That a bear?'

'City people think the bear is a killer,' said Billy. 'To us, the bear is a survivor—on sea, land, ice and in all weather, she can live.'

Gallen looked at his talisman. 'Survivor, huh?'

Billy shook his hand. 'Be safe, Mr Gerry.'

Winter organised the baggage loading, walking the suitcases and bags through to the rear luggage compartment of the Challenger jet.

'Where's Durville?' said Gallen, as Winter re-emerged on the tarmac, the morning taking forever to be warmed by the watery sun.

'Sleeping it off,' said the Canadian. 'Florita slipped him a Valium.'

Captain Martin fired the plane and Gallen joined the pilots in the cockpit. As they swung away from the tiny terminal, giving them a view of the endless white, he saw something beside the airport building.

'Any glasses in here?' he asked, and Martin reached down beside him, coming up with a mid-sized set of Nikon binoculars.

Concentrating as the Challenger made for its take-off position, Gallen scoped Reggie's convoy in the car park but there wasn't much to look at. Reggie and his bodyguard had moved into the tiny terminal to wait for their plane.

Sweeping the snowbound airport as the Challenger turned for its take-off run, Gallen's eyes focused. Was it a black SUV, parked behind a snow bank? He thought he saw a set of field-glasses looking straight back at him from the front seat.

The aircraft turned away from the SUV and Gallen pushed through to the cabin.

'Kenny! Take a look through the window.' He thrust the glasses at Winter. 'Check the black SUV beside the terminal building.'

Winter pointed the binoculars through the cabin window, his fingers dancing slowly on the adjustment buttons. 'Can't see anything, boss.'

Taking back the field-glasses, Gallen searched the snow bank but couldn't find the SUV.

'Abort the take-off,' he said, raising his voice so the captain could hear. 'Bring it into the hangar.'

Winter found his explosives detector and for the next half-hour they went over the plane and through the bags, checking in the lavatories, the galley and the large luggage compartment itself, which was situated behind the aft washroom. The captain and co-pilot even pulled on their parkas and checked the undercarriage and landing gear, looking for anything that wasn't supposed to be there.

When they decided to try again, Reggie and his party were boarding their own private jet.

'Thank God for some engine noise,' said McCann as they took off one hour late and climbed into the blue. 'That Durville ever stop snoring?'

Two hours out of Kugaaruk, Gallen was roused from his reverie as Durville woke with theatrical stretches and groans.

'Chrissakes,' said the oil man, staggering to his feet, hitching up his jeans and making for the aft washroom.

Moving down the plane, Gallen took a seat opposite Florita, noticing she'd let her hair out of the bun. 'He's back with us, I see.'

'I only gave him half a Valium, but it helps with his hangovers.'

Gallen kept it casual. 'He talking about the meeting, his drinking with Reggie?'

'He just woke up, Gerry,' she said, a small smile creasing the side of her mouth.

'Sorry,' he said. 'I'm curious about this Reggie and his posse.'

'He's TTC. But he's from the other side.'

'Other side?'

'Of the North Pole,' said Florita. 'They're all Inuit, but Reggie's from the Siberian side, while Kugaaruk is the Canadian side.'

'Reggie's Russian?' said Gallen.

Florita chuckled. 'I'm not saying anything, Gerry, 'cept that Reggie comes from the other side of the Pole is all.'

The hissing sound from the washroom rose above the twin jet engines. Durville was having a shower.

'Any ideas why someone would be glassing us on the runway this morning?'

'*Glassing?*'

'Using field-glasses to observe us.'

'Oh, you mean binoculars. No, Gerry, I have no idea. I didn't see this vehicle.'

Gallen looked away. His anxiety wasn't always something he could substantiate.

'What about Reggie's men?' he pushed. 'They wanted to come into the meeting.'

'Perhaps they wanted to sit down, get warm.'

'They were armed.'

Florita looked out the window.

'You know Reggie's senior bodyguard? The big Russian?' said Gallen.

'No.'

'You seen him before?'

'Yes.'

'Where?'

'In Vlad.'

'Vladivostok?'

'Like I said.'

'What's his name?'

Florita sighed. 'Gerry, I don't know his name. The only reason I know yours is that we coordinate Harry's schedule.'

Gallen nodded. 'Could you find out for me? It would help.'

Florita nodded too, looked back at her paperwork, nothing else to say.

'Okay, then,' he said, standing.

Durville burst out of the washroom as Gallen took his seat opposite McCann. There was a kerfuffle, and rather than twist to see what the commotion was about, he gave McCann a soft kick.

'What's the fuss back there?'

Squinting through a half-closed eye, McCann focused on Durville. 'He's waving something around, looks like a BlackBerry.'

'Look at this thing,' Gallen heard Durville say. 'A phone covered in abalone. I love these Eskimos. A BlackBerry covered in *seashells*? I love it.'

It was when Durville said the phone was a gift from one of the tribal members that Gallen felt his pulse roar in his ears. As he lurched from his seat, he almost collided with Winter, who was also heading for the oil man.

CHAPTER 18

The abalone-encrusted BlackBerry glinted in Winter's hand.

'This came from Reggie?' said Gallen, looking down at Durville, whose rough confidence was gone.

'Gave it to me last night,' said Durville, slurping at coffee. 'Told me it was a special gift from the first nations. There a problem?'

'Sure it was from Reggie?' said Gallen.

'Sure as shit,' said Durville, his breath smelling of booze. 'What's this about?'

'We were under surveillance at the airport,' said Gallen. 'Not Reggie's people—another car, mile away from the terminal.'

'That a bad thing?'

'You glass me when I'm packing a plane and readying for take-off,' said Gallen, 'then, yeah, that can be a bad thing. Can mean you want to see what I've found in the bags, where I'm searching, see what I'm worried about.'

'Shit,' said Durville. 'I didn't think, I—'

'Don't matter now, sir,' said Winter. 'Please tell me: have you used this phone?'

'No, I just found it in my jeans when I took a shower,' said Durville. 'Forgot all about it.'

Winter carried the device back to his seat, handing it to Ford.

'What's goin' on?' demanded Durville. 'What's he doin'?'

Gallen put a hand on the overhead racks, leaned over his employer. 'Kenny's got a detector. We'll see if there's any explosive.'

'Explosive?' said the oil man, mouth hanging open. 'Holy shit.'

'Let's wait for Kenny,' said Gallen, trying to quell the man's nerves. 'It could be nothing.'

Looking to the front of the cabin, Gallen saw Winter and Ford hunched together, the beeps of the detector quite obvious above the roar of the engines.

'What's that?' said Durville, sitting up. 'What's that sound?'

Gallen moved towards Winter. 'Can we turn down the sound?'

Winter hit a button on the wand. 'Okay, boss. Mike says it's RDX.'

'Fuck,' said Gallen, rubbing his chin as he looked at the sparkling BlackBerry sitting on the fold-down table between the Canadian and the Aussie.

Winter took his voice lower. 'We've also got a live circuit.'

'But it's a phone. Of course there's a circuit.'

'The circuit's live,' said Ford, 'but the phone is switched off.'

'So?'

The Aussie took a quick look over his shoulder. 'So, there's explosive and it's wired. It's live.'

Kneeling, Gallen looked at the BlackBerry. 'What have we got, and what do we do?'

'We used to see these in the Gulf,' said Ford. 'We'd cuff the tangos, collect the collateral—the phones, laptops, files, maps, address books.'

Gallen nodded. He'd loaded a lot of that collateral in the field. 'Were they wired for the phone's switch?'

'I asked you a question, Gerry,' said the oil man, coming down the aisle, glass of Scotch in his hand. 'What the fuck is going on?'

Standing, Gallen tried to get Durville back to his seat, but the man stood his ground, fronting Gallen with his chest.

''Less I missed something, Gerry,' said Durville, 'I employ you, not the other ways around.'

Gallen stayed friendly. 'I understand how the money flows, but right now my job is to secure everyone on this aircraft. I need you to sit down, sir.'

'The fuck you telling me to do on my own fucking plane?'

'Sit down!' said Gallen, eyeballing his employer. 'You wanna sack me in Edmonton, you go right ahead. Right now, let us do our job.'

Durville didn't back away one inch and Gallen waited for a punch or at least a poke in the chest, but it didn't come.

'Okay, Gerry,' said Durville, his jaw clenched. 'You do your stuff, then you come report to me. I'm sitting right here.'

Gallen kneeled beside Ford and Winter. 'So, a bomb is triggered if we switch on the phone?'

'No, boss,' said Ford, his blue eyes sparkling with adrenaline. 'The tangos realised we were on to that by the end of oh-three.'

'And?' said Gallen.

'They started installing timer switches,' said Winter. 'Cheap circuitry from a digital watch will do it. Small, reliable, don't need much battery.'

'They can go off any time?' said Gallen, hissing with stress.

'Once put a hole in a Navy IRB,' said Ford, talking about the rigid-inflatable craft that Navy commandos used to board ships. 'It was an IED sitting in the spine of a ring-binder file. They're simple systems but this'll put a hole in the cabin.'

'Can we open it? See what the timer says?'

'I wouldn't do that,' said Winter as Ford shook his head.

'Booby-trapped?' asked Gallen.

'About ninety per cent likely,' said Ford. 'All you need is one extra wire, that pulls across the detonator terminals when you open the case.'

McCann leaned over Gallen's shoulder, whispering, 'I vote we get the thing out the motherfucking door, tout fucking suite.'

Gallen looked at Winter for guidance. 'Kenny?'

'Get the captain to take her down,' said Winter. 'Everyone get strapped in and I'll throw the thing out the door.'

'How much time we got?'

'No idea, boss. Mike's right. These things are simple timers. Could go off any minute.'

'Okay,' said Gallen. 'I want Durville and Florita in the washroom, door locked. Kenny, that's your job, and if he argues, drop him.'

'Okay, boss.'

'Mike, I want you in the cockpit with the pilots, keeping them calm, talking them through it, okay?'

'Got it,' said Ford.

'Break out the parkas and thermals,' said Gallen, pointing to Ford and Winter. 'Get your people in every layer you can find.' Turning to McCann, he smiled. 'Donny, you're gonna help me throw a bomb out the door.'

The Challenger jet had dropped low enough that Gallen could see the crests and valleys of snow and ice as they screamed past at a relatively slow four hundred mph.

After talking it over with the captain, Gallen had decided to throw the BlackBerry out through the forward cabin door just behind the cockpit and on the left of the aircraft. It would have been safer to dispose of it through the cargo door under the left turbo-fan engine, but the cargo door was a 'plug' type—once it was pushed from inside, it was gone and the plane would be depressurised all the way to Edmonton. They might save themselves from a bomb, but they wouldn't have enough oxygen and the sub-zero temperatures would turn the plane into a freezer inside of one minute. By using the forward cabin door, they could at least reseal the plane.

Gallen needed to have enough freedom to open the main hatch, but he didn't want to be sucked out of the plane. So they fixed a cargo strap around his waist which connected to the lap-belt of a forward-facing seat behind him. McCann would be belted into the same seat and he'd control the tension on the cargo strap, but if he couldn't hold on, the lap-belt should hold.

Gallen stood in front of the hatch, thinking about the directions from Captain Martin: the lever had to be extended fully upwards to open the cabin door. The pilot had completed his instructions with a small stutter. 'Then you have to push, which will be hard at this speed. While the inside and outside pressure equalise, the door will fly open and try to suck you out.'

Gallen focused on the arming lever but could see only Martin's eyes—eyes that revealed the captain thought the whole idea was madness.

Martin's voice crackled over Gallen's radio earpiece. 'We're flying at two hundred feet. Now's as good a time as any.'

Turning, his arctic gear cumbersome in the warmth of the cabin, Gallen gave McCann the thumbs-up.

'I gotcha,' said McCann, giving Gallen a wink. 'Let's get it done.'

Taking a deep breath, Gallen put his hands on the down-facing lever, feeling McCann put some tension on the cargo strap.

The lever came up easily; as it reached its open point and clicked into place, Gallen felt the cargo strap pull back on his waist. He was scared, but felt safe with McCann at his six.

'Okay, Donny,' he said into his mic. 'I've got it up, now I'm gonna push this fucker out.'

'I gotcha, boss.'

Gallen felt the cargo strap solid against his belly, pushing up slightly against the abalone BlackBerry that was sitting in the front pocket of his arctic parka.

He shoved, but the door wouldn't budge. Gallen repositioned his feet and pushed with his body weight. Still nothing.

'Think like a defensive tackle,' said McCann and Gallen shifted his feet again, this time putting his legs and hips into it, not just his arms and shoulders. The door gave slightly and an unholy hissing started from the crack, turning to a high-pitched howling as he got it open three inches. As he pushed more and got it to four inches, he flinched as a siren screamed. The emergency lights went on in the cabin and oxygen masks fell from the capsules over the seats.

From the washroom, he could hear a female's scream.

'One more block, boss,' said McCann, and Gallen drove up with his legs and hips. As he did so, the door was ripped away, thrown outwards along its horizontal hinge.

The cold tore the air out of Gallen's lungs. Immediately his body went into shock, the same kind of reaction the Marines had tried to induce in the special forces guys all those years ago at the Mountain Warfare Training Center in California, where the instructors would make the candidates take a plunge in ice-cold water and then get them to perform small actions like unlocking a padlock or dialling a phone. By the end of that day, the trainees got the point: the cold makes you uncoordinated, it makes you slow, it makes you fuck things up. The lesson: don't get cold.

As the noise and cold ripped at him, messing with his orientation, Gallen could feel the air trying to drag him out while McCann pulled on the cargo strap.

The wind smashed the hood of the parka around his face, deafening him, as he peered out of the Thinsulate balaclava, trying to concentrate on the job. Reaching for his parka pocket, against the pressure of the wind, he found the BlackBerry but couldn't make his gloved hand close around it. The wind-driven cold was intense and he could feel his body shutting down fast.

'Fuck,' he said, as the BlackBerry refused to stick in his hand. He couldn't form a grip, couldn't make his hand operate properly.

'You got it, boss,' said McCann. 'Take your time.'

Gallen realised he was running out of oxygen. He couldn't take a breath of the fifty-below air and his lungs were shutting down. He couldn't feel his legs or his face, didn't know if he could move his lips to talk. Grabbing at the BlackBerry again, he finally held it in his hand with a chicken-grip, his vision blurry as ice formed over his eyeballs.

'Throw it,' said McCann over the headset and Gallen pushed his hand outside the plane, where the rushing air tried to rip off his arm. He was clumsy now and didn't realise until he focused on his hand—as if it were some disembodied thing hanging outside the plane—that the BlackBerry was no longer in it.

'Did I get it?' said Gallen, slurring like he was tired and drunk.

McCann's voice screamed over the radio: 'It's on the floor! You dropped it!'

Looking down, slowly, as though walking on the moon, Gallen saw the glittering abalone of the BlackBerry between his feet, like it was a hundred miles away, separated by a storm of noise and confusion.

'Kick it, boss!' McCann's panicked voice rose above the terrible noise.

Using his last vestiges of consciousness, Gallen wondered what would happen if he kicked the bomb. Would it trigger the timer? He kicked at the phone clumsily, connecting with his toe.

The BlackBerry slid with aching slowness to the aluminium rails along which the door would seal, and then the air caught the device, hurtling it to the left so fast that it disappeared. Leaning back to concentrate on closing the cabin door, Gallen saw a flash of orange and white and felt the quick scorch of heat. The blast knocked him back into the cabin and falling to the floor he felt the plane lurch and a new sound start, a screaming death-noise.

'Fire,' said McCann, pulling back on the cargo strap and dragging Gallen into the cabin. Gallen's legs and mind had become useless; he felt like a passenger in his own body, as if he was looking down on his lethargic self in a dream. He was in shock from the cold and felt McCann pull him into the forward-facing seat, giving him an oxygen mask; he was gasping to breathe, but had no strength for it. McCann wrapped him with the cargo strap as the open door continued its screaming suction attempts, creating a tornado of paper and cushions, shoes, coffee cups and pens.

Gallen wanted to tell McCann to look after himself, to stay away from the suck of that door, but he couldn't speak, couldn't breathe.

Then there was a loud bang from the aft cabin area, way down behind the washroom. It shook the cabin frame and one of the cabin windows popped out, creating another source of the screeching howl, and then the air was filled with clothes, swirling at high speed and blowing out the door like smoke in an exhaust fan.

Looking back, McCann's mouth fell open. 'Fucking cargo hold exploded!'

Gallen tried to voice a question but the plane lurched violently, first left and then to the right, in a swinging barrel roll that didn't stop, just took them over and over like a clothes dryer.

The hastily secured cargo strap gave way on the third loop and as Gallen's face raced down towards the ceiling console, he wondered if that was smoke he was smelling.

The ceiling accelerated at him and then there was nothing.

CHAPTER 19

The light came in slowly, edging into his head like a flashlight beam under a door. Gallen was aware of warm on cold, and pain, a dull ache in his head, not unlike a hangover, not unlike the morning after a fist-fight.

Opening one eye, he saw snow and rapidly closed the eye again as a splitting, glare-induced headache threatened. Moving his mouth, he felt blood and missing teeth: the upper right incisor and the one behind it.

As he sucked, he opened his eyes again. He was surrounded by snow, with daylight visible, and he could hear a groaning sound.

Trying to keep his breathing low, remembering the arctic survival lessons about not panicking when buried in snow, he moved his head and found an air pocket.

Breathing shallowly, he made a quick check of his faculties: he could see, he could hear and he could distinguish hot and cold. Wiggling his left toes, he could just feel them. Didn't feel like anything was broken, but his foot was certainly cold. It was the same on the other foot and he wondered how long he'd lain like that.

His arms moved too, and by circling his wrists he managed to hollow out a small passage so he could bring his hands up to his face. Touching his cheeks and jaw, he found no breaks, at least not bad enough that he couldn't eat.

He looked at his gloves in the snow-filtered light and saw a wet sheen. Licking it, he confirmed blood: his face had been smashed and he'd lost some teeth, but the pain was being managed by the intense cold of the snow.

Moans rang out. He had no idea which way was up or down, and pushing his hands down to the front pockets of his arctic parka, he fossicked for a cigarette lighter. His hands were too numb and he couldn't find the lighter, but as he dragged his hand back, it rubbed against something under his parka. Pulling at the chin domes, Gallen got his thumb under a cord of some sort and pulled out the bear's head he'd been given by Billy and Sami at the kayak workshop. The black eyes glinted and what was yellowish tusk in daylight now came into its own: it had a faint luminescence in the half-light, its carved face glowing at the edges, creating a mesmerising effect. As he held it up by the cord, the head dangled down by his chin, telling him that upwards was a line that rose perpendicular from his left shoulder.

'Bear's not a killer,' he mumbled. 'She's a survivor.'

Hearing the moans again, he started burrowing upwards.

The sun made him wince as he broke out of the snow drift. As his eyes adjusted to the intense brightness, he got an idea of how lucky he'd been.

About a mile distant, a pall of black smoke rose thousands of feet into the still air, a furrow twenty feet deep leading to where the plane's fuselage had slammed into a rock face. On the left side of the deep furrow, there was a section of wing from the Challenger. Random pieces of debris from the corporate jet were littered around the rolling dales of snow, a piece of leather chair here, a landing wheel there.

Looking down, he saw red splashes, and pushing his tongue into his cheek he realised there was a deep gash on the left side of his face. Refastening the wolverine-lined hood of the parka to keep his head warm, he pulled his glove off and immediately felt the cold, which he estimated was at least minus thirty on the ground. Warmer than he'd been at altitude with the wind-chill factor, but colder than any daytime temperature he'd ever experienced, either in Afghanistan or Wyoming.

His de-gloved hand still had a silk liner over it but the chill went into his bones like someone had hit him with a mallet. Exploring in the chest pocket of his parka, Gallen pulled out an unused handkerchief and quickly got the glove back onto his hand. Laying the opened handkerchief on the ground, he filled it with snow and tied the ends of it together as best he could. Then he held it against the facial gash, hoping to staunch the wound before he lost too much blood.

As the cold dug deep into his facial tissue, making tears of pain run, Gallen raised his G-Shock. The watches were favoured in the military because they were simple to use and because of their toughness: Gallen had started life with a stainless-steel analogue watch from the Pendleton PX but he'd switched to a G-Shock after a troop truck had driven over a colleague's and the thing had still worked.

Now he was on to his second, a present to himself when coming back through Guam for the last time after his final tour in the Ghan. He'd discarded his old trusty and bought himself the top of the line. Looking at it now, it worked fine: 11.18 am, it said. Gallen remembered a feature that he'd never used, thinking it too gimmicky for a military professional. Pressing the 'comp' button on the lower right of the dial, he watched the face blink twice and a black display came up showing 'SE'. Turning slowly, Gallen brought the G-Shock around until the dial showed a large 'N'. Fixing his north as a mountain saddle in the distance that had a distinctive U-shape followed by a sharp peak, he turned back to the plane and fixed it in a south-west position.

The moaning continued and Gallen looked around, trying to find the source. He could vaguely remember McCann holding him down in the seat, and then not being able to hold on anymore. What had happened to them? Had they been thrown from the plane?

Tramping north, struggling in snow up to his armpits, Gallen croaked through the hoarseness in his larynx.

'Donny!' he said, trying to put strength into it. 'Donny, talk to me.'

The moans got louder as he struggled over a crest and looked down into a bowl, his energy sapped after just ten minutes of moving through that terrain.

There was no sign of his colleague in the bowl and Gallen paused: he either used his energy to find Donny McCann or he used it to get to the plane wreck, look for survivors and ransack the cabin for food and fire. He breathed deep, turned, saw a trek of perhaps a thousand yards to the plane, then looked back at the endless snow bowls in front of him. Fuck it: he'd give it thirty minutes to find his man, and then he'd summon the energy to get to the plane. He had the whole day to find food but he may have only a few minutes to find Donny alive.

He heard the moan again.

'Donny!' he yelled.

Stepping over the crest, Gallen started downwards into the bowl but he only took one step and he was through the snow layer, dropping like a stone. The snow raced past him and then his feet were hitting something solid and he bounced across a hard floor until he came to rest on a small knoll of ice.

Looking around, he saw an ice cave formed by the winds and covered over by a crusted bridge of snow, just waiting for someone to tread on it and fall to their death. The moan of pain was closer now and, turning to find it, he gasped as his ribs spasmed.

'Shit,' he said to himself, his body in a rictus of pain. He could barely breathe and he knew why, having sprung a rib as a hockey player in high school.

Struggling to his feet, trying to find a pain-free way of moving, he stood still on the subterranean ice knoll until he could balance without flashes of light at the edges of his vision.

Moving gingerly through the cave, avoiding the large fissures on the floor which seemed to go forever into the earth, he followed the moans, yelling his encouragement, trying to hear McCann's echoes long enough to get a fix on him.

Pushing through a small gap in the ice wall, Gallen padded into a larger ice gallery and found Donny McCann lying on the ice floor, a hole in the roof above.

'Shit, Donny,' he said, wincing with pain as he kneeled beside his comrade. 'What's up?'

'Back,' whispered McCann, his mouth quivering with cold. 'Broke my fucking back.'

'You sure?' Gallen looked down the inert length of what had once been the most vital person he'd ever known.

'I'm sure, boss,' said McCann, lips dark blue. 'Anyone else make it?'

'Don't know,' said Gallen.

'Take the headset.' Following the line of the injured man's nod, Gallen saw the radio headset and cabling lying in the ice. He retrieved it and, reaching down to McCann's belt, plugged it into the radio set and installed it around his head and throat.

'Kenny, Mike, anyone there?' said Gallen into the mic, blood dripping off his face again.

'Try all the channels,' said McCann in a hoarse whisper. 'There's five.'

Reaching into McCann's parka, Gallen tried each channel, his fingers barely able to grasp the tuning button.

'You got the volume up?' said McCann, eyelids drooping.

Looking again at the radio set, lost in the layers of clothing at McCann's belt, Gallen found the volume control and turned it up. The headset crackled and Gallen heard a voice.

'Boss, that you?' came the Canadian drawl. 'Donny? Gerry? This is Kenny Winter, copy?'

'Gotcha, Kenny,' said Gallen, his jaw seizing. 'We're in an ice cave, I've got a man down. Can you assist? Over.'

'Can try. Where are you?' came the voice.

'Look for a dome of snow, directly north-east of the plane wreck. My guess, eight hundred to one thousand yards.'

'Got no compass, boss,' said the Canadian, his voice wavering in and out.

'Okay, take a fix on the saddle in the distance, along the line the plane landed on,' said Gallen, the rib starting to ache. 'There's a U-shaped saddle on the mountain horizon, with a sharp peak right beside it. Walk towards it and after eight hundred yards, look to your right for footprints around a big snow dome.'

Gasping for breath as the rib muscle gripped like a clenching fist, Gallen fought for consciousness. He panted as Winter's voice surged into the headset.

'On our way, boss,' said the Canadian.

'Bring ropes,' said Gallen through his gasps. 'And don't walk on the dome. Repeat, do not walk on the dome, it's hollow underneath.'

Gallen heard the crackle of reply but passed out before he could make out the words.

CHAPTER 20

Gallen came out of a deep dream to a knocking sensation on the back of his head: Donny McCann, head-butting him.

'Get up, boss,' said McCann. 'Got company.'

Pushing himself off the ice, groggy as a drunk, Gallen shook his head clear and looked around. 'Where?'

'In the roof, boss.'

Looking up, Gallen saw a dark shape flat against the snow, about fifteen yards from the hole McCann had fallen through.

'Kenny?' he said, as loud as he could before the rib spasmed again.

The reply echoed around the ice walls. 'Boss.'

'Don't come any closer, I can see your body through the snow.'

'I'm roped,' said Winter. 'Got Mike anchored in the hard stuff.'

The shape wriggled further along the snow and Gallen hunched his body over McCann, giving him some protection should the roof cave in.

Winter looked down through the hole. 'You two okay?'

'No,' said Gallen. 'Donny's got a broken back. I've got a rib and hypothermia.'

Rope appeared in the hole and then it was falling to the floor about nine feet from McCann. Picking it up, Gallen checked it was still attached to Winter.

'I'm going to move back to the anchor,' said Winter. 'Secure Donny and give three tugs when you want him outa there.'

As carefully as he could, Gallen attached the end of the rope under McCann's armpits and around his chest. In all other circumstances, the military advised against moving a man with spinal and neck injuries. But this was different. Donny McCann was dying of hypothermia and shock from the broken back. He needed a hospital.

Gallen was about to tug on the rope three times, but he realised McCann was unconscious again. Slapping him, he felt emotions coming up. 'Don't slip away on me, you tough bastard. Don't you dare.'

McCann mumbled something and Gallen slapped him again.

'We okay, boss?' came Winter's voice from topside.

Gallen yelled, tears in his eyes, almost unable to articulate a single word. 'Wait a minute—Donny, wake up,' he said, giving him a third slap.

McCann's eyes opened and he spoke. 'It's over, boss.'

'No,' said Gallen. 'It's over when I say it's over, Corporal.'

'Momma gets my payout, okay?'

'Shut up,' said Gallen, pulling three times on the rope.

The rope tightened and Donny McCann started his ascent, the rope tearing through the roof so that Donny kept falling back to the ice floor before the rope hit the hard stuff and the lift got purchase.

'Tell her I forgive her.' McCann's eyes rolled back in his head as he rose to the top.

'Shut up,' said Gallen.

'Terry weren't her fault,' said McCann. 'Tell her that.'

'Tell her yourself,' said Gallen, warm tears falling down his face as he watched the broken body ascend.

Hands tore at McCann as he reached the surface, the still body too much for Gallen to stomach.

'Okay, your turn, boss,' Winter called, and the rope came down again. Wiping his tears on the back of hands he could no longer feel, Gallen used the last remaining dexterity in his hands to tie on to the lift and pull the rope three times. He felt the rope go taut and let himself be pulled upwards, clambering at the precipice as he reached the surface and then was dragged over the dome and onto the downward slope, sliding until he came to rest.

Hands reached for him, untying the rope.

'Can't breathe,' he gasped, trying to stand as his ribs spasmed. 'Fucking cold.'

Winter led him by the arm to a makeshift sled. It was the upright section of a leather seat on the Challenger, now with ropes attached to the front. McCann was already laid along its length and Mike Ford was waiting for Gallen to lie on it too.

'Cuddle up to Donny,' said Winter, 'and hold on tight. Might warm you up—might be the only way you make it through the next twelve hours.'

Lying alongside McCann, Gallen put his arms around him and immediately felt sleep claiming him. He fought it, trying to stay awake as Ford and Winter grunted and strained through the chest-high snow, pulling the makeshift gurney like a couple of mules. Drifting in and out of what Gallen knew were hallucinations, he remembered the fireman lifts at Pendleton: two men buddying up for a two-hundred-yard race. One carried for the hundred yards going out and the carrier became the carried on the inbound hundred. Not even the toughest Marine liked that weekly test of character, but by the time the Force Recon candidates were assigned to a unit, they understood what the fireman lift was all about: I bust a gut for you, so you can bust a gut for me. Gallen remembered how the load changed when you knew it was going to be subsequently taken by your buddy. It was a load shared, after all, and once he'd realised that, it was lighter all round.

The noises and shapes whirled around him, it was hot and then cold and smells blended together in an indistinguishable blur. Gallen slept deeply, occasionally conscious of someone trying to wake him and open his eyelids. He went deep into a world of brothers and sisters, of summers baling hay and winters testing the pond to see if it was ready to take skaters; of a mother beeswaxing the furniture and hockey games where all he could hear was the sound of his father telling him to get off the damn ice: 'Don't you dare stay down.'

Gradually, slowly, Gallen came out of the dream world, until he opened his eyes, finding himself in a room that was dark save for a small fire burning a few feet from him. Beside him was another body and they were bundled together, thick layers of clothes and blankets across them.

As soon as he took a breath he started coughing, the soot from the fire too much for his lungs.

'Kenny!' It was a woman's voice. 'He's awake.'

Gallen tried to sit up but couldn't because of the layers. The air around his face was very cold and as his eyes became accustomed to the gloom, he could make out Florita sitting on the other side of the fire.

She moved around to him. 'Welcome back.'

'Where have I been?' he asked.

Winter appeared from under a hanging tarp. 'You've been in a coma, boss,' said the Canadian. 'Hypothermia. Real bad.'

Turning his head, Gallen came face to face with McCann and realised they were both naked under the layers. 'Hey, I love Donny like a brother, but it stops at a hug.'

Florita laughed softly, her face kind in the firelight. 'I think you're much better.'

'How's Donny?' Gallen looked for signs of consciousness.

Winter shook his head. He helped Gallen out of the layers, then handed him his dried kit. The last thing Gallen put on was his Goodhue boots, fire-dried and warm.

Hissing out the pain in his ribs and needing Winter to help him into the parka, Gallen took a cup of warmish tea from Florita. For the first time he made out the form of a man lying still in the shadows on the other side of the fire, only his face showing.

'Harry,' said Florita, following his gaze. 'He's vomiting blood.'

Durville groaned like a drunk man dreaming, and rolled slightly to his back, exposing what looked like a briefcase with a strap wrapped around his neck and shoulders.

Taking a seat so he could almost touch the fire, Gallen swapped a brief look with Florita. He'd ask her later; he wouldn't make the query public.

'Kenny,' he said, 'wanna brief me?'

'Both pilots dead on impact,' said Winter, whose mouth and eyes operated from the gap in his black balaclava which was tucked back behind the wolverine-fur hood of his parka.

'Where are we?' Gallen looked at the ceiling and saw the oxygen masks still dangling.

'Fuselage, the middle section,' said Winter. 'The rear exploded from the bomb—we salvaged a bunch of clothes and other stuff from the luggage area, but we lost most of it. It's lucky we got into the arctic gear before the bomb went off.'

'We got a flare gun?'

Winter shook his head. 'Looked for it all yesterday. It was either in the cockpit or the luggage area, both destroyed.'

'What about the front section?' said Gallen, wondering about comms and navigation.

'Mike's been going up there as long as his fingers are working, trying to get the radio operating again. He's got a battery that works good, but too much of the circuitry was burned out.'

'So, there's six of us?'

'Soon to be five, maybe four.' Winter nodded at McCann. 'I don't know what we can do for him.'

'What's our situation?' said Gallen, wanting food.

'The av gas was stored behind the baggage area. One of the tanks survived and that's what we're burning, using soaked rags.'

'Food?'

'The galley was stocked with cold cuts, muffins, milk, tea, coffee, bread,' said Winter. 'Florita and I went over the supplies a couple times.'

'And?'

'We can feed six people for four days,' said Florita. 'Five people a bit longer.'

'There are firearms on board, so hunting is an option,' said Winter. 'But I'm advising against it. This is really tough country and the last thing we need is a fresh case of hypothermia.'

'Agreed,' said Gallen.

The tarp flipped up and Mike Ford dropped to his knees as soon as he entered, hands out to the fire. 'Hey, boss. You're back?'

'Sure am,' said Gallen. 'How we looking in that cockpit?'

'Got a battery with charge and a few circuits connecting,' the Aussie said, rubbing his hands together. 'But the radio is fire-damaged. I can't get it to work. Its receive function works sometimes, but that's useless to us.'

Gallen sipped the tea then asked, 'Any idea where we are?'

'Nah, mate,' said Ford. 'Lost the avionics, so there's no coordinates.'

'We were flying south-west for, what, an hour?' said Gallen. 'Any idea where our nearest town or settlement might be?'

Reaching behind him, Winter produced a fold-out map of North America.

'That's the best we have?' said Gallen.

'Planes don't really carry maps anymore,' said Ford. 'The navigation system is in the computer. These maps are just Oasis notations for where the fuel depots are.'

'So where are we?'

Ford put a finger on a place on the map and made a vague circle. 'West of Baker Lake.'

The Aussie's finger was in the middle of a wilderness so vast and so devoid of human settlement that it made northern Wyoming look like midtown Manhattan.

'What's the scale on this?' Gallen could barely comprehend their predicament. Putting three fingers together and measuring the distances, he looked up at Ford and then Winter. 'There's no settlement within five hundred miles of us,' he said.

'Five hundred would be Baker Lake, and that's the closest,' said Ford.

'Okay,' said Gallen, realising there wasn't much more than morale to keep them going, 'let's keep the injured alive, and then in the morning we'll work on a way to attract those search planes.'

'Roger that,' said Winter.

Feeling something in the breast pocket of his parka, Gallen fossicked it out and smiled at his find. 'Look what I got.'

Smiles ripping their faces, hands went out for Gallen's full and unopened pack of Marlboros. Lighting up from the fire, Winter sucked on the smoke and leaned back. 'That's what I call leadership.'

Gallen nodded at the men, pleased he could make a small difference. But it was Florita's eyes that told the real story. They were realistic female eyes; they had seen the end of the road and were resigned to it.

CHAPTER 21

The peak of the cliff that the Challenger had crashed into formed
a convenient lookout platform and Gallen sent the men up in
shifts to search for aircraft. If any were spotted, the lookout would
signal to the others below, who would throw the foam cushioning
from the leather cabin seats onto the fire and create a mass of black
smoke.

It was a treacherous climb to the top, so Gallen excused Florita
from that duty. Florita was charged with keeping blankets and clothes
dry. If the sun was strong enough, she could suspend the clothing
and blankets on salvaged rope and air them as much as possible. She
was also the sole arbiter of food rationing and kept a distillery going
all day that created fresh water from the snow.

Winter took the first watch on the lookout, taking with him the
radio headset that they'd managed to recharge from the spare battery
in the fuselage. Gallen worked with Ford to shore up a warmer
environment for the nights, when the temperature would get to
minus forty if the winds rose.

Checking on McCann every hour or so, Gallen couldn't shake
him from the coma. Among the debris, Ford had found a large
medical kit and they searched it for something that might
wake McCann up.

'That Harry Durville's rooted,' said Ford, as they sorte
the medical supplies. 'Once you're bleeding inside, it's
Donny can recover if we can keep him conscious. W
adrenaline?' He held up a large syringe.

Gallen wasn't convinced, slightly suspicious of the Australian use
of adrenaline. But as the afternoon wore on he approached Ford.
'Let's try it. Once only, okay?'

Peeling back the layers of blankets and clothing, which Florita
whisked away to dry, Ford plunged the needle into McCann's neck
muscle and depressed the syringe until half of the adrenaline was
expelled into McCann's bloodstream.

The result was instantaneous, McCann's eyes opening wide and
his face taking on a surprised look, like a baby waking from sleep.

Florita had food and tea ready, and fed him while Ford created
a better bed for the former Marine. The talk was forced and
empty, the survivors saving their energy for the task ahead.

They laid McCann in the remade bed, with dry blankets and a
fresh set of thermals. Gallen lowered his ear to McCann's lips when
he realised the man wanted to talk.

'It's important, what I said,' said his former corporal in a
deathly rasp.

'Your mother gets the payout,' said Gallen.

'I forgive her for Terry.'

'I'll tell her that.'

'I woulda found a way to juvie anyhow, didn't have to beat him
to do it.'

'Who's Terry?' said Gallen.

'Stepfather.'

'Okay.'

'He hit my sister, so I beat his ass—put him in the hospital.'

Gallen pretended not to notice the wetness in McCann's eyes.
He was a tough, proud Marine with a combat history and a kick-ass
reputation. He didn't need to go out like this in front of his old CO.

'I was fifteen, boss, and, you know, the things that happen in—'

'You don't need to tell me,' said Gallen.

McCann sniffed, tears running down his face. 'I was fucked up,
man. Hurt, scared and fucked up, and I blamed Momma.'

'Look—' started Gallen.

'I said some things, terrible things, to that woman. But it weren't her fault for all that. So you get her the money and you say I's sorry. Donald loves her and forgives her.'

Gallen couldn't meet his eyes.

'Boss?' said McCann, a new tone in his voice.

'Yep.'

'I ain't no homo—I mean, it happened and all but I don't go for dudes.'

Gallen laughed. 'You can bivvy down with me any day, brother.'

'Brother?!' said McCann, a return to his usual cockiness. 'What we got here? Vanilla Ice made cap'n?'

The winds rose in the night, screaming around the fuselage at what Winter estimated was a sixty-mph northerly. They slept and dozed upright, taking turns with feet to the fire, backs to one another, sharing blankets and body heat. Gallen was glad they'd collected as much insulation as possible and tried to seal their tubular shelter. It wasn't perfect, but with a system of dropping tarps, snow banked up against the gaps and insulation packed around holes it kept most of the wind out.

When Gallen opened his eyes in the morning half-light, the wind had died and he was aware of weeping behind him. Climbing out of the shared blankets he found Florita leaning over McCann, sobbing.

'What?' he said, before meeting Florita's eyes.

'I can't do this, Gerry,' she said, gasping back the tears. 'I can't.'

Kneeling, Gallen put an arm around her heaving shoulders. 'Guess what, Florita?'

'What?'

'You're already doing it.'

'I can't—'

'And you're doing a damn fine job.'

They buried McCann against the cliff face, rolling what rocks and stones they could find to make a basic cairn, puny and out of place in the eternal wilderness. Mike Ford made a cross from pieces of a suitcase and they gathered around the Marine, silence descending on the group as they stood in snow to their hips.

Gallen became aware of the eyes on him. He wasn't religious, even though he'd gone to church as a youngster and been confirmed, at his mother's insistence. Winter nodded at him and for the first time in a long time, Gerry Gallen couldn't think what to say.

'Um,' he said slowly, self-consciously, in the vast silence of the morning, hoping some words would come. 'The first time I shipped out for combat, an old staff sergeant in the Corps gave us a pep talk. He told us that being a combat Marine was different to anything else we'd ever do in our lives. I remember he said there's only one thing more powerful than putting your life in another man's hands, and that's knowing he's good for it.'

'Fucking eh,' said Winter.

'Got that right,' added Ford.

'That reliance on other men is not something we talk about much in the military,' said Gallen, hoping he was giving the folks what they wanted. 'We're either totally hyped up or we're too embarrassed about how scared we are, or we're just too busy drinking and forgetting. But that old staff sergeant was right: there's this bond that happens when there's only us, and that's all there is.'

'Fuck yeah,' said Winter.

'Donny McCann was a tough guy from Compton and he was one of the best Marines I ever worked with. He was a ladies' man and he liked to party but I never saw him disrespect a woman, although I saw him get into fights to stop others doin' it.'

Florita looked up.

'He was a corporal in my unit when I was a captain, up there in the hills of the northern Ghan. Donny was a rear-facing turret gunner in the convoy and he was the last man standing, the guy still hammering away with that fifty-cal while the rest of us were hiding under the vehicle, hoping the incoming would stop. That's who he was.'

Gallen looked around at the faces, saw Florita crossing herself, saw Winter and Ford staring at him.

'So, Donny,' said Gallen, turning to the grave, not wanting anyone to see what the cold was doing to his eyes. 'I wish I had some church words for you, brother. But for now, let me say that you were always a thousand per cent. You were the real deal. I put my life in your hands, and you were good for it.'

Gallen took the lookout shift himself, finding a rocky outcrop at the top of the cliff where he could sit without getting the seat of his arctic fatigues wet. He had a set of naval binoculars around his neck, huge things that had been stashed in an overhead locker by persons unknown. Leaning against the rock was the Heckler G36 assault rifle. If he saw a fox or a hare, he was going to try and shoot it, but he wasn't going to stalk it. Winter was right: the country was too tough. Chasing the wildlife would take more out than eating it could put back in.

He tried to clear his mind, stay focused. There was the immediate concern of survival but there was also payback. Ford and Winter wanted to strike back at the bombers and they were annoyed that Durville wasn't forthcoming about who might have done it. Never mind that Durville was close to death.

He'd heard a couple of comments from Winter, and the way the two had looked at him when they buried McCann was a pure call to arms. In officer school, they were trained to think like a leader so that potentially negative responses among the men—revenge, lust, rage, fear—could be used to create a positive energy for the whole team. But Gallen didn't know if he had the right to manipulate the men away from their sense of vengeance. Having a goal—any goal—was sometimes fuel to keep going.

Standing to stretch his legs, Gallen glassed the horizon. It was a landscape of mid-sized hills and small mountains, escarpments and glacial riverbeds, covered in snow and ice and seeming to stretch forever in all directions; from one angle it looked like an ocean of white, while from another perspective it was a desert of snow. The sun bounced off each surface in a slightly different way, giving the terrain the creepy quality of being both uniform and constantly changing. It was an optical illusion and one that—once you watched it for too long—left the observer with almost no sense of distance or height or depth. Luckily they'd managed to recover enough polarised sunglasses that no one had to go without. Adding snow-blindness to their impossible situation would have been cruel punishment.

A figure walked slowly up the side of the cliff, a ramp-like block of snow and ice that led around the long way to the top of the escarpment. Gallen saw the red parka, black backpack and blue arctic pants and knew it was Florita.

She took half an hour to reach the rocky outcrop and was exhausted when she arrived, sitting heavily beside Gallen.

'You didn't need to do that,' he said. 'I would have come to you.'

He could see her smiling, way back in her parka hood, hiding behind fur trimming and a Thinsulate balaclava.

'I needed the air, needed to talk,' she said breathlessly.

'Should have made an appointment. Can't you see I'm busy?'

Florita laughed and shrugged the pack off her shoulders. 'Look what I found.'

She pulled out a bright orange plastic box with a lid. It could have been a fishing tackle box, but Gallen knew it as an emergency flare kit.

Taking it from her, he opened it and looked inside: there was a white pistol with a blue handle, while an array of twelve flare charges in two rows of six gave the user a choice of white, red, blue, green and orange.

'Nice work,' said Gallen, smiling as he handed back the box.

Florita put it in her pack. 'I know you want more from Harry, especially after Donny.'

'You noticed?'

'And I know that Kenny and Mike will leave him till you give the word.'

'They want some answers and so do I,' said Gallen. 'I mean, you like being out here 'cos someone bombed your plane?'

Florita shook her head, a plume of steam erupting from her hood as she sighed.

'So, who's Reggie?'

'He's Russian, his name is Kransk, and Harry believes he holds the key to the richest oil and gas reserves since Saudi was opened up in the 1930s.'

'Where? Out here?'

'Under the Arctic Ocean,' said Florita. 'Harry and Oasis Energy are working on cornering a resource that will control the world's oil and gas supply for the next century.'

Gallen fished out a smoke, lit it. 'Where does Reggie come in? He an oil guy?'

She shook her head. 'Harry has been trying to flush him out, see exactly who he represents and what he can do.'

'So that meeting in Kugaaruk.'

Florita looked away. 'I've said too much.'

'You haven't told me a thing.'

'You wouldn't believe the confidentiality contracts I signed to get this job,' said Florita. 'And I'm not throwing it away because I can't keep my mouth shut.'

'Good job, huh?'

'I was a fourth-year associate in a big LA law firm, beavering away for my theoretical chance to make partner, some day, perhaps, if I kept wearing the tight dresses, if I kept being the cute Latina laughing at the stupid Anglo jokes.'

'Then along comes Harry.'

'The Oasis partner was in Tokyo and his associate was on compassionate leave in Dallas. A contract needed to be checked and signed overnight, and when I saw it I called the number on the cover page to make sure they understood what they were signing.' Florita warmed to the story. 'So Harry Durville picks up the phone, and here I am talking with this big-time oil guy, this billionaire you see on the cover of Time and Forbes, and we're taking clauses out and putting others in.'

'Saved his ass, right?'

'Next thing you know, I'm on the Oasis jet, doing the deals, meeting the Arabs and the Indonesians, and my firm doesn't like it, tells me to move over, let the Oasis partner back in the game.'

'I had no idea it worked like that.'

'Sure,' said Florita. 'So about three weeks later, when I'm back in the tight dress, pretending to laugh at some lame prank, Harry asks me out for lunch. He makes me an offer: he'll double my salary, give me stock options and a VP title—chief legal counsel.'

'And he paid for discretion.'

'Absolutely,' said Florita.

Gallen wanted to argue, to put on some pressure. But he admired people who stuck to their undertaking. It was the single most important character trait for a combat soldier, in his opinion, trumping bravery and strength and even intellect.

'I understand that,' he said, realising her face was close to his.

'You do?' she laughed. 'Wish you'd tell Kenny that. Harry's scared of him, doesn't want to be left alone with him.'

'Heard of his reputation in the Ghan,' said Gallen, thinking about the Canadian's past.

'No,' said Florita, confused. 'Harry used to watch him in the Western Hockey League. Says Kenny once put his stick through the plexiglass.'

The shape started as a speck on the horizon. Gallen stood, dislodging the hand that Florita had placed on his leg, and pressed the field-glasses to his eyes.

He was sure he'd seen movement against a small mountain range about fifty miles away. Scanning the whiteness, the maritime glasses good at cutting out glare, he strained his eyes to catch it again.

'A snow flurry?' Florita stood beside him. 'Maybe a bird?'

Letting the binoculars fall to his chest again, Gallen put his sunglasses back on, not taking his eyes off the horizon. 'It was something,' he said. 'Maybe a bird, but maybe a reflection.'

'Which means glass or steel?' said Florita.

'I was hoping.'

They stood awkwardly, jostling for position.

'Well,' she said. 'I suppose I'd better get back to the water still.'

'Yeah, um . . .' Gallen tried to think of something mature to say. 'I guess.'

She turned to him and leaned in, and as Gallen saw the look in her eyes—way back in the darkness of the snow hood—he caught movement at the edge of his vision. Pushing her away, he lifted the glasses again, his heart pumping into his throat.

Scanning across the mid-distance, concentrating on the ten-mile zone, he picked it up.

'Shit,' he said. 'Helicopter . . . Kenny, Mike!' he yelled into the radio mouthpiece. 'Pick up! Kenny, Mike!'

As he waited, he motioned for Florita to get the flare box.

The Aussie snarl came on the radio. 'What's up, boss?'

'Get the cushions on that fire!' he yelled. 'I got a black helo doing grids about ten miles north-west of our position. Get that black smoke in the air!'

The helo was going back and forth as shouted voices rose from the crashed plane below them. It looked like a small MH-6, the kind the US military called a Little Bird. It wasn't what he'd expect for a search-and-rescue helicopter, but he'd fly out of there hanging off a kite if that was what was available.

'Florita, got that flare gun?' he said, eyes locked on the helo.

'How does it work?'

'Take out the gun, grab the barrel and break it,' he said.

She fumbled for a few moments, the cold and gloves making small movements hard. The sound of the gun breaking echoed through the silence.

'Put a red charge in the barrel, and make sure the solid end is facing you.'

She did as she was told and closed the breech before Gallen could tell her to.

'Point straight in the air and pull the trigger,' he said. 'It won't hurt you.'

The flare rocket exploded on its way with a whooshing sound and Gallen pulled his eyes from the glasses long enough to see it arc five hundred feet in the air before bursting, then floating.

'They'll see that, won't they?' she said, both of them breathless with excitement.

'We got smoke yet?' asked Gallen. 'Shit!' The helo was flying away.

'Is it going?'

'Hope not.' Gallen watched the low-flying helo duck behind a ridge. 'Hope they're doing a search pattern.'

Lowering the glasses, he looked down and saw thick black smoke rising to their position at the lookout, the chemicals in the foam cushions doing their job.

The radio crackled. 'We got all the cushions on the fire,' said Winter. 'This is it, boss. You set that flare?'

'That was us,' said Gallen. 'Florita found a box.'

'Then where's that helo?'

'Headed west.' Gallen ran arcs with the glasses, trying to catch another glimpse. 'Keep the smoke coming.'

Waiting for three minutes, their breathing rasping in the cold, they could hear the occasional shout of urgency and excitement coming from the camp below. The smoke billowed and the tension built as Gallen wondered what he would do if this failed. There was no Plan B except to get that radio working. As people started dying, there would be the issue of eating the flesh, and for him the answer would always be 'no'; once the sanction on cannibalism was lifted, when would hungry men make the decision to kill another to eat him, rather than waiting for him to die?

The noise started as a low throb, not unlike the distant undercurrent of an ocean hitting the beach. Turning his head and the field-glasses, Gallen swung for the direction of it. The throb started to come in sets of two and then three.

'Hear that?' he whispered.

'Yes,' said Florita.

The throb grew and then Florita was shouting, hitting Gallen on the back.

Letting the glasses fall, Gallen turned to her and saw it, the Little Bird hovering two hundred yards behind their position, where it had obviously emerged having circled through a valley. As they watched the nose of the rescue craft pointed their way.

'Over here, over here!' she said, at a volume that took Gallen by surprise. Stashing the flare box in her pack, the executive started running for the helicopter.

The radio crackled. 'We can hear the helo, boss. You see 'em?'

'They're here,' said Gallen, waving his arms. 'They're here.' He followed Florita towards the aircraft; as they struggled in snow up to their armpits, they yelped and whooped like young children.

'They've seen us,' said Florita, crying with joy. 'Thank you, Jesus.'

Gallen was getting short of breath in the snow, his bruised ribs aching, and was thankful when the helo dipped its nose at the two survivors and accelerated across the forbidding terrain. The speed with which the helo crossed that impossible ground brought tears to his eyes.

'They've located us,' he said into the mouthpiece. 'We'll be down there in a couple minutes.'

Winter sounded excited. 'Copy that, boss.'

Resting while Florita continued on through the snow, Gallen waved again at the helo as it closed on them. He looked for markings, but couldn't see any. He wondered if an oil rig helo had joined the search for the downed Challenger.

Florita jumped at the top of a snow bowl and slid on her back to the bottom, her laughter rising above the din of the closing helicopter, which banked over her and hovered.

Something clicked in Gallen's brain before he saw the man. Something reptilian, something that made him shrug the Heckler from his shoulder into his gloved hands. Then the man in the left side of the helo's rear compartment pushed back the small hatch in the main plexiglass door and Gallen's instincts were confirmed: it was the stance of that figure in the chopper, and the stillness of his eyes as he focused on Florita in the snow.

It was the appearance of a rifle and the movement of a man about to take a shot . . .

CHAPTER 22

Gallen cupped his hands and yelled, 'Florita! Get out of there!' His voice was barely audible over the vibration of the helo.

The shooter at the rear door of the helo pushed a muzzle through the gap of the smaller window and Gallen lifted his Heckler, flicked the safety. The rifle coming out of the helo looked like an M14, what the US military called a DMR, or a designated marksman's rifle. It was accurate at two miles.

Finding a good shoulder and bringing the G36 to his eye-line, Gallen squeezed at the target and watched the shooter fall back from the door as a star appeared in the plexiglass.

'Florita! Get down!' he shouted, panting cold air out of his lungs.

The woman turned, confused, her face hidden by the wolverine fur around the hood.

The helo swept quickly away from the bottom of the bowl and Gallen started running, trying to reach Florita. Looking up, he saw the Little Bird standing off, the shooter now pushing back the entire rear compartment door and assuming a professional's kneeling stance.

Surging to his left, clumsy in the deep snow, Gallen crawled and swam through the white hindrance to the cover of a large rock as the bullets whistled and sang around him.

Gasping for breath as he climbed behind the rock and checked the Heckler for load, he keyed the radio. 'Kenny and Mike, this is lookout, do you copy, over?'

'Gotcha, boss,' came Winter's voice. 'This is home base. Those gunshots?'

'Affirmative, we're under fire! Repeat, under fire! Don't come up here. Find cover and break out the rifles.'

'Can do. Anyone hit?'

'Negative. They have a sniper in the rear of the bird. Out.'

Shouldering the German rifle, Gallen rose over the rock and scoped the ground along the barrel of the G36, an old habit from special forces: in a gunfight, never let your head and eyes work independent of your weapon. The half-second that you lose is the half-second in which you die.

The helo hovered over Florita's position; judging by the lack of gunfire, they couldn't find her. Good girl, thought Gallen: she must be burrowing into the deep snow drift.

The helo swung about so Gallen could see a second shooter aiming from the right side of the Little Bird. Gallen ducked as chunks of rock and ice exploded five feet in front of him.

Kneeling behind the rock, Gallen scooped snow and patted it to the size of a bowling ball, his lungs struggling for air in the intense cold. He tore off his Thinsulate balaclava inside the arctic parka and stretched the material over the snowball as three shots sounded above the helo's thromp.

Waiting, trying to make himself breathe slowly through his panic, he counted down from five and threw the balaclava-covered snowball as far to his left as he could.

The shots came fast, sending shards of black Thinsulate flying into the snow.

Breaking cover from the opposite side of the rock, Gallen got a bead on the shooter and put three bursts into the side of the helo. The shooter leaned back in surprise, but not before Gallen drilled him in the left kneecap, the stomach and the upper chest, just below his chin.

The shooter fell from the helo into the snow on the ridge. Banking away, the aircraft headed back towards the bottom of the bowl, and this time Gallen tried to run through the deep snow, knowing that Florita had no chance if the other shooter got even a glimpse of her.

As he reached the edge of the bowl, readying to throw himself down the toboggan track created by Florita, he watched the muzzle flashes from the side of the helo and saw the snow and ice coughing up chunks.

He now had a shot of almost one hundred yards to the helo. Lifting the G36, he conserved his loads by switching to single shot and trying to scare the pilot—few pilots enjoyed stars appearing in front of them and would generally stand off until the shooting stopped. But before he could put a bullet in the cockpit windshield, the sniper's fire stopped and the helo banked away, keeping a wide arc as Gallen aimed-up.

'They're coming,' he said into his mouthpiece, ripping his eyes off the helo disappearing over the ridge.

Heaving for breath, he looked back at where the snow and ice had been churned up over Florita's body, knowing she couldn't have survived. His job now was to help the living defend themselves.

Forcing his weakened legs to cover the thirty yards to the edge of the lookout precipice, he saw the red flare still burning in the air, its last glimmer of brightness about to expire as the shooting started out of view.

Scores of volleys sounded over the harsh noise of the helo as Gallen finally made it to the precipice. Exhausted, fighting for oxygen, he looked down along his rifle and saw muzzle flashes pouring out of the helo at the camp, and muzzle flames firing back. Winter was visible from Gallen's position, shooting from behind the starboard engine that lay fifteen yards from the tarpaulin entrance to the fuselage. Ford was behind a rock, close to Donny McCann's cairn.

Checking his magazine, Gallen found he had two-thirds of the loads left and he aimed-up, hesitating as he did so, watching the helo back off out of the range of the small-arms fire.

The sniper had pulled inside the cabin and Gallen let his rifle drop, knowing it was a waste of ammo at that distance. As the helo throbbed in the still air, he heard a whirring, squealing sound. Lifting the field-glasses to his eyes, he found the source of the sound: mounted beneath the cockpit of the helo was a black minigun; the squealing sound was the six barrels spinning in preparation to fire.

Gallen keyed the mic. 'Kenny, this is Gerry. They've got a minigun. Get down.'

'Copy that,' said the Canadian, and then the most ungodly sound on a battlefield tore the air apart in a banshee's shriek of lead. Fire spewed forty feet from under the helo as the electrically powered mini Gatling gun opened up at a cycle rate of twenty rounds per second, chewing a hole in everything in its path.

The first five-second burst reduced the Challenger's starboard engine to shreds of metal but Gallen couldn't see Ford's body or any blood. As the helo swung to take out Winter's position, the pilot's profile was too tempting for Gallen: adopting a kneeling marksman's pose, he started squeezing head shots at the pilot. The second caught the frame beneath the pilot but the man didn't notice and opened up with the minigun. As fire flowed from the minigun, Gallen's fourth shot starred the glass beside the pilot's head, surprising him and making him bank away, the line of continuous fire creeping up the cliff face and sending cascades of rock fragments into the air.

'He's backing off,' said Gallen into his mic. 'We have to hit that engine or the tail rotor.'

'Hearing you, boss,' came Ford's Aussie twang.

'Okay, on my five,' said Gallen, and counted them in.

As the helo righted itself and drifted back to firing position, Gallen reached 'five' and the three Heckler & Koch G36 rifles opened up on the helo, which banked again and tried to circle back.

'Shit,' said Gallen, wanting the helo within range.

'I'll get him in,' said Ford.

'Nothing stupid, Mike,' said Gallen, struggling to breathe.

The Aussie emerged from his hide a few yards away from the destroyed jet engine, and raised his rifle in plain sight. The helo twisted slightly and the shooter in the back aimed-up with the DMR.

Firing again, Gallen missed on the first but hit the man's shoulder with a lucky shot on his second, dropping the shooter.

The pilot forgot about being careful and, dipping the nose, charged at the fuselage, the minigun spinning.

'Okay, boys,' came Winter's voice. 'Mike, get down, let's finish this prick.'

Ford dived to his left, back to the dugout he'd found in the snow, and Winter and Gallen opened up on the helo as it went through its ammo cans faster than any other gun on earth. Gallen's shots found their mark in the helo's tail section and rotor turret, but with no impact. Then his G36 clicked empty.

Finally, the fuselage looking like Swiss cheese, the helo banked out of the bowl and circled, Winter having stopped shooting too.

Gallen's heart sank. 'Guys, I'm out. Get down, wait for them to deboard and then let's take 'em.'

'Wait,' came Winter's voice. 'Think I scored in the engine bay.'

They waited for the helo to circle, coming back to finish them with the relentless gun. Then Winter's voice was in his head.

'Smoke! Look, boss!'

Squinting into the sun, Gallen saw a vague tendril of brown smoke wafting from the helo and then realised the engine note had changed from roaring power to a lawnmower with a dirty spark plug.

Standing, he watched the aircraft limping away from their camp, the engine note becoming more uneven as the smoke from the turbine grew browner. There was a flash of flame and then the smoke was black like a steam locomotive and the engine was struggling, the rotor losing revs.

'You seeing this?' said Gallen, but he could see the Canadian and Aussie already emerging from their hides, running through the snow after the crippled helo. 'Bring ammo for me,' he said, dragging his feet back into action as he headed down to the camp. 'And bring a pack full of food.'

'Got it,' came Ford's voice.

'And fellers,' said Gallen over the mic, his lungs burning for air, 'whatever we have to do, I want that radio in one piece. Can do?'

'No one touches the radio,' Winter panted. 'No one even looks at it funny.'

133

As Gallen found the ice ramp down to the fuselage a shot of orange flame burst from the stricken helicopter.

Keeping his eyes on the point where the aircraft disappeared over the ridge, he threw himself forward on his stomach and let gravity take him on a toboggan ride to the valley floor.

CHAPTER 23

Gallen met his men at the bottom of the lookout cliff, dusting snow off his parka as he took the spare mag. He was exhausted, fighting for breath as the three of them looked at a point on the horizon about five hundred yards north where the helo had dropped, flames pouring from it.

'Shit, guys,' he said, hands on his knees, his face almost hitting snow as he leaned forward. 'I'm beat.'

'We can't keep running around in this snow,' said Winter, mouth hanging open like a hound dog's. 'We don't have the food supply to support it, and we can't afford to get covered in sweat. It just ices over.'

Catching their breath, they looked at where they had to trek to, simply to get into a gunfight on the other side of the hill.

Looking at his G-Shock, Gallen had 3.42 pm. The sun was low and the temperature was starting its drop towards the overnight extremes of minus forty or fifty, the killer temperatures they didn't want to endure in the open.

'If the wreck's one thousand yards,' said Gallen, 'we can get there and back before nightfall proper. Let's say a return trip of ninety minutes?'

'And if we get to the top of the hill and the chopper's two thousand yards, with shooters waiting?' said Winter.

They looked at one another, caught between the uncertainty of waiting in the fuselage for search and rescue, and the uncertainty of finding the Little Bird's radio and calling for help.

'How's Harry?' said Gallen, changing the subject.

'On his way out,' said Ford. 'But he's dry and we got food into him a couple of hours ago. Where's Florita?'

'They got her at the lookout,' said Gallen, unable to look them in the eye. 'Starts running towards the chopper like her Christmases have come at once, and then—'

'Shit,' said Ford.

'Okay.' Gallen took a calming breath. 'There's only way home, and it starts with a radio. What's our food?'

Opening his pack, Winter revealed a plastic bag of muffins and a Tupperware container of cold cuts: ham, salami and pressed chicken. Beside the food stash were two large bottles of water, distilled by Florita.

'That's maybe enough for twenty-four hours,' said Winter. 'We'll have to get to that helo and get on the radio tonight.'

The helicopter was perched on the end of a large ice escarpment, lying horizontal about two hundred feet over a partially frozen lake. As the sun edged towards the horizon to their left, pushing down the temperature to twenty below, Winter handed the field-glasses back to Gallen.

'Seven hundred yards,' said Winter. 'I agree with Mike. There's one set of tracks away from the machine.'

'One survivor?'

'One who can move on foot,' said Ford. 'Doesn't mean there's not a dude in the bird with broken legs, waiting with an M4 on his lap.'

'Where would the tracks go?' said Gallen.

'The fit one's gone wandering, or he's waiting for us to arrive, going to ambush us for our clothes and food.'

Gallen looked at the scene again, saw the last light of the day and felt the cold numbing his feet and face. A puff of wind hit the ridge they were standing on, and the cold cut through to his ribs like someone had hit him with a chisel.

'We go the long way,' he said, knowing he wasn't going to be popular. 'There's one survivor on foot and he's probably got the DMR. He could be waiting for us, so we have to come in from his six.'

Ducking into the lee side of the ridge, Winter led the team in a long semicircle. As their feet started breaking through the crust of the hardening snow, Gallen knew he'd given them a better chance of taking the helo unchallenged, but he also knew the journey would take about an hour longer than the direct route.

Gallen's legs gave out halfway up the large snow drift. Falling sideways, he felt himself drop until the drift held him as if weightless. He struggled for balance as Ford and Winter got him upright.

'You okay, boss?' Winter whispered. The wind had died and the terrain had an eerie stillness, the pale blue dome of dusk bouncing the smallest noises for a thousand yards.

'I'm okay.' Gallen knew he should have had more recovery time from the hypothermia. The truth was, he was running on half-strength and he was having trouble balancing.

'Have some water,' said Winter, pulling it out of his waistband, where it was being carried to keep from freezing.

Sipping, they watched Ford slide down from the top of the drift where he'd done a recce with the glasses.

'I make one body at our eleven o'clock,' said the Aussie, taking his turn on the water bottle. 'Not moving, rifle lying beside him. He's been waiting at the top of a drift.'

'Dead?' asked Gallen.

'Sleeping, maybe hypothermia. Christ, it's cold.'

As they huddled in, trying to breathe through their noses to stop plumes of steam moving into the air, Gallen saw something extraordinary and for a second thought he was hallucinating.

'The fuck's that?' He cowered away as what looked like an ice fairy floated past them on the air.

'Ice,' said Winter. 'Gets cold enough out here, ice crystals form in the air. It must have fallen through fifty below.'

'Jesus,' Gallen said, tongue cold simply from opening his mouth. 'We have to take out that shooter, get to the helo.'

'I'll do it,' said Winter. 'Just gimme cover.'

Slinging his rifle diagonally over his shoulders, Winter checked the Ka-bar in its rubber belt scabbard and crawled over the ridge on a journey that would cover about a hundred and twenty yards to the next ridge, where the shooter was lying.

The moon rose from the north, favouring Gallen and Ford. They could keep their heads up without worrying about their silhouettes on the horizon.

Gallen tracked Winter's progress with his G36, jaws clenching in the cold. The exertion of moving through the deep snow may have been exhausting but it had kept them warm. Now he had to consciously move his toes and twirl his wrists, making the blood run to the extremities as his nose ran freely, the mucus freezing solid on his top lip.

Winter crawled to within twenty yards of the prone man, the air alive with the man's snoring. The shooter partially rolled sideways, made three snores, and then his head collapsed into the snow, hypothermia reducing him to a near-comatose state.

Winter must have seen this before, decided Gallen, because as soon as the snores had finished and the head slumped, he stood and walked the last few yards, picked up the shooter's rifle and rolled the man onto his back.

'Okay,' said Winter, his voice carrying across the snow bowl as if he were standing beside them. 'We're clear.'

At Gallen's request, Winter ratted the man, turning out his pockets, finding a wallet which he looked inside then handed over to Gallen. The Canadian found a support-belt under the man's clothes, the mark of a former soldier whose back had taken one too many jumps off a helicopter or landings with a parachute.

'He's a pro,' said Winter, panting in long plumes of steam as he stood with Gallen and Ford. 'Hi-Tec boots, back belt, military thermals. It's all generic, Canadian and US military issue.'

'No ID?' said Gallen.

Winter shook his head. 'Check out the wallet.'

Looking at the wallet reflecting the moon, Gallen couldn't see anything strange about it. 'What are we looking at?'

'No cards, no memberships,' said Winter. 'It's all cash; even the brand name of the wallet has been cut out. Who, these days, has a wallet that looks like that?'

'You mean, besides a spook?' Ford checked the man's arms for tattoos but instead came up with a G-Shock watch, which he pocketed.

Gallen pushed back the man's parka hood and grabbed the double-layer balaclava off his head, shoving it thankfully onto his own skull, which had gone naked since creating the snowball diversion. The sleeping man was swarthy, like a Spaniard. He didn't look like any of the men they'd encountered with Reggie's crew at the meeting house in Kugaaruk.

Gallen nodded at the man. 'Can you get him talking, Kenny?'

'I can try, boss. But it's over for him.'

'I want to know who's in that helo,' Gallen said, looking across the snow to where the helo lay buried in the ice like a massive dragonfly.

Winter and Ford worked on the shooter, waking him and trying to get him talking while Gallen scoped the helo with the glasses. More ice crystals floated past, suspended in the frozen air, and Gallen felt the cold driving up into his boots, sitting on his back like a gorilla.

'Is that Russian?' said Ford, as they got a few slurred words out of the dying man.

'No,' said Gallen. 'Let's go.'

They took turns at the lead as they tramped across the deep snow bowl towards the helo, gasping the freezing air while trying to stop it going too deep. The moisture in the air was frozen and Gallen's injured rib was aching with every breath. He worried about what was happening in his lungs, worried about frostbite and hypothermia. He could sense his team were desperate to get into the helo and get warm as the temperature crushed in on their skulls.

Approaching the helo, almost unable to stand, Gallen raised his G36 and gestured Ford and Winter to close on it from opposite flanks. The ice creaked as the men approached the downed aircraft and Gallen could see the patches of clear lake water below, reflecting the moonlight.

Pushing into the cockpit, Winter poked and prodded the pilot and gave the thumbs-up to Gallen. The ground creaked again: were they on a glacier, or was it the deep snow contracting with the cold, having warmed in the day?

'Let's get on that radio,' said Gallen, his voice sounding far away with fatigue.

Putting his boots on the Little Bird's step, Winter froze. 'What the fuck—' he started, and then he was turning, the helo moving as the ice emitted a ripping sound.

'Shit,' said Ford, moving to Winter as the helo slid deeper into the snow.

Gallen looked down at the source of the ripping sound and saw a crack opening a few feet in front of him.

'It's going,' he said, the creaking and ripping joined by a crashing as tons of ice hit the lake's waters below.

Grabbing Winter by the arm, Ford pulled the big man off the helo's step and ran with him through the snow as the gap opened in front of Gallen. The two men ran, Gallen screaming encouragement as the helo disappeared from view and the noise of the ice hitting the lake reached a crescendo.

Shoving his rifle's muzzle into the snow as hard as he could, Gallen sat straddling it and called for the men to leap as the gap opened to six feet in front of him. The whole scene unfolded in slow motion, the ice opening at a steady but slow pace and the two men struggling through deep snow which reduced their progress to the most excruciating pace.

Winter leapt first, pushing off the receding precipice of the crevasse and landing with his hands on Gallen's fatigues belt. Ford leapt a second later and disappeared into the darkness of the opening maw.

Screaming at one another above the cacophony of the sheering ice cliff, Gallen leaned back, driving his ass into the snow, hoping for enough purchase with the rifle and his heels to hold up the Canadian.

'Climb!' screamed Winter, and Gallen felt the rifle start to slip through the snow, pushing the heels of his boots over the edge so they were dangling under Winter's armpits.

Why was Winter telling Gallen to climb?

Then he said it again. 'Mike, fucking climb!' and Gallen saw

Ford's hands gripping into Winter's shoulders, tearing at the arctic parka's heavy fabric.

Reaching down as they all teetered on the edge of the yawning crevasse, Gallen gripped Winter by the shoulder of his parka. With his other hand, Gallen gripped Ford's glove and took the weight, the rifle sliding a few inches more through the snow towards the gap. Once it reached the edge they'd all be going into the lake and certain death.

Gallen's balls ached as they bore the weight of two men. 'Make it fast,' he said with a grimace as Ford clambered over Winter's shoulder and hit the ground behind Gallen.

The movement made the rifle slide through the ice precipice and Gallen felt his momentum taking him over as Ford grabbed him by the back of his belt. The rifle gave way and clattered into the darkness as his legs and hips extended over the edge, Winter holding onto his legs and front pocket, the lake gleaming below. Gallen could now see the waves made by the falling ice and submerged helo. He didn't want to die—not down there, anyway.

Yelling at the top of his lungs, Gallen pulled up on Winter as Ford pulled back on his belt. Twisting around, he came face to face with the icy edge as Winter clambered over him and helped Ford drag him to safety.

Panting in the moonlight, lungs aching with the cold, they caught their breath as the lake slowly returned to its millpond stillness, with not a sign that the helo had ever existed.

'Well, that was a fuck-up,' said Ford as their pulses returned to normal, triggering a laughing fit among them. Gallen laughed until his eyes ran; for the first time in three years, he felt a sense of joy.

'Drove a corporate jet into a cliff, dropped a helicopter into a lake,' Winter chuckled. 'And we're just getting warmed up.'

Sitting up, Gallen pulled the last of the Marlboros from his parka, fished out three that were unbroken and offered them to the other men. As Winter proffered flame from his Zippo, they sucked on their smokes like men attending their own funerals.

'Well,' said Gallen, as they smoked, 'we have to go back, hope the fire hasn't gone out.'

It was the death option and none of them expected to make it. At least one of them would fail and the still fit wouldn't have the strength to drag an exhausted man through chest-high snow at fifty below. They'd arrive back at the shelter, physically spent and with no fire and no food. They were already struggling to breathe and talk, and their uncoordinated movements were consistent with the early stages of hypothermia.

'Or,' said Winter, sucking on his smoke from way back in his parka hood, 'we can check that out.'

Following his gaze, Ford and Gallen looked across the lake, getting a clear view now the helo wasn't in the way. On the other side of the lake, between two large snow dunes, was a shape that didn't look natural, a white sphere hovering over the snow.

'What is that?' said Gallen.

The moon had risen further and although it wasn't full it was casting a strong light in the still air. Winter raised the field-glasses and took his time investigating the sphere.

'I make it a compound,' he said. 'Got a large dome, sitting on a building of some kind. Demountable, maybe? Whole thing inside a fence.'

Gallen had a look, saw the white sphere balanced on a rectangular single-storey building.

'That's four miles, maybe five. You guys up for it?'

'Weren't doing nothing anyhow,' said Winter. 'Diary's free.'

Gallen looked at the Aussie. 'Mike?'

'Pope shit in the woods?' said Ford. 'How about you, boss? Got the gas?'

'Nope.' Gallen stood and brushed himself off in the moonlight. 'But that never stopped me before.'

CHAPTER 24

Winter cut the last of the muffins into even portions with his Ka-bar knife and handed them out. They were hard, like stale ship's biscuit, but the men chewed at them and swallowed them down, knowing that the next several hours would sap their last reserves. They'd talked it through and Gallen had insisted on a vote: either trudge for an hour back to the fuselage to the certainty of no food or radio, but a guarantee of heat; or spend maybe three hours in the snow at fifty below to get to a small chance of food, heat and radio. No guarantees.

They voted unanimously: risk all for the strange building in the snow.

Spooked by the collapsing lake frontage that had claimed the helicopter and the radio with it, they took a wide track around the north end of the long lake, staying fifty yards away from where they expected the lake started. What had scared Gallen most about the helo's submersion was the fact that the lake had eroded so far under the land ice. There was no telling how far back the lake extended under the ice and he didn't want to test it with the boots of three men.

Urging each other on, they took turns in the lead through the snow, the lead man acting as a sort of ice-breaker to ease the passage of the men following. The temperature was brutal and they tried to keep rests to a minimum, the sweat on their backs and legs freezing as soon as they stood still for more than thirty seconds.

Stopping briefly at the top of a large snow drift, Ford pulled his ratted G-Shock from the front pocket of his parka and read the time: 11.54 pm. They'd been travelling just over three hours and the sphere had disappeared from view.

Gallen's left lung ached under his injured rib. In the past half-hour, the pain had deepened so it was no longer purely external. His breathing was faint and he was losing strength. He reckoned he had another thirty minutes of exertion.

'Hey, look at this,' said Ford as they prepared to set out again. 'Dude's watch has a temperature gauge. It's fifty-two degrees below zero, Celsius.'

By the time they'd negotiated two major snow bowls, Gallen was no longer asked to lead. He was falling behind and Winter had pushed him into the middle of the pack. He was running on instinct, his legs numb with fatigue and cold and his breath ridiculously shallow, as if he was sucking breaths through a straw.

At the bottom of a bowl, where the snow was head-height and had to be fought through like a jungle path, Gallen looked to the top of the drift that loomed over him and his legs stopped.

As he lost his balance, he felt Winter grab him under the armpits; there was shouting and then Ford was in front of him.

'Ten more minutes, boss,' said the Aussie.

Winter whispered in his ear, 'We're gonna do this. We're not stopping now.'

Planting one foot in front of the other, his balance kept largely by leaning on the snow wall as he followed Ford's trail, Gallen managed to get himself to the top of the drift. They all panted as the zenith moon illuminated the ground in front of them. It was dominated by a large white dome sitting on a square scaffold which in turn sat over a long, white demountable.

'Holy shit,' said Winter, out of breath.

It took them five minutes to get to the fencing around the structure, their enthusiasm and panic combining for a renewed sprint through the snow. Winter smashed the padlock on the gate but they couldn't swing it open through the deep snow, so the

Canadian threw his pack over the cyclone fencing, climbed to the top and put his hands down for Gallen, who allowed himself to be man-handled over the fence by the two men, falling into deep snow on the other side.

Walking around the seemingly abandoned structure, they could find only one door that wasn't completely snowed over. It had been a long time since someone had shovelled snow around this building.

Kneeling, Winter scraped at the snow until a sign on the door appeared: Property of the Royal Canadian Air Force. Trespassing at this facility is prohibited and punishable under national security laws.

'Ooh,' said Ford facetiously. 'I'm gonna tell on you, Kenny.'

The snow was hard-packed and the three of them cussed as they dug it out, down to the door handle and then down to the step, Winter getting into the subsequent hole and kicking a pathway so the snow didn't fall in when he broke down the door.

Reaching up, he took a rifle from Ford and cocked the slide, aiming at the lock and putting a protective flat hand across his eyes.

'Fire in the hole,' he said, and put a three-shot burst into the heavy locking mechanism. Dropping his shoulder into the door, he bounced off it.

'Again,' said Ford. 'Can't hold out forever.'

After another three-shot burst, the shots echoing for several seconds in the still night, Winter forced the door and it swung inwards. Sliding down the side of the hole, Ford and Gallen followed him into the darkness.

Pressing the backlight buttons on their G-Shocks, they walked through anterooms and storage areas that contained the detritus of an abandoned military outpost. Pushing on, they found themselves in the room that obviously sat beneath the spherical dome on the roof, a core of wires and cables descending from the sphere into the centre of the room. Computer screens, radars and comms equipment were arrayed around the core.

'Listening station?' suggested Gallen.

Winter had a closer look, and raised his eyes to the ceiling. 'I think this is a distant early warning facility, what they called the DEW Line.'

'The what?' said Ford.

'Cold War stuff,' said Gallen, remembering the story. 'Detect the Ruskies before they flew their bombers over the Arctic. Right, Kenny?'

The Aussie snarl came from the darkness. 'Bingo, boys. Check this out.'

Following Ford's voice, they walked through a door and into a room that made Gallen's heart sing: a series of dry stores, then a kitchen with a stove with a stack of wood beside it.

'There's a washroom in there,' said Ford. 'Shower too. With any luck the stove heats the water.'

'Mike, get the fire going.' Gallen moved back to the main door, which he shut against the brutal cold. As he turned, the rooms lit up with an amber glow as the other men found a kerosene lamp and Ford kneeled in front of the stove's open door.

'We're gonna make it, boss,' said Winter, his hood and balaclava down and showing a rare smile.

'It's a start.' Gallen tried to smile, but felt suddenly very weak.

'Boss,' said Winter, dropping the lamp and running to him.

Gallen felt his weight collapsing on Winter's chest, heard the Canadian calling for Ford and then his head was lolling, his feet dragging.

He knew what it was, but he was beyond speaking. He hadn't taken a proper breath for five minutes. His lungs had failed.

CHAPTER 25

Gallen opened his eyes, the overhead lights making him wince. His mouth was dry, his lips fat and cracked. He turned his head, realising he was dressed in a body bag made of what looked like aluminium foil. He was naked beneath the bag and his fatigues were hanging up to dry along with Winter's and Ford's. The throb of a generator sounded and the electric lights were working.

Leaning over the stove, Ford was also in a foil body bag which he'd taped at the ankles. The BBC World Service played on the radio and Gallen realised what felt strange: for the first time in several days, he was warm.

'There you are.' Ford smiled as he turned. 'Cuppa?'

'Coffee, black,' said Gallen, his voice croaking as he tried to sit up, triggering a fireworks display behind his eyeballs.

'Don't get up,' said Ford, coming over. As the Aussie sat down on the bunk, Gallen realised there was a large medical kit open on the floor beside his bed.

He knew he'd passed out and he could remember it was because of the pain in his ribs and inability to get air.

'What's up?'

'Been feeding you paracetamol in your sleep,' said Ford, fitting a stethoscope to his ears. 'Trying to get the swelling and fluid down.'

'Fluid?'

'Yeah.' Ford stood and poured coffee into an enamel mug. 'Been stething you every half-hour. There's a huge haematoma on your left ribs, but under it is a growing reservoir of fluid. In the pleural cavity of your lungs.'

'Speak English, you damn Aussie,' said Gallen, pushing himself onto his elbow and taking the coffee.

'Pleurisy, mate,' said Ford, his bedside manner belying the fact he was a trained saboteur and killer. 'You take an injury to your chest in this kind of cold, and pleurisy is highly likely.'

'Pleurisy? Like pneumonia?'

Ford looked up as Winter entered the room. 'The two often go together, but pleurisy is water between the outside and inside lining of the lungs. If we let it go too long, your lung will collapse. It won't take air.'

'That's why I passed out?'

Ford smiled. 'Amazed you made it that far, frankly. I was sucking up some big ones getting through those drifts.'

'So?'

'So I was feeding you paracetamol, to reduce the swelling, but we have to drain that lung.'

'Drain?' Gallen sipped at the coffee and felt his ribs pound with the exertion of talking.

'Take the fluid off and then pump you with antibiotics, which we have right here,' Ford said, holding a jar of capsules that looked like they'd passed their use-by back when a genuine actor was in the White House.

Gallen looked at Winter as he approached. 'Hear that, Kenny? Take fluid off?'

'Thought we'd lost you, boss,' said Winter. 'I've seen this done before, in the Ghan. It's no biggie.'

'How small is no b . . .?' said Gallen, the question cut off as he ran out of breath.

'I put a tube into the cavity,' said Ford, 'then draw out as much fluid as I can with a large syringe.'

Gallen looked from one set of eyes to another. 'You're serious. You think you're gonna put a tube into my chest?'

'I did this once in a cave in Helmand,' said Ford. 'He was American, too.'

Gallen shook his head. 'He live to talk about it?'

'Sure,' said Ford, deadpan. 'He lived to tell me that if I ever set foot in the state of Mississippi, he'd hunt me down like a fox.'

The BBC World Service had the disappearance of Harry Durville's plane at the top of its 'Americas' section. The announcer started reading the story of the eccentric, tough oil billionaire as Ford finished his painkiller injections around the side of Gallen's chest. Hiding the catheter in his fist, Ford lifted it to the rib cage and pushed in hard, the sensation numbed until the spike slipped between two ribs and into Gallen's lung tissue.

Gasping with the pain, Gallen stayed still, held down by Winter. 'Shit, Mike. Think you got me?'

'Hold on, mate. Gimme ten minutes, that's it.'

Ford sealed the catheter in place with a piece of bandage tape and fitted a clear plastic tube to it. Then, having pushed a large syringe into the base of the tube, Ford pulled out with the plunger, immediately drawing a reddish-amber fluid into the syringe.

'If you can relax, the fluid will drain faster,' said Ford, changing syringes for another extraction. He went through seven syringes in the next twelve minutes, taking the fluid off the lung.

As Gallen took the penicillin at the end of the extraction, Winter sat beside him. 'The radio's not transmitting. Mike and I have been trying to find the problem but it looks like an antenna malfunction.'

'Can't we put a makeshift on it, try some rabbit ears?' said Gallen, remembering some of the quick fixes they used to do on radios in the field. 'We just need to get a signal out, even a weak one.'

Ford shook his head. 'They didn't want that happening at this facility. It was an early warning base where comms security was pretty important, so the radio system ain't like the Harrises we trained on.'

'What is it?'

'It's what they used to call a tropospheric scatter wave,' said Ford. 'I trained in comms when I was doing my time in the Navy, and we were only ever told about these things—never seen them before.'

'What's the problem?'

'They're custom-built and hard-wired into the antenna systems. The antenna itself is part of the radio. No antenna, no comms.'

Gallen breathed out.

'The base that picks up our signal has to be using the same scatter wave receiver as we're putting out,' said Winter. 'It looks like a giant relay system.'

'So we're going to have to go out there, climb the tower and find the break,' said Ford. 'Sun rose about three hours ago. We were going to eat and get out there.'

'Okay,' said Gallen. 'But be careful. One of us with pleurisy is enough.'

Gallen lay on the bunk, drifting in and out of sleep in the warmth of the stove-heated room. Ford had found a box of VCR tapes, and *Rain Man* was now playing on the TV—*Rain Man* because the copy of *Die Hard* was worn out from too much play. He flipped through a *Time* magazine from 1988, in which George Bush senior was running against Michael Dukakis and someone was trying to explain why the USS *Vincennes* shooting down an Iranian airliner and killing two hundred and ninety people was a bad thing yet also justifiable.

The idea of justifying the unjustifiable was playing on his mind. Harry Durville was not his favourite human being, but they'd left him back at the fuselage camp to die a lonely death. They certainly had their reasons, and Winter had tried to make it more comfortable for the billionaire. Yet Gallen felt guilty about it. 'No man left behind' wasn't a cliché of war movies: it was a real commitment in Gallen's world and he wanted to return to the camp, at least check on Durville.

The door burst in before the end of the movie, and Ford and Winter were standing in the room, dripping sheets of ice and snow from their parkas and gloves. Leaving the wet gear on the racks in the corner, they moved to the stove in their thermals, Ford stoking it with more wood as they got themselves warm.

'So?' said Gallen.

'It's been disabled,' said Winter, reaching for a smoke and offering one to Ford. 'Guess when this place was decommissioned, they did a total job.'

'We can't fix it?' said Gallen, unable to disguise his disappointment.

'It's rooted,' said Ford, pushing himself back onto the stove as he sucked on his smoke. 'It's fucked, mate.'

'Any ideas?'

Winter cleared his throat. 'Mike found a garage and workshop.'

'And?'

'And there's a snowmobile parked in there.'

Gallen shook his head, not wanting to hear it.

'Looks like it works, boss,' said Ford.

'Holy shit,' said Gallen, wishing he could smoke. 'We gonna travel five hundred miles across this country on a snowmobile that hasn't been used for twenty years?'

Ford and Winter looked at him and Gallen could tell that neither wanted to be the one to say it.

'Well?' he said. 'What's that look?'

'Three wouldn't make it,' said Ford.

'But two might,' said Winter.

Gallen nodded, reality setting in. 'Don't tell me—two fit guys, right?'

'We'd come straight back,' said Winter.

Gallen snorted. 'How nice of you, Kenny.'

CHAPTER 26

Ford dragged an aluminium medical sled into the heated inner room and started packing it with supplies. It looked like the kind of emergency capsule in which injured skiers were transported off the mountain but it was now going to carry food, shovels, tents and spare clothing, and a replacement snowmobile track they'd found in the garage. But mostly it was going to carry two hundred pounds of gasoline in jerry cans.

'Okay, boss,' said Ford, the sound of the snowmobile's revs coming from the garage area. 'We're gonna shut down all the electrical points in this building except the ones you have in here. Lights and TV.'

Gallen nodded, still too tired to talk properly.

'There's enough diesel for the generator to tick over for five or six days,' said the Aussie. 'And that wood pile is good for a week, just don't overdo it. Keep it on the slow combustion and stay in your foil bag.'

Looking down at the table in the heated room as Winter came through, Gallen saw the map from the Challenger lying open, saw the guesstimates for where they were and the various routes to Baker Lake, the only settlement in the southern region of Nunavut; it was, they all agreed, at least five hundred miles away.

The calculations were stark in their simplicity: two men would have to travel at least one hundred miles per day, in an east by northeast direction, hoping to find Baker Lake, which was not exactly a massive metropolis. The terrain was as bad as any of them had seen, just an endless procession of ice, snow and water, arranged in various obstacles and traps. Snowmobiles were useful machines—Gallen had grown up using them on the farm—but they bogged in deep snow, and once you broke a track, you were finished.

Gallen had already resigned himself to waiting in this concrete igloo for at least a week. If no one came, he'd starve, if he didn't get a secondary lung infection and die from that first. It was Ford and Winter he was worried about: there were so many things that could go wrong on their mercy dash that their calmness was both disturbing and inspirational.

Watching them put on their layers and adjust the snow goggles they'd found in the stores, Gallen felt a pang of sadness, something he hadn't felt since he'd been to the Joe Nyles fundraiser in Florida.

Winter saw the look, cracked a smile as he slipped on his Thinsulate balaclava. 'No speeches, boss. None of us asked for this—we just do what we can, right?'

Gallen slumped. Two weeks ago these two men were making a living with their skills, free from the dangers of a military life. Now they were in the middle of the Arctic tundra, having to make a trek that was probably going to end in death.

'We do what we can,' said Gallen, short of breath again. 'No heroes, okay?'

The VHS copy of *Wall Street* was good enough that Gallen could follow the story, and when it finished he ate a cup of dried raisins and dried apricots and made a pot of coffee. He'd promised himself to preserve the generator's diesel consumption by limiting himself to one movie per day, and he already had them lined up as a countdown to when Ford and Winter should return with the search-and-rescue helicopter: *Predator*, *The Untouchables*, *Beverly Hills Cop II*, *Robocop* and *Twins*.

Gallen took his penicillin and lay in the cot with two cardboard boxes of magazines beside him. The room was warm and he was tired again, although breathing was slightly easier than it had been before Ford drained the fluid off his lung.

As he dozed, he tried to put some of the pieces of this disaster back together. He'd been targeted to form a crew and take on the bodyguard assignment of a person who lived a dangerous life. Responsible for the security issues surrounding Oasis Energy's global interests was Paul Mulligan, a former intelligence bigwig from DIA. Mulligan had stalked him to a motel in Red Butte before making his offer. Where else had he been followed and put under surveillance? And why was Mulligan in that motel car park? It was like asking the Secretary of Defense to make a purchase order for infantry boots. It was an unlikely role.

Gallen ached for a cigarette but kept with coffee. Then there'd been the tails that had been on Winter and Gallen in Los Angeles, and probably also in Denver and Calgary. Gallen thought about the LA tail and Reggie's security crew in Kugaaruk: were they the same people? Working for the same employer? He'd have to do work on that if he ever got out of the Arctic.

But the biggest concern was the man called Reggie Kransk and an admission that the TTC wasn't as legit as it sounded. There was a massive oil and gas field under the Arctic Ocean which, Florita had implied, would keep the West going on its petroleum habit for several decades.

If Gallen ever got out of his predicament, he was going to start with a person who should have known better than to mess with a former special forces captain. He was going to find Paul Mulligan, and he was going to get some answers.

The noise woke him from his sleep. The fire in the stove had burned down and he listened to its soft hiss, audible above the howl of the wind around the spherical dome.

Looking at his G-Shock beside the cot, he saw it was 9.53 pm, a few hours into nightfall. Ford and Winter were out there somewhere, weathering what sounded like a fifty-mph wind.

Something else niggled at him, but he couldn't place it. Emerging from the bed, he padded over dry concrete to the wood pile, opened the stove door and put two pieces of wood into the box.

Something made him hold his breath, as if a spider had run up his spine. A faint bang, coming from the garage area of the building. He wasn't experienced with Arctic storms but it sounded like something more than wind hitting a roller door.

Pulling on his hypothermia suit, which looked like a giant roasting bag for a turkey, he picked up the SIG handgun left to him and moved to the door that sealed the warm room from the draughty building. As he leaned his ear to the door, he heard it again: a thump and then a whir. Someone was opening the garage door?

His heart pounding, Gallen thought of possible explanations. Maybe the hit men in the helo had radioed to their back-up, who were now scouting the area? The snowmobile tracks would have led directly to the Canadian Air Force building.

Checking the SIG for load and safety, Gallen tried to get deep breaths into his lungs without coughing. He needed to stay calm: whoever was entering that garage door had the disadvantage of not knowing the layout.

Slipping into his boots, he moved into the main room of the building, feeling the cold as he crossed the floor, past the old terminals and radar consoles, to the far side, where the garage was located. The lights were down, a faint illumination coming from the bunk room where Gallen had left one bulb burning.

The roller door clanked and then the building was filled with the noise of a snowmobile, revving above the sound of the garage door coming down again as men yelled at one another.

Ripping open the door, Gallen held the SIG in cup-and-saucer, keeping his forehead lined up with the gun as he scanned for unfriendlies.

A light went on. He was blinded momentarily then realised it was Winter at the light switch, sheets of ice falling off him like a barn in spring. Ford was huddled over the snow patrol capsule behind the snowmobile.

'What the fuck?' said Gallen, moving into the garage which was now wet with snow and ice.

Ignoring Gallen, Winter moved to Ford's side and then they were lifting something out of the capsule.

'Quick, boss,' said the Canadian as they marched past. 'Get another foil bag, woollen blankets.'

Shutting out the cold from the garage, Gallen followed the two men into the bunk room, where the heat was sealed in again as he shut the insulated door.

Unzipping a foil emergency bag, Gallen handed it over as Ford tore open what had been a folded tent and was now a covering of some sort.

'Get a double bag,' said Ford.

Gallen saw a body beneath the tent, Ford and Winter tearing wet clothes from it.

'In the bunk,' said Winter as Gallen unzipped a double hypothermia blanket. 'Quick!'

Panting with exertion and panic, red-faced with cold, the Australian and Canadian got the naked body into the rustling metallic bag alongside Gallen, making him flinch at the shock of incredibly cold skin. As they fastened the hypothermia blanket he saw glimpses of the body, bluish pale, translucent with cold, dark hair in a tangle around a handsome face.

'Florita?' said Gallen as Ford and Winter wove woollen blankets around the duo.

'Correct,' said Winter, lock-jawed with cold as he raced to the stove where he checked the coffee pot for contents and put it on the front burner.

Ford's jaws clattered as he pulled pills from his medical kit and forced them into the woman's mouth, his hands as stiff as timber.

'I don't understand,' said Gallen, as he felt her wet hair against his face.

'You don't have to.' Winter's face was a mask of exhaustion and worry. 'Let's call it a miracle and not push our luck.'

156

CHAPTER 27

Florita's pulse was faint and slow against Gallen's mouth, which Ford had encouraged him to place on her neck. It was eight o'clock in the morning and Gallen wanted to use the washroom almost as much as he wanted to remove himself from the embarrassing physical intimacy.

'She needs all the warm contact she can get,' said the Aussie, kneeling beside the cot with his stethoscope. Pulling back the blanket, he listened to the woman's heart and then restored her sleeping arrangement.

'She's alive,' Gallen whispered.

'Yeah, she's doing better than the alternative,' said Ford, rummaging in his medic's kit. 'But there's no substitute for sharing bodily warmth. Can you hang on for a couple of hours, at least until she regains consciousness?'

Gallen agreed and tried not to move as Winter returned from the shower cubicle and warmed himself against the stove.

'One of you going to tell me why you're here with Florita, not halfway to Baker Lake?'

'Shit.' Ford shook his head slightly as he selected a vial and a syringe. 'Florita happened.'

'We were half an hour east when we saw the flare,' said Winter. 'It was coming from the Challenger so we headed back, looking for Durville.'

'And?'

'Durville was dead.'

Ford injected something into Florita's neck. 'We headed out again and there was another flare—a green burster—coming from up behind the lookout.'

Gallen felt a wave of guilt. 'Shit, she was up there?'

'Found her in a snow cave, dug down,' said Winter. 'She wouldn't have survived in the open.'

'That was her last flare,' said Ford. 'What a tough chick.'

When Florita had stabilised, Gallen climbed out of the hypothermia bag, had a hot shower and dressed in dry thermals and clothes. The three of them sat at the table as the executive slept.

Gallen sipped coffee. 'Okay, so what did you do with Durville?'

'Buried him,' said Winter, lighting a smoke.

'Can we find him?'

'Right beside Donny,' said Winter. 'You wanna make sure you can hand back a body?'

'Something like that.'

'We grabbed his bag.'

Gallen paused. 'His bag?'

'Yeah,' said Winter. 'You didn't see that thing he was clutching in the fuselage?'

'Thought he was trying to stay warm,' said Gallen.

Winter smiled. 'When we found him, it was wound around him so tight I thought he'd been strangled.'

The bag was a satchel-style leather briefcase with a shoulder strap. Gallen dragged it across the table. Pulling out the contents, he placed them on the table: the ream of white foolscap paper was slightly damp. Feeling the outside pockets, Gallen came up with a BlackBerry, a charger and a Bluetooth earpiece-mic. Pushing the on-off button, Gallen started the device but it immediately asked for a password.

'Have a go at that,' he said, passing the BlackBerry to Ford.

Picking up the papers, Gallen scanned them one by one. The top sheet was a weekly run-down of Durville's movements and appointments, printed from an Outlook program—Florita's, judging by the tiny signature line on the bottom of the page. All of the entries duplicated what was on Gallen's own running sheet. As he put down the sheet though, a name caught his eye, one that he hadn't seen before: Tommy Tumchak, followed by a phone number.

'Kenny.' Gallen looked up. 'What's nine-oh-seven?'

'Alaska, ain't it?' said Winter. 'Not Anchorage. Probably Barrow.'

The date for the phone call was the day after the Kugaaruk meeting. It meant nothing to Gallen, but he decided to keep the diary anyway.

The rest of the documents were backgrounds on Gallen, Winter, McCann and Ford. They seemed to have got Gallen's details correct and he smirked at the mention of the Silver Star, a medal for gallantry in action. It distinguished the combat Marine from the pen-pusher but the clipboards had been trying to erode that over the years, awarding themselves Silver Stars for the most tenuous connections to combat. The enlisted men called them Fobbers—a reference to the heavily fortified Forward Operating Bases, or FOBs, and the fact that many of the military careerists went to Afghanistan to have 'combat' stamped on their CV without ever leaving the safety of the FOB.

Winter's sheet showed entries for Royal Canadian Infantry Corps, JTF2 Assaulters with specialties in marksmanship, field survival and hand-to-hand combat. Then there was a long period seconded to NATO's intel command in Afghanistan. Ford, meanwhile, had taught comms and fieldcraft to other Navy combat divers. McCann's Silver Star wasn't news to Gallen; he'd earned it in the same action as Gallen himself.

Sifting through the papers again, Gallen looked for the sheet on Bren Dale, the person who was supposed to be on the detail. It wasn't there. Gallen wondered about it: given that Dale had pulled out at the last minute, shouldn't the brief still be in there?

There was something strange about the briefcase, and he had another look, opening all the inside pockets. 'This is it?' he asked the other men. 'Nothing fell out?'

'Didn't even look in it,' said Winter. 'What's wrong?'

'I'll be happier if we can access that BlackBerry, see who Harry was talking to. But for now, I dunno. Would have expected more in a billionaire's briefcase.'

'Like?' said Winter.

'Like draft agreements, MOUs, maps, proposals. He's an oil and gas guy who's travelling with his top legal person to meet with a Russian to discuss some of the biggest untouched oil deposits on earth,' said Gallen, lifting the foolscap pages. 'But all he has is a BlackBerry and intel notes on his bodyguard?'

'What're you saying, boss?' asked Ford.

'I'm confused, is all,' said Gallen. 'Either the meeting was very informal—just getting to know you—or he brought some documents that were handed over to Reggie.'

'With no copies?' said Ford. 'And no documents handed to him?'

'Precisely,' said Gallen. 'Or . . .'

'What?' said Winter.

'Harry was hugging that briefcase because there *was* a document, and he didn't want anyone to see it.'

Ford gulped his coffee. 'So where is it?'

'It was taken, I suppose,' said Gallen. 'From when he packed at the hotel to when he died in the fuselage, he thought he had something in that case worth holding on to.'

'That's about two days, boss,' said Winter. 'You can search my stuff. I ain't got it.'

'Neither have I,' said Ford.

Turning as one, they looked at Florita.

'I'll talk to her when she comes around,' said Gallen. 'For now, let's talk about another shot at Baker Lake. I'll take the trip this time.'

'You look like shit, boss,' said Winter. 'It's cold out there and that snowmobile ain't the Orient Express.'

'I can't ask you guys to take all the pain.'

Winter gave him a look. 'We're beyond that, don't you think?'

'I don't—'

'You got pleurisy, boss—you'd be a liability,' said Winter. 'Besides, her toes are no good. She needs a hospital. If there's a third person on the sled, it's Florita.'

'Frostbite?'

Winter shrugged. 'Why Mike was rubbing on her feet all night.'

Looking over, Gallen saw the Australian rubbing Florita's feet through the foil bag.

'We have to talk,' said Gallen.

'Don't worry. I don't want to eat you, boss.' Ford smiled.

'Look,' said Gallen, glad someone had come out with it, 'we're low on wood, low on diesel and now we have four mouths to feed. So our food supply just shrank to three days.'

'We'll try again,' said Winter. 'But we'll need food.'

'What we really need,' said Gallen, 'is comms.'

'No luck,' said Ford.

'Well,' said Gallen casually, 'there's a Harris at the bottom of that lake.'

The conversation halted like someone had lifted the needle off an LP. Ford grabbed a Camel and avoided Gallen's eyes.

Then the sceptical Aussie drawl started up. 'Between *lake* and *bottom* you missed the part about freezing.'

'I saw the suits in the garage,' said Gallen, as softly as he could. 'Hanging on the wall.'

'I *told* you.' Ford pointed at Winter. 'Told you he wouldn't miss that.'

Winter slowly fixed Gallen with a look, not of hostility, but certainly that of a man who'd told a few COs to go fuck themselves in his time. 'Boss, I know what you're thinking, but that diving gear is, what, thirty, forty years old?'

Gallen shrugged. 'Looks okay.'

Winter raised the intensity slightly. 'That's a freezing lake and we don't know how deep the wreck is sitting. What we do know is that exposure is our big enemy. It's already given you the pleurisy.'

'Can we do it?' Gallen looked at Ford.

'Fuck's sake,' said the Aussie, leaning back on his chair legs, his blue eyes crackling through blistered cheekbones. 'You think because I'm a clearance diver I'm crazy?'

'No,' said Gallen, keeping his voice soft. 'I thought because you're a Navy commando that something this impossible might be possible.'

Winter slowly shook his head.

'It'll feel warmer under the water, right?' said Gallen.

Ford's eyes widened. 'You're nuts.'

'Let's check the gear,' said Gallen, standing.

'No, I mean it, mate. You're a fucking lunatic.'

CHAPTER 28

They watched Mike Ford as he sorted and arranged each dive rig, separating and checking every moving part. It was like watching a sniper take apart his rifle, except that Ford seemed to feel the need to blow on every piece, screw it, shake it, bang it and hold it to the light, squinting.

'What's that?' asked Gallen, noticing that Ford was particularly fixated on a valve system.

'That's your basic sealed diaphragm,' said Ford, smiling as he held it in his fingers. 'Environmentally sealed, to be precise. Supposed to trick the regulators into thinking they're in normal water.'

'What happens otherwise?' said Winter.

'The water would freeze the air-mix so the regulator would seize, and then your lungs would really have something to complain about.'

'I see,' said Gallen, secretly glad that he wasn't going in that lake.

'It's natural to worry about your dry suit in arctic diving, that's what everyone is concerned about,' said Ford, replacing the diaphragm. 'But you have to start with the breathing apparatus. If that doesn't work then we're not going far.'

'The seals and connectors working?' said Gallen.

'Pretty well preserved,' said Ford. 'This is high-quality stuff. It's US Navy spec.'

When Ford and Winter returned from the garage workshop, they'd filled the tanks with air from the compressor and found a flashlight that was not as strong as the modern ones, but which was the only one on the base. They also had a selection of tools that they would use to remove the Harris military radio without damaging it too much.

Directing Winter into the rubberised thermal undergarments, Ford laughed at the other man's idea that only one frogman needed to dive.

'Something you landlubbers gotta know,' he said with a wink as he stretched the rubber vest over his head and pulled it down. 'If you have the choice, you always dive with a buddy. It's the first rule of diving.'

Winter's thermal pants wouldn't sit properly on his hips and when Ford had to wrench the vest down, there was a one-inch gap between the top and bottoms.

'Geez, you're a big bastard,' said Ford. 'You should be okay when we get the dry suit on.'

Stepping into the silvery dry suit, Winter tugged on the leggings but they wouldn't pull up far enough. 'Shit. We got a bigger one?'

'This is it,' said Ford. 'But you can't wear that. You won't be able to move.'

'Need someone more your size, eh Mike?' said the Canadian.

Looking from Ford to Winter and back again, Gallen tried not to grimace. He believed that a commanding officer should only ask of his men what he was prepared to do himself. And he'd come up with this crazy idea.

'You're, what?' Ford looked Gallen up and down. 'Five-eleven, one-ninety, two hundred?'

'Fuck's sake,' mumbled Gallen.

Ford smiled. 'You're up, boss.'

Winter drove the spike into the hard ice with a large sledgehammer, steam bursting from his fur-lined hood as he worked the four-foot length of steel in far enough to hold two men.

Tying off the rope under the spike's flange, Winter threw it over the edge and onto the lake at the iced-over point where the helicopter had sunk two nights earlier.

Gallen coughed. The cold air was going down hard, his infected lungs not ready for the intense, paralysing temperature. The cold tore at the exposed flesh on his face, whistling at the wound in his cheek and attacking the broken teeth in his bare gums. The rest of him was insulated against the cold by the dry suit, a partially air-filled rubberised garment that started at insulated booties, enveloped the hands in gloves and ended in a waterproof hood that covered his entire head save for a rectangle that exposed his eyes, nose and mouth.

Gallen was over the edge first, the cold oozing through the booties as he struggled for a grip on the ice cliff. Giving up the idea of abseiling against that cliff, he opted for an adaptive rappel, sliding down the rope, bouncing off the ice cliff-face.

Hearing a shout, he looked up into the blue sky where Ford was leaning over the edge. 'Don't burn your gloves,' said the Aussie, louder than he had to. 'They need to be sealed when we hit the drink.'

The weight bore down on him and Gallen took it as slow as possible, trying to preserve his gloves. After two minutes of exertion, he hit the ice ledge beside the lake, exhausted already. Heaving for breath, which triggered a hacking coughing fit, he doubled over and tried to spit out phlegm. Then he tugged on the rope and waited for Ford.

Holding the rope steady, Gallen looked across the lake, a long piece of still water which was about a quarter of a mile across and maybe three miles long. The shore ice crushed up against the cliff, having repaired itself over the hole created by the helicopter, and Gallen looked for the hole they'd have to dive through.

The rope came down and he unclipped the scuba rigs and pulled the rope, which was retrieved quickly. Then Ford was on the line, ankles crossed over on the thick rope as he wormed his way down. If Gallen had been an instructor at Pendleton, he'd have given Ford a nine out of ten; he'd have given himself a three and a bawling-out.

Ford landed, his tool bag across his shoulder and flashlight clipped to his weight belt. After checking and rechecking the regulators, breathers, mouthpieces and masks, Ford picked up a set of fins and jammed them under Gallen's weight belt.

Gallen shrugged into the scuba tank harness held by the Aussie and allowed him to come around and buckle the rig across his chest so it was tight. The air was at about minus thirty and Gallen was having a mild panic attack about going into that water. He'd completed the Marine Corps Combatant Dive School, but he'd never really used the training in operations because he'd been sent to Mindanao instead. It didn't matter that he knew he could dive in the dark; this was different. This was Arctic diving with lungs that had just been drained of fluid. And he was scared of how his body would react, that the old Marines' mind-over-matter approach would not be enough with pleurisy in his lungs.

'We have to go through that?' said Gallen, anxiety creeping over him as he pointed across the shore ice to a gap between two floes. It was a hundred and fifty feet from the shore.

'That's it,' said Ford, testing the ice with his bootie-clad foot.

A breath of wind flashed across the frozen lake, so cold Gallen felt it could peel off his face, nose-first.

'Shit,' he said, looking away from the wind, feeling like he'd been fed the world's worst brain-freeze. Pain exploded in his sinuses and he held his hands over his nose, trying to regain composure as tears ran off his face and mucus poured out of his nose. 'Holy fuck.'

Tying a bowline, Ford attached the main rope to his waist and tied a thin line between himself and Gallen. They walked across the creaking ice, the sound of the lake lapping beneath it as creepy a sound as Gallen had ever heard. His anxiety rose as they got closer to the hole in the ice, a pulse banging in his head.

Following Ford's lead, Gallen sat on the ice and put his feet in the water. The cold shot was instant, such a sudden sensation that he saw stars.

Ford looked at him. 'You've done this before, right, boss?' he said as they pulled on their fins. 'I mean, Force Recon and all that. Just tell me if I'm teaching you to suck eggs.'

Gallen gulped down the stress and thought about transferring the adrenaline into positive action, not fear.

'Yeah, I've dived before,' he said. 'Just not under the ice.'

'It's basic. Just follow my lead and stay focused.'

Gallen nodded but Ford shook his head. 'No, I mean it. You let your mind wander down there and you'll drift away. The cold'll do that, so stay close and stay focused on the job. It helps, believe me.'

'Okay,' said Gallen, as they pulled the fins over their booties.

Ford looked at the G-Shock on his wrist over the dry suit and turned his body towards the spot where the helo had sunk. It was Gallen's watch, on loan to Ford so the Aussie could make a compass-navigated swim back to the site of the helo.

'Lids down,' said Ford, and they pulled down their masks, which formed a seal around the facial gap in their hoods. In theory, at least, no water should break that seal.

'Mouthpiece in, boss, and then three-breath test.'

Gallen did as he was told and gave the thumbs-up. His heart banged erratically in his temples and he heard Ford yell 'Divers below' to Winter, who stood on the cliff.

Then Ford was tapping him on the shoulder and showing two fingers. The Aussie slid off the ice shelf into the freezing abyss, the ropes following him like snakes. And then, as though in a nightmare, Gallen was leaning forward, the water claiming him like an ice-demon.

167

CHAPTER 29

The sound of his own screams would have deafened him if any sound was able to escape his throat. The cold lake water wrapped around Gallen's chest, throat and head like an angry squid and tried to choke the life out of him as he drifted in the first few seconds of the dive. Feeling virtually paralysed, he did what Ford had suggested and focused on what was in front of him and kept it real simple: follow the leader, don't lose eyes on the man in front, don't panic.

Slowly Gallen's breathing started coming in short sharp chunks of air as he forced his chest to operate and made his legs and arms move. Finning behind Ford, the strange light filtering through the ice, he looked into the blackness beneath him and hoped this wasn't going to be a deep dive. The lakes in this region were probably U-shaped glacial valleys and that could mean a steep side and a dive of a hundred feet.

The cold pressed on his temples like a vice, his breathing sounding like a saw, but Gallen kept paddling, trusting that the sooner they salvaged the radio, the sooner he'd be back in front of that stove breathing in warm air.

After forty seconds of finning, Gallen almost ran into the back of Ford, who trod water under the ice floe, the bubble of an air pocket visible between water surface and ice.

They were fifteen feet from the steep-sided shore and Ford pointed downwards. As Gallen followed him into the darkness, the flashlight came on, illuminating the maw of cold and black. The cold got worse, along with the pressure on his skull and chest, and Ford stopped again, pointing. Below them, in the yellowish light provided by the weak old batteries, was the Little Bird helo, upside down, its plexiglass cockpit embedded in lake mud, the deadly minigun sitting on top of the wreck like a suitcase handle.

His breathing rasped and bubbles flew upwards as Gallen leaned over and finned downwards after the Aussie to a point where there was no more natural light.

Handing Gallen the tool kit, Ford gestured for the bag to be opened. Looping his arm around one of the fuselage pillars, Gallen steadied himself and opened the diver's mesh bag, his face now numb at the edges of his mask. He could see Ford's hands in the spill of the flashlight beam, could see him moving them furiously to get blood into them, and then the Aussie dipped his hands into the toolkit and drew out a small crescent spanner and a rubber-handled Phillips screwdriver.

Taking the flashlight, Gallen aimed it into the cockpit, getting a fright as he saw the pilot hanging upside down in his harness.

Scanning the cockpit with the beam, Gallen picked up the flight deck and located the Harris radio, planted in a ceiling bracket in front of the pilot's head.

Ford moved into the cockpit and, unhooking the pilot, sent the blond flier to float with the fishes. Moving closer to the cockpit, Gallen gave a full beam to the radio as an aluminium briefcase floated in the slipstream of the pilot's exit.

Ford swam to the radio as Gallen reached for the briefcase, placing it in the tool bag before it could descend to the bottom. His hands were already frozen numb and the cold sat on his chest like a piano; Gallen had to fight the panic, making himself focus minutely on where the flashlight beam was pointed and how many times Mike Ford turned the spanner.

After two minutes, Gallen watched a screw from the radio bracket float to the bottom. When he looked back into the cockpit he realised that the flashlight was failing. Its weak yellow light had faded to a sepia tone and he could see Ford hurrying to get the job done while the beam held out.

Gallen was at the end of his endurance. He needed to be out of that water and he urged on the Aussie, cursing loudly to himself about the situations that his life had forced him into. For the last four days he'd felt constantly on the edge of disaster, unable to change a thing. He'd simply been hanging on, trying to inspire others to do the same, and he was exhausted.

Ford's elbow came up and down and then the spanner was flying free, spinning into the darkness. Lunging at it, the Aussie tried to get his hand on the tool but it went out of his reach. As Ford pulled back into the cockpit, his rig snagged on a broken piece of the door frame and instantaneously the air started rushing out of the tubes into the water.

His eyes growing wide, Ford signalled he was going up. Gallen prepared to fin to the surface but Ford was already untying the main line to Kenny Winter on the cliff and pointing at the tool bag.

Before Gallen could argue, Ford was ascending and Gallen tied the main line around his own waist, cursing the lake gods as his flashlight faded to a mushroom-coloured smudge of light.

Moving to the cockpit, he looked in the tool bag and found another crescent spanner. His body wanted to shut down as he kneeled on the ceiling of the helo and concentrated the beam into the radio bracket. His hands were locked in place like a chicken's claws and he could feel his body going into shock as it became painful to draw breath. The piano that had been sitting on his chest had changed to a church organ and he groaned into the mouthpiece, trying to make the oxygen flow. Even as he felt himself expiring, he had the strangest thought: that there was an entire specialty in the military that did this work, totally hidden from the sight of all but those involved in it. If he ever got out of this shit, he'd never again take a clearance diver for granted.

The second screw that held the radio in place was much smaller than the first one and he tried in vain to wheel the spanner to a smaller size, yelling in frustration as his thumb slipped on the wheel. His wrist ached, his fingers wouldn't respond, his other hand couldn't hold the spanner properly. He'd done these coordination exercises in special forces divers tanks and in the ocean waters of Okinawa in summer—but trying to make a spanner work in this cold was beyond a joke.

As tears of frustration formed in his eyes, the flashlight went dead and he reached up to the pilot's seat and dragged the spanner wheel across the fabric. Pushing his gloved finger into the new gap, he sensed it had worked and he tried it on the radio screw. Still too big.

He banged the flashlight; it briefly sprang to life and Gallen rolled the spanner wheel along the pilot's seat again, further reducing the spacing of the crescent.

His breath now coming in erratic jags, Gallen reached for the second screw, completely missing it. The cold had taken his co-ordination and he did what he'd been told: tried to focus totally on the job. Not the cold, not his breathing, not the darkness. Just the job.

He hooked the spanner onto the screw on the second try and it fitted. As he turned the spanner as slowly as he could, the flashlight died again, plunging him into primal blackness, a void that could send otherwise tough soldiers into wild, thrashing panic attacks. Gallen had seen it, seen what this environment could do to a man who wasn't psychologically prepared for it.

Making himself breathe and focus, he lowered his free hand and tried to move it. When it finally did, he held the spanner on the screw and turned slowly, ensuring the spanner stayed on the head, not entirely sure what was moving through the thickness of the gloves and the intense cold. After a minute, the screw came free.

Pulling the Harris out of its bracket, Gallen saw for the first time the cables bolted into the back of it.

'Shit,' he said to himself, unsure how many of the cables had to be preserved.

Now breathing as shallowly as he had before the pleurisy made him pass out, Gallen reached behind the radio in the inky black and felt as best he could for the types of cable: one of them pulled away—a simple plug. Another wouldn't budge and he could feel a spinning washer at its base—like a cable TV connector—which he tried the spanner on. He needed it slightly smaller and rolled the spanner wheel on the pilot's seat for a third time, wondering when he was going to simply black out.

Bringing the spanner back to the rear of the Harris, Gallen found the washer turned easily; as he tried to rush it, though, the spanner fell out of his hand and into the dark.

Panting for his life, he decided to go up. With a hard pull, he tore the final connecting cable out of the back of the radio and placed the unit in his bag. Then he started his ascent. After thirty seconds of slowly rising, he felt less pressure on his chest and could see the ice above. He stopped, trod water and looked at the G-Shock he had swapped with Ford; unable to use the buttons to make a countdown clock, he counted three minutes off the display. To his left he could see a set of scuba tanks suspended in the water, being jiggled like a huge tea bag. It was Ford marking Gallen's escape route.

His mind played tricks as he trod water and looked at the G-Shock, and then he was dreaming: dreams of childhood, of being in the jungle. A dream about hitting the ice in a game they once played in Gillette, when Gallen's cheek was split open and he lay there on the cold, concussed and coming to with the arena ice for a pillow.

The ice! The cold! The feeling he could sleep forever . . .

Opening his eyes, Gallen realised he'd stopped treading water and that he was sinking slightly. Shit! He'd fallen asleep.

Releasing the small valve on the chest of the dry suit, he let air out of the suit and kicked upwards, hoping he'd decompressed all he had to. He'd forgotten what time it was when he checked the watch.

Making it to the hole in the ice, he didn't have the strength even to break the water. Then he felt the rope pulling him up out of the hole and into the cold sunshine, where he flopped onto the ice like a sack of salt.

The mouthpiece was ripped away and then his mouth was being cleared and his tanks pulled off and he was gasping, coughing. As he twisted and turned onto his knees, he vomited, the action forcing blood into his face with excruciating pain.

Taking the bag from him, Ford helped Gallen across the ice, both of them stumbling to the ice cliff, their joints frozen stiff, their blood sluggish in their veins. Winter looked down from the cliff and Gallen could see that the main line was now attached to the rear bar of the snowmobile. Tying them on together, leaving the scuba gear on the shore ice, Ford waved to the Canadian and then they were being pulled up the ice wall, bouncing against it as they were hoisted up and over the precipice by the snowmobile. Winter untied the rope and accelerated back to the divers, who lay in the snow, exhausted.

Gallen felt himself being loaded into the rescue capsule and then they were travelling, a deep warm sleep finally enveloping him like a drug.

CHAPTER 30

Sitting on a cot with his back to the wall, Gallen sipped on black tea, the coffee having run out as the last scavenged food was about to. He felt a little stunned and the dive in the lake had left him unable to hear very well.

Lying under blankets in the cot beside him, Florita turned away from the old *Sports Illustrated* she'd been reading.

'So, this building was part of a line?'

'The Pentagon wanted a line of radar stations that would give an early warning to our air force bases, allow us to scramble fighter jets against the Soviets,' said Gallen. 'The only place that line would work would be across the Canadian Arctic, over to Greenland I think.'

Florita made a face. 'Sounds like a Maginot Line. It was a success?'

'Don't remember any big US cities being visited by missiles,' said Gallen, getting a smile from Florita. 'They started shutting them down in the mid-1980s.'

'And shut down the radios too, huh?'

Gallen looked at the table in the middle of the room, where Ford and Winter were working on the Harris. The Harris was the radio unit carried by most Western combat forces, whether you were special forces, artillery or logistics. It had a design so basic that most Vietnam War veterans would be able to operate the modern ones, and they had a reputation of being able to go to hell and back and still be reliable.

'That radio was in a frozen lake for twenty-four hours,' said Florita. 'Do you guys really think it will work again?'

'I was once in the field,' said Ford, as he held up a component and blew on it. 'An APC ran over our Manpack, and twenty minutes later our comms guy had us back on the net. He didn't buy a drink for two weeks after that.'

'What's a Manpack?' said Florita.

Ford pointed to the parts arrayed in front of him. 'This is the Manpack, the Harris we're all trained on in the forces. They had one mounted in the chopper.'

'The antenna going to be a problem?' asked Gallen.

'Think I got the solution,' said Winter, picking up a long piece of metal.

He'd stripped down a piece of aluminium window frame as an antenna and Ford had wired it into the Harris.

'This is looking okay,' said Ford, clicking a dried piece into place and observing the completed machine. 'Our big worry is the battery, but Kenny's got that sorted.'

Winter left the room and came back a minute later with the snowmobile's battery. Hooking it up, Ford made some of the lights work on the radio's small screen, but he shook his head slowly.

'I can get a scan going,' said the Aussie, twirling the switches. 'But it reverts to the preset.'

No one spoke. The preset from the radio would go to the people who'd tried to kill them.

'Can we get an emergency channel? What is it? One twenty-one point five?' said Gallen.

'That's civilian aviation emergency,' said Ford. 'I can dial that in, but the radio seems to flick us back to presets. We'd broadcast to the emergency channel in bursts.'

Gallen paused. He needed to get this right. 'What do we know about the presets?'

'One is hidden. It's programmed into the Harris as "Home",' said Ford. 'The other is one twenty-three point oh-two-fiver.'

The information clicked in Gallen's mind. 'Isn't that—?'

'Yes it is,' said Winter quickly, clearly wanting to avoid worrying Florita.

'What is it, Gerry?' she said, eyes flashing with annoyance as she sat up. 'What is this frequency, this preset?'

The men looked at one another, Winter breaking the deadlock. 'It's an air-to-air frequency. The one helicopters use.'

They watched her as she processed the information, her face dropping as she realised what it meant. 'Oh no,' she said, hand going to her face, which suddenly wore the nightmare of her ordeal in the snow. 'There's another helicopter?'

'That seems to be the case,' said Gallen.

Tears formed in Florita's eyes, her hands fidgety. 'So, so . . . what do we do? I mean, we can't just sit here.'

'We have to put out a call,' said Gallen. 'Or we'll starve.'

Florita's bravery fell to pieces in front of the three men, her sobs snapping them all back to the reality of their situation. Not every person forced into such circumstances was motivated to keep going till they found a way out. Florita was reality, the rest of them were the aberration, the people who were trained over many years to keep moving regardless of their peril. They'd waited for Florita to talk about her experiences in her own time—the way it was done among men in the field. But Gallen realised his mistake. She was a woman, a civilian, and what they'd taken for bravery may have been trauma and fear.

'They're out there!' said Florita, lips quivering, looking at Gallen. 'I'm sorry, Gerry, I'm so sorry. I tried to be brave, I'm trying. I—'

Winter gave him the dirtiest look, flicking his head, and Gallen moved to Florita's cot, put his arm around her shoulders.

'They won't hurt you again,' he said as the high-flying lawyer sobbed and clung to his chest. 'We're getting out of here.'

When Florita had succumbed to Ford's offer of Valium, Gallen tucked her into the cot and joined the men at the table.

'Okay, so we put out a mayday on the emergency frequency. Who hears us?' he asked.

'Just about every aircraft is preset to one twenty-one point five on their secondary channel,' said Ford. 'The people looking for that helo are also looking for us, and they'll be listening to that channel.'

'So there could be another helo waiting in the vicinity that was working with the one we put down?'

'I'd say so,' said Ford.

'We need to give our location in coded form,' said Winter. 'Something the locals would understand, but not a bunch of mercs flown in to kill us.'

'Ideas?' said Gallen.

'The name of this base,' said Winter. 'Found a label on a box of oil in the garage. It matches with some others I found.'

'And?'

'This base was called CAM fifteen. If we put a call out with that location, some of the local search-and-rescue people might know what it is . . .'

'But not the unfriendlies?' said Gallen.

'Worth a try?'

Gallen thought about it. 'How are we for weapons, ammo?'

'Two handguns, about forty rounds,' said Ford. 'Three rifles, half-loaded—let's say forty, forty-five rounds.'

'Okay, Mike.' Gallen rubbed his stubble with his fingertips. 'Get a mayday on the net. Call it CAM fifteen, and no more. Not even the word *base* or *facility*. Okay?'

'Got it, boss.'

'And as soon as we send that mayday, Mike, I want us all over those presets.'

'Pick up the chatter?'

'Damn right,' said Gallen, aching for a cigarette. 'If they're coming in again, I want to know in advance.'

Ford dialled in one twenty-one point five on the MHZ band and started relaying the message.

'Mayday, mayday. Aircraft down. Survivors at CAM fifteen. Repeat . . .'

Before he could finish the message the display switched from one twenty-one point five to *Home*. After it happened several times, Gallen asked him to simply say 'CAM fifteen' and then switch to 'Mayday' on the next burst.

They sent the mayday for twenty minutes and then reverted to the presets on the mercenaries' radio. They stayed silent, waiting for a giveaway voice or comment, but whoever was sitting at 'Home' had discipline and was not answering.

Gallen led Winter out of the room, into the main buildings. 'I don't want to have the discussion where Florita can hear it. But let's find our shooting points in case we have another wave of mercenaries.'

'That roof gantry?' said Winter.

'What I was thinking. This time, they won't be able to stand off and mop us up with the minigun. They'll have to come in, so we get to counter-attack.'

'If it's a Little Bird again, they'll only have three shooters and the pilot,' said Winter. 'You'd like to take 'em out on the ground?'

'Without losing the helo,' said Gallen.

They secured the ladder that led to the trapdoor in the ceiling and Winter climbed it first, knocking his big shoulder against it until the door gave way. Pushing through drift snow, they clambered onto a gantry that ran in a square around the white dome.

'This goes around the whole facility,' said Winter, zipping his parka further to his chin as the wind squalled. 'There's also a door into the dome.'

'What's in there?' said Gallen, scoping the area around the building and deciding that a roof vantage point was about the best they'd get if attacked.

'It's radar scoops, back to back,' said Winter. 'The thing is, it's enclosed. If we decide to use a sentry, there's at least shelter from the wind.'

Lifting his binoculars, Gallen swept the terrain on a three-sixty-degree scan. 'What's that, from the north?'

Winter squinted. 'Storm, big one by the height of it.'

About fifty miles away, a wall of white and purple-black rose out of the tundra, thousands of feet into the air. Another squall struck them, this one forcing Gallen to move his feet.

'Let's get inside,' he said, moving back to the trapdoor. 'We'll take two-hour revolving shifts up here. I don't want anyone freezing to death.'

As Gallen got to the door, he turned and saw Winter squatting slightly, the rifle sliding off his shoulder.

The Canadian lifted a finger to his lips and then trained the weapon. Looking out into the glare, Gallen couldn't see what he was aiming at but unholstered his SIG as a precaution.

The rifle jumped and a puff of cordite wafted away on the breeze.

'What's going on?' said Gallen.

Winter smiled. 'Dinner.'

CHAPTER 31

The fox stew tasted better than anything they could have served Gallen at the Ritz. Certainly it beat the Denver Hilton's lobster mac and cheese, the single most expensive item he'd ever ordered at a restaurant.

But it didn't stop Florita holding forth on the rights and wrongs of killing and eating an arctic fox.

'It's endangered, isn't it?' she demanded of Gallen, even though he hadn't shot the beast.

'Is now,' said Winter, chewing.

'That's not even funny, Kenny,' she said.

'Try some,' said the Canadian. 'It's pretty good.'

'I'd rather starve.'

'Nice you got the choice,' said Winter.

'Actually,' she glowered, 'the choice was taken when you shot that poor animal, Kenny.'

'Like we say in the military . . .' Winter paused to wipe juice off his chin.

'What?'

'Sometimes a simple thank you would suffice.'

Florita stood in a huff and sat on her cot, flipping through a *Time* magazine but not reading it.

Gallen checked his G-Shock: twelve minutes before he relieved Mike Ford on the gantry and the winds sounded as though they had risen to beyond fifty mph—the speed at which things broke and people got swept away.

Getting up, he eyed Durville's satchel and had an idea. 'Florita, can you get us into Harry's BlackBerry? It's password protected.'

'I can't do that.'

'Don't you want to know who bombed us? Who shot at you in the snow?'

'Of course I do, Gerry,' she said, looking both annoyed and scared. 'But that could be a job for the police.'

'That could be a job for the head of Harry's personal security,' said Winter, shovelling stew. 'They killed Harry too.'

Turning for her magazine, Florita sighed. 'I don't know the code.'

The remains of the stew sat on the back burner of the wood stove, waiting for Ford to devour it when he came down from his shift. Gallen and Winter were hungry and both eyed the mound of fox stew that sat on Florita's plate.

'So, you really don't want the stew?' said Winter.

'Kenny!' Gallen growled. 'No one touches Florita's meal.'

The gantry was buffeted by high winds and visibility had reduced to about ten feet as the blizzard developed into a white-out. Climbing into the dome, Gallen stamped his feet and took a look at the six holes Ford had dug in the tin with his Ka-bar knife. The dim half-light of the northern night permeated the landscape as the snow was thrown across it by the ton.

The last surviving radio headset sat on Gallen's ears, with the agreement not to use it unless there was danger. The batteries were close to expiring and they didn't have rechargers. Below, Gallen knew that the maydays would continue to be broadcast every five minutes and, in between times, they'd be monitoring the Home frequency for traffic.

Stamping to keep the blood flowing into his toes, Gallen kept moving from hole to hole, preventing himself from thinking about the obviously dire circumstances by doing what they used to do while on combat tours: dream about what you'd do when you were back on civvie street.

He thought about the family farm and Roy, and what he'd have to do to bring the place back into the black. His pay cheques were being diverted into the Sweet Clover account, so the trust lawyer would have some funds to pay the creditors. But Gallen needed a bigger plan than that; he needed to decide what he was going to do with his life, a life no longer owned by the Marine Corps.

As he watched the ground, listening to the increasing howl of the blizzard, the radio headset crackled: Ford was on the line.

'Good news, boss. Baker Lake Mounties are sending a chopper. They're advising five hours but they don't have this weather in town.'

'You spoken with them?'

'Yeah. Bloke called Detective Sergeant Jim Ballagh. He asked for the cords but I said I didn't know—just said it's a building called CAM fifteen, out in the snow.'

'Yeah?'

'Got back three minutes later, said they had the location and were on their way.'

'What about our friends?'

'Getting faint chatter but can't confirm. Could be someone else. You'll know when I do.'

Swapping shifts with Winter twenty minutes later, Gallen warmed himself by the stove as Ford monitored the radio.

Looking around, Gallen couldn't see a spare plate of fox stew. 'She eat it?' he asked softly.

Ford smiled. 'Kenny apologised, said he felt terrible about it—'

'Yes, he did,' said Florita, sitting up from what looked like a sleep. 'And I ate it, only because I'm starving.'

Gallen laughed. 'How was it?'

'About the same as goat.'

'Well I thought it was better than roo,' said Ford, and both Gallen and Florita made faces.

'What's wrong with kangaroo?' said Ford, going back to the radio. 'If it's good enough for me dogs, it's good enough for me.'

Thawing out, Gallen noticed something beside the stove, against the wall. It was the aluminium briefcase from the sunken helicopter, now dried out.

Placing it on the table, he flipped the latches and opened the lid. Inside was a black ionised-steel box with a flip-up lid. Opening it, he saw the screen and a keyboard. He knew what this machine was, he just couldn't put his finger on it.

'Mike, what's this?'

Ford looked at it and reached over, pulled out a retractable aerial that extended from behind the box. 'Location receiver. You follow people or cars or luggage with it.'

Gallen stared at Ford, looked down at it again, his pulse hammering. 'What could it track?'

Ford left the radio, turned the briefcase towards him and had a closer look at the water-damaged machine. 'Micro-beacons the size of the smallest watch battery. Standard homing beacons the size of a casino chip. Magnetic beacons that are more the size of a cell phone and give a signal for almost two hundred miles. Transport companies and bus fleets use them.'

'It'll track anything?'

Ford nodded. 'Pretty much. If it gives a signal in the right range, you lock on to it and track it until you lose signal. The Pentagon operates the world's largest container shipment operation, and it's all tracked on large versions of that.'

Gallen thought about it: there was nothing to tie Reggie's people to the attack helo or to the tracking technology. Yet that was the only connection he could see.

What really concerned him was the chance of another merc helo in the vicinity, waiting to complete what the first team couldn't. They'd have the same locator boxes.

'What's up, boss?' said Ford, getting more static on the Home preset.

'If the bad guys had beacons on us, then the beacons are probably still among us, right?'

'Could be,' said Ford.

They had all the fatigues and weapons on the table inside of thirty seconds, Gallen and Ford picking off the RFDs and throwing them in the fire—the tags on the guns requiring the flat side of a knife, given their solid bonding to the gunmetal.

Taking apart Durville's BlackBerry, they searched for tags and came up empty. When Winter came down for his break, they stripped the tags off his parka and fatigues, but the only location technology was the RFDs Aaron had claimed were innocent.

Gallen took the next turn as sentry: he wanted Ford working the radio. Taking a look through every hole in the radar dome, he started his routine for keeping the blood moving: gripping his hands, stamping his feet, flapping his arms. The wind was dying and the blizzard abating, but he had the temperature up there in the dome at minus forty, at least.

The blasts of drift made reconnaissance difficult. With the half-light of the northern spring and the rising moon, the light was bouncing strangely off the snow and ice. The noise was still deafening, which was why Gallen missed the first words of Ford's radio message.

'Repeat.'

'That watch with the temperature in it?' said the Aussie, yelling over the howl of the northerly.

'What about it?'

'Donny gave it to me, boss.'

Gallen wasn't getting it. 'So?'

'So it was the only thing that the three of us down here couldn't vouch for,' said Ford. 'We opened it up.'

'Yep?'

'There's a beacon in it. Flat model, like a sticker, with circuitry in it.'

'Crap,' said Gallen.

'Doesn't sound private, right?'

'Fuck it,' said Gallen, not able to help himself. The beacon Ford was describing was used by government intelligence agencies.

Then he was distracted by something through the west-facing hole in the dome. He thought he saw a different kind of light about a hundred yards away, but in the wind-driven drift he couldn't be sure. Looking harder, he saw a yellowish shading that didn't fit with the white swirls of snow.

184

'Search-and-rescue call lately?'

'Yeah, boss,' said Ford. 'Just told us they're ten minutes away.'

'Ten?'

'That's right.'

'Okay, Mike. Send Kenny, tooled up,' said Gallen, convinced there was an electronic light west of the base.

'Seen something?'

'Just send him. You're staying with the girl,' said Gallen, breath coming fast and shallow.

'Wait,' said the Aussie, his voice breaking up.

'You there, Mike?'

'Got traffic on the preset,' said Ford.

'What?'

'Sounds like a pilot. Said, "We're in position." Their base told—'

The voice crackled out and there was dead air. Checking the Heckler & Koch for load and safety, Gallen focused through his peephole, wiping the back of his nose with his glove. The yellow glow disappeared and he strained his eyes in the gloom of the moonlight as the dying wind left calm patches between the squalls.

The trapdoor clanged and Winter's boots sounded on the gantry before the big Canadian squeezed into the dome, panting with the shock of the cold air in his lungs.

'What's up?'

'Possible boogies, your eleven,' said Gallen, letting Winter get close to the peephole.

'Don't see anything,' said Winter.

'Keep watching. How's your mag?'

'Four-fifths. Yours?'

'Two-thirds.' Gallen pushed Winter aside for another look. 'I saw something out there.'

'Yeah, I know,' said Winter.

Gallen paused, sensing a joke. 'You *know*?'

'Lost you on the radio,' said Winter.

'So?'

'So the Harris went down, too,' said Winter.

'Even to search-and-rescue?'

'That went down first, just after you came up here,' said Winter, eyes steady.

'Oh, shit.'

'Yeah, boss. Mike thinks we're being jammed.'

CHAPTER 32

They took a revolving sentry, Winter and Gallen at opposite sides of the dome, but moving to the hole to their left every minute. The snow drifted and abated, swirled and then wound down like a huge jet motor being de-throttled. The light changed with each squall, bringing different pieces of ground into focus and then covering them over again.

'What's this about Donny's watch?' said Gallen, nibbling on two raisins he'd found in his parka pocket. He was sensitive about Donny McCann being disrespected, but he still had to know.

'Mike and Donny swapped watches back in Kugaaruk,' said Winter. 'Mike was amazed at the cold—him bein' an Aussie and all—and he kept askin' what the temp was. So Donny says, *Here, swap with me—this G-Shock gives you the temperature too.*'

'You see this beacon?'

'Sure did, boss.'

'And?'

'And I ain't seen that kit since I was in the Ghan, and from time to time we was working with the Agency.'

'This beacon is CIA?'

Winter moved to the hole on his left. 'Or Pentagon. It's government spook gear. Hell, when I was at ISAF they'd put that shit in our watches, in our weapons, underneath our radios—you name it, boss, the Agency and the Pentagon was tracking everyone with those stickers.'

'Shit,' said Gallen softly. He remembered once seeing one of those circuitry-loaded stickers on the back of a map he was returning after a ten-day recon stint. It was the size of a quarter, had a green base and gunmetal circuit board, and he'd decided not to follow it through.

They swapped a look in the dark. 'Probably tracked you too, boss.'

Gallen saw a movement in the snow. 'Got something, Kenny. My two o'clock.'

Joining Gallen, Winter had a look.

'See where that long ridge dips back to the bowl?' said Gallen.

'Yep,' said Winter. 'I make two boogies, snow-cam suits.'

When Gallen looked through the hole again, the drifts had closed the sight-line.

Unsheathing his Ka-bar, Winter hacked another hole in the alloy dome, pulling the blade down and across to create a triangle and a shooting point.

'I want you up here,' said Gallen. 'Give me cover. I'm going to flank them from the left. When the shit starts, you come at 'em from this side.'

'No offence, boss,' said Winter, 'but you're not well, and this is my line.'

'You're saying?'

'I'm saying that I'd rather you cover me from up here. The way I can do this means we might keep the helo.'

Gallen took a breath, coughed out the cold air in a plume of steam. 'Okay, Kenny, but tell Ford to stay with Florita, okay? And kill the lights. Let's make these assholes work for it.'

The squall lifted for several seconds, revealing one man lying in the snow behind the long ridge. Raising the Heckler to his shoulder, Gallen was tempted to take the two-hundred-yard shot, but kept his finger along the trigger-guard. He wanted Winter to start the assault when he was good and ready. That way, they could take out the first two mercs and even up the odds for the remaining boogies.

He'd allowed Ford to open one of the side windows of the base, giving him a sweep of the rear of the demountable. It was going to bring the temperature of the base down dramatically, but they needed someone in the rear.

'What the fuck are you waiting for?' said Gallen to himself, checking the other peepholes and returning to the shooting point Winter had carved out.

Through the snow, lights cast an eerie path, sometimes hitting the snow in front of the base, other times diffusing into the endlessly dancing drift. Taking a breath, he aimed in the direction of the lights, now hearing the thump of rotors and the scream of a turbine engine. It was a helicopter, but whose?

Slowly the snow flew in a slightly different pattern and a huge yellow machine appeared out of the whiteness. It looked like a Cormorant CH-149, the search-and-rescue aircraft of the Canadian military.

Moving out of the dome, Gallen braced himself on the gantry as the snow and drift was driven into him by the rotor downwash, pushing the fur-lined hood back onto his shoulders. Lighting up the area with its floodlights, the helicopter depowered as Gallen looked for the mercs.

Carefully descending the ladder from the gantry, he hit the deep snow and waded to his right, around the back of the helicopter. Crouching behind a ridge, Gallen looked for the mercenary but could see nothing among the flurries.

Circling further around, shoulder-deep in drift, he almost ran into a merc—the third one, walking towards the helicopter in a snow bowl, oblivious to the intrusion. Gallen raised the Heckler and made a single chest-shot from the high ground then waded through the snow to the fallen merc.

Kneeling over him, he saw the eyes still fluttering and felt the Kevlar vest. The fallen man's arm swung sideways, knocking the rifle out of Gallen's wrist, making his arm flap. The merc's knife arced upwards at his chest, slicing through the arctic parka as though it was paper.

Rolling away, Gallen went for the SIG on his waistband but the merc was too quick, coming at him with another knife strike, which Gallen fended by attacking the man's wrist with the back of his forearm. The snow made it like fighting in mud and Gallen could see the merc was as tired as he was after only a few seconds of struggle.

Punching the merc hard in the left temple as he lost his balance, Gallen swung, driving a flat hand into his nose and then grabbing the man by the throat as he held the knife wrist with his other hand.

The man bled freely from the nostrils but he threw his knife hand under Gallen's chin and hit him in the throat. Gasping slightly, Gallen felt the man slide from underneath him and tear his knife wrist free as Gallen was thrown on his back. Kicking out, Gallen got the merc in the jaw with his JB Goodhue, snapping the man's neck back and stunning him. Pushing his attacker's jaw, Gallen finally found his own Ka-bar and sliced down into the carotid artery, bleeding the man by the throat while shifting his hand to cover the mouth.

Crouching over the man as the last twitches jumped in his hips, Gallen looked around, panting for air and knee-deep in snow. His parka was in tatters up the front and he'd lost his rifle.

Kneeling, as the cold attacked his torso, he undid the merc's jacket and put it on. It felt warm and as he zipped up he felt the wetness of blood on the collar. Checking the man's Beretta 9mm handgun for loads before he put it in his waistband, he saw it had a full fifteen-shot magazine.

Crawling around, looking for the Heckler, he realised it was futile. There wasn't enough light and they'd struggled over a large area. Seeing something sticking out of the snow, he waded to it and picked up what he hoped was the Heckler. Looking at it, his heart jumped: it was a Russian-made hand-held rocket launcher, of the type favoured by the jihadists in the north of Afghanistan.

If this was what they were armed with, what was the mission? Looking at the helicopter, whose rotors were almost stopped, Gallen saw it at once.

'Get out,' he screamed, wading towards the yellow beast and the rescuer in the red exposure suit.

The rescuer, who was wearing a full-face safety helmet, didn't hear Gallen, and when his buddy joined him on the snow and looked away at CAM fifteen, he didn't hear either.

Following them, with barely the energy to stand, Gallen tried to catch their attention, but they were walking to the building.

'They're gonna bomb it!' he cried, but it was too late. The shrieking whoosh snaked through the snow storm and, missing the helicopter by inches, piled into the white dome at eighty mph, instantly turning it into a sphere of fire and debris.

CHAPTER 33

Gallen found the merc thirty feet from him, still kneeling from launching the rocket—he could smell the smoke from the tail. Pulling out his SIG, he waded towards the man as pieces of burning timber and steel rained into the snow, leaving deep hissing holes. Turning to look at Gallen, the merc raised his rifle but muzzle flashes erupted from the snow storm—from the other side of the bowl—and part of the merc's head disintegrated.

Watching him sag to the red-splattered snow, Gallen crouched, waiting for the shooter. As Winter emerged from the flurries, a rocket launcher slung across his back, he eyed Gallen across the snow bowl and brought his Heckler to the sight-line.

Realising he was wearing the dead merc's parka, Gallen shouted, 'No! It's me, Gerry!' He waved his arms and Winter edged forward, the rifle not budging from its aim despite the blizzard conditions.

Gallen gingerly grabbed the front of his wolverine fur-lined hood and pulled it back, only to realise he had his black balaclava on underneath.

Heart pumping, waiting for the shot, he heard Winter's voice. 'What's your name?'

'Gerry,' he said into a lull. 'Gerry Gallen.'

As Winter approached, he could see blood up the Canadian's

right sleeve. 'They're packing rocket launchers,' said Winter, heaving for breath.

'We put down three?'

Winter nodded. 'If you killed one to get that parka, that's three. So we have maybe one more shooter and definitely a pilot.'

The search-and-rescue men in their red coveralls ran for the burning building, unaware that their helicopter had been the target.

'We have to find that other chopper, boss,' said Winter. 'We can't let them blow up our ride.'

Above the roar of the flames, the faint throb of a helicopter could be heard. It sounded as if it was everywhere at once.

'You think the bird's carrying rockets?' said Gallen.

'If they have another minigun, it'll hardly matter about rockets.'

'Let's guard the helo,' said Gallen, although his instinct was to race into the building, whose roof was starting to catch.

Handing over his Heckler, Winter started to speak but sagged into the snow before he could finish, hand clutched to his thigh.

Ducking to the ground as a bullet sailed past his ear, Gallen pulled the Canadian down further into the snow bowl, his eyes scanning for a shooter. Cocking the Heckler, Gallen leaned over the prone shape of Winter, who was going into shock; blood drained into the snow, Winter's moans soft but audible over the wind.

'Our four o'clock,' snarled Winter, fighting for consciousness as he pointed over the highest edge of the bowl. 'One guy.'

'Wait there,' said Gallen, moving towards the ridge line, faint in the occasional moonlight, holding a good shoulder to the weapon. Swaying his hips into the thick layer of light drift that suddenly became heavy pack snow about two feet down, he kept his sights on the ridge as he moved forward, hoping surprise would be enough to get the first shot off.

Climbing the side of the bowl, the snow getting deeper and heavier, he felt the sweat running down his back and off his face, his weakened lungs fighting for every ounce of air.

Blinking the sweat off his left eyelid as he crested the edge of the bowl, Gallen was blinded by the search lights as they swept over him, so low that he lost his balance and fell backwards. As he dropped he saw the fourth shooter riding on the landing rails of the Little Bird, the minigun's six barrels spinning under the cockpit in anticipation of firing. There was only one target in front of that deadly gun—the search-and-rescue Cormorant.

Locking eyes with the shooter, he watched the merc point and then the helo was swinging away from its intended quarry, banking steeply as it hooked back to finish Gallen and Winter. Lying on his back, Gallen shifted the Heckler & Koch G36 to full auto and waited for the helo to make a death-pass. He aimed at the shooter riding on the rails—Delta Force-style—and they shot at each other simultaneously, the bullets raining around Gallen's body as he launched a magazine of 5.56mm loads.

Gallen held his finger on the trigger as the bird shrieked overhead, low enough that he could hear the shooter screaming with pain above the turbines and rotor.

Trying to turn in the snow, Gallen pushed himself onto an elbow as the helo banked again, its black bodywork looking ominous against the ever-changing dance of drift snow. The shooter now hung limply, one leg hooked over the landing rail, his broken body straining on the harness as his head lolled.

Seeing the minigun spin again as the bird swooped over, Gallen aimed up and felt the click of an empty magazine and the bolt retracting back, with no reason to hammer forward again.

He realised it was over for him and his team. In one strafe that minigun and its fifty-rounds-per-second firing rate could finish himself, Winter and the search-and-rescue Cormorant, before mopping up any of the survivors.

Waiting for the coup de grace, Gallen's mind spun out a reel of memories, of hockey fights, of high school kisses, of bad combat and good horses. His mouth was slack and his lungs had passed their use-by date about five minutes into the wreck dive. He was screwed, and as he waited for the burst of orange from the minigun to chew him into a thousand pieces, he thought of the weirdest thing: Marcia had once told him that his stubbornness was both his weakness and his strength—that his complete inability to accept defeat was more suited to a special forces command than a suburban marriage.

And she was right.

Eyes focusing on that spinning gun, Gallen smiled and summoned his last breath. 'Fuck you!'

A long streak of white and blue plumed through the half-light and then the air expanded in a super-heated ball of flame. Turning his face from the exploding black helicopter, Gallen faced the kneeling form of Kenny Winter, who promptly keeled over sideways as he dropped the empty rocket launcher.

Voices sounded through the deafening blast of the Little Bird exploding as a burning piece of fuselage landed six feet from Gallen's head and the smell of av-gas soot permeated the atmosphere.

The two search-and-rescue guys in their red exposure suits waded down the side of the bowl in a panic, one of them waving a fire blanket—something Gallen hadn't seen since bunker drills in Okinawa. He heard Ford's Aussie twang instructing someone to roll and, looking around, he couldn't see who the ocker was talking to.

As he felt sleep coming on—the soft snow like a featherbed— the search-and-rescue guy with the blanket finally reached him and dived at his legs.

He looked down to see what was happening. The last thing he saw was his pants on fire.

CHAPTER 34

The news segment on the wall-mounted TV continued its report on the death of Harry Durville but this time named the two pilots of the Challenger, and Donny McCann, showing a picture of the Marine when he was nineteen years old and topped with his USMC dress-lid.

Allowing himself a small smile at the old photo, Gallen noticed that four days after the airlift out of the snow the North American news media still didn't have the full story on the two helicopters that had been sent to finish what the BlackBerry bomb had started. They didn't even have a confirmed case of sabotage or terrorism. It smelled of an intelligence officer's media management and he wondered who had done the managing and which organisation was calling the shots.

Clicking the off button on his remote, Gallen eased himself carefully onto his left foot, now strapped from below his knee to the edge of his toes. Angry purple colouring ran up his thigh above the strapping and on the other leg the purple down the side of his calf was peeled back, showing wet flesh, covered in what looked like Vaseline.

Hobbling to the window, he looked out on a plutey Calgary golf club from the third floor of Rockyview Hospital. His face had taken two stitches, and he was being driven to a dental surgeon in half an hour to have his broken teeth fixed. Running his tongue over the jagged stumps of the teeth he lost when the Challenger went down, he let his eyes scan the grounds of the enormous hospital, looking for people sitting in cars, watchers on park benches and white vans with too many aerials.

'Sign the damn thing and let's get out of here,' came the man's voice, and Gallen turned quickly to see Aaron crossing the floor to join him at the window.

'I was about to,' said Gallen, eyeing the insurer's death and disability forms sitting on the table. 'Just wanted to make sure Donny's payout goes to his mom. He asked me specifically.'

Picking up the form with the McCann stickie on it, Aaron flipped through. 'In the beneficiary box, it says "next of kin". There a problem?'

'No,' said Gallen, looking at the green of the golf club's fairways trying to poke through the patchy spring snow. 'But he was married twice and he's got a sister he don't like. I wanted his momma's name, so we can name her in the payout.'

Aaron lifted his phone from his pocket and turned away, issuing a command to an assistant to get the name of Donny McCann's mother. He was tanned for Calgary in March and Gallen noticed he'd dropped his business shirt and suit in favour of jeans and a leather jacket.

'How're the legs?' said Aaron, eyes scanning the hospital campus as instinctively as Gallen's.

Sitting on the bed, Gallen stretched them in front of him. 'Took the shrapnel out of my calf and the doctors are happy with it. The burns are going to heal, but they'll always be ugly.'

'Pity. Those were some gorgeous legs,' said Aaron.

'They were my best feature.'

Silence sat between them like a canyon as their smiles faded. Aaron's face sagged, the real man glimpsing through. 'I did what I could, Gerry.'

'Maybe,' said Gallen, keeping it light. 'But someone didn't.'

Aaron nodded, stepped back from the window. 'When I saw you, I just happened to be standing by the fire blanket box. It was luck.'

Gallen was confused. 'What?'

'But shit, that thirty yards to get to you,' said Aaron, shaking his head. 'That was the longest thirty yards of my life. I couldn't go any faster through that snow, honest to God.'

'That was you?'

Aaron shrugged. 'No one told you?'

'I thought that was search-and-rescue.'

Gallen thought back to that night in the snow, looking down at his burning legs as the man in red leapt on them with the fire blanket, the flames taking ten seconds to smother, a bat of an eye in real life, but a marathon when your body's going up in flames.

'I was in Baker Lake when the call came through,' said Aaron. 'I'd been hassling them, ordering them to fly grids, and then Mike comes on the emergency channel and I suited up, went with them.'

'Thanks,' said Gallen. 'You trained for that?'

'I was in the Navy,' said Aaron. 'Bunker drills, fire blanket training. Years ago now, but the training stuck I guess.'

'So,' said Gallen, finally getting somewhere with Aaron. 'You ONI?'

They stared at each other for several seconds. 'We need to talk, Gerry, but not here.'

'I'm due at the dentist soon.'

'I'll ride with you.'

The dentist mapped the molars on the other side of Gallen's mouth, fed the information into a machine, and they talked while replacement teeth were machined out of a ceramic composite material. After two hours in the surgery, Gallen emerged into the cold sunlight with two new crowns.

'Feel like a drink?' said Aaron.

'Four or five should do it.'

Gallen ate soup and drank cold beer at the bistro that was set back from the street. He was half in the bag by the time they cut the small talk.

'My nurses and doctors call me Mr Brown,' he said, raising his finger at the waitress for another Bud. 'And I can't find my team. Where's Kenny and Mike?'

'We're in a security situation right now,' said Aaron. 'Our CEO's plane is bombed, and his bodyguard hunted down.'

'I noticed.'

'So I had everyone in different hospitals, under assumed names.'

Gallen looked at him. 'Thanks.'

'You're wondering about Ford?'

'What happened to him?'

'He's okay but I sent him on leave for a while.'

'Where?'

'Can't say, Gerry,' said the spook. 'But he didn't want to go and he wanted to see you and Winter.'

'What about Florita?'

'Her frostbite was contained and she's back at work. I asked her to stay away from here, for her security and yours.'

'We still employed?' said Gallen as more beer arrived.

'Of course,' said Aaron. 'You did your job.'

'So you read the RCMP interviews?'

'I spoke with Clancy,' said Aaron, meaning Detective Inspector Charles Clancy, who'd interviewed Gallen at his hospital bed as soon as he was conscious. 'Given that Harry brought a gift on board, I don't see the crime. I would have missed that too.'

'Yeah, but I missed it.'

'Like I said, you still got a job,' said Aaron. 'Take a few days off and I'll see you back here Monday. I'd like a full report on all this, by the way. You can email it.'

'So I don't have a few days off?'

'You can drive a laptop?'

'Sure.'

'Then gimme a report, Gerry. Do it from the farm and when you get back Monday, we'll talk about the gig.'

'Who would I bodyguard?' said Gallen.

'You haven't read the papers?'

Gallen shrugged.

'Florita Mendes was named the acting CEO yesterday.'

'Shit,' said Gallen, surprised.

'I'm now the VP security.'

'What happened to Mulligan?' said Gallen.

'He's not around.'

They looked at one another, deadpanning.

'He resigned?'

'Harry sacked him the day before he flew to Kugaaruk,' said Aaron. 'He left and hasn't been seen since.'

Gallen drank deeply. 'That's not like Paul Mulligan, walk away from a trough when his snout was just getting wet.'

'You can sort that out, and while you're at it, you can launch an investigation into who bombed our plane.'

'You want me to head an investigation?' said Gallen. 'What happened to bodyguarding?'

'You're taking my job, should you want it,' said Aaron. 'Almost twice the pay and you won't need snowshoes. That MasterCard of yours is now unlimited. Well, almost. Just make sure you can justify the expenses—the accountants are tough at Oasis.'

'Thanks,' said Gallen.

'Not me, the new CEO demanded it.'

Gallen smiled. 'Okay, we'll investigate. But I'm not a spook or a cop.'

'I've seen your file and you were always half-spook.'

'Bullshit,' said Gallen.

'Pretending to be a logging contractor in Mindanao, collecting better intel on the Moros than we got through NICA or the Agency— if that ain't spooking, what is?'

Gallen laughed. 'That was a frustrated first lieutenant who talked his CO into getting some first-hand intel.'

'I asked around, you were pegged for DIA, but you said no. Twice.'

Gallen looked out at the street. 'Not everyone wants to jump head-first onto an av-gas fire. So thanks, man. I owe ya.'

'I'm no hero, Gerry,' said Aaron, finishing his beer. 'I just reacted.'

Gallen smiled. That was what the really brave ones said.

* * *

When he got to the airport the next morning, Gallen checked for eyes in the terminal and then checked his bank account at an ATM, confirming payment of the leave bonus he'd been promised.

Buying his ticket to Cheyenne on the Oasis MasterCard, he rang ahead and hired a Chev Equinox for a week. He made sure the basics were in the Oasis name so he could save his cash for more interesting things. Because the one thing Gallen hadn't mentioned to the RCMP investigators was the beacon planted in Donny McCann's watch. Aaron may have wanted him back at the farm, but Gallen had a stopover planned before he got there.

CHAPTER 35

The East Side Motel on Highway 220 looked half full as Gallen pulled into the reception drive-through at 7.13 pm. The drive up from Cheyenne Airport to Red Butte had been easy if you discounted the aching ankle and the burns that he wanted to scratch.

Paying in cash and checking in as Roland Smith, Gallen showed a British Columbia driver's licence he'd claimed at the bar at Calgary Airport. There were three lost licences jammed in the mirror behind the cocktail station, and he'd been close enough to read the name and see the real owner had dark hair.

Taking a large room on the second floor—two along from where he'd stayed during Tyler Richards' fundraiser—he looked down on the internal courtyard and waited to see if the manager would double-check the false vehicle rego he'd listed on the guest information form.

Sipping on a beer from the minibar, Gallen cased the motel, looking for surveillance, looking for a tail. It looked clear and, finishing the beer, he went down to the business centre, a small room with a table, a computer and a scanner-printer. Creating an iGoogle account under the name Igor Olafnowsky, he accessed his new account and Googled the story on Harry Durville's death. The *Calgary Herald* had the best photo spread and when he'd found Donny's USMC picture, he printed it and switched off the computer tower, in contravention of the sign that said: *Do Not Turn Off This Computer!!!*

Gallen got to the motel's restaurant a little after eight o'clock, and taking a corner booth saw a face he recognised.

'Hi,' said the girl with the biker rings as she dumped a menu in front of him and poured a glass of water. 'Soup of the day's minestrone. Chef's special is barbecue pork ribs with ranch fries and beans.'

'I'll take 'em both,' said Gallen with a smile, not touching the menu. 'And in the same order. A handle of Miller too, thanks.'

The waitress returned his smile, having just been introduced to the easiest table of the week.

'Your leg okay? Need a cushion or sumpin?'

'I'm fine,' said Gallen, winking. 'It only hurts when I run.'

'You were here a couple weeks ago, right?' she said. 'Marines get-together?'

Gallen saw her name tag, saw a figure that was holding together for someone north of thirty. 'Fundraiser, actually, Glenda, for an old brother in a wheelchair.'

'Oh no,' she said, shaking her head. 'I hate that, hate this fucking war.'

'There's nothing to love.' Gallen nodded. 'But those of us over there, we do our best.'

'No, no,' said Glenda, embarrassed. 'Not the guys. Not the *guys*. You know what I mean—the oil people: Cheney, Halliburton, the Bush family. All those shitheads wouldn't know a yellow ribbon if it ate them in the crotch.'

Gallen laughed as she stalked off, wondering if she knew there'd been a new president in the White House for two years.

The tab came to $34.85 and Gallen left five tens on the table. 'Keep it,' he said as Glenda scooped up the notes.

'You from around here?'

'Down from Clearmont. I was actually trying to find what happened to my buddy.'

'Who?'

Gallen shrugged. 'Old Marines buddy who was here for that fundraiser.'

'Perhaps I can help?' said Glenda, putting her weight on her left hip. 'I'm outa here at ten-thirty.'

'Great,' said Gallen. 'The name's Roly, by the way.'

They sat on stools at a roadhouse bar, watching bikers and cowboys shooting pool around a red baize table. The juke box seemed to have nothing but Jennings, Cash and Haggard, and Gallen let his strapped leg swing free to the music he'd grown up with.

'So, she happy now?' said Glenda, who looked a lot sexier in her jeans and tank top than she did in her waitress dress. 'This Marcia?'

'Who knows?' Gallen sipped at his beer. 'She wanted more than a Marine, and she got it. End of story.'

'I think she's nuts,' said Glenda, drinking bourbon and Coke.

'You don't know me like she knew me.'

She smiled. 'Well, Roly, we can fix that.'

'I have to find out what happened to Donny. I feel terrible for his family.'

'What do you need?' said Glenda.

'I'd love to know who he was kicking with when he was staying at the East Side.'

'Gotta picture?' she asked, flicking her hair and giving Gallen the eye.

Pulling the printed picture out of his inside pocket, he handed it over. 'That's Donny, nineteen years old.'

Her face lit up. 'Oh, so that's Donny.'

'What do you mean?'

'I mean, I remember this hound,' she said, grabbing him by the hand. 'Let's go.'

Staying seated, Gallen pulled her back and Glenda leaned into him, kissed him on the lips. 'I have someone you should meet, so let's go, Marine!'

The house sat on a secondary street, a wood-sided Wyoming house with a brick chimney and a closed-in porch which was a boot room in winter.

Pulling him inside, Glenda left him in a living area where a blonde woman lay on a sofa watching *Cops*.

'Beer okay?' came Glenda's voice from the kitchen.

'Beer's good,' said Gallen, smiling at the blonde as she sat up and arranged her hair.

'Hi,' she said, reaching out her hand. 'Ellen.'

They shook and Gallen introduced himself once more as Roly.

'Wanna seat, take the weight off that leg?'

'Thanks,' said Gallen, removing magazines and chocolate wrappers and taking a seat beside the woman.

Handing him the Coors as she came into the living room, Glenda sat on the arm of the sofa. 'Meet my roommate, Ellen,' she said with a laugh. 'Donny's girlfriend for just one night.'

'Shut up!' said Ellen, wrapping a cardigan around her breasts.

'Roly's trying to find out what happened to Donny. Remember Donny, from that Marines night down at the East Side?'

Ellen lit a cigarette, grabbed Glenda's beer and took a slug. 'Well, the first place I'd look would be in the morgue up there in polar bear land. What the fuck they call that Indian reservation?'

'Nunavut,' said Gallen. 'I know he's in a morgue. I'm trying to work out who put him there.'

'Donny's dead?' said Glenda, shocked.

Ellen looked at her. 'Don't you watch the news? He was killed in that plane crash where the oil billionaire died—whatsisname, Durban or Durville or sumpin?'

Gallen focused on Ellen. 'You knew Donny?'

'I did that night,' said Ellen, not so cocky. 'We were fooling around, you know?'

'Yeah,' said Gallen, remembering Donny partying in his Cutlass. 'You were fooling around in a red Oldsmobile.'

'Yeah, I remember 'cos he was looking out for someone and then he suddenly stops when this dude goes up to his room.'

'What kind of dude?'

'White guy. About six foot, athletic. I only saw him from behind. Looked like a bull rider.'

'And?'

Ellen thought. 'Donny says, *Okay so the pigeon has landed*, or sumpin like that.'

'Like he was waiting for the white guy to show?'

'Yeah,' said Ellen. 'So he tells me he's going up there in a few minutes but there's still time for—'

'Okay,' said Gallen, getting the picture. 'What then?'

'About five minutes later, there's this banging sound and Donny's looking in the mirror and freaking, saying *Shit* and *Fuck*, and something like *He doubled back*, then he's out of the car and running across the parking lot in his shorts.'

Gallen remembered the night well. 'And then?'

'There's this talking and arguing behind us, and then Donny comes back, gets in the car and lets me keep the whisky and the smoke. Tells me the party's over, see ya later.'

'That was it?'

'Yeah,' said Ellen. 'I was getting my shirt done up and this guy turns up beside the car, and Donny is outa there, snapping to attention.'

'Like Donny's boss, maybe?'

'Just like that,' said Ellen. 'Except Donny was scared.'

'Know the guy? This boss man?'

'Well, I thought you all knew each other,' said Ellen.

'What do you mean?'

'I saw you in the restaurant. I work in the kitchen.'

Gallen was confused. 'So?'

'I work the breakfast shift, Roly,' she said, like it was elementary. 'You had breakfast with the boss guy.'

CHAPTER 36

It was low cloud and not much above freezing when Gallen picked up the mail, dropped the red flag and drove up the drive, aiming at the big white sign that said *Sweet Clover*.

The muffled bark of a dog sounded from inside the farmhouse as Gallen eased himself onto the muddy turning area. A red Dodge Ram was parked alongside the farm labourers' bunkhouse. The house door opened and a black retriever limped out, barking like Lauren Bacall.

'That you on the TV?' said Roy, stretching on the porch.

'Not the dead one,' said Gallen, patting Roy's old dog as she sniffed his foot.

'Coulda called.'

Gallen handed over the mail as he walked past. 'Anyone been here?'

'Like who?' said Roy, shutting the door as he followed Gallen into the warm kitchen.

'Like men wanting to check the gas or the power lines; someone who turns up, says you need your satellite dish adjusted?'

'Just your girlfriend,' said Roy, face flushed with last night's whisky. 'She's riding that jumper.'

'Yvonne?'

Roy smiled. 'Like I said.'

* * *

The weak sun warmed his back as he watched Yvonne take Peaches over the low practice jumps in the arena. The front hooves were hitting the top rails and they weren't yet the height she'd be jumping at the first competition in Douglas County.

Smirking as he heard her cussing, Gallen resisted the temptation to light a smoke and instead lowered himself to the sandy surface and walked to the second jump, tender on his leg.

'What's going on?' she said, walking the horse to where Gallen stood at the jump. 'This was working yesterday.'

'Eye-line,' said Gallen, replacing the rail and walking across the arena to the fourth jump.

'Where am I looking?' said Yvonne. 'At the cute cowboy?'

She was joking, but Gallen didn't get that immediately, and in the time he took to turn and squint into the sun at her face, he blushed.

'Sorry, just kidding around,' said Yvonne.

Gallen recovered but the moment was lost.

'So,' she said, 'Kenny got a few days off?'

'Kenny's not working here no more,' said Gallen.

'Saw him at the supermarket last night,' she said.

Gallen tried to act natural. 'How's he doing?'

'He asked after you, Gerry,' she said, dismounting. 'Told me he had a new cell number, asked me to give it to you.'

'Really?'

Yvonne reached into the back pocket of her jeans, pulled out a piece of paper. 'Yeah, he wrote it down.'

Gallen took the paper, still a bit flustered. 'By eye-line, I meant you were lookin' at the rail, not at the landing ground.'

'Yeah, I know,' she said. 'I gotta work on that.'

Gallen flipped the stirrup over the saddle, undid the girth. 'I didn't know you were divorced.'

'Well, I knew you were,' said Yvonne, rubbing the horse's nostrils.

Gallen went to talk but laughed instead.

'What?'

'Nothing.' Gallen shook his head as he lifted the saddle and its blanket off the animal's back. 'Women seem to know all this stuff.'

'Maybe we listen better,' said Yvonne.

'Sorry, what was that?' Gallen turned for the barn.

Giving him a slap on the bicep, Yvonne flicked the hair from her face, becoming serious. 'It was hard, living in that house, waiting to settle on my new farm, and here's my ex-husband just walking in and out like I'm still his, his . . .'

'Property?'

Yvonne's eyes widened. 'Yes, just like that. After you left with Kenny I thought maybe I should have told you about the divorce, but . . .'

'It's okay,' said Gallen, walking to the tack room in the barn.

'So how did you find out?' Yvonne said, following.

'Girls' talk,' said Gallen, heaving the saddle on the saddle rack.

'Who?'

'Frank Holst.'

'Hmm. Frank the Octopus, huh? Not much changes in Clearmont.'

''Fraid not,' said Gallen, pointing at a hook where Yvonne could hang the reins.

'Least of all the music.'

'Sorry?'

'The Muskrats are still playing, down Arvada.'

'Didn't they play—' His mind wandered back to a yee-haw band that played their prom night almost twenty years ago.

'That's them. Remember Katy Shanahan kept harassing them to play "Achy Breaky Heart", and when they finally did, she slipped over in that spilled punch and knocked herself out?'

'Yeah,' said Gallen. 'And that good ol' boy finished the song and says, *And that, kids, is why I don't play no Billy Ray Cyrus.*'

'That's the one,' she said, looking at her feet. 'So, you wanna . . . ?'

Gallen felt himself turning away from those brown eyes and clearing his throat. He wasn't ready for dating.

'Yeah, so I'm up tomorrow,' said Yvonne, recovering fast. 'You be here?'

'I'll be here,' he said, annoyed he'd fudged the invite to the Muskrats.

Watching Yvonne peel out in her new red Dodge, Gallen leaned into the boot room and grabbed the keys to the truck.

The transmission behaved impeccably on the drive into Clearmont. The mechanics had used the reconditioned tranny that'd been on order for months and the whole job had come in at just under twelve hundred dollars, not a bad price for another hundred thousand miles of towing. Now all he had to worry about was the diesel, which had started losing power.

Pulling in to the dispatch compound at the rear of the post office, Gallen got out and walked towards the overweight man in the US Postal Service windbreaker who was tapping on a clipboard and talking to another man as a large van was loaded with mail bags.

'You know that half of that bag is stamped day before yesterday?' said the overweight man. 'This is the US Postal Service, not a fricking river boat in Indonesia!'

'Barry,' said Gallen, giving the underling a break. 'You old dog.'

'Gerry.' Barry turned. 'Aren't you dead?'

'Wishful thinking, dude,' said Gallen, amazed at the jungle drum in small towns. 'Got a sec?'

Moving away from the mail van, Barry Teague—a high school buddy—lit a smoke and offered one. 'So that was you, that shit up in Canada?' he said, exhaling as he put away his smokes. 'That limp—that's part of it, right?'

'Don't worry about me, Barry,' said Gallen. 'They won't let me pass till I've paid my taxes.'

Barry was angling for good dirt, first-hand gossip. 'You still doin' that black ops stuff, GG? You are, aintcha?'

'I told you, Barry, I drove a truck. Most danger I ever saw was dealing with the Marines equivalent of you.'

'I'm a softie, Gerry.' Barry jacked a thumb over his shoulder. 'That's why they walk on me. Had a no-show yesterday, now I'm taking attitude from some Mexican who talks like a gangster.'

Gallen cringed. Wyoming was the most Anglo state in the US and he never liked to have those demographics supported by bigoted attitudes. 'They all talk like that, these youngsters. It's just a pose.'

'Hmmm,' said Barry sceptically. 'So what's up?'

'Need to borrow your phone. Mine's dead and I need to make a quick call.'

Pulling out his cell phone, Barry sighed. 'We should have a drink sometime.'

'Sure,' said Gallen, fishing Winter's number from his jacket pocket.

'Bunch of us heading down to the Spotted Horse tonight. Few brews, bit of a laugh.'

'Sounds cool,' said Gallen, dialling the number.

'Pick you up at six,' said Barry. 'It's wings night down there. We'll get in early, grab a table.'

'Sure,' said Gallen, walking away as the number rang. As Winter picked up, Gallen could have sworn Barry said 'the Muskrats'.

The hawk swooped again as Gallen made his way around the southern boundary of the farm and had his horse climb the snow-covered levee. Along the old dike that kept the swamp on one side and the hay fields on the other, Gallen let the horse walk, his foot still too sore for a lope. After five minutes he came up to the hunting hide that Roy had built almost fifty years ago, when he was still a kid growing up on Sweet Clover. It was a twenty-by-twenty shack, with a shooting porch that looked out over the swamp for duck season, and a mess of sticks and branches on the other side, where it overlooked a stand of cedars and aspens—the deer stand.

A wisp of smoke drifted out of the steel chimney into the still, cold air and Gallen tied off the horse and entered, thankful for a warm stove.

'That mare's sore, right hock,' said Winter, looking up from the table. 'Might take a look.'

'I'll tell Roy,' said Gallen, pushing his fingers into the bullring on the trapdoor beside the table, pulling up to show a six-pack of Coors Lights in the cage. Pulling off two of the cans, he let the beers back into the snow and peered through the slit windows as he cracked the beer. 'I gather we're alone?'

'Did a three-sixty,' said the Canadian, dressed in a black Tough Duck and jeans, his socked feet aimed at the stove. 'We're alone.'

'How's the leg?'

'In and out, through the thigh,' said Winter. 'Just a nick on the artery, but it was lucky the medics were there.'

'Okay—'

Winter shook his head and looked at the floor, tough guy dissolving to sombre. 'Thought we'd lost you, boss. Shit! That fireball!'

'Don't remember it.'

Winter looked at him. 'The fuel tank ignited and bounced twenty feet in front of you, boss, then a piece of the fire breaks off, lands on your feet.'

'I remember the smell of being on fire.'

'Better than the smell of me shitting myself—I never saw a fireball hitting a man before.'

'It's not something I recommend.'

'I never liked that Aaron,' said Winter. 'But he came through. Not every man has the heart to jump on a fire with nothing but a blanket.'

Nodding, Gallen raised his beer and touched cans with Winter. 'We still gotta job, believe it or not.'

'Yeah, Aaron told me. You believe him?'

Gallen shrugged as Winter lit a cigarette. 'My pay's landing when it should.'

'Same here.'

'He wants me to lead the investigation, find these pricks.'

'You want volunteers?'

Gallen looked into the eyes of a killer. 'Kenny, it would have to be an investigation.'

'Sure,' Winter said.

'I mean it. Once we start hunting these cocksuckers, we'll leave a trail a mile wide and you can bet that the Mounties and the FBI have us as people of interest.'

Winter looked away. 'You're right.'

'Okay,' said Gallen. 'So let's start with what we know.'

'Mulligan hires us, Aaron puts tags on our stuff.'

'Aaron's tags are declared, they're from the accountants.'

'Okay,' said Winter. 'So we bodyguard Harry Durville and a dude called Reggie gives him a fancy Inuit BlackBerry. Turns out to be a bomb.'

Gallen sipped on his beer. 'We survive and when the helicopters roll in to grab what they want to grab, they're surprised that we're running around and shooting back.'

'So they send another helo: this time they try to clean us up along with the search-and-rescue team.'

Gallen leaned forward. 'This is the part I'm confused about: Durville's bag doesn't have any documents in it. If the mercs weren't sent to retrieve them, what was their job?'

'To kill Durville and anyone else who saw the meeting,' said Winter. 'The bombing was a hit.'

Gallen wasn't convinced. 'Harry Durville was involved in something huge up in Kugaaruk. I can't believe he wasn't carrying at least one piece of paper from that meeting.'

'You think?'

'Not even a memo, minutes of the meeting?' said Gallen. 'This is the CEO of a Fortune 500 company and he's accompanied by his chief legal counsel. What kind of attorney comes out of a meeting to secure the largest oil deposits in the world without documenting it?'

'So we're back to that,' said Winter. 'Someone stole the documents from his bag before he died. It wasn't me, it wasn't you and I'm fairly sure it weren't Mike.'

'Someone who knew where the documents were and how important they were,' said Gallen.

'So that leaves Florita and Donny,' said Winter.

'What did you say?'

Winter recoiled slightly. 'Whoa, boss.'

'I'm sorry,' said Gallen. 'Donny?'

'Just saying.'

'It's okay,' said Gallen, slumping and drinking. 'It could be Donny.'

'You sure?'

'No, I'm not.' Gallen exhaled. 'But Donny was secretly working for Paul Mulligan.'

'What?!'

'He was supposed to engineer a meeting between me and Mulligan when I went down to that fundraiser for Richards,' said Gallen, massaging the bridge of his nose. 'I assumed Mulligan had used Donny to get me into the Oasis gig. But given all this, it may have been deeper. Maybe he paid Donny to steal whatever documents came out of that meeting with Reggie.'

'Donny woulda done that to *you*?'

Gallen nodded. 'Donny wouldn't have seen the damage. He'd have seen it as grabbin' some lame-ass shit from some lame-ass corporate dude. No hurt, no foul.'

'Well you know what that means, right, boss?'

Gallen put his elbows on the table, rubbing his temples. 'Given that Durville sacked Mulligan the day before we flew north, it means we have an enemy who could be anywhere and who probably hasn't secured those documents yet.' He drank deeply. 'It means we'd better make sure Florita doesn't have them, because Mulligan might already be treating her as if she does.'

Winter tapped a big finger on the top of his beer can. 'Wasn't what I meant, boss.'

'No?'

'No. If your mission was to secure those documents, would you bomb the plane?'

Gallen's left temple bulged with his pulse. 'No. I'd want the documents, not a bunch of ashes.'

'Okay,' said Winter. 'So whoever wanted the documents didn't bomb the plane.'

'And whoever bombed the plane wasn't after the documents?'

'Right.'

'You're saying there's two crews, working separate?'

'I can't see it any other way.'

Gallen's burns itched in his right leg. 'Shit.'

Winter nodded. 'I think we're being sandwiched.'

CHAPTER 37

They bought pitchers of beer and made pigs of themselves with the wings special, but it didn't feel like old times. It felt like a bunch of guys in their mid-thirties in a sea of people in their early twenties.

Barry Teague wouldn't shut up about his internal postal service politics and Murray Davis, who'd lost as much weight as hair since his senior year of high school, sat looking morose. Tony Eastman tried to get Gallen to support his post-divorce misogyny.

The Muskrats appeared on the tiny corner stage just after eight o'clock and Barry's shepherd's whistle sounded wrong in an atmosphere where the youngsters were pretending they didn't care. Which they probably didn't, thought Gallen, seeing how many of them were fiddling with their cell phones.

The four-piece looked like the kind of men that Roy used to employ in the old days: lots of moustaches and beards, non-ironic cowboy hats and old Wranglers with a new seat sewed into them. It was the same look Gallen remembered from the prom, except back then the Muskrats had turned up in their tuxedos and played a selection of songs that didn't stray too far from Lynyrd Skynard, Garth Brooks and Hank junior, perhaps throwing in some Creedence and Chuck Berry to boogie it up.

Ensuring the waitress was happy with her tips, they kept the pitchers coming, and when Gallen turned to signal for another he saw her: Yvonne, dolled up, looking hot in jeans, boots and a down-filled vest. She saw him and waved, smiling. Gallen wondered if he should go to the bar and apologise for not taking her out, or sit and wait for her to come over.

Turning back to his buddies, he caught the smiles.

'Jesus, look at Yvonne,' said Barry, raising his eyebrows. 'Shit, she gets better with age.'

'She's out of our league,' said Tony, sneering.

'Try telling GG that,' said Barry.

Gallen smiled in his beer. 'Cut it out.'

'Yvonne's back on the market.' Barry winked at Tony. 'She's divorced. Know that, Tones?'

'Really?'

'Yeah, another chance for the sisterhood to destroy us, right? Steal our balls, hide 'em in a vice.'

The rest of them laughed and Tony put his beer down, looking betrayed. 'You won't be laughing when you wake up one day and they're runnin' the joint. Day's comin'.'

The Muskrats were ending their first set and, leaping to his feet, Gallen decided to cut off the innuendo before Yvonne wandered into the ambush.

'Thought I'd scared you off,' she said. She was standing beside the bar with her arms crossed, smelling great.

Gallen smiled. 'You did.'

'So?'

'So I was kind of tricked into this by a bunch of idiots,' said Gallen, throwing a thumb over his shoulder. 'Nothing like a wings night to get this crew off their asses.'

Behind Yvonne, a man in a sports jacket and chinos ordered chardonnay and was told all they had was white wine.

'You know Rob—Rob Stansfield, a lawyer in Clearmont?'

'Sure,' said Gallen, shaking hands with Wes Carty's partner in law. 'How you doin', Rob?'

'Good, thanks, Gerry,' the lawyer said, trying to divert Yvonne to a booth at the rear of the bar.

'You could join us,' said Gallen. 'We're up the front.'

Seeing Rob hesitating, not wanting his date to be hijacked, Gallen pointed to the gents and walked away, heart thumping.

As he stood at the urinal, he felt a buzzing from the pre-paid cell phone he'd bought in a Clearmont convenience store. Only one person knew his new number.

'Kenny,' he said, lowering his voice.

'. . . news . . .' said the Canadian as the noise of an argument drifted through the slat window over the urinal.

'What's that?' said Gallen, zipping and trying to keep the phone to his ear.

As he tried to pick up Kenny Winter's words, raised voices came from outside the washroom. He heard Yvonne, and she was shrieking.

Pushing through the rear door into the car park, Gallen scoped the ground: Rob the lawyer, doubled over against a dark F-250, a man about to kick him in the stomach. Closer to the door, Yvonne struggled with a tall blond man who had her by the wrists.

'Piss off, Brandon,' said Yvonne, trying to kick her former husband. 'Piss off!'

'Where's ya boyfriend now, eh, Evie?' said Brandon, enjoying himself. 'What's he gonna do about it?'

Pushing Yvonne away as Gallen approached, Brandon Robinson faced off. Ignoring the former football star, Gallen walked around him to where Rob groaned on the concrete. His assailant saw Gallen and reached into his windbreaker.

Pulling up, Gallen saw a dark Beretta 9mm levelled at his forehead as the man smiled. He was taller than Gallen and younger, with a short haircut and a swarthy complexion that made him look part-Mexican or Hawaiian.

'This what you lookin' for, brother?' said the man, extending the gun at Gallen's face. 'Huh?'

'Looking out for Rob,' said Gallen, slowly raising his hands as he nodded at the writhing lawyer. 'Dude's a lawyer. He's not in this.'

'Oh, he's in this,' said the man. 'Touchin' what ain't his puts him right in this.'

'You mean Yvonne?'

'The fuck you think, Einstein?'

'Well, lookee here,' came Brandon Robinson's voice from over Gallen's right shoulder. 'It's our war hero.'

'Gotta stop drinking, Brandon,' said Gallen, still looking at the gun. 'Brings out the bitch in you.'

'Stop it, Brandon,' yelled Yvonne, and Gallen heard the door to the bar swing open.

'Hear that, hero?' said Brandon, putting his hand on the back of Gallen's neck. 'Evie's gonna save—'

Gallen swung a reverse punch, opening his hips and straightening his right fist with the forearm as it accelerated into Brandon Robinson's face. It felt like hitting a watermelon, a few sobs of pain the only indication that he'd just flattened Robinson's nose.

Keeping his eyes on the shooter as Robinson fell to the ground, Gallen put his hands up again. 'Put down the gun, eh, sport? What's your name?'

'Don't worry about my name,' said the thug.

'Not worried. Just asked you what it was.'

'Gerry, don't,' came Yvonne's voice, but Gallen was focused on the tough guy with the gun.

'You want my gun?' said Gallen as softly as he could and still be heard. Behind him the bubble of voices suggested drinkers spilling into the car park with the promise of a fight.

His eyes darting to Brandon Robinson and back, the shooter gulped again. 'Sure. Let's wrap this up.'

'Let's,' said Gallen, pulling his cheap Nokia from his back pocket and throwing it through the night air at the gun man. As the thug's eyes followed the arc of the phone, Gallen moved forward, sliding his boots across concrete in a boxer's shuffle. The gunman recovered and brought the Beretta level again as Gallen hit the gun hand sideways with a left block and drove a fast punch into the other man's mouth. As the shooter lost balance, Gallen grabbed the gun wrist and threw a savage elbow into the thug's teeth, developing power with a turn of his hips.

Feeling the gunman trying to regain control of his weapon as he fell into the truck, Gallen increased his grip on the gun wrist, stabbed his fingers into the man's eyeballs and then got both of his hands onto the gun wrist.

The thug regained balance against the truck and lashed out with a knee which caught Gallen in the groin. But the hold he had on the man's wrist was firm and, pushing the gun down against the inside of the man's forearm, Gallen forced all of his weight behind a downwards jerk of the wrist lock, breaking the gunman's wrist and forearm in one quick movement.

Screams echoed as Gallen watched the gun bounce on the concrete.

'Y'all hold it right there,' came the deep drawl from behind him as Gallen retrieved the Beretta from the ground, steam blowing out of his panting mouth.

Turning, he came face to face with Will Andrews, the owner of the bar, Winchester .30-30 tucked into his right armpit.

'Actually, you can hold it right here, Willy,' said Gallen, handing him the gun as Yvonne helped the lawyer to his feet. 'I got a beer to finish.'

'What about this shit?' Will's moustache twitched with annoyance as he looked around the car park.

'Call the sheriff,' said Gallen, as Yvonne took a free kick at her ex-husband's face. 'I'll be at the front table.'

CHAPTER 38

Barry stood on the brakes and readied to swing his truck into the farm's driveway.

'I still don't see how no Army truck driver could do that, Gerry,' he said, flicking his smoke into the darkness. 'You telling me everything?'

'I just reacted,' said Gallen, tired and a bit drunk.

'The dude had a gun, Gerry! Chrissakes.'

In the distance, Gallen saw something. Putting his left hand out, he grabbed Barry's forearm. 'Just a minute.'

'What?' said Barry, pausing in the road outside Sweet Clover. 'Deer?'

Gallen scanned the darkness of the road. 'Hit the lights, Barry. Dash lights too.'

Turning off the headlights and reducing the dash lights to zero, Barry eased back in his seat, rubbing his face. 'What's going on?'

'There,' said Gallen, as headlights a half-mile down the road flashed on and off several times.

'What is that?' said Barry, his voice betraying nerves.

'It's morse.'

'I don't know about—'

'Let's go,' said Gallen, pointing at the flashing headlights.

'Look, this is not really—'

'He's friendly.'

Barry's voice squeaked like an adolescent's. 'How do you know?'

''Cos he just called me.'

'With those flashes?'

'Yeah. They said B.O.S.S.'

Gallen thanked Barry for the ride and climbed into Kenny's truck.

'What's up?' said Gallen, smelling hours of cigarettes as he sat on something in the passenger seat.

'That phone of yours don't work,' said Winter, eyes focused on the faint glow of the farmhouse lights. Roy was probably drinking, watching the NHL highlights.

'It smashed,' said Gallen, lighting a smoke and pulling the envelopes from under his ass. 'This yours?'

'You had mail.'

Looking at it, Gallen saw two envelopes: one, a white foolscap with the logo of Marcia's lawyers in Tucson. Throwing it onto the back seat, Gallen saw the brownish security envelope and registered-mail stickers of the second one. Tearing it open, he pulled out his new passport.

Shoving it in his inside pocket, he followed Winter's gaze to the farmhouse. 'What've we got?'

'Bell TV van turns up half an hour after you left,' said Winter. 'You expecting maintenance?'

'Nope.'

'Dish upgrade?'

'Nope. So Roy let 'em in?' said Gallen.

'Yep. I was watching from the tree line. They spent thirty-five minutes in there.'

'How many?'

'Two technician guys,' said Winter. 'Coveralls and clipboards. But there was this other dude in the van.'

'He get out?'

'No. I saw him between the front seats; he was sitting in back.'

'And?'

221

'And I was wondering what he was doing in there when I realised the air vent was turning on the top of the van. With no wind.'

'Surveillance camera?'

'That was my guess.'

'Okay,' said Gallen, hissing out the tension between his teeth.

'I tried calling but you answered and then, I dunno. Sounded like a woman screaming.'

'I'll tell you about it later,' said Gallen, his senses on alert. 'So I guess the house is bugged. You speak to Roy about this?'

Winter shook his head, eyes not leaving the farmhouse. 'Nope. Grabbed the truck and been sitting out here half the night, trying to make sure you don't go in.'

'Out-fucking-standing,' said Gallen. 'Which way they leave?'

'This way,' Winter said, jacking his thumb in reverse. 'I been up and down this line for an hour and they ain't parked down here.'

Gallen thought about it. 'On a neighbouring property?'

Winter shrugged.

'Got any glasses?'

Pulling a set of Bushnell night-vision binoculars from the door pocket, Winter handed them over. Getting out, Gallen leaned his elbows on the hood of the truck, slowly scanning the area around the farmhouse and the road with the illuminated black-and-white view. He could see a horse tail flashing in the yards past the house and the binoculars also picked up a large porcupine trying to climb a cedar that grew between the farmhouse and the old orchard. But no human shapes, no men moving around, no plumes of steam erupting from people talking in their hide.

It wasn't just the immediate danger of an assassin or a snatch-artist who would be lurking close to the house, waiting for him or Winter to show up, that worried Gallen. There was also the matter of the listening post: where it was, what vehicle it was sitting in and who was inside listening.

Some transmitters had ranges of up to ten miles but most professionals in the surveillance game preferred the reliability of the short-range bugs. It meant there was likely a van with a bunch of coffee-drinking listeners in a close radius; they weren't on the road but that didn't mean they weren't around.

Gallen got back in the truck, which had the interior light switched off. 'Well, I guess we're blown,' he said, wishing he hadn't drunk so much beer. 'We can't stay here.'

'I was hoping you'd say that,' said Winter.

'Any ideas on who they are?'

Winter ground his teeth. 'I saw something when I caught that dude hiding in the van.'

'What?'

'He looked familiar. Black guy, about thirty. Only caught a glimpse of his face through the windscreen, but I think I've seen him before.'

'Military? Intel?'

'Maybe, Gerry—but the other one? I was certain about him.'

'The other one?'

'The lead guy, when they were knocking at the door.'

'Who was it?'

'It was the dude who looked like a lawyer in the SUV behind the bar.'

Gallen shook his head in confusion.

'In Los Angeles,' said Winter, dragging on his smoke.

Gallen envisioned the scene behind the Spanish bar at Marina Del Rey. 'Shit, those guys?'

'It was him,' said Winter. 'We've been made.'

CHAPTER 39

It was just after ten when Gallen and Winter pulled in to the Higgins family farm. The front door of the ranch house opened, spilling yellow light onto the porch before Gallen's boots hit the gravel.

'Keep him on the leash, Billy,' said Gallen. 'It's me. Gerry.'

Behind the screen door, a large German shepherd called Zane barked into the night.

'You comin' in?' said Higgins, thick woollen socks on his feet and holding a can of Bud. '*Major Dundee* just started.'

'Nah, Billy,' said Gallen, walking towards the porch. 'Emergency. Gotta take a horse to Oklahoma first thing in the morning and the fricking gooseneck is cracked.'

'Take the Dodge,' said Higgins, belching.

'I'll leave you the Ford. She's running, just don't use the gooseneck hitch.'

The dog stopped barking. 'When you back, Ger?'

'A week,' said Gallen. 'That a problem?'

'Nah, we're sweet,' said Higgins, heading back inside. 'Key's under the seat.'

* * *

They made good time north and at Billings they stopped at a drive-through ATM where Gallen withdrew six thousand in cash from his corporate MasterCard. He was going to need money but didn't want to be on the grid, didn't want to leave any electronic paper trails. Across the road from the ATM was an all-night convenience store where he bought two pre-paid Nokia phones that would fit the car charger in the Dodge. Then he bought ten fifty-dollar Verizon top-up cards, registered the whole lot in the name of Roland Smith from BC.

They avoided the I-90 and stuck to the big white signs that signalled Montana 3, the state highway that took traffic north into Alberta. The big Dodge Ram purred along, its diesel thirsty but smooth, the phones charging as they drove. Gallen felt relatively safe travelling across Montana in a borrowed truck. In his world, a local sheriff or highway patrolman knew how the rednecks swapped vehicles, but he was hoping that it would take a suit from the government longer to get it.

Pulling into the Shelby trucker's roadhouse at 5.41 am, they parked in the rear among the semis and took a seat in the diner back from the window. Sipping coffee and eating eggs with biscuit as the sun touched the mountains, Gallen decided he'd sobered up enough to take a driving stint. The next stretch of road joined with the famous I-15 North, the CANAMEX highway that connected Mexico to Alberta.

'Don't matter if they're Agency, Pentagon or NSA,' said Winter, mulling over the Spanish bar crew who were now at the Gallen farm. 'They're from Washington and we still have a border crossing, right?'

Around them truck drivers watched the morning TV news and slapped down their money for a hot shower.

'There's not a lot we can do about that,' said Gallen. 'If the CIA or the Pentagon really wants to talk, they'll come and talk.'

'How you want to play it?'

Gallen had a good idea what Winter was talking about but he didn't want to do it that way. 'Kenny, I'd as soon talk our way through this,' he said, eyeing the sign that offered towels and showers. 'We haven't broken the law yet.'

'Just so you know,' said Winter.

'Yeah, I know,' said Gallen, slapping his pockets for change as he made for the towels. 'We'll do it easy, okay? Right now I need a shower.'

The line crawled through the US side of the border crossing while the trucks got the express treatment in the other lanes. Peering through the top of the windscreen, Gallen pulled down the peak of his cap as he saw the arrays of cameras that automatically scanned the passing parade. It wasn't the licence plate that concerned him—it was his face being captured and run through the intel databases operated by the US Government.

The Americans waved them through and Gallen let the Dodge idle to the Canadian side where a young woman in a dark CBSA parka gestured them to an inspection lane.

'Shit,' said Winter under his breath.

Parking the Dodge in the inspection bay, Gallen switched off. 'Just relax, Kenny.'

The woman was tall and athletic, pretty too. They watched her walk to the front of the Dodge and scan the licence plate with a hand-held attached to an iPad device, before arriving at Gallen's open window.

'Good morning, sir,' she said with a smile, her lanyard identifying her as Officer Langtry. 'American?'

'Yes, ma'am,' said Gallen, handing over his passport.

She scanned that too and Gallen killed the radio as 'Hot Child in the City' ramped up.

'So, Mr Gallen,' she said, looking into his eyes. 'I see you've renewed your passport?'

'Yes, ma'am.'

'Military passports with no orders—that's not a good mix.'

'No, ma'am.'

'Anything to declare this morning?'

'No, ma'am.'

'Any firearms, explosives, alcohol, tobacco?'

'No, ma'am, 'cept a couple packs of Marlboros.'

'No cash in excess of ten thousand Canadian dollars?'

'No, ma'am.'

'You carrying any blood samples, any used veterinary equipment?'

'No, ma'am.'

'You currently under criminal indictment in the United States?'

'No, ma'am.'

'Parole or suspended sentence?'

'Nope.'

'This your truck?'

'No, ma'am.'

'Those your mineral blocks in the back?'

Gallen craned his head but couldn't see the supplies in the tray of the Dodge. 'No, ma'am.'

Officer Langtry looked past him to Winter. 'And this would be Mr William Higgins?'

Gallen craved a smoke but didn't want to light up. 'No, ma'am.'

Moving to the other side of the truck, Langtry scanned Winter's passport but paid particular attention to his face.

'Kenny Winter?' she said. 'Not Kenny Winter, defenceman for the Hurricanes?'

Winter smiled. 'Yes, ma'am, but don't hold it against me.'

'I don't,' said Officer Langtry, beaming. 'Lethbridge is our team. We're all 'Canes fans down here.'

'Glad to hear it. Thought I was non grata?'

'Forget that crap,' she said, waving it away. 'Those animals from Spokane been getting away with it for years. You just gave a little back is all.'

Walking back to Gallen, Langtry leaned on the door. 'So, you're not William Higgins but you're in his truck?'

'My gooseneck hitch is broken so I borrowed Billy's.'

'You're not towing, sir.'

'I'm looking for horses, at the auctions,' said Gallen. 'If anything's worth buying, we'll hire a trailer.'

'Looking for horses?'

'We're trainers. Roy Gallen's my father.'

Langtry Googled him on her iPad. 'Sweet Clover, huh? Roy Gallen and family—stock contractor for the rodeo, trainer of ropers and cutting horses.'

'That's him.'

'Which auctions?'

Gallen hesitated. 'Up Stettler and Big Valley. Maybe try Leduc, around there.'

'Stettler's a meat auction,' said Langtry.

'Only if they go for meat,' said Gallen. 'Otherwise they're a cheap roping horse.'

Langtry's face softened. 'You do that?'

'He does,' said Gallen, pointing at Winter. 'You wouldn't believe how many hundred-thousand-dollar roping horses were bought at meat auctions.'

She looked back at the customs office, where faces peered out of the plate glass in the early morning light. Then she scribbled something on a sheet of paper, tore it off.

'Okay,' she said, lowering her voice as she handed back Gallen's passport. 'Next time, bring a signed declaration that this vehicle is in authorised third-party use. Have a nice day, sir.'

The slap on the roof sounded friendly enough as Gallen started the Dodge. Easing out of the customs enclosure, onto Canadian territory, Gallen could sense Winter craning his neck.

'Don't attract attention, Kenny.'

'Sorry, boss. Can't keep my eyes off that ass.'

Handing Winter his passport, Gallen swung the Dodge onto Highway 4 for Lethbridge and hit the gas. 'Keep your eyes on that instead.'

Opening the passport, Winter pulled out the scrap of paper that Officer Langtry had placed there.

'What does it say?'

'Says, *US intelligence about to be notified that Gerard Gallen just crossed the border.*'

'Shit,' said Gallen.

'Least she gave us a heads-up,' said Winter, turning in his seat and looking behind. 'Nice work on the meat auctions.'

Gallen lit a smoke and inhaled deeply as he keyed his Nokia and looked at the list of call centres he could use for his long-distance card. He rang the Miami one, then input his PIN and the number he wanted to call in Jakarta.

The call went to voicemail and he hung up before the beep sounded.

He was sinking off the grid, just like he'd been trained. The fear he'd been feeling at the border crossing was evaporating into a cold, hard sense of what he had to do.

He was back in the game, and he was liking it.

CHAPTER 40

Pulling into a shopping centre on the north side of the Crowsnest Highway in Lethbridge, they found a parking spot and changed their US dollars at a bank that was just opening. They walked to a line of used-car lots on the south side of the highway where Gallen found what he was looking for: an eight-year-old Chev Impala for $2499, before taxes. After he'd changed the registration with his Roland Smith driver's licence, they took the closest on-ramp and gunned the car north for Calgary.

Gallen grabbed his phone as he found a comfortable speed between the armada of trucks that were heading for Calgary and on to Edmonton. This time he dialled the call centre in Boston then, after inputting his PIN, the Jakarta number.

'Pete,' he said as the American voice answered. 'Gerry.'

'Hey, Gerry,' said the intel man. 'You in Boston now?'

'Alberta's too cold, even in spring,' said Gallen.

'Maybe getting even colder when you lose a billionaire, hey, Gerry?'

'It wasn't a great first week.'

'I haven't spoken to Piers yet, but he's in town next week.'

'Thanks, buddy,' said Gallen. 'But it's not that.'

'What you need?'

'You must know a good hacker, someone who can access a file on a corporate server?'

Morton sighed. 'Shit, Gerry. You had to do this on the open air? You clean?'

'I'm clean, Pete,' said Gallen as he overtook a line of semis. 'Are you?'

'Don't get smart,' said the ex-DIA man. 'Maybe you don't need a hacker. What are you looking for?'

'You remember my employer?'

'Yep.'

'I need a residential address on two names. Can do?'

'Spell them,' said Morton. The NSA's voice-recognition software scanned for names, numbers and words. It was less efficient with strings of letters.

'Why don't I just tell you their positions?' said Gallen as he slipped back into the long line of trucks.

'Try me.'

Gallen listed the acting chief executive and the vice-president, security and after thirty seconds of tapping and clicking, Morton came back on the line.

'Can't break in. I'll ask my guy. Where do I send the results?'

'I'll call in an hour.'

Morton laughed, a cackling smoker's laugh.

'What's funny?'

'You, buddy,' Morton said. 'You're obviously dodging our friends in DC and, just so you know, it suits me that I think you're in Boston. Clear?'

'Crystal,' said Gallen. 'I'll call in an hour.'

The Elf cafe was perfect for Gallen's needs: the internet bunker was tucked away in Calgary's Chinese-Korean sector, on the corner of 17th and 34th streets. The place had no coffee, no trendies and no one wanting to be friendly.

Setting up a Gmail account under the name 'Zamboanga1103', Gallen went into settings and set up email forwarding. Opening another window, he went to a website that collected spam databases and cut and pasted two thousand email addresses into the forwarding rules of his Zamboanga1103 account. Scrolling down the addresses he stopped about halfway and inserted his Igor Olafnowsky email address and then shut down the computer.

Opening his Igor Olafnowsky Gmail account, Gallen looked around and saw Winter smoking on the street outside the window. Selecting the Fort Worth number on his long-distance card, Gallen got Morton on the second ring.

'I've got 'em,' said Morton. 'What have you got for me?'

'An IOU you can cash in anytime, so long as it doesn't endanger my life.'

'I'll hold you to it,' said Morton. 'You want this on the air?'

'Gmail,' said Gallen, looking around at the Asian faces in the bare room. 'The city we met in plus the month and year. Thirteen characters.'

'Gotcha, buddy,' said Morton. 'On its way now. Don't be a stranger.'

The line went dead and Gallen hunched over the monitor as youngsters milled. Hitting the refresh button on the Gmail program, he waited for a shade over a minute. The email arrived and he scribbled the addresses on a piece of paper as fast as he could.

Turning off the server stack and the monitor too, Gallen paid with a Canadian ten-dollar note and left before the owner could complain.

Winter drove for two blocks to a drive-through McDonald's before heading down to a river park where they decamped and ate at a picnic table in the weak sun.

'So, Aaron's got a surname and he hasn't listed his Calgary address?' said Winter, burger spilling from his mouth as he looked down at Gallen's scrap of paper. 'Think they put him up at the same hotel where we stayed?'

'Not a bad bet.'

Finishing their lunch, they made a plan. They'd book into the Sheraton: Gallen would case Florita's house; Winter would source firearms and try to find Aaron.

'What are we looking for?' said Winter, sipping on Sprite.

'I want to know who Florita and Aaron are talking to and where they're going,' said Gallen.

'I know you keep saying that they've done nothing wrong, that we're just doing recon,' said Winter, slightly exasperated, 'but shit, Gerry, you must have some suspicions.'

Looking at two scullers powering down the river in the lee of the skyscrapers, Gallen wiped the grease of the French fries off his fingers before opening his new pack of smokes.

'Suspicion might be the wrong word,' he said, lighting up. 'Let's just say that a week ago I was blown out of the sky, and only two people seem to have gained from the experience.'

Winter took a smoke. 'I hadn't seen it that way.'

'I lost Durville to a bomb, but they want me back? With a promotion?'

'Not like any army I ever fought in.'

'No,' said Gallen, turning for the car. 'So let's do this the military way.'

'Remind me.'

'We start at the beginning,' said Gallen. 'By understanding how much we don't know.'

233

CHAPTER 41

The news backgrounder on CNN showed a group of European and American activists from an organisation called ArcticWatch parading a few bedraggled Inuit in front of a press conference in Paris. A woman with a strong French accent said something about global warming and decimation of hunting grounds for the Inuit and tied it all up with a bromide about corporate greed, Big Oil and the global mining oligopoly.

Gallen sipped on his beer and rolled to his side to check the time on the bedside table: 3.37 pm. Winter was seven minutes past the RV. Even though he was buying handguns, Gallen trusted him. He'd panic at nine o'clock.

Taking a bite from one of the perfect meatballs ordered in from Joey Tomato's Grill across the road, he was about to check the news on Fox and MSNBC when the CNN story grabbed his attention. The ArcticWatch woman swept her hand to her side to indicate the Inuit and then called them the Transarctic Tribal Council.

Grabbing for the remote, he sat up and increased the volume in time to hear the journalist's voiceover pick up the story.

'*It has been almost a decade since the United Nations oversaw the creation of the Inuit Circumpolar Council—or ICC—in response to Inuit complaints that decisions about their livelihood were being made thousands of miles from their homelands. Inuit* argued that while their Arctic hunting grounds were under the technical sovereignty of nations such as Russia, Canada, the United States and Denmark, they were a distinct ethnic people who had interacted, intermarried and traded with one another for thousands of years. The Inuit put their case as an ethnic nation with their own territorial, economic and social interests, quite separate from the interests of their imperial masters in Washington, Ottawa, Moscow and Copenhagen.'

Gallen watched the Frenchwoman on the screen, the show using file shots of her protesting on the ice in Greenland, meeting with Vlad Putin in a Moscow drawing room and marching with Eskimos in Ottawa. Her name was Martina Du Bois, and apparently she was a Sorbonne-educated left-wing lawyer who came from a famous military family.

The reporter interviewed her and soon they were talking about the Transarctic Tribal Council—Reggie's outfit. Gallen focused on the story, his heart rate lifting. She spoke about the TTC representing Inuit whereas the ICC represented the governments of the various Arctic nations. Apparently there was a difference.

It was the first Gallen had heard of the Transarctic Tribal Council being a new or rival organisation; especially that it rivalled the United Nations-sanctioned group.

The CNN report switched to voiceover again.

'With the discovery of the world's largest oil and gas deposits outside the Middle East on the floor of the Arctic Ocean, Du Bois' ArcticWatch has become closely aligned with the Transarctic Tribal Council. The TTC was set up to counter what Du Bois sees as the increasing encroachment of government policy friendly to big oil and mining companies in the Arctic Circle.'

As the report broadened to describe how global warming was opening oil fields and sea lanes to the exploration companies, making the extraction of oil and minerals profitable, Gallen eased back on the pillows and wondered about what was not being said; what was the propaganda component?

The screen was now dominated by an aerial shot of a giant ship with two hulls, each the size of a container ship. This enormous catamaran was called the Fanny Blankes-Koen, and as the helicopter circled it the reporter's voiceover explained that the ship was an Oasis Energy venture to test the Arctic Ocean floor. Sitting on the bow gantries of the dual-hull vessel was a shape that Gallen had seen as a model in Durville's office. It was a large pod not unlike a flying saucer from a 1950s movie.

The reporter got to the heart of it.

'This massive commitment from one of the world's largest oil companies will seek to overcome the problems of drilling in arctic conditions by simply ducking most of the conditions altogether. The Oasis-led venture will bolt this oil rig to the sea bed and on top of it place a small town called Ariadne. In this, the largest saturation-diving platform ever built, up to one hundred oil workers will live and work around the clock for three months at a time before being replaced by a new crew. ArcticWatch has opposed the building of the Ariadne submerged oil rig, citing pollution and degradation of the Inuit's hunting areas . . .'

The door's electronic lock clicked and Kenny Winter was inside, throwing his backpack on the bed.

'Go okay?' said Gallen, watching the door until it shut itself and locked down.

'Two SIGs, nine-mil,' said Winter, pulling off his jacket and scooping a handful of fries off the Joey Tomato's plate. 'Not new but they've been maintained. Army surplus.'

Pulling one of the black SIG handguns from Winter's pack, Gallen tore it down and laid the pieces on the bed cover. It was well used but seemed to have a new firing pin and newish spring on the slide. He didn't care too much; the SIG P226 was a classic sidearm in special forces and he felt comfortable with the weapon's strengths and limitations.

'Let's split up,' he said. 'You can make a friend at security, chat up one of those girls on the front desk. Let's see if we can learn something about Mr Aaron Michaels.'

Gallen left the room first, hiding the SIG in his waistband and tucking it under his Carhartt jacket. He hailed a cab from the front of the Sheraton Suites, then waved it on. He took the third cab that stopped and directed the driver across the river and west, without stating a destination. Stopping two streets back from the river, Gallen got out and paid cash, then stood in the shadows of a tree until the taxi was out of sight.

He walked for three minutes north, through the leafy area of Westmount, an inner-city enclave of lawyers, doctors and well-to-do gays.

Turning onto Florita's street, Gallen made a pass of her house, a ninety-year-old three-storey place with colonial features on the balconies. Her mailbox was devoid of a name and the front entrance was accessible.

Walking around the block, he strolled down the rear lane that separated the large houses. Stopping behind Florita's, he pulled a garbage bin to the fence and climbed it. To his right was a double garage that opened onto the laneway and in front of him was a large garden, dominated by a lawn and then a swimming pool that ran up to an entertaining area at the rear of the house.

The nights were still cold, but Gallen could see what a mini country club this would be in the summer.

Leaping to the lawn beside the garage, Gallen listened for sounds and stayed in the shadows. Through the side window of the garage he could see a small silver BMW.

There was a light on in the second floor of the house, but not on the ground floor. Moving towards the house, he scanned for light beams or pressure pads, even though he knew there was no chance of seeing them in the dark. There were small solar lights planted in the shrubberies and flowerbeds and they shed a slight glow.

Pausing beside the kidney-shaped pool, Gallen saw leaves on the cover. Looking up, he looked at the light in the second-storey window and thought he saw movement. Freezing as he wondered if he'd stepped on a pressure pad, he reached for the SIG jammed in the small of his back. Easing it out, he became aware of a red dot in the darkness beside the pool. The dot enlarged and moved to one side.

'The gun's a bit much, isn't it, Gerry?'

Dropping to a crouch, Gallen aimed at the dot in the dark, his night sight ruined by staring too long at the upstairs light.

'Who's that?' he snarled, more surprised than scared. His pulse thumped in his temples and the burns on his left leg ached.

Slowly the shape of a man in a recliner revealed itself, then light was spilling onto the pool area and the French doors swung open.

'Aaron,' said the woman as she pulled her robe around her hips and leaned through the door, 'you okay?'

* * *

237

They sat on opposite sides of the large kitchen island, Gallen feeling unwelcome. 'After Aaron told me I'd been promoted, I was still being followed and I decided to avoid the offices, approach you directly.'

Florita handed him a bottle of European beer, swapped a look with Aaron and plunged her coffee. 'So you crept into the backyard?'

'I was going to knock on the back door, make it as non-scary as possible,' said Gallen, smiling. 'Whoever is watching me is probably watching you and I'd bet the phones are tapped. I needed a conversation, below the radar.'

'What about?'

'If we're going to chase the bastards who bombed us, I need to start with everything you know.'

'I think I told you,' said Florita, clearly nervous. 'I've got that new contract for you, by the way. It's in the study.'

Aaron slugged at his beer as Florita left. 'Could have called me, tough guy.'

'You weren't made CEO a few days after the old one was bombed out of the sky. I'm looking for a thread, and—no offence intended—I don't think you're in it.'

'None taken, Gerry.'

'What are you doing here, Aaron?' said Gallen carefully. 'Besides the obvious.'

Aaron laughed, throwing his head back and slamming his hand on the counter. 'Shit, man. Rednecks! What would we do without 'em?'

'I mean it. You bodyguarding? Doing a bit of the Kevin Costner?'

Aaron shook his head slowly as Florita swept back into the room, throwing the blue-bound contract on the marble counter top.

'Gerry thinks we're girlfriend and boyfriend,' said Aaron, still laughing.

'Shit, so much for secrets,' said Florita, slumping. 'Christ, I need a drink.'

As Florita poured from a bottle of red wine, Gallen looked between the two. 'She say secret?'

Aaron stretched and smiled at Florita. 'Sure. Tell him.'

'I was robbed tonight, Gerry,' she said, sipping the wine as she leaned against the counter. 'They went through the study but the only thing they took was a few files.'

'Where were these files?' said Gallen.

'In the safe. That's why Aaron's here. I found out an hour ago, by accident. I'd just got out of the bath.'

Gallen looked at Aaron. 'So they're pros?'

Aaron nodded. 'Looks like it. No damage, no explosive, no blunt screwdrivers—just put in the code and opened that thing.'

Gallen tried to slow his mind. These two would have kept the robbery from him unless he'd turned up. 'So what'd they take?'

'Handover documents, mainly,' said Florita, relaxing with the wine. 'Taking the CEO position has been a bit of a shock, so I stashed the confidential stuff from Harry in my safe, to read at home.'

Gerry finished the beer. 'Forgive my ignorance, but handover documents?'

'All the memos and contracts and relationships that aren't necessarily in the public domain, but which you need to run a publicly listed oil company,' said Florita. 'And with Harry—because of the informal way he operated—there's a ton of side agreements and handshake contracts that I needed to know about.'

'It's all gone?' said Gallen.

'All of it. They left my gold bars.'

'What could they do with the documents?'

Florita pointed at Aaron. 'I've already been through this. There's perhaps some material that could be used by blackmailers—'

'Like?'

Florita shrugged. 'Like what we had to do to get drilling leases in a certain national park, like what Harry promised to an EIS auditor if he just ticked the box on groundwater and aquifer degradation.'

'EIS?'

'Environmental Impact Study,' said Aaron, with a big smirk. 'Just learned that one myself.'

'You think another oil company, or Greenpeace, waited for Harry to die so they could steal his secret papers from the new CEO?' It didn't stack up.

'I don't know,' said Florita.

'Well, what I know,' said Gallen, 'is that Harry Durville spent his entire career getting hammered drunk, getting into fights and threatening just about anyone who dared to stare him down. He left a trail a mile wide for anyone who wanted to get to him, extort money, embarrass him into paying up or changing his actions. But you're telling me the blackmailer waited until he was *dead* before moving?'

Aaron spurted beer as he laughed.

Florita dropped her gaze. 'Don't you two laugh at me.'

'So tell us what's going on,' said Gallen.

'Okay.' She exhaled. 'But this conversation is never going to be repeated.'

'You got it,' said Aaron.

Gallen nodded.

'Harry commissioned a report on something called Operation Nanook,' said Florita. 'Two copies were delivered, but when I cleared Harry's safe there was only one. I assume the other was with him when we went down.' She stood, grabbed two more beers from the stainless-steel fridge.

'What were they?' asked Aaron, flipping the bottle top.

'I believe it's a backgrounder on Reggie Kransk and the TTC. Mulligan commissioned the report to be clear on Oasis's partners. Harry thought it was bullshit.'

'Why did Harry think that?' said Gallen.

'The report was very negative about Kransk: who was controlling him and what those controllers wanted.'

Gallen drank, craving a cigarette. 'Who wrote the report?'

'A crowd called Newport Associates,' said Florita.

'Ex-DIA,' said Aaron.

Gallen clicked. 'Mulligan's buddies?'

Florita nodded. 'Harry thought that.'

Gallen looked at Florita. 'You read it?'

'No, I hadn't got around to it,' she said. 'It came in about the time you were hired and I didn't feel I needed to read it—Harry wasn't talking about anything else right up until his death.'

'What was Nanook?' said Aaron.

'I think Nanook was the Oasis strategy for securing the Arctic Ocean leases.' Florita poured herself more wine. 'Harry decided

Mulligan was working for another oil company, against Oasis. They had a big fight and Mulligan was sacked the day before we flew up to the meeting in Kugaaruk.'

'You think Mulligan bombed our plane?' said Gallen.

'She doesn't know and neither do I,' said Aaron. 'That's why you're investigating.'

'You said there were two reports,' said Gallen. 'There was one in your safe.'

'I'm pretty sure Harry carried the other to Kugaaruk. I saw a red cover in his satchel.'

Gallen stopped speaking, silence descending.

'What?' said Florita, looking from man to man.

Aaron cleared his throat. 'I think Gerry wants to know what's really in that report from Newport Associates.'

'I told you, Aaron, I didn't read it.'

Aaron stood up, leaned into her. 'Florita, what did Harry say was in it? It's probably important.'

Looking into her glass, Florita swirled the wine before draining it in one gulp. 'Okay, but this never goes beyond this room, okay?'

'You're the boss,' said Gallen. 'Shoot.'

'Newport Associates thinks Reggie Kransk's Transarctic Tribal Council is a front for several Russian oil and gas companies.'

CHAPTER 42

Gallen's head spun as the cab pulled up to the Sheraton Suites. Asking the driver to keep going, he slipped down in the back seat, scanned for surveillance vehicles as they raced past the lit-up foyer.

Coming around the block again, Gallen had the cab stop short of the hotel and walked the rest of the way.

Gallen knew that he'd taken this gig too soon after coming back from Afghanistan. After drifting around the States for a few months, catching up with old Marines buddies, he'd hoped to lay low on the family farm for while. He'd needed it: just a period of normalcy, with nothing but horses and cattle, bank overdrafts and diesel bills to worry about. Now he realised he'd fallen into precisely the role he didn't want to play back in civvie life: the messed-up, broken-down war vet who couldn't let anything go.

Worse than that, some of his paranoia was proving justified. Florita knew more than she was saying about Mulligan and his investigation of Reggie Kransk. Perhaps she didn't want too many people knowing where Kransk fitted in, but that still made her someone willing to lie to Gallen.

Cracking a beer from the minibar, he sat on the sofa, pulled off his boots.

'Get anything?' said Winter, wandering through, rubbing his eyes.

'I got a headache,' said Gallen, throwing his boots at the door.

'See her?'

'Drank beer with her. And Aaron.'

Winter grabbed a beer for himself. 'Aaron? He screwing her?'

'No. She had a robbery. Thieves took her Oasis files and papers. All of Harry's secret papers.'

'Shit.'

'Yeah. There was one from a private intelligence firm in LA. They wrote a background report on our friend Reggie Kransk.'

'So?'

'So it's very unflattering. It links Reggie's little tribal council to Russian oil interests.'

'They stole it? Wonder what else is in it.'

'I wonder who feels implicated enough to steal it,' said Gallen.

'Any ideas?'

Gallen shrugged. 'What's important now is that we have some action here in Calgary. Whoever's been stalking us is around, so why let that go to waste?'

'You wanna bait them?' said Winter. 'If they're watchers, that's okay. If they're shooters, that's not so good.'

Gallen drained the beer and thought. 'They wanted a document, and now they have it.'

'So why would they stay around?'

Gallen let the facts fall into place. 'Because they know Newport delivered two reports: one original and a copy.'

'And they think we have the original?'

Gallen stood, walked to the curtained hotel window and stood at the side of it, peeking out through the gap. Traffic sped across the city, steam from exhaust pipes rising in the cold night air.

'They know that we walked away from that plane crash, and that we worked personal security for Harry,' said Gallen. 'They haven't struck us off the list yet.'

'Shit, Gerry,' said Winter, standing. 'They'll never stop looking.'

'So let's flush 'em out,' said Gallen. 'I was gonna find a new hotel tomorrow, book it in my name, use the Oasis MasterCard, basically put up a flag for these bozos. Any ideas?'

'We need a flat layout, front and rear exits,' said Winter without hesitation. 'Maybe an upmarket motel, with a forecourt. Use a room decoy and put someone in the car.'

'Maybe make a new buddy in the front office?'

'You've done this before, right?' said Winter, cracking a smile.

'Only twice.'

'There's something else,' said the Canadian, having his own look from the side of the window.

'Yep?'

'We need Mike back.'

When Winter turned around, Gallen held the strip of paper up to his face.

'Mike's number?' said Winter. 'Aaron give you that?'

'Yep,' said Gallen. 'Think it's too late to call?'

'He's a fricking Australian,' said Winter, grabbing his Nokia from the table. 'It's eight in the morning for him.'

CHAPTER 43

The first rays of warm spring sunshine fell on the twenty-ninth-floor window as Gallen watched the seven Oasis vice-presidents file out of the chief executive's office. Kenny Winter had just updated him by phone: Ford had joined Winter at the motel suites. They were rented in their own names with the Oasis MasterCard. The trap had been laid.

Getting to his feet as Aaron beckoned him, Gallen smiled at the executive assistant and walked into the large office.

'Everyone calm?' he said, instinctively moving to the window and surveying the view. To his right, sitting on a sofa, he saw a businessman he hadn't met.

'No,' said Florita, sliding into her leather chair as she breathed out. 'There's a feeling that we're vulnerable, that we're caught in something we don't understand.'

'That true?' said Gallen.

'The boss was appointed by the board last week,' said Aaron, 'but they want a plan at the extraordinary board meeting this Friday.'

'So you need some answers?'

'I need something,' said Florita, throwing a folded copy of the *Calgary Herald* across the desk.

Picking it up, Gallen saw the front-page headline: OASIS STOCK PRICE SET TO PLUMMET ON RUSSIAN RUMORS.

'What the heck is this?' said Gallen.

'Third paragraph,' said the man on the sofa. 'It's underlined.'

Looking at Aaron, Gallen raised an eyebrow.

'Meet Dave Joyce,' said Aaron. 'Vice-president, corporate communications.'

'PR guy?' said Gallen as Joyce stood and offered his hand.

'Something like that,' said Joyce, his puffy eyes suggesting overwork and stress.

Glancing down past the byline of senior writer Lars Flint, Gallen found the highlighted section:

> The spokesman for Oasis refused to comment on allegations that the late founder and CEO of Canada's largest oil company, Harry Durville, was in secret negotiations with several Russian oil companies to control drilling leases in the Arctic Ocean.
>
> When questioned specifically on Mr Durville's involvement with an Inuit organisation called the Transarctic Tribal Council (TTC), the spokesman terminated the interview.

Tossing the newspaper on Florita's desk, Gallen looked at Joyce and saw a man in his early forties who was finally being put under the kind of pressure he was paid so well to handle.

'You're the spokesman mentioned in here?' said Gallen, tapping the newspaper.

'Yep.'

'When did this happen?'

'Last night,' said Joyce. 'Halfway through the family meal and this journalist is on the line.'

'He tell you what he knew about the Russians and the TTC?'

'I told Aaron this,' said Joyce, swigging at a bottle of water.

'So tell me.'

Joyce sat back on the sofa, closing his eyes. 'He asks if I've heard the rumours about Durville doing a secret deal with the Russians to control the drilling rights on the Arctic sea bed.'

'And?'

'And I said no.'

'And then?'

'I think I asked him where the hell he was getting this from.'

'Flint tell you?'

Joyce shook his head. 'He went straight into these allegations about Oasis's support for the TTC, and once that started I just hung up.'

Gallen stole a glance at Aaron, who mouthed the word 'no': Dave Joyce didn't know about the Newport Associates report or the burglary at Florita's house.

'Dave, did it sound like this reporter was reading from something?' said Gallen. 'Or was it more like he had half the story, trying to flush you out?'

'The second one,' said Joyce, sitting up. 'With a major story like that, the reporter would email the evidence across to me or they'd tell me where it came from. It would strengthen their own story, make it bigger and more solid.'

'You dealt with Flint before?'

'No, he doesn't usually write on business.'

Gallen didn't understand. 'What do you mean?'

'On newspapers, there's a business and finance section,' said Joyce. 'Flint doesn't work there. He's a senior writer, usually does think-pieces, op-ed and he writes the editorials.'

'Op what?' said Gallen.

'Op-ed,' said Joyce. 'You know: opposite the editorial, the opinion pieces.'

'But not in the business and finance section?'

'No,' said Joyce. 'He's never written about business, to my knowledge. He usually weighs in with opinions about cuts in defence spending, increasing the deployment in Iraq, that sort of thing.'

'You speak to him this morning?'

'Receptionist couldn't put me through.'

'Couldn't? Or wouldn't?'

'She said his line wasn't answering,' said Joyce, slumping. 'This is the worst time for this crap. The very worst.'

Gallen looked to Aaron and Florita for a clue, then turned back to Joyce. 'What's up?'

'This,' said Joyce, tossing a glossy Oasis marketing folder across the coffee table. Picking it up, Gallen saw a white cover that proclaimed

'Ariadne: *Queen of the Arctic*'. On the bottom right were the words: Media Pack, Ariadne Launch, April 10.

Opening it, Gallen saw press releases, photos and diagrams of the flying saucer-type structure he'd seen on CNN, which also sat in model form against the wall.

'April tenth, that's . . .'

'This Friday,' said Joyce, as if Gallen was simple. 'You *did* know about the *Ariadne* launch?'

Looking at Florita and Aaron, Gallen made a face. 'Well, of course I didn't.'

Aaron cleared his throat. 'It wasn't going to be an issue, Gerry, until Florita decided she wanted to go down on the first journey.'

There was silence in the room as Gallen stared at Florita.

'I was going to tell you this morning,' said Florita. 'Feedback from the Street wasn't good.'

'Wall Street?'

'Yep,' said Florita. 'There's an idea that a female can't run an oil company. We thought this would be a good way to make the analysts and fund managers see me as a chief executive, not a woman.'

'By going to the bottom in this tin can?' said Gallen, holding up the photo. 'You coulda gone sky diving, taken a raft down some rapids.'

'It'll be a photo op,' said Joyce, defending what was obviously his idea. 'She won't go to the bottom. That's almost a thousand feet.'

'So?' said Gallen.

'We'll submerge her with the *Ariadne* for the networks and news channels, but only fifty feet down. Then we'll just bring her to the surface.'

'Oh, you will?' said Gallen. 'How will *you* do that, Dave?'

'Well . . .' Joyce looked at Aaron.

'Gerry, the take-off would be your team,' said Aaron.

Breathing out, Gallen tried to stay calm. 'I think everyone in this room should remember that two weeks ago the former chief executive of this company—sorry, the managing director—was bombed out of the sky in his corporate jet. I remember it well 'cos it was my third day on the job.'

'I'm sorry, Gerry,' said Florita. 'This was dreamed up yesterday, after a link-up with our New York PR firm. They thought it was time to redefine the story; take it away from Harry and the plane wreck, make it about the future.'

'It's high-impact stuff,' said Joyce, leaning his elbows on his knees as he gained confidence. 'After BP's image disaster in the Gulf of Mexico, this is a game-changer: female CEO, ecologically responsible drilling, might even have a penguin swimming nearby, right, Gerry? Networks will love that.'

Gallen looked at the communications man in his four-thousand-dollar suit and Italian shoes and all he could see was the kind of administration fool that the Pentagon produced like spring flies.

'That's great, Dave,' he said. 'But penguins live in Antarctica, okay?'

'Really?' said Joyce, trying to make a joke of it.

'Yeah, really. Secondly, I think BP's spill in the Gulf was slightly more than an *image* disaster.'

'Of course, of *course*,' Joyce said, waving it away, now red in the face.

'And lastly, Dave, let's talk about high impact.'

Joyce gulped.

'High impact is a hit team killing Harry Durville and trying to bring the rest of us down with him.'

As he waited for Joyce to leave, Gallen could feel Aaron's gaze on him.

'So that went well,' said Florita, walking to the side-board and pouring herself a glass of water. 'Can we finish with the pissing contest already?'

'Sure,' said Gallen. 'I'll work up a security plan for the dive, but I think we have to find this newspaper reporter.'

Florita grabbed the TV remote as the Oasis logo appeared behind a business anchorwoman. The woman told the audience that Oasis had lost eleven per cent of its stock price in early trading on the NYSE based on unconfirmed rumours that the late Harry Durville had been secretly dealing with the Russians over Arctic Ocean oil.

The anchorwoman switched her attention to Microsoft sales and Florita hit the mute button again. 'Right now, I need less details, more results.'

'We're on it,' said Aaron, gesturing for Gallen to leave the office.

* * *

Gallen raced south along the river to the southern rail yard precinct of Calgary, an area known as Ogden. The text message from Winter had been brief: *2 @ Fallback 1*.

He was driving too quickly and his head was filled with plans and contingencies: the CEO was going down in the submersible, only to be taken off to a waiting boat. That'd be a job for Mike Ford. The reporter on the *Calgary Herald* would have to be collared and questioned. He still had the broader question of who bombed the plane. And where was Paul Mulligan?

Pulling off the Deerfoot Trail, he negotiated the maze of warehouses and truck loading hubs and drove along alleys filled with containers and machinery, loaders and security dogs.

At the end of a cul-de-sac called Ogden Dale Plaza, Gallen aimed under a sign for Britannia Oil Refining and drove into an abandoned oil storage area that Oasis had bought and mothballed six years earlier. Parking beside a white Chev van, Gallen scanned the area for unwanted eyes and climbed the outside stairs that led to the old administration offices looking over the Britannia switching yards and storage tanks.

Pushing into the building that doubled as the 'Fallback 1' in Winter's text message, Gallen pulled the SIG from his waistband. 'Anyone home?' he called as he scanned the panoramic view available from the elevated offices.

The internal door inched open twenty seconds later and a handgun was pointing at his chest.

'What have we got?' said Gallen, as Winter lowered the gun and walked to him.

'Two unfriendlies.' A shiner was starting around Winter's left eye. 'Followed them into the motel room and persuaded them to leave with us.'

'Put up a fight?'

'Sure did,' said Winter, reholstering his SIG. 'The big dude wanted to fight—Mike dropped him with a leg shot.'

'Cops?' Gallen looked across the vast rail yards for movement.

'I think we're clean,' said Winter.

'Think?'

'No tails, but you never know with these guys.'

'What do you mean?'

Winter shrugged. 'If they're Agency, then they're being tracked as we speak.'

'You got their phones?'

'No phones.'

That was good news and also bad news.

Moving towards the door, Gallen realised Winter wasn't getting out of the way.

'What's up, Kenny?' he said, trying to look over the big man's shoulder.

'I don't know who they work for, but I've seen these guys before. One is that lawyer dude from behind the Spanish bar in Del Rey.'

'The other one?'

'Remember I told you I saw someone in the back of that Bell cable van at Roy's?'

'Big black dude? Stuck his head between the front seats? That's when you knew it was a surveillance truck.'

'Yeah,' said Winter, biting on a new smoke and offering Gallen one. 'Him.'

'They alive? Talking?'

'Yep, and just.' Smoke streamed through Winter's nostrils. 'Mike's playing good cop, getting them coffee and donuts. I'm Freddy Krueger.'

Inhaling and looking away, Gallen thought about the next few minutes and how it could be crucial not only to doing their job for Oasis, but staying alive in the medium term. One lesson he'd learned in Mindanao and Afghanistan was that the intelligence fraternity was much harder on itself than it ever was on civilians or the hapless mules who got in the way. Once you declared for one side in the spy world, you were playing for keeps. When Gallen walked in that room and started insisting on answers, there'd be no going back. It would move from a simple snatch that could be explained away as an accident to a hostile act that would certainly be responded to.

'Before we go in there,' said Gallen, 'I need Roy off the farm.'

'It's done,' said Winter.

Gallen's blood pressure was ticking. 'Where?'

'Asked him not to tell me,' said Winter.

'What about his cell?'

'In the mail to a history lecturer at the University of Texas, in Austin.'

Gallen sucked on the smoke and ground it into the floor as he exhaled. 'Let's do this, Kenny.'

The room was a wooden-floored space that would have accommodated a tennis court. Natural light streamed through the glass panels in the roof as Gallen strode towards the backs of the two people duct-taped to the chairs. One was a normal-sized Anglo, judging by his shape, and the one on the right was larger—a leg wound was making a pool of blood around his left boot.

Nodding a greeting to Ford, who was making coffee at a small kitchenette, Gallen rounded the chairs and stood in front of the two captives.

The smaller man looked upset, quite unlike his cocky act behind the Spanish bar in Del Rey. The big one had a strapped leg and a smashed nose. He tried a smile. 'Howdy doody, cap'n.'

Gallen froze. He was looking at his old gunnery sergeant, Bren Dale.

CHAPTER 44

The revving of diesel locomotives wafted into the room, along with the clanking of rail cars and yelling brakemen. Gallen dragged a chair in front of Dale as Mike Ford escorted the other captive out the door.

Then they were two war veterans left with shared memories and not much more.

'You want to tell me what this is about?' said Gallen, sipping at the surprisingly good coffee.

'Why don't you start?'

'Okay. A special forces guy leaves 1st Recon and goes spying,' said Gallen, lighting a smoke. 'But he's spooking on his old CO, being a pest.'

Dale's head shook slowly, the pain from his leg obvious on his face. 'Shit, cap'n. Let me out of this, and we all walk away.'

'Like I walked away from that bomb in Harry Durville's plane?'

Bren Dale eyeballed Gallen. 'Didn't bomb no plane, boss.'

'Someone did.'

Dale looked away. 'I didn't ask for this.'

'You like going to my childhood home, pretending to be a fucking cable guy?' said Gallen softly. 'That a fitting finale to what we did on Basilan?'

253

'You like creeping round my daddy's offices?' Dale took a deep breath, his broken nose running with blood. 'Remember I asked you to reposition our direct action, that night on Basilan?'

'I do,' said Gallen.

'Remember I told you that the intel from the Philippines side was no good? That it was a fricking ambush?'

'I do,' said Gallen again, remembering a night that triggered a three-day retreat from the Moro stronghold. 'Christ. You were a spook all along?'

'I didn't say that,' said Dale, in a tone that meant Gallen had got it right. 'Point is, I told you something and you acted; you saved a lot of lives and you got a promotion out of it, last I heard. Now I'm telling you again.'

'Fuck, Bren,' said Gallen. 'You were DIA? Why didn't I know?'

'War on Terror, all that shit. The units had their staff intel briefings, business as usual. But DIA had their own embedded guys.'

Gallen could feel the anger welling in his neck. 'Why would DIA do something like that?'

'Same reason we invaded Iraq when we hadn't secured Afghanistan: clowns running the circus, know-it-alls who know nothing. Point is, I tried to warn you off this time round too.'

'When?' said Gallen.

'Suddenly pulling out of the gig,' said Dale, his face softening. 'Shit, boss, I thought you'd work it out: ol' Brenny just bails out, won't return your calls? He must be workin' again.'

'So who're you working for?'

Dale shook his head. 'The who don't matter.'

'What don't matter is that you hold out, Bren,' said Gallen. 'Kenny wants a close chat with that boy of yours.'

'Jesus,' said Dale, shaking his head and closing his eyes. 'You know about Winter?'

'Some.'

'No, I mean, you seen his sheet?'

'The Assaulters? ISAF?'

'You know what he did before they cut him loose?'

'Canadians set him up for a DD. Sign this or we fuck you.'

'Canadians had nothing the fuck to do with nothing, boss,' said Dale. 'He was on payback duty for the Agency.'

'Payback for what?' said Gallen, lighting another smoke.

'For that Jordanian bomber up in Khost,' said Dale, talking about the al-Qaeda double agent who talked his way into the CIA compound in Khost and detonated his bomb, killing seven Agency officers.

Gallen checked his surprise. 'Kenny?'

'Made six hits in thirteen days,' said Dale, smiling with the information ascendency. 'High-level dudes—al-Qaeda bankers and lawyers. Gaza, Penang, Amman and . . . Colombo I think it was.'

'Bullshit, Bren. Kenny was on secondment.'

'Bullshit, yourself,' said Dale. 'What you think all them Canadian and Aussie special forces dudes were doing in Kabul in the first place? Helping the Eurocrats fill out their paperwork?'

'ISAF head shed, in Kabul?' said Gallen, knowing the headquarters compound well. 'That's NATO, not Agency.'

'Sure,' said Dale. 'But not after the X Rotation.'

Gallen thought about it; Rotation X had been a controversial reorganisation of the ISAF system in February 2007, in which member nations started to contribute their own forces in a 'composite' structure, rather than the old integrated NATO command. It was seen as Washington trying to insert its own strategy and operations under an international banner.

'Well, after that, it was the sadists running the joint,' said Dale, grinning at the military's word for the Special Activities Division of the CIA. 'Fucking Bank of Langley, my brother. Holy shit.'

Gallen knew about the Agency's SAD, their paramilitaries and political operators. They appeared in forward operations bases, kept to themselves and only referred to themselves by first names. And when they needed to be saved from their own ventures, people like Gallen's Force Recon units and the Army's Green Berets were sent out into the night to retrieve them.

Standing in frustration, Gallen walked to the window and looked out over the rail yards. A police helicopter moved across the horizon in the distance.

Something tweaked a vague memory. 'Bank of Langley?'

'Billions in cash, boss,' said Dale. 'Sadists were buying up the warlords, trying to speed up the end game.'

'Just one big pool of deniable assassins, feeding at this lake of cash? That it?'

Dale shrugged, still smiling to himself.

'Forget about Kenny,' said Gallen, bringing the conversation back. 'You broke into my employer's house and stole something. Where is it?'

Dale deadpanned. 'Don't know what you're talking about, boss.'

'I can get Kenny in here.'

'But you won't.'

'Okay, then let's ask it another way,' said Gallen, annoyed that Dale was wasting time. 'Why the tail?'

'Orders.'

'Why? You've already got the Newport file.'

Dale's face creased in confusion. 'Newport?'

The floorboards creaked at the other end of the room. Gallen reflexively launched himself at the floor, rolling into the wall behind a storage cupboard as rifle fire whistled above his head.

'Stop,' yelled Dale, as Gallen pulled his SIG free of his waistband and shot at the door, where two men with rifles were posted. 'Stop, Gerry, I'll tell you, I'll tell you.'

One of the shooters at the door seemed to sag from a leg shot. The other hesitated, allowing Gallen to find his feet and get a proper grip on the SIG. Standing, he moved sideways from behind the cupboards so he was behind Dale as he poured fire into the far doorway, forcing the remaining shooter to yield.

Gallen estimated he had seven shots left in the fifteen-shooter. Standing slightly taller, he watched the door close as the door behind him opened: Winter.

As Gallen tried to calm his breathing, the door at the far end of the room was thrown open once more, and as Gallen and Winter shot at it, a rifle muzzle pointed into the room and fired a burst on full auto. Throwing himself back to the cupboard as the splinters flew, Gallen heard the screaming whine of a helicopter outside the window.

Standing slowly, he swapped a look with Winter, who crabbed down the other wall towards the shooters' door.

Holding his SIG in a cup-and-saucer grip, Gallen aimed it at the shattered window. Down on the concrete apron, two men—one of them limping—ran for the helo and jumped inside. Leaning out the jagged window and aiming, Gallen took five shots. The sixth created a spark off the rotors. As he steadied for the last shot, the helo lifted skywards, banking away into the clear Alberta skies.

Struggling to get air into his lungs, Gallen walked towards Bren Dale, freezing as he stood over his former sergeant. Dale's chest was torn open with a bullet wound, his eyes rolled permanently to the ceiling.

'Everyone okay?' said Gallen, checking himself as he said it.

'Mr Kevlar isn't so happy,' said Winter, walking back from the shooters' door, pulling up his shirt to examine a slug in his vest.

Gallen gulped at a dry throat as he walked through to Mike Ford in the other room. 'Where's the white dude?'

Ford pointed at the door flapping in the breeze.

'Ran?' said Gallen, moving to the door in time to see the man disappear behind an abandoned railway oil tanker.

'Like a robber's dog,' said Ford, looking through the empty window pane at the retreating helicopter. 'How's Dale?'

'Didn't make it,' said Gallen, still panting. 'Get anything from your guy?'

Ford and Winter swapped a look.

'Well? This is turning into a cluster. I hope we got something.'

'The bloke told us they didn't take a file from Florita,' said Ford. 'And they aren't investigating Oasis. Didn't know what we were talking about.'

'So who are they?'

'Don't know,' said Winter, lighting a smoke as he scanned the rail yards. 'But I think the lawyer dude is the boss.'

'Why?' said Gallen.

'Before you got here, he wouldn't let the black guy speak,' said Ford. 'Tried to do all the talking.'

Gallen and Ford followed Winter towards Bren Dale's sprawled body. Kneeling, the Canadian slit the flexi-cuffs on Dale's wrists and motioned with his head for Ford to help him. They eased the large body to the floor and Gallen smoked as Winter meticulously went through the former Marine's clothing and shoes. There was folded cash in his right chinos pocket, about $500 American and

$380 Canadian. Winter handed it to Gallen and then pulled a set of keys from the left pocket.

'Dale was the driver,' said Winter, handing over the keys. The black plastic grip of the main key featured an oval decal for the Ford Motor Co., but the keys had no identification on them, not even a registration number.

'There'll be a dark Crown Vic somewhere near the motel,' said Gallen, knowing that Winter already had it logged in his mind.

Gallen and Ford watched in silence as Winter undressed and searched Bren Dale, the Canadian doing a thorough but unpopular job—in special forces, every dead and injured body was a potential gold mine of information. Because special forces was largely recon, you had to get used to inspecting clothes and then orifices to see what could be learned.

Finding nothing, Winter walked to the kitchenette and washed his hands. 'Your buddy's working clean,' he said, shaking off his hands and then wiping them on his jeans.

Gallen looked down on the body, the USMC tattoo on Dale's left pec destroyed by the fatal bullet. 'You sure?' he said.

'No phone, no credit cards, no room key. Not even a watch.'

'That's pro,' said Gallen.

'That's deniable,' said Ford.

258

CHAPTER 45

After they'd searched around the motel for Dale's car and come up empty, they met back in the room Winter had rented. Whoever was chasing Gallen had a professional clean-up team to go with the helo and spooks.

Ford made coffee as Gallen tried to set them back on course. 'So let's go through it: about ten to midnight on the first night you're in here, you watch a heavily built black man move along the lower level, duck into a maintenance alcove and then through the door?'

'Right there,' said Winter, standing and pointing through the muslin curtains at a janitor's lock-up on the ground level.

'So you give him a few minutes and then you pick up a small movement?'

'See those bars, up high in the wall?'

Gallen saw an air vent in the cinder blocks. 'Yep.'

'The white boy leaves about ten minutes later. I took that to be the midnight change-over,' said Winter.

'And what happens?'

'Just before six in the morning, the white boy is back,' said Ford, handing out coffees. 'That was my shift.'

'So you wake Kenny and move on them while they're in the same room?'

259

'That's about it,' said Ford. 'The rest you know.'

'We need an ID on this leader. He had to be staying nearby. What's across the road?'

'Another motel,' said Winter.

'Let's rattle a cage,' said Gallen.

Winter was back in the car thirty-seven minutes later.

As Ford accelerated into the traffic, Gallen leaned over his seat. 'What we get?'

'Found this.' Pulling a white DVD from the inside pocket of his jacket, Winter handed it over. 'Told the maid that the night manager had left my umbrella in the room behind the counter.'

'So when she couldn't find it, you just helped yourself?'

'Something like that. Check the dates. I think that's the CCTV for yesterday.'

'Might be useful.' Gallen handed the disc back to Winter. 'We need something to play it on.'

'In my bag,' said Ford over his shoulder as they merged with traffic and got southbound on Crowchild.

Winter pulled a black laptop from the side storage compartment of a Cordura overnight bag and booted up. Inserting the DVD, he manipulated the images back and forth, reverting to the 'gallery' function that allowed him to select views around the motel.

'That's Dale, right there,' said Winter, turning the screen so Gallen could see. It showed a side view of the big man at a second-floor ice machine. He was dressed in a dark polo shirt and dark shorts and the time code had it as 11.52 pm.

'Bren making a drink before he takes his surveillance shift?'

'Looks like it,' said Winter. 'Let's find his room.'

Winter found another camera angle, froze the image and turned the screen for Gallen. It showed Bren Dale emerging from a motel door on the second level. The image wasn't clear enough to see the number on the door.

'Can we get it clearer, Mike?' said Winter.

'Yeah,' said the Aussie. 'Take a grab of the door, drop it into Photoshop and click on the button that says *Resolve*.'

'Shit,' said Winter, smiling as he shook his head. 'You're running Photoshop?'

As they passed McMahon Stadium, Winter looked up. 'Room number two-fifteen.'

Keying his cell phone, Gallen asked directory for the Capitol Motel and waited for the connection.

'Hi, John Green here, financial controller at Akron Precision Machinery, down in Ohio,' said Gallen, giving his cheeriest mid-western greeting. 'Could I speak with the manager of the Capitol Motel, please?'

A woman named Lucinda Davies came on the line and Gallen introduced himself again. 'Listen, wondering if you could help me with some housekeeping at this end?' said Gallen.

'Sure, Mr Green. What do you need?'

'This is embarrassing,' said Gallen. 'I'm going through an electronic expenses claim from two of our salespeople who stayed with you last night, in room two-fifteen?'

Gallen heard tapping on a keyboard. 'Yes, two gentlemen stayed with us, under the name Simon Smith. Is that the party?'

'Simon—that's him,' said Gallen. 'Top guy in our Rockies division, but, well, this is nothing to boast about.'

'I've seen it all before, Mr Green,' said the manager. 'If you're asking me to help you with a fraud inquiry, I can certainly do that for our corporate clients. I mean, you're paying the bills, right?'

'That's my point exactly, Lucinda,' said Gallen. 'Thank you for understanding.'

'What's the problem?'

'We've had this issue with salespeople claiming on a top-of-the-line rental vehicle, but they're actually driving a little Toyota.'

'Driving a hatchback, claiming for a Navigator?'

'That's it,' said Gallen. 'If I could get the vehicle rego they booked under, I can trace it back with the rental company. We have thirty-five reps on the road. This could be costing us thousands a week.'

'Okay, Mr Green,' said Lucinda. 'The vehicle is a Cadillac Escalade, Colorado plates.' She read out the plate number which Gallen transcribed on the back of a CAA map of Alberta.

'But this is weird,' said Lucinda. 'You said Akron Precision something?'

'Precision Machinery, yes,' said Gallen.

'Mr Smith paid with cash, but his card imprint was a Visa in the name of Royal Enterprises.'

'Royal?' said Gallen. 'Umm, yeah. That's our aviation parts division. Listen, thanks for the heads-up. I'm going to get my assistant to call back, set up an account with you guys. Might smooth things in the future.'

Gallen hung up and thought about the conversation. 'Kenny, go back to the security footage. Look for an Escalade with Colorado plates.'

'Why does that ring a bell?' Winter tapped at the laptop.

'That white guy who escaped. One of the crew behind the Spanish bar in Del Rey? He's travelling as Simon Smith and his Visa card is in the name of Royal Enterprises.'

'You got a rego number?'

They met the new recruit in a cafe on 8th Street south-west.

From the three names Aaron had provided, Liam Tucker's fitted best with what Gallen wanted for his fourth man: a retired Marine who'd served in Afghanistan and spent almost three years guarding high-ranking officers in Helmand Province before walking with his pension. Thirty-four years old, a little lost and openly glad to be sharing coffee with some military guys.

'How's the 'burbs?' said Winter after they'd made their greetings and been served their coffees.

'Christ.' Tucker whipped off his Orioles cap and ran his hand over his hair. 'My brother gets me this job as a mortgage broker and, holy crap, I don't know how people do it.'

'Gotta have stamina for them office jobs,' Ford smiled. 'All the incoming from behind.'

'Gets you between the shoulder blades,' said Winter. 'You worked personal security detail?'

'Sure,' said Tucker, sipping on the coffee and eyeing another table of customers who were hugging and calling each other darling.

'Worked PSD convoys, mainly out of D-2, and up to Marjah. All the pleasure spots.'

'Busy up there?' said Winter.

'Some,' said Tucker, not excited about it. 'It was okay, I guess, unless the routes leaked to Towelie, and suddenly there's no such thing as an abandoned car or a rock on the roadside. It's IED alley.'

'But you were doing an electrical trade,' said Gallen. 'Before you transferred to an oh-three.'

Liam Tucker turned and looked at him, and Gallen gave him a wink. An 03 occupational speciality—known as an MOS in the Corps—was a combat position like a mortar man, a rifleman or machine gunner. A Marine smart enough to demand an electrical trade did not generally switch to an infantry MOS. It translated to no career when he signed off.

'Shit,' said Tucker, slumping back in his chair, slapping his cap on his leg.

'Didn't have something to do with this concussion?' said Gallen.

Winter sat up. 'The what?'

'It's in his file,' said Gallen. 'But let's ask Liam.'

Shaking his head, Tucker looked beaten. 'Okay, I was two years in and I got concussed playing football. I recovered but I weren't seeing colours so well.'

Mike Ford laughed. 'So you couldn't see if a wire was yellow or red?'

Tucker fiddled with his cap. 'You know what the Corps's like, Gerry. They find you're colour blind and the clipboards take over.'

Gallen nodded. He knew about that particular bureaucratic hell. 'So you skipped the doctors and became a machine gunner?'

'Yep.'

'And then you're working personal security?' said Gallen. 'Why?'

'Cos I was tapped for PSD after my first tour in Afghanistan,' said Tucker. 'They needed gunners. I trained in Florida and they threw me in.'

'You okay?' said Gallen. 'I mean, after the shit?'

'Never did drugs, stopped drinking whisky,' said Tucker. 'Got a divorce. That what you mean?'

'No psych?'

'No, sir.'

'Okay, but understand: we work dry, we get hammered later. That work for you, Liam?'

'Like a dream, boss.'

Gallen dropped Ford and Tucker at Florita's house as the sun set. It was Sunday night and the security detail was going to co-locate in the house with Florita, drive her to work each morning and act as a bodyguard shadow.

Gallen was nervous, eyes darting to parked cars and people in the street as Aaron opened the door to the large house and ushered in the two bodyguards.

'I'll hitch a ride with you,' said Aaron. 'Got an address for Mr Flint, our reporter.'

Lighting a smoke on the approach path while Aaron got Ford and Tucker settled, Gallen scanned the street for people in cars and unwelcome eyes. His vision was acute and scattered, zooming from one potential hide to another. The attack in the Britannia Oil yards had put him on edge in a way that the bombing of Durville's jet had not. The crash in the snow and subsequent events were all reaction and counter-punching—just a blur of survival and necessity. This was stressful in a different way; it was like being a rat in a maze, someone waiting for him to take a wrong turn. Gallen wanted to get out of the maze for a while, have a chat with the watchers. His cell phone rang and Gallen mumbled his hellos on seeing the caller ID.

'Gerry.' It was Rob Stansfield, calling from Wyoming. 'Everything okay?'

'Sure,' said Gallen, surprised the lawyer had returned his call. 'I was remembering that night down Arvada, and after all that entertainment in the parking lot, you told me that if I ever needed a favour . . .'

'Sure did,' said Stansfield.

'Tell you what—gimme an hour of your time gratis, and anything over that you can bill to the Sweet Clover trust account. Fair?'

'Like I said, Gerry.'

'I need a company search on a Royal Enterprises. That's all I got, no location, no principals. It's a name on a credit card.'

'Okay. Royal Enterprises,' said Stansfield. 'You want the directors, right?'

'I want it all, Rob,' said Gallen. 'And I have a Hail Mary, if you're inclined.'

'Like what?'

'Colorado registration on a Cadillac Escalade,' said Gallen, hoping he wasn't pushing the friendship. 'You have any contacts in law enforcement?'

'I play golf with the sheriff on Sunday mornings. That count?'

'I like the sound of it,' said Gallen, then read out the rego. 'By the way, you ever hear from Yvonne's husband again?'

'Heard from his lawyers.'

'What they want?'

'To give me an apology, wanting to know if I was going to sue.'

Gallen laughed. 'She's a nice woman, Rob. You look after her.'

'About that,' said Stansfield.

'Yeah?'

'You don't know?'

'Know what?' said Gallen.

Stansfield sighed. 'I made my play, Gerry, but honestly? She talks about you more than she talks about those damn horses.'

Gallen ended the call as Aaron emerged from Florita's house, and they made for the van.

'So,' said Aaron as they sped back across the river to the Sheraton Suites, 'that wasn't you down at the Ogden yards this morning?'

'No comment,' said Gallen, eyeing the driver of an SUV beside them as they waited at a red light.

'You want to tell me what's going on?'

The light turned green, and Gallen let the SUV go in front. 'Why don't you start?'

'On what?' said Aaron.

'You think our new CEO is telling us everything?'

'She told us what she could.'

'Could?'

'She runs a public company,' said Aaron. 'Some of what she knows about Harry might not be for shareholder consumption. The New York Stock Exchange and the SEC may have something to say about it, see what I mean?'

'Is the Oasis deal with Reggie Kransk legal?'

'I don't know,' said Aaron. 'But Florita's a lawyer and if she's nervous about the subject, then Harry Durville might have left a headache. So, the Britannia yards, huh? Cops talking about a shoot-out, a body found with bullet holes in it?'

'Not now, Aaron.'

Aaron lit a smoke and gave a direction that would swing them south onto the Macleod Trail and down to Pump Hill. 'Thought I might be able to help.'

'Help with what?'

'Any problems.'

'I didn't shoot anyone, Aaron,' said Gallen.

'I know.'

Gallen gripped the wheel and made to swing to the shoulder but in Alberta they didn't put shoulders on their expressways. There was only concrete wall, and he straightened the van a few inches from the grey barrier and moved back to the speed of the traffic.

'Whoa,' said Aaron, legs stiff against the bulkhead.

'You know what, Aaron?' Gallen made himself breathe out. 'The fuck do you know?'

'One of the old crowd called me a few hours ago.'

'What'd he want?'

'Wanted to know the score.'

'Why?'

'Pentagon's been following an ex-spook's movements, Gerry, and the trail ended with a Calgary police report of a helicopter, gunshots and a former US Marine lying dead in a property belonging to Oasis Energy. As far as these things go, it was a courtesy call, see what's up.'

Gallen cheered up slightly. 'They said ex-spook?'

'What my man said.'

They drove in silence, the buzz of adrenaline filling up the car.

'So who's the ex-spy?' said Gallen. 'You get a name?'

'No. What's your involvement?'

'We abducted a team that infiltrated my father's house. They'd been tailing us since we met Mulligan in Del Rey. You wouldn't judge me for that.'

'No judgment,' said Aaron. 'But tell me you didn't kill the Marine.'

'It wasn't me,' said Gallen, watching the lights flickering on over the expressway.

'Who? Winter? Ford?'

'This going back to your buddy?'

Aaron snorted. 'I don't have a choice, Gerry. Don't play naive with me.'

'Okay,' said Gallen. 'We set a trap in a motel up near the university—'

'U of C?'

'Yep,' said Gallen. 'I got the call during that morning meeting with the PR guy. My team was holding them at the Britannia yards.'

'So?'

'So I go down there and discover that one of the team is my old gunnie, Bren Dale.'

Aaron's forehead creased. 'The guy who was suddenly unavailable for this gig?'

'That's him.'

'Who killed him?'

'I don't know,' said Gallen, shaking his head.

'So there was a helo?'

'I was about to let Bren go,' said Gallen. 'He would have backed off. He had a bullet hole in the leg and his heart wasn't in it, anyway.'

'So?'

'So I wanted to know why he's following me and suddenly there's shooters bursting into the room. They're firing at me, but when it's over there's a hole in Bren's chest.'

'What about the other guy?'

'The small white guy? We think he's working as Simon Smith—he didn't kill Bren, if that's what you're asking,' said Gallen. 'So, can we still operate?'

'I assume so, but we won't be welcome south of the border. Unless—'

Gallen looked sideways. 'Yes?'

'Unless we can give them a name.'

'The shooter?'

'The thought had occurred.'

'Shit,' said Gallen. 'What are we getting into?'

'We're in it already,' said Aaron, chaining a fresh smoke. 'Take this exit.'

CHAPTER 46

They watched the street from the van, the large houses of Pump Hill looking like mini-mansions in the dusk light. Gallen wasn't up-to-date on what print journalists earned, but this street seemed a long way above what most of them could afford.

Reaching between his feet, Aaron pulled up a black laptop bag and opened it.

'What's the plan?' said Gallen, lighting a smoke and letting his eyes wander along the street. A woman walked a dog, a man swept a driveway.

'Thought I'd return Mr Flint's laptop,' said Aaron, opening the laptop and booting up a blank MS Word document. Pulling down one of the menu bars, he selected 'record' and a red dot glowed at the bottom of the document.

Carefully closing it, he slid the computer into the bag and opened his door. For as long as the battery held out the laptop was now a voice-activated recording device networked to the other laptop in the van; whatever was recorded on the Word document's sound file was accessible on Aaron's computer.

'I'll give you fifteen minutes, then I'm coming in,' said Gallen, reflexively checking his SIG.

Aaron smiled. 'I'm gonna do this the subtle way, if you don't mind.'

Watching Aaron walk up the cobbled driveway, Gallen thought he saw a movement at a curtain upstairs.

The front door opened and a sensibly dressed woman made an inquiring face at Aaron, who went into his song-and-dance act.

Ninety seconds later, he was back in the van.

'How'd that go?' asked Gallen.

'Just Barry Long, from the subs desk at the *Herald*, returning Lars's laptop,' said Aaron.

'She say where he is?'

'Called away on assignment,' said Aaron, looking at the house. 'Urgent matter, had to go last night. Hush-hush.'

'Believe her?'

'No.'

'Why not?'

'Because Lars and Wendy don't have kids living at home. It's just them.'

'So?'

'So why does a housewife need two BlackBerries charging on the hall table?'

Aaron had barely clicked on the cellular networking icon when the MS Word document started transmitting.

'*The fuck was that?*' came the grumpy voice of a stressed man.

'Barry,' said Wendy. '*Barry Long? From a desk at work. Submissions?*'

'*Subs desk,*' said Lars, anxiety in his voice. '*Barry? The fuck he want, this time of night?*'

'*Dropped off your laptop, darling. It's right there.*'

'*My laptop's upstairs. What the—*'

In the van they could hear the sounds of a bag being unzipped and the shuffles and scrapes of the laptop being picked up.

'*This Barry—what'd he look like?*'

'*Tall, well-dressed. Quite stylish.*'

'*On all counts, that wouldn't be a sub-editor,*' said Lars, snarling. '*And if it was Barry, he'd be half in the bag by now. Was this guy drunk?*'

'No. *Very sober, very charming.*'

'Shit!'

'*What's wrong, darling?*'

The voices became more faint until they were mumbles. Then a door slammed and the muffled conservation ceased.

'Lars has left the building,' said Aaron.

'Backyard?'

'Probably,' said Aaron.

'You stay here, I'm going for a stroll down the alley.'

Gallen walked around the block, turned into the back lane behind the house and felt his phone buzzing against his leg.

'Yep.'

'The garage door is going up,' said Aaron. 'Lars is moving.'

Gallen jogged around the block, wondering how he got here, in the middle of Calgary suburbia. When he was in the jungles of the Philippines and then the hills of Afghanistan, it used to suddenly occur to him that the life he'd chosen always seemed to drop him someplace he didn't belong, to wander through someone else's life. To operate in a place you knew nothing about, amid people you didn't understand, you had to burn at a high adrenaline rate, had to maintain hyper-vigilance and observation until it became automatic. And once you lived your life in that way, long-term paranoia was the inevitable result.

He felt that now, breath coming fast, heart banging in his temples, total, full-body alertness—a two-legged wolf padding across the concrete, eyes scanning, ears straining, and pity the poor motherfucker who threatened him now, 'cos he'd draw down the SIG and drop 'em where they stood. And he'd do it like he was in a trance.

First the tyres screeched with the over-revved engine and then came the sickening crunch of steel on steel, shattering the serenity of the evening.

Picking up the pace, Gallen rounded the corner and saw a blue Nissan Maxima buried in the front of their white van.

Drawing his handgun, he approached the crash site at a fast jog as the driver of the Maxima got to the passenger window of the van and started screaming.

Gallen saw Aaron's hands held up in surrender and a man—Lars Flint—shouting at him. 'I told you fuckers, I'm not doing it anymore. I'm not playing this game no more!'

Lars was purple in the face with rage. Porch lights came on along the street and Gallen stowed his weapon as he closed on the man.

'Lars?' he said, as the newspaper man kicked at the front tyre of the van.

'I want them out of my life,' screamed the journalist. 'Okay? This ain't 1992 no more, okay? I'm fucking sick of this shit.'

Looking at Aaron, Gallen mouthed the word 'drive'.

As his partner jumped across to the driver's side, Gallen had a quick look around and decided he was well situated in the darkness afforded by the van.

Slapping the reporter hard on the face, he walked around the stunned man and put a fast carotid hold on him, cradling his fall as he fainted.

Dragging him backwards across the pavement, Gallen saw the van door slide back and Aaron's hands reach out for the limp journalist, pulling him in as Gallen shut the sliding door.

Leaping into the passenger seat, Gallen put his hand over his face as Aaron backed away from the smashed Maxima and then gunned the van's engine as they raced down the street, right front fender scraping on the tyre.

'Fuck,' Gallen panted as they took a left and then right and got onto Southland, aiming for the rush-hour crowds on the Macleod Trail.

'You got a plan for Lars?' said Aaron, eyes in the rear-view mirror as much as they were on the road in front.

'Plan was to shut him up, get him off the street.'

'Like they say in the classics,' said Aaron, sweat on his forehead, 'you break it, you own it.'

'Find us a quiet spot,' said Gallen. 'It's time for a chat.'

CHAPTER 47

At the dark edges of a trucking hub beside Union Cemetery, Aaron stopped the van and turned in his seat.

Gallen sat on the bench seat beside Lars Flint, whom he'd handcuffed with duct tape and blindfolded with a sweatshirt tied around his face.

'You know who I am?' said Gallen, soft and friendly.

'No,' said Flint, a quaver in his voice. 'I don't even know *where* I am.'

'Are you Lars Flint?'

Flint's throat bobbed. 'Yes. Are you going to kill me?'

'Are you a journalist?'

'Yes.'

'Are you a senior writer on the *Calgary Herald*?'

'Yes, sir.'

'Have you recently written about Russian oil companies?'

'Shit,' said Flint, hysteria in his voice. 'You're the *Russians*? Oh, for Christ's sake.'

'Who told you to write the story?' said Gallen, maintaining calm, just like they taught you in special forces.

'Fuck!' said Flint, back heaving. 'I'm so sick of this.'

'Who gave you the information, Lars?' prompted Gallen. 'You help me with this and I'll help you with your problem. That fair?'

273

Gallen swapped a look with Aaron as Flint cried softly. Across the huge concrete apron, trucks emitted their high-pitched beeps as they reversed into loading bays. The nocturnal mission of shifting stuff all over North America was going about its business, but Lars Flint wasn't going anywhere.

'Who made you do this, Lars?'

'A man.'

'What kind of man, Lars?'

Flint sniffed back his tears; his BO smelled of fear but at least he hadn't peed himself. 'Calls himself John Leonard, he's been feeding me for years.'

'Feeding?'

'You know—twigging me to stories, pointing me in a direction?'

'No,' said Gallen. 'I don't know. Tell me.'

Flint sighed. 'He's a businessman, based in Vancouver. But he's usually got a tan so I assume LA. He never denied it.'

'So what does John do for you?'

'He might bump into me in the street, take me to lunch, that sort of thing.'

'What do you talk about?'

'He usually has a snippet, an insider view, on something interesting.'

'Such as?'

'Well, the Oasis connection with Russian oil was fairly interesting. Or Canadian government interests in the US defence industry, or details of a left-wing politician's secret bank accounts, or a bureaucrat's undeclared share trading. That sort of thing.'

'The sort of thing that makes Canadians look bad?'

Flint fiddled his fingers. 'Okay, so he's probably a spook. Big deal. The stories are always true and that's my job: to tell the truth.'

'So you're working on a piece about how a senior writer at the *Herald* is a cipher for US foreign policy?'

'Fuck off.'

'Perhaps a story on how a lifelong newspaper guy is buying a mansion in Pump Hill? How, in a row of million-dollar houses, he was offered one for four hundred thousand and all the paperwork and bank loans were all ready to sign? Just a fluke, really.'

Flint turned his sweatshirt-wrapped head towards Gallen. 'You Greenpeace or Save the Whales? Something like that?'

'I'm the guy who's gonna make the pain go away, Lars,' said Gallen.

'Just like the others, right? You people are all so full of shit.'

'Others?' said Gallen. 'What others, Lars?'

'The ones who came into my house this morning,' said Flint, exasperated. 'Came downstairs for a cup of coffee and they're standing there, in the damn kitchen, while Wendy's at the supermarket.'

'Who?'

'Spooks, heavies. They didn't have name tags.'

'What did they want, Lars?'

'The leader wanted to know what you want to know.'

'About John Leonard?'

'Yep, and I couldn't help him any more than I can help you,' said Flint. 'I don't have a number; he always contacts me.'

'And that was it?'

'No, this guy wanted to see the report.'

'What report?'

Flint chuckled. 'That's what I told this guy, and he hit me.'

'The report,' said Gallen. 'Does it have a name?'

'No,' said Flint. 'But it has a colour. Red.'

'What's in it?'

'He didn't say. He just accused me of having been given the report before I wrote the story.'

'Did you have a report about Russian oil interests and Oasis?'

'No,' said Flint, 'I just took notes. When I said I'd have to see something, Leonard laughed and told me to ring Oasis and see what happened when I repeated the allegations.'

'So who's the guy?'

'The leader?'

'Yeah.'

'Early forties, receding black hair,' said Flint, with a reporter's eye for detail. 'About six-one and strong, but not athletic, if you see what I mean.'

Gallen saw exactly what he meant but refused to jump to that conclusion.

'What did he sound like?' said Gallen.

'Like a businessman more than a heavy,' said Flint. 'And he had a weird way of addressing me.'

'Yeah?'

'Yeah, he kept calling me "Ace".'

CHAPTER 48

Dropping Flint gently to the ground behind a series of large headstones, Gallen checked the darkness of the Union Cemetery and jogged back to the van. They accelerated along one of the wide boulevards and swung into the sweep of traffic on 25th, before joining the Macleod Trail, which would take them north and back to downtown. It was four minutes before either Gallen or Aaron said a word.

Gallen lit a smoke, turned down the radio. 'So, I guess this is the part where I demand an explanation or I'm taking my crew and going home.'

'Shit, Gerry,' said Aaron.

'Shit yourself, Aaron Michaels. I signed on to this in good faith, but I ain't putting my boys out there until someone fills me in.'

Aaron exhaled. 'How do I make it good again?'

'You can start by telling me why Harry cut Mulligan loose,' said Gallen. 'Then we can discuss what it is about this Nanook report that makes Mulligan want to double back and make life difficult. I have a CEO to protect, remember? And to do that I have to keep my team in one piece.'

'Can we get a drink?'

'We can get a haircut, if that's what you want,' said Gallen. 'I just want answers.'

Gallen finished a phone-in with Winter as Aaron arrived at the booth with two beers.

'I was Mulligan's 2IC,' said Aaron, opening a bag of nuts and pouring them into a wooden bowl. 'I was new, learning the ropes, realising that Harry was a bit of a handful.'

'With the company he kept?'

'Yeah, the drinking and fighting, the whoring. The whole nine yards. I'd been on the job ten, eleven days and Harry wanted to hit Vegas—it was two in the freaking morning. He was on the tables and drinking by five am and he went for fifteen hours straight.'

'Really?' said Gallen.

'I swear to God. And I mean those were hard hours, man.'

'Tough gig.'

'Shit, yeah,' said Aaron, leaning back and sipping at the beer. 'In my previous life I'd spent time in-country, running counter-intel around the consular community, so Mulligan thought I was the guy to create a perimeter on Harry.'

'Get to the spies before they got to him?'

'Precisely,' said Aaron, casing the bar. 'The job description was basic, but you try doing that with Harry Durville when he's drunk and dragging a posse of hookers up to his suite. You can't be with the man all the time, so we had Piers and the other Brits.'

'What happened?'

'We were starting to do these meetings up in the Arctic Circle with the Inuit and it became obvious these natives had some serious muscle and intel behind them.'

'You knew this?'

'No, Gerry,' said Aaron. 'I just knew, right? Just like you know there's pros around when you walk into an airport concourse that's under surveillance. You just know.'

Gallen nodded. 'So what happened?'

'I went to Mulligan and told him that I'd like to do a project on the natives and the TTC, the Transarctic Tribal Council.'

'Just get the upper hand?'

'Sure,' said Aaron. 'So Mulligan, who knew exactly what I was saying, 'cos the asshole's been a military spook in combat zones, he stonewalls me.'

'How?'

'Says he's got it covered, says I'm imagining things, says he has total one hundred per cent faith in me and the Brits.'

'Okay,' said Gallen, chuckling at the fob-off.

'It annoyed me but I decided to do it from the bottom up instead, and I briefed the Brits. Turns out Piers—the ex-Para—had been getting the bad vibe too. We'd been at a settlement in the Davis Strait, between Baffin and Greenland, and the Brits had been screwing around with their Harris, scanning channels while they waited for the meeting to end.'

'And?'

'And they picked up the kind of interference that one of them—a Royal Marines Commando—had been trained to detect during Operation Iraqi Freedom.'

'What was it?'

'Signal jammers.' Aaron shrugged. 'What are the chances that you fly to an isolated bunch of Nissen huts on an ice floe in the Davis Strait and Eskimo Nell is running a signal jam from her kayak?'

'Chances are slim,' said Gallen.

'So I told Piers I'd been cut off from this subject by Mulligan, and Piers told me he'd take it up with Harry himself.'

'He could do that?'

'Yeah, Harry and Piers got along well. Couple tough guys with hard backgrounds. Shared the belief that just about everyone else was a complete fairy.'

'So?'

'I didn't learn all this until the dust had settled,' said Aaron, 'but basically, Harry rings Newport Associates, who do a lot of private intel for the oil and gas industry.'

'Tell me about Newport,' said Gallen.

'Newport is to private intel what Halliburton is to oil services or Blackwater is to private armies,' said Aaron. 'They used to run reports for foreign governments until 9/11 came along, and then Uncle Sam got the shits with that. So they reverted to their core business—doing intel and counter-intelligence for North America's largest corporations.'

'Never heard of them,' said Gallen.

'But they've heard of you, Marine.'

'Okay, so Harry goes to Newport?'

'But he does it without Mulligan knowing,' said Aaron.

'Ouch,' said Gallen, smiling. 'He cut out the main man?'

Aaron laughed. 'Totally cut him out.'

'So?'

'So,' said Aaron, 'I'm working up a security schedule for Harry one morning, up in head office, and Mulligan storms in.'

'Angry?'

'Purple. Asks me what the fuck I know about the TTC and Reggie Kransk and why he's been ant-fucked.'

Gallen drank the beer.

'I knew nothing about it—then,' said Aaron. 'My ignorance must have been obvious. I didn't even know who Reggie Kransk was. Mulligan left me alone after that, but that must have been the morning that Harry got the report from Newport and challenged Mulligan with it.'

'Why?'

'Because the Brits were suddenly sacked, but Mulligan was telling Harry that they got a better offer in Iraq and just fucked off.'

'So Mulligan was working for Reggie, keeping his agenda secret?' said Gallen.

'I assumed that—so did Harry,' said Aaron.

'And that's where we come in?'

'And that's where you come in,' said Aaron. 'I'm sorry about the icy reception but you were a Mulligan hire, with Mulligan loyalties.'

'You ever see the report?'

'No, just what Florita told you, which is pretty much what she told me.'

'Pretty much?'

Aaron sighed. 'Okay—she told me no more details, just that the report could never see the light of day.'

'Why not?'

Aaron ignored the question. 'The point, Gerry, is that with Newport's regular accounts, they offer a burn service.'

'What's a burn service?'

Aaron looked around. 'Let's say you're a CEO of a big corporation, and you're in discussions with new partners in . . . shit, I don't know, Rwanda—but you want to know more about them.'

'Okay,' said Gallen. 'I call Newport Associates, right?'

'Sure,' said Aaron. 'But because you don't want your company annoying a regulator, or the shareholders, you want to be sure that having been informed of something, you can turn around and disavow.'

'Disavow? You mean, deny that I know anything?'

'Yes.' Aaron smiled. 'Newport informs you that your new partner, the Minister for Resources, is also a trafficker in stolen children, or an opium grower. But you look at that information, and as repulsed as you are, you don't see how that is going to mess with your intention to take as much copper ore out of there as possible.'

'Jesus,' said Gallen, shaking his head. 'Newport tells me more than I want to know . . .'

'So you pay an extra million for the burn service, and Newport will burn any evidence or paper trail that led to that report.'

'Burn?'

'Wipe, eradicate, burn,' said Aaron. 'The slate is clean—there're no files slipped to journalists, no whistleblower sending copies to the SEC, no tree-hugger standing up at the AGM and waving a bunch of papers, asking embarrassing questions about what happened to a tribe in the Andes.'

'So the only evidence that I know the truth about Reggie Kransk and the TTC is sitting in the actual report, which is in my possession?'

'Hah!' said Aaron, leaning back, slugging his beer.

Gallen was missing something. 'What's funny?'

'Newport Associates' burn service doesn't come with one report,' said Aaron. 'It comes with two.'

'So one report goes missing from Florita's safe . . .' said Gallen. 'And the other?'

Aaron raised his glass. 'The other, my captain, is a mystery.'

Gallen's memory swirled in and out of focus, the days peeling back, the layers coming off, thinking. Thinking!

As he looked at Aaron, he remembered Harry Durville's empty satchel, remembered wondering aloud why the managing director of a massive company would go all the way to a meeting and not carry any papers. He recalled a girl in Red Butte, drinking beer and telling him that Mulligan was cosy with Donny McCann.

'You okay, Gerry?' said Aaron. 'Looks like you seen a ghost.'

'I think I know where that second report is,' said Gallen, finishing the beer in one draw.

'Where?' Aaron leaned forward.

'Don't worry about where,' said Gallen. 'Just get me a helo.'

'No, Gerry. I have to know.'

'This is a burn service.' Gallen stood up. 'You get to disavow.'

CHAPTER 49

'This Martina Du Bois . . .' said Kenny Winter, two hours into the flight to Baker Lake. 'I don't get where she fits in.'

Taking the *Ariadne* launch document that Winter had been reading, Gallen snapped out of his obsessive thinking about the hit teams.

'Isn't she that ArcticWatch activist?' said Gallen, looking at the page of the document entitled *Personnel*. 'I saw her on CNN.'

'Yeah, so why's she on the maiden dive of this *Ariadne* thing?' said Winter. 'I thought the green protestors were against drilling in the Arctic?'

Reading down the list of the vessel's complement, Gallen saw Martina Du Bois' name and three men from ArcticWatch.

'It must be some publicity stunt.' Gallen flipped through the file of backgrounders at the back of the press kit and found the one headed: Ariadne *gets the thumbs-up from environmentalists*. 'There it is,' he said, handing over the press release.

Reading from it, Winter raised an eyebrow. 'Who's this Dave Joyce, at the end here?'

'Vice-president, corporate communications. The head PR guy for Oasis,' said Gallen.

Winter smirked. 'He sure writes a pile of shit for a veep. Listen to this: "*ArcticWatch has awarded the Oasis Energy Ariadne Project five 'Polar*

Bears'—the highest award *ArcticWatch* can bestow on a company for actions that support the environment and the indigenous concerns of the Arctic Ocean." '

'Five Polar Bears,' said Gallen as the stewardess brought him a coffee from the kitchenette at the back of the Challenger jet. 'That sounds important.'

'Well it must be, because these ArcticWatch people are going down there with the Oasis drilling crews and engineers.'

'You sure?' said Gallen.

'What it says.'

Picking up the phone built into his seat, Gallen put in a call to Aaron.

'Gerry? Where are you?'

'In the air,' said Gallen. 'Just going through the plan for the *Ariadne* launch. What's this about the ArcticWatch people going down there? I assume we're taking them off with Florita?'

'Ixnay on that, Gerry. They're down there for the first three-month shift.'

'Why?'

'I'm just the security guy, Gerry, case you hadn't picked it. This comes from above.'

'This a Joyce thing?'

'I think Joyce helped create ArcticWatch,' said Aaron.

Gallen paused, the bullshit factor too strong. 'Okay, Aaron. So nothing to worry about?'

'Nothing.'

The Oasis Challenger landed at Baker Lake Airport, powering through the slush and ice, past the famous green terminal, to where an Oasis Sikorsky S-92 was waiting.

Putting on their arctic gear, Gallen and Winter checked their SIGs and deplaned, walking across the wet surface to where a pilot was giving the thumbs-up in the cockpit of the large yellow helicopter.

'You really think that retrieving this Newport Associates report is going to stop the teams?' said Winter as the beeping of the turbine's starter motor sounded.

'I don't know,' said Gallen as he took the loadmaster's hand, 'but if we have the thing, we at least control that much.'

He let himself be pulled into the cargo hold and took a seat as Winter was hauled in to join him. Leaning into the flight deck, Winter handed over the coordinates and joined Gallen in the load space seats.

'You okay?' said Gallen, as the Canadian was seated. He seemed nervy.

'Remember I said that there was probably more than one team out there?' said Winter. 'There was something weird about those shooters at the Britannia yards.'

'You mean they didn't come on like a rescue team?'

'I guess that's it,' said Winter. 'You think they killed Dale?'

'Rather than let him talk with me?'

'Yes.'

Gallen took the helmet and visor offered him by the loadmaster as the side door was slid shut with a bang. 'I don't know, Kenny. I'm all out of answers. Could be nothing to do with Oasis—could be other shit.'

Kenny turned slightly as if to talk, but Gallen pulled on his helmet and the conversation was over.

The loadmaster joined the pilot on the flight deck and the helo lifted into the sky.

It was early dusk when the helo crested the ridge and flew down towards the site of the crash.

Gallen and Winter leaned into the flight deck, watching the site in the red glow as the pilot banked off to land. Feeling emotional, Gallen pulled on his mittens and his Thinsulate double-layer balaclava before pulling the fur-lined hood forward and zipping the arctic parka all the way to his nose.

Helping each other put on their military snow shoes, they prepared to trek across the drifts. The Marines also issued hard plastic snow shoes for icy conditions, but Chase Lang had supplied the 'tennis racquet' variety—the much-hated footwear that 1st Recon Marines were forced to patrol in during their stints at the Mountain Warfare Training Center in Bridgeport.

Throwing the small backpack over his right shoulder, Gallen waited for the loadmaster to drop the fold-out stairs and walked down them into snow.

The two men struggled through the deep snow to where a hump of packed powder was all that showed the world what had happened in this place. The snow was about to start its thaw, but there'd been enough flurries to cover the whole crash site in a white veil.

Halfway down the gentle fifty-yard slope to the plane wreck, the area was illuminated as the helicopter's floodlights went on. The last rotations of the rotors whooshed through the air and then Gallen was alone with his breathing.

Arriving at the starboard side of the fuselage that had sheltered the survivors from the elements, Winter pointed to where the entrance should be. Removing their fold-up shovels from their backpacks, the two men dug for several minutes until the snow caved in and the doorway to their hut was exposed.

The air accident investigators and the RCMP detectives had torn down the sacking and insulation that had once formed a door, and as they looked around the fuselage, illuminated by their flashlights, they smelled the burning rags and gasoline soot that had defined their survival.

Going to the ruined cockpit, Winter announced that the investigators had removed the flight deck avionics and probably the black box too. Harry Durville's corpse was gone and so were those of the two pilots. Donny McCann's body was back in Los Angeles, where his mother had buried him.

They stood in silence, looking at the beds that Harry and Donny had been afforded as they died, given pride of place closest to the meagre fire.

'So,' said Gallen, 'Donny McCann was probably working for Paul Mulligan. His job was to steal the documents Harry Durville was carrying . . .'

'The documents that were safe inside the bodyguard perimeter, but which weren't so safe when one of the bodyguards was the thief,' said Winter, lighting a smoke and offering one to Gallen.

'Now, we know that Donny didn't have the documents on him when he died.'

'Check that, boss,' said Winter. 'We buried him naked, and there weren't no documents.'

'Correct,' said Gallen, exhaling a thick plume of smoke into the cold air. 'When we retrieved Harry's satchel, there was nothing in there.'

'That's right. Which means he stashed them somewhere in the wreck.'

They searched the fuselage in a grid pattern for half an hour, establishing where Donny McCann could have hidden Durville's documents. They went through every leather-bound seat that hadn't already been stripped for its insulation. They searched all the overhead lockers—which were underfoot—but came up empty.

'He couldn't move,' said Winter, exasperated and panting for breath as he finished sorting through a pile of debris. 'So I don't know that searching in the snow is going to achieve anything.'

Taking a seat, Gallen realised the helo's spotlights were illuminating the fuselage and he switched off his flashlight.

'It's like Donny just chucked the documents down a hole,' said Winter, hawking and spitting.

'A hole?' said Gallen. 'A hole!'

'Yeah?'

'That's where Donny was thrown when the plane landed,' said Gallen, standing. 'I found him in that ice cave, under the dome.'

'He couldn't move, even then,' said Winter.

'Yeah, but he was conscious and he'd been that way longer than me.'

'You think Donny did the theft on the plane?'

'I don't know,' said Gallen, moving out of the fuselage and into the night. 'But we're going to find out.'

The two of them slammed their shovels into the peak of the dome as they were held suspended in their safety harnesses beneath the thumping Sikorsky.

The lights from the undercarriage made Gallen squint and the noise and wind effect was terrible as they tried to break through the dome, a death-trap that turned solid as concrete when you needed to dig through.

After ten minutes, Winter broke through the crust and promptly disappeared into the dome, the safety rope tensing as he was held aloft. A split-second later, Gallen also fell into the cavern.

'Okay, Oasis One,' he said into his mic, as he dangled in the dappled light. 'Take us down.'

The winches let out the cable and the two of them landed on the wet floor of the cave, the noise and light from the Sikorsky bouncing around crazily.

'This way,' said Gallen, unclipping from the safety line.

Leading Winter through the cave, he struggled to get his bearings: which way had he walked when he'd regained consciousness that afternoon? The light effects from the helo were disorienting and within minutes every twist and turn looked the same.

'Let's try that again,' said Gallen, as the cavern reduced suddenly to a tunnel that a medium-sized dog would have to squeeze through.

Retracing their steps, both of them slipped on the ice as they struggled to make headway up the slight incline, the snow shoes giving no purchase on the shiny surface. Small gutters had been cut in the ice where the melt water flowed.

'Need my golf shoes,' said Winter as they crested a small rise and paused.

Panting, Gallen looked around, the air temperature dropping into the minus-twenty range with the coming of night. 'This way,' he pointed, and stepped out.

The first slip was comical and as he swung his arms around for balance, Gallen almost laughed. Then he slipped again, his feet going straight upwards, leaving him horizontal in mid-air.

'Gerry!' yelled Winter above the din of the helo, and as Gallen hit the ice slopes his snow shoes broke off and he was accelerating like an Olympic luger. Gathering speed across the surface, Gallen plummeted and bounced towards the ice wall at the bottom of the slope, screaming as he did so and praying to a God he hadn't spoken to since his teens. Gallen's head bounced off the concrete-like floor, and he looked ahead and saw the ice wall approaching at twenty-five mph.

Readying himself for death—or life in a wheelchair—Gallen shut his eyes and tried to relax his body. The final ground before the collision suddenly gave way, and he was falling and accelerating. And then the momentum had ceased and Gallen opened his eyes. He was lying in a pool of water, in a wide guttering at the edge of another ice cave.

Pulling himself out of the incredibly cold water, Gallen gasped for air, the nightmare memory of pleurisy returning. All around him was the noise of the helo and Winter's shouts.

'Kenny, Kenny,' he said into the mic, scared he was going to pass out with the shock of the cold water, 'I'm okay. I went under the ice wall. Repeat, I'm okay but wet.'

Shaking as he turned, he made his fingers wrap around the flashlight in his parka pocket and fumbled with the power switch. 'Shit,' he said to himself, not wanting to ever feel as cold as he had after that plane wreck. He'd promised himself it would never happen again.

Finally getting the flashlight powered up, he swung it around as his jaw seized shut.

'Gerry,' came Winter's voice in the helmet. 'I'm coming. Stay dry, I'm coming.'

'Roger th-th-that,' said Gallen, forcing it out as his nervous system tried to shut down. Turning slowly with the flashlight, he recognised the cavern; it was where he had found the prone form of Donny McCann.

Movement came from the corner of his eye, and in the gloom he could see a fluoro-yellow helmet poking through the ice culvert that he'd just slid through.

'Here, boss,' came Winter's voice over the speakers in Gallen's helmet, but now the voice sounded like it was echoing up from a well. The cave was starting to take on a dream-like quality as Winter arrived in front of Gallen.

'Shit, boss. Fuck!' he said.

Gallen, his brain swirling towards unconsciousness, was unable to talk or smile or even shut his mouth; his face had completely seized up.

Tearing off his own parka and balaclava, Winter ripped at Gallen's sodden clothes as he stood like a helpless infant. Gallen's brain was taking him into dream realms, back to the hot baths his mother used to run him after hockey, young Gerry soaking in the warmth while his parents argued about turning a sensitive boy into a hockey thug, Gerry lying there in a halfway world between his mother's desire for him to be educated and his dad's need to have at least one son who could spend time in the bin without it ruining his day.

The life was draining out, it felt like the end, as Winter pulled the dry balaclava and parka onto Gallen. And here he was sixteen years after refusing to take the hockey scholarship to the University of North Dakota, because he wanted to join the Marines instead. Turning his back on the one thing that would have made both his mom and dad proud—getting a degree while playing for the Fighting Sioux—to become a soldier.

His mother. Why didn't he call his mother?

The first slap felt like a dream. The second made his eyes open and focus.

'Gerry!' the man shouted, and slapped him again.

'Th-th-th . . . there,' said Gallen, his whole body shaking with the exertion of speaking. He couldn't make his arm move and so he pointed with his forehead.

Winter aimed his flashlight at the floor in the middle of the cavern. 'Here, Gerry? This it?'

Closing his eyes, Gallen made himself nod once.

Winter walked away into the cave, the beam from his helmet fixed on the ice floor. He was wearing a layer of thermals and a jumper and nothing else. The flashlight beam crisscrossed in the gloom and then it was pointed in one direction.

Gallen's head felt disembodied, as if it was floating away. He felt a sadness, as if he was closer to his mom than he had been since he was sixteen, yet still so far from her.

He felt like crying but his face wouldn't work. And then Winter was in front of him again, slapping him and pointing, and then the Canadian's arm was around his shoulder and under his armpit and they were moving, Gallen forcing each slow step as his body cried to shut down, brain-first.

Standing against the wall, Winter put on his helmet and Gallen listened as he told the pilot and loadmaster what to do. The noise

290

built and then the entire centre section of the roof was collapsing, the Sikorsky's landing gear sticking through, the landing lights lighting up the cave like a Broadway stage.

The loadmaster lowered the harnesses and Gallen watched helpless as Winter—now suffering from the cold himself—clipped Gallen onto the line and gave the thumbs-up.

As Gallen was raised into the Sikorsky's belly, he watched Winter disappear like an apparition.

Hands grabbed at him as his mind floated away, into a dream of hot baths and a mother who had left him, but still cared.

And then the sleep came.

CHAPTER 50

His mouth was glued shut. He became aware of the crunch of the
cotton pillow case and the soft sound of a TV on low volume.

Opening his eyes, Gallen let himself acclimatise as he did his test
of toes and fingers. He was dressed in a foil suit inside several quilts.
Feeling okay, but groggy, he tried to raise his head and was hit
by a swoon that made him groan and hit the pillow again.

'Shit, boss,' came Winter's voice, as Gallen squinted to stop his
mind spinning. 'Don't move till I get the quack, okay?'

The doctor arrived eight minutes later and spent an hour going
over Gallen's vital signs, his eyesight, cognition and blood pressure.

'So, it's a Monday, you say?' she said, getting Gallen propped up
on several pillows against the hotel bedstead. 'Want another guess?'

Squinting against the daylight, he felt a Krakatoa-size headache in
its early stages. 'I give up,' he croaked.

'Try Wednesday,' she said, standing and packing her bag. 'You'll
be okay, but you're lucky you have a fast-thinking friend.'

'And a helo on standby,' said Winter, winking.

'He needs a day of rest, okay, Mr Winter?'

'Gotcha, Doc.'

'I mean it. A full day. I'm holding you responsible.'

Giving Winter her business card, she said goodbye and left.

Grabbing a cold beer, Winter sat on the end of Gallen's bed and handed him a water-damaged manila file. 'I've read it—your turn.'

Gallen looked: inside were the red pages of the Newport Associates report, titled *Operation Nanook*. Behind it was another report which, Gallen realised, contained the original backgrounders on Gallen and his team as prepared for Harry Durville.

'You want tea, coffee, water?' said Winter.

'Tea, thanks,' Gallen croaked.

Shaking out the report on Operation Nanook, Gallen sipped as he read: Rurik 'Reggie' Kransk, born 1952 in the Arctic Siberian city of Naryan-Mar; son of a visiting Russian scientist and an Inuit woman who died young from alcohol-related illnesses when Reggie was four; raised by his uncle as a fisherman; left school aged twelve, became captain of a fishing boat when he was sixteen, bought his own boat when he was eighteen.

Never a dissident in the strict Soviet sense of the word, Reggie was nonetheless associated with organised crime in the major cities. Under the Soviet commissars, all produce had to go through the state-owned agencies for distribution to shops and restaurants. Local gossip said Reggie got rich fast because he supplied the mob-run restaurant trade of Moscow and Leningrad with the best seafood, without it having to spend days in a ministry warehouse while the paperwork was completed.

By the time he was twenty-five, he owned a flotilla of fishing boats and a fleet of planes that flew the catch directly into Moscow. Taking advantage of Moscow's indifference to its Inuit citizens—known as Nenets in Siberia—and its desire to 'autonomise' them out of sight and out of mind, Reggie Kransk established the Gruppa, a collection of Nenets families around the Barents Sea who had long attempted to keep their fishing grounds free of Soviet control and commercial intrusion, and now had a focal point with Reggie's money and his influence in Moscow. With the Gruppa, Reggie controlled a million square miles of Arctic fishing grounds by the mid-1980s.

Gallen speed-read the details. He chuckled as the writer of the report noted that Reggie had skilfully cultivated the West's adoration of ethnic minorities by getting the Gruppa included in various United Nations and World Bank development programs. Greenpeace had made them immune from protests about whales and seals, because they were an oppressed ethnic minority; the Soviet Union had honoured their claim on 'traditional' fishing grounds, largely under pressure from the UN; the British television network ITV had made a documentary on the Nenets, and Reggie's cohorts had flown in from their villas in Monaco and Sardinia to dress up for the cameras.

At one point Gallen laughed out loud.

'What is it?' said Winter.

'This writer has it in for poor old Reggie,' said Gallen.

He skipped to the part headlined *Perestroika*. In 1988, said the report, as the Soviet Union was collapsing from within, the Gruppa's identity changed from a simple business box at the Naryan-Mar Post Office to a corporate address in Zurich, with Swiss lawyers, accountants and bankers. On the same date as the corporate shift, the Gruppa was renamed the Transarctic Tribal Council and was registered with the United Nations Development Programme.

'Holy shit,' said Gallen.

'What?'

'That Transarctic Tribal Council? It's owned by Reggie Kransk.'

'You can own something like that?' said Winter.

The report's author concluded with a mix of facts and speculation. From Gallen's perspective, it looked as though Reggie's move to Zurich had thrown a veil over his and the TTC's affairs.

There was a final paragraph which surmised that the TTC had started as a group of Nenets fishing families, defending their ethnic rights from an oppressive regime, but had morphed into a powerful front for the Bashoff crime family. The Bashoffs were a Moscow-based operation that throughout the 1970s and 1980s had run the unlicensed restaurants, nightclubs, casinos and brothels frequented by the Soviet elite. They had formed a company called ProProm, taken over a small Siberian state-owned oil and gas company in 1990, renamed it Thor Oil, and promptly secured the sea-bed drilling rights in the fishing grounds once controlled by the Gruppa. As the Arctic Ocean opened up with the melting ice caps and the increased viability of the North-West Passage and Northern Sea Route, the Bashoffs used the Inuit territorial claims via the UN not simply to secure drilling rights across the Arctic Ocean, but to shut out the companies that comprised Big Oil: Shell, BP, Chevron, ExxonMobil, ConocoPhillips and Total.

Effectively, Reggie Kransk's connections with the gangster-owned nightclubs and restaurants under Soviet rule had turned into a force to rival the world's largest oil companies. Most of this extraordinary expansion had been hidden behind the Inuit claims of the TTC, claims willingly taken up by the West.

The final line of the main report said it all: *It is the view of this firm that Oasis Energy—by entering into heads of agreement with the TTC—is not securing cooperation from the true tribal inhabitants of the Arctic Ocean, but is an unwitting participant in the true aim of this agreement: Russian domination of oil-drilling rights in the Arctic Ocean.*

An appended report at the back was called *Risk Assessment*; Gallen skimmed it. It was only three pages and was filled with small sub-heads entitled *Personnel Risk*, *Finance Risk* and *Political Risk*. It was Newport summarising the obvious: partnering with people like Reggie Kransk and the Bashoff family delivered a lot of power to the partners who controlled a flawed or corrupt political process. Just as such connections could aid Oasis Energy, so too could they scuttle their plans without legal recourse.

Gallen flipped to the final page and was about to close the report when he saw a hand-scrawled notation in the margin, just below the sub-head *Technology Risk*. Turning the page on its side, he saw the words *Star Okay* and a line drawn from those words to underline a phrase in the risk assessment. The underlined words were *strategic power source* and *negative potential*.

Gallen dropped the report on the bed. He was too exhausted even to feel outraged by what he'd just read. Outrage would have to take a back seat while he let the fear sink in.

'This isn't the kind of thing we can speak about,' he said, almost in a whisper.

Winter nodded. 'I know. We go to all this trouble to grab something, and it's no better than a death warrant.'

'This goes straight to Florita and Aaron. It's now their headache.'

'No arguments here,' said Winter.

'By the way—thanks, Kenny,' said Gallen. 'For, you know, back there and all.'

'Gave me a scare, boss,' said Winter, sipping on his beer. 'When I found you in that cave, you were like dead but still standing.'

'I think I was hallucinating,' said Gallen, his own voice sounding far away.

'I know you were.'

'How?' said Gallen.

'You were talking to your mom,' said Winter, avoiding Gallen's eyes.

CHAPTER 51

Gallen watched a replay of the Bruins and Maple Leafs on the hotel TV while sipping herbal tea to stay warm. Winter got off the phone to Calgary and shook his head. 'Can't get the Challenger up here till seven tonight at the earliest. Larry's saying it'll be more like nine.'

The alternative was a ten-hour milk-run flight that hopped to either Edmonton or Winnipeg before catching a jet into Calgary. In Canada's north, cold wasn't the only problem; distance was equally daunting.

'Well, maybe that gives us a chance to look into something,' said Gallen.

'Like that Jackie?'

'I think we can assume Jackie didn't own that house, and that Jackie isn't a tribal elder in the *National Geographic* sense.'

'Okay,' said Winter, grinning. 'So what?'

'You might want to call up the Sikorsky.'

'Why?'

'Because I want to get back to basics, see what's what.'

'Like?'

'Like the soldiers from the Little Bird helo,' said Gallen. 'One we found dying in the snow and we ratted him.'

'He had that accent, you didn't think it was Russian. But we found nothing on him.'

'And I shot another out of the helo, up behind the lookout.'

'Yeah, you did,' said Winter, keeping one eye on the Bruins. 'So?'

'We didn't rat him,' said Gallen. 'Judging by the newspaper reports, the Mounties never retrieved his body.'

'Why are we going to do this?' said Winter. 'You're supposed to be resting, boss.'

'Because now we've seen this report, it's time to assess our watchers. Who's to say this other guy was working clean?'

'Long shot,' said Winter.

'We're up here anyway. What's the harm?'

Winter wasn't convinced. 'So you think Mulligan is trying to retrieve the Newport report?'

'Someone is; why not Mulligan?'

'And Bren and Simon Smith may have been another group?'

'Sure.' Gallen nodded. 'But if you can have two crows on the road kill, why not three?'

'So, Reggie's men bombed the jet?'

'Well, I keep thinking about that soldier's language and his accent,' said Gallen. 'And I don't believe it was Russian.'

'No?'

'No, Kenny. I think there's another crew in this.'

'I promised that doctor you'd rest, Gerry.'

'And you promised Jesus you wouldn't swear,' said Gallen. 'How's that goin' for ya?'

The skies were clear and there was no wind as they poked the snow banks with avalanche probes: long, thin poles that rescuers used to find bodies under the snow.

The weather being fine, Gallen had asked the pilots to leave and give them two hours alone. Now, after the first hour, Gallen sat panting beside Winter as they ate sandwiches from the hotel kitchen.

'Coulda sworn it was around here,' said Gallen, still feeling weak.

298

In front of them, halfway into the large snow bowl that Florita had slid down for her life, was the chopped-up area they'd just covered in a grid about thirty yards wide. Gallen had been certain the shooter had fallen into this part of the bowl.

'I shot from this rock, and the helo was right there,' he said, happy at least for the sun on his head. The northern tundra played tricks on the eyes, making everything look the same. They'd tried to trig it back by sight-lines, but the area wasn't yielding a body.

Looking across the snow bowl to the other side, Gallen focused on the overhang at the top of the opposite rise. The thick ice and snow cascaded off the lip of the overhang but there seemed to be a space under the cascade and a small trail in the snow leading away from it.

'What would that trail be?' Gallen pointed across the bowl.

'That'd be a fox,' said Winter.

Gallen looked at the Canadian. 'Would a fox show interest in our shooter?'

'Sure,' said Winter. 'They'd save the carcass, bury it somewhere.'

Gallen looked up the slope. 'It'd be too heavy to drag up to the den.'

'So they'd drag it downhill,' said Winter, pointing. At the bottom of the bowl was a small ravine that led into the neighbouring bowl. 'They'd want it where the sun don't shine, down there in the shadows.'

Finishing their lunch, they waded down the side of the bowl to the ravine and walked through it, shoulder to shoulder, probing the snow with their poles at every step. They worked their way into the next bowl then came back through the ravine, probing again. Nothing.

'Shit,' said Gallen, gasping for air. 'I can't do too much more.'

'Let's think like the fox,' said Winter, looking around. 'I want to keep the meat preserved, so I drag it downhill to a ravine and bury it . . .' He pointed his probe at the ravine. 'There. Under the overhang.'

'The fox could drag the body that high?' said Gallen.

'No, the fox would dig straight back from the floor of the bowl.'

Probing along the flat face under the overhang, they still found nothing, until Winter put his hand up. 'That's hollow.'

Pulling fold-up shovels from their backpacks, they scooped away the snow under the ravine's overhang until there was a small cavern in front of them. Hands on knees, catching his breath, Gallen looked up and into the darkness. At the base of the hollow was a body in black arctic fatigues. The shooter from the helo.

'Shit,' smiled Gallen, stepping towards their prize.

'No,' said Winter, hand slapping across Gallen's chest.

Pulling up, Gallen looked at Winter, who was pointing at the overhang. 'You don't wanna be under that when it comes down, boss.' Pulling a climbing rope from his backpack, Winter made a loop in it and beckoned Gallen forward. 'Use your pole to push up his ankle.'

Leaning forward, Gallen got the twelve-foot avalanche pole under the soldier's booted left foot and levered the ankle up so Winter could get a rope under the heel. The Canadian got the loop over the ankle at the fourth try and they dragged the body out into the open. The man's face had been eaten off and most of his entrails pulled out.

'Is the fox going to take exception to this?' said Gallen, looking around, trying not to focus on the partly eaten soldier.

'Fox will stay away, but we could always get a visit from Mr Grizzly, wanting to know what we're doing in his meat-locker.'

Winter kneeled beside the soldier and started with the pockets in his parka and insulated fatigue pants. There was a packet of PK gum in a chest pocket of the parka, and two full rifle magazines in the other. They were twenty-five-round clips from the Checkmate company and had rubberised pull-grips on the bottom of them, a sign that the shooter had experience.

'Pro,' mumbled Winter, checking the other pockets and opening the parka. Against the man's left armpit, where there were still military thermals, was a small military two-way radio which was slung across the chest, a mic attached to the man's throat.

On his belt was a 9mm SIG Sauer handgun, which Winter checked for load and action and pushed into his own parka pocket. There was a G-Shock on his right wrist.

'Much the same as the other dude,' said Winter, standing. 'Hi-Tec boots, generic arctic fatigues and thermals, standard mags and ammo for an M14 DMR—M1A, if you're getting fancy. Even the watches are straight out of the PX. Nothing to ID these boys. They're working clean.'

Gallen thought about it, his breath having returned. You could often get a feel for an enemy by ratting him—small elements usually provided clues. Elements on this shooter suggested Western forces, probably North American. The clothing and weapons could have come straight out of Chase Lang's warehouse in Longbeach. The watches were a favourite of US soldiers and even the gum was standard North American. Yet the swarthiness was not right and neither was the accent of the other soldier they'd found.

It was almost as if this crew had dressed themselves deliberately to deceive people like Winter and Gallen.

'PK?' said Gallen, accepting a smoke from Winter. 'Don't the boys all chew Extra these days?'

'Yep,' said Winter, dragging on his smoke. 'And there's this.'

Looking down, Gallen watched Winter's boot hit the shooter's hip, where the thermal leggings met the shredded thermal top.

'What?' said Gallen.

'If you're from Wyoming or Saskatchewan, would you wear your cotton underwear *underneath* your thermals?'

Gallen laughed. Once cotton was wet, it made life uncomfortable, so North Americans went naked under their thermals. This shooter's white cotton underwear was sticking out above the thermal leggings.

Winter kneeled, put his smoke between his teeth and pushed the thermals down. 'The dude's not used to snow, is my guess.' Pulling out the back of the underwear, he tore the elastic band off and gave it to Gallen.

Reading the label of the underwear, Gallen laughed. It said, *Delta Galil Industries. Made in Israel.*

301

CHAPTER 52

Gallen woke to a beeping sound as the cellular network kicked in again. As he opened his eyes the Challenger's engines depowered slightly and he felt the aircraft tipping for an approach into Calgary.

'Coffee, boss?' came Winter's voice from behind.

Turning, Gallen croaked a 'yes' at the Canadian, who was poised at the kitchenette. Above his head, on the bulkhead, the middle nautical clock labelled *Calgary* said it was 2.19.

Shaking out the fatigue, Gallen accepted the mug of coffee as Winter took the facing leather-bound seat and offered him a smoke.

Lighting up, they looked out the window where the darkness was touched only by the intermittent red flash of the Challenger's lights.

'What if they're Israeli, but working private?' said Gallen, picking up the conversation they'd been having before he'd fallen asleep. 'I mean, have we really picked a fight with the Mossad?'

'I've been thinking about the private angle,' said Winter. 'But even the ex-IDF, ex-Mossad dudes, they only work private 'cos Tel Aviv is getting something out of it.'

Gallen sipped coffee. 'In that case, we're back to what I was saying before.'

'What's a bunch of Israelites doing in the snow, taking shots at us?'

'Yep,' said Gallen. 'That.'

'You gonna take that?' Winter nodded at Gallen's cell on the wide armrest. 'Got a message, didn't you?'

Picking it up, Gallen cleared the text message and dialled into voicemail: Rob Stansfield, calling from his law offices in Wyoming, five hours earlier.

Grabbing at the pen and pad on the armrest, Gallen scribbled on it as Rob's voice gave him the details.

'The owner of the dark Escalade at the Capitol Motel is Royal Enterprises,' said Gallen, reading from his note.

'Same as the Simon Smith Visa card.'

'Correct,' said Gallen, waking up with the coffee and cigarette. 'Royal Enterprises has lawyers and accountants acting as its directors and its bank is in Los Angeles. But Stansfield recognised the company secretary's name. He's based in Denver.'

'Colorado plates.' Winter stared out the window.

'You okay, Kenny?' said Gallen.

Winter nodded, still looking out the window. 'Yup.'

'I mean it, man,' said Gallen. He'd seen this sudden change in his men when he was in the field and it usually suggested unspoken fears about a gig, or it came after a soldier had received bad spouse-mail. Either way, Gallen's job had been to pounce on that introversion before it acted out in ways that got people killed.

Winter sucked on his smoke and massaged the bridge of his nose as he winced.

'Better out than in, Marine,' said Gallen, bringing the volume down to a whisper, increasing its impact.

Deciding to give Winter some time free of eye contact, Gallen stood and walked to the head. Washing his face and drying off, he ran a comb through his thin dark hair and stepped back into the cabin where Winter was looking at the ceiling.

'So?' Gallen sat down and grabbed his coffee.

'So,' said Winter, the prairie drawl so slow that a casual observer would think this man simple. 'That Escalade at Del Rey, with Colorado plates?'

'Yep?'

'I thought it might be a coincidence,' said Winter, tapping ash, his face having set solid. 'But it ain't no coincidence, not after that shit in the Britannia yards.'

'What coincidence?'

Winter sighed. 'They ain't chasing you, boss. They're after me.'

'They?'

'Old shit, from the Ghan,' said Winter.

'Who?'

'Don't have a name.'

'What *do* you have?' said Gallen, annoyed at the evasion.

'Unfinished business,' said Winter.

'They don't want to kill you,' said Gallen. 'So what? Snatch you? Interrogate you?'

'Both,' said Winter. 'You don't need to be involved.'

'I'm already involved, Kenny—'

'I'm sorting it out, soon as we land.' Winter nodded slowly in the same way Mike Tyson used to before a fight.

They held stares for twenty seconds, before Winter turned away. 'Sorry, boss. That's the best I can do.'

'Roy,' said Gallen. 'He really safe?'

'Safer than me or you,' said Winter. 'Please trust me to sort this out.'

'Can I trust you, Kenny?'

'With your life,' said Winter. 'I'm good for it.'

Zipping his Carhartt jacket against the cold, Gallen hurried across the car park blacktop, tiny ice crystals crushing under his boots as they approached the white van in the yellow glow of the flood-lights.

Waiting at the passenger door while Winter put a mini Maglite between his teeth and did a quick IED check under the vehicle, Gallen reached into his pocket and came out with a depleted pack of Marlboros. Pushing his fingers into the soft foil, he found the last smoke as the steel pressed firmly into the indentation behind his left ear.

Gallen dropped the Marlboros and spread his fingers as he lifted his hands. A man's hand gripped his right elbow and pushed upwards.

'Hands on your head,' the man whispered.

As Gallen put his hands on his head, the man's hand dropped to the SIG in his waistband and whipped it out in a fast, smooth action. The opportunity to attack was gone and as the barrel pushed harder into his head, Gallen watched another man, dressed in black, shuffle to the side of the van with a handgun held cup-and-saucer.

As Winter emerged, Maglite between his teeth, Gallen was about to warn him but something heavy descended behind his right ear and the last thing he saw was the tarmac racing towards his face.

Gallen, his hands flexi-cuffed behind his back, opened his mouth and allowed the man who called himself Simon Smith to put two Tylenol 3s onto his tongue. Gulping at the offered bottle of water, Gallen got the painkillers down as the volcano in his skull started to erupt.

'Didn't need to hit me,' he said, shifting his butt backwards along the lino flooring to get better support against the wall. The room was large and looked like it was part of an abandoned showroom.

'No I didn't,' said Simon, who looked to be in his early thirties, sandy hair, pale eyes. He was dressed in a pair of chinos and a plum-coloured polo shirt. 'But it's not every day I render a couple hard-ons like you and Winter.'

Gallen detected an East Coast born-to-rule accent beneath the tough-guy act. 'Could have asked me what you wanted,' he said, the throbbing lump behind his ear making him nauseous.

Simon laughed. 'Really?'

'Yes, really.' Gallen shut his eyes against the stars dancing in his vision. 'At the very least, you want a man to get hit? Hit him yourself.'

Simon's face hardened very quickly. 'Who said I didn't hit you?'

'Hah,' said Gallen, smiling. 'No soldier's gonna boast that he hit a man from behind.'

Simon stood up, a sneer on his face. 'You're cocky for someone in such a lot of shit.'

'Cocky is relative,' said Gallen.

'Yeah?'

'Yeah,' said Gallen, conversational. 'Like, the guy who's gonna kick your ass, break your jaw? He's relatively more cocky than the dude who slaps other dudes from behind.'

'Shut up, Gallen,' said Simon, hand reaching for his pistol.

'You office guys sure like violence for a bunch of pansies who spend their lives avoiding it.'

The 9mm handgun came out, and found its level at Gallen's forehead. He looked back, making himself control his heart rate. 'Safety's on, Simon. Use your right thumb.'

'Fuck you, Gallen,' said Simon. 'The whole war-hero thing doesn't impress me.'

'I need the news, not the weather,' said Gallen, flinching from a piece of spittle. The 9mm's barrel pressed into his forehead and he relaxed, knowing he'd beaten the spook, or whatever he was.

'You could die here today.' Simon's face twisted. 'Medals or no medals, it doesn't worry me.'

'Where's Kenny?' said Gallen.

'Mind your business.'

'You got nice legs, Simon. You do ballet?'

The pistol slapped across Gallen's left cheek and blood flowed freely out of his left nostril.

'I said, shut up, Gallen!'

Gallen had won: the office boy was losing it. Now he wanted him slightly closer.

'That's a real sissy slap, Simon,' he said with a smile, as the blood ran onto his lap. 'Back home there's girl hockey players with more stand-up than you.'

A cloud formed under Simon's face and he stowed the 9mm in his belt as he reached forward and grabbed Gallen's hair. Simon's fist drew back; as he readied to throw the punch, Gallen leaned to his right and hooked his right leg, sweeping it back hard against the outside of his assailant's left knee, dropping Simon to the mat.

Rolling his left leg across Simon's body as he fell to the lino, Gallen kneeled over him and ducked into a punch that glanced off his left cheek. Using his momentum, Gallen threw a fast head-butt directly into Simon's front teeth.

Hearing the teeth snap and the involuntary gasp of pain, Gallen used the brief moment of shock to force his manacled hands down behind his hips to Simon's belt. Grabbing the handgun, he rolled away and sprang to his feet.

Fumbling with the weapon, trying to get the safety off from a back-to-front position, Gallen turned away from Simon and aimed the pistol. The first shot went off before he had full control and the bullet hit the plasterboard. As Simon panicked and tried to crawl backwards on his ass, Gallen felt his hair being grabbed and a barrel being forced into his eyeball.

A deep voice told him to drop it.

Gallen's adrenaline was peaking but the man behind the weapon had killed before, judging by his voice.

Dropping the 9mm to the floor, Gallen stood straight, panting as he looked at the man behind the pistol.

'Shit,' he said, looking at the big dark face as he caught his breath. The pieces of the puzzle were falling into place. 'Royal Enterprises, huh?'

'King of Chev,' said Ern Dale. 'And don't you forget it.'

CHAPTER 53

'I didn't kill Bren,' said Gallen, fast as he could.

'I know,' said Dale, eyes steady.

'You know? Then what's this about?' said Gallen, nodding at Simon Smith.

Several yards away Simon groaned as he found his feet, gingerly touching his mouth, which was bleeding down his shirt.

Dale shook his head. 'It's about boys and men, right, Gerry?'

'Story of my life.' Gallen sniffed back blood. 'Where's Kenny? We've got things to do.'

'Kenny's gonna be spending some time with me, Gerry.'

'He works for me, Ern.'

'Have a seat,' said Dale, trousering the pistol and walking to a picnic table with three steel-framed chairs around it. 'Maybe you can help me.' Pulling a chair out for Gallen, he yelled across the room, 'Simon, get us some coffee and bring those cookies you hidin'. The chocolate ones.'

Simon left the room, dripping blood.

'That's some fancy fightin', Gerry,' said Dale, lighting a smoke. 'Takes me back to the old days and those instructors at Bragg. Made us fight with wrists tied up, with ankles tied up. Hated that trainin'.'

'Fort Bragg?' said Gallen. 'That's Army. Green Berets?'

'Maybe.'

'Thought you was Corps? Thought Bren was in your footsteps?'

Ern Dale laughed. 'No, Bren knew if he walked into an Army recruiting office, I'd know before the day was out.'

'So he joined the Marines?'

Dale shrugged. 'I told him, Gerry. I told him, *Son, one Dale, in one war—that's enough for Uncle Sam. I gave up my youth for that shit, and I ain't giving up no son for that too.*' He looked away and when he looked back his eyes were wet and his face was hard. 'And he goes out on one job for me, and . . .'

'I'm sorry.'

'His funeral's tomorrow, Fairmount. Fourteen hundred. Bren would want you there.'

'Fairmount?' said Gallen. He would have expected Dale to be buried at the military cemetery. 'Not Fort Logan?'

'You think that's selfish, Gerry?' said Dale, a challenge more than a question.

'Just surprised.'

Ern Dale played with his fingers. 'Yeah, well. He's in the military section of Fairmount. You be there?'

'I'll try. If I get out of this alive.'

'Then be straight with me and we all walk away. My word on that.'

'Shoot,' said Gallen as Simon arrived with a thermos flask and two plastic mugs. He poured the coffees, his face a mess of drying blood.

'Black and one,' said Gallen, not taking his eyes off Simon, who threw a handful of sugar sachets on the table and dropped the cookies.

'Hands,' said Dale, pointing at Gallen.

Simon started to argue, but Ern Dale's sudden eyeballing worked faster than a TV remote. Snipping Gallen's wrists free, Simon took a seat away from the table and sat with his 9mm on his lap.

Dale's face changed as he turned to Gallen. 'So, where's the money, Gerry?'

Gallen poured the sugar into his coffee. 'What money?'

'Don't be clever, Gerry. I don't want you, just the dough.'

'I don't know enough to be clever, Ern,' said Gallen, picking up Dale's disposable cigarette lighter and using it as a swizzle stick in the coffee. 'This about Durville money? Oasis money?'

Dale's nostrils flared and he offered Gallen a cigarette. 'You want me to believe you spend all this time with Kenny and you don't know about the money? Shit, Gerry. Soldiers only talk about two things, and the other one's women.'

Gallen shrugged. 'I mean it, Ern: what money?'

'A lot of money, Gerry,' said Dale. 'That's what money.'

Gallen's mind was doing backflips. Kenny had told him on the plane that he was going to deal with the Royal Enterprises connection. But he only said it once the company was connected to Denver— and, thought Gallen, to Ern Dale. Who was Dale working for? He had to tread carefully because a lot of money and a lot of ignorance was a dangerous combination. He didn't want to mouth off and get someone killed.

'Tell me, Ern.'

'No,' said Dale, sipping the coffee. 'You tell me, Gerry. Where's the money? Where's it stashed?'

'You think I'm running around in the snow, getting shot at, 'cos I've got a stash?'

'I don't know,' said Dale. 'But I know something belonging to my friends is now in the possession of a certain Canadian shooter.'

'Your friends?'

'Let's just say that Kenny goes out to do a little job for some important people and he don't come back with what he should come back with.'

'I don't follow.'

'My friends expect their operators to skim a little, take what they can hide in their pants,' said Dale, opening his palms in the gesture of a reasonable man. 'It's hard out there and no one gets paid what they worth. But when you take the whole fleece from these people, there's consequences.'

Gallen sagged a little, dragged on the smoke as he thought about it. What had Kenny got himself into? 'So this is a spook thing, right, Ern? You doing clean-up duty for the Pentagon? Bunch of spooks missed their pay-day, they call in their old buddy Ern to track it down?'

'Don't play games, Gerry,' said Dale, crushing out his cigarette. 'Where is it? On the farm? You got Roy on the job?'

'No, Ern.'

'That lawyer, right? Or that bank? You were in there an hour and they got safe-deposit boxes down there, Gerry.'

'I didn't know that.'

'Yeah, but Kenny does, I bet.'

'Look, Ern—'

Dale held up his hand as if something had just occurred to him. 'Hey, how about this, Gerry? That girlfriend of yours. She keeping something for ya?'

Gallen blushed. 'I don't have no girlfriend.'

'Sure you do, Gerry. Fine-lookin' filly. Looks like . . .' He turned to Simon and clicked his fingers. 'Who that Hollywood actress you and Bren say she look like?'

'Diane Lane,' said Simon through the bloody rag he was holding to his mouth.

'That's it,' Ern said, facing Gallen. 'Diane Lane. That's who—'

'Her name's Yvonne and she knows less than me, Ern,' said Gallen, understanding that Dale was trying to push him.

'Or Momma? She doing well for herself, Gerry. Got that nice place round Diamond Head.'

Gallen tried to control his response. Ern Dale was doing to him what he'd just done to Simon. Trying to bust him up a little, get him talking loose and emotional.

'Well, Ern,' he said through clenched teeth, 'just as we're getting all friendly, you have to make it like that.'

'Don't have to be like that, Gerry.'

Gallen took a deep breath. 'You're not talking to Kenny?'

Dale swapped a look with Simon.

Gallen didn't like it. 'Where's Kenny? He okay?'

The noises started as a distant scuffle and the three of them stopped and listened.

And then a shot rang out.

CHAPTER 54

'Simon,' said Dale, raising his 9mm and waving it at the door. 'Check it out.'

Getting to his feet, Gallen looked to the door as multiple shots suggested people firing back.

'Let's wait, Gerry,' said Dale. 'We still got business.'

The gunshots abated and male voices yelled from another part of the building. Gallen's instincts were to take shelter, find a weapon, organise a defence or counter-attack. He could now see a second doorway at the other end of the empty showroom and he wondered what was behind it.

As the voices got closer, Gallen noticed Dale's expression changing.

'Stay there,' said Dale, checking his pistol as he moved towards the door Simon had just exited.

Gallen moved in behind Dale, not wanting to stand out in the open.

'You deaf, Gerry?' said Dale, swinging around and levelling the handgun. 'I said stay there.'

Gallen raised his hands slightly and stopped. As Ern Dale turned back to the door, a dark-clad figure appeared in the doorframe, his handgun rising at Dale and Gallen.

'Shit,' said Gallen, diving for the wall to his right. It was Paul Mulligan.

The gunfire started as Gallen slid against the wall and dropped to a crouch. Splinters flew off the doorframe where Mulligan had just been as Dale returned fire.

'Ern, it's me—Mulligan,' came the voice from around the corner. 'Paul Mulligan.'

'The fuck are my boys,' yelled Dale, aimed-up at the door. 'What you do with my guys?'

'It's a misunderstanding, Ern,' came Mulligan's syrupy voice. 'Gallen's got something of mine, that's all.'

'So join the club,' said Dale.

'We've got Winter already,' came the spook's voice. 'Let me have Gallen and you walk. I got no fight with you.'

'Got no fight with you neither, Mulligan,' said Dale, 'so you be on your way and I'll get on with my business.'

Gallen had heard enough. If Mulligan and Dale were going to make a deal, he'd be the loser. Eyeing his backpack on the floor at the far wall, Gallen broke from his position and sprinted the twenty yards to the second door.

Spinning, Dale let a shot go at Gallen and it zinged into the lino in front of his feet, making him stumble. As he dived behind the picnic table and chairs, sliding into his backpack, he watched Dale swing back to the main doorway in time for Mulligan to enter again, this time with an M4 assault rifle.

Grabbing the backpack, Gallen got to his feet in a panic and made the door as Dale took a hit and went down. Bullets smashed up the doorframe and the ceiling of the stairwell on the other side as Gallen burst through.

Panicked, gasping for air, he took the stairs three at a time as he made for the fire exit at the bottom of the stairwell. As he hit it and threw his weight into the locking bar, he felt his shoulder almost break as he bounced off and fell to the concrete.

Locked. Who the hell locked a fire door?

Looking around, Gallen struggled for air. There was no other exit. He was trapped. He'd just disobeyed one of the first commandments of special forces training: don't enter a situation you can't get out of.

He thought about running back up the stairs, but as he looked up a leg kicked back the shredded door and then Mulligan was standing on the landing, black overcoat over a dark suit with no tie. With the M4 carbine held across his midriff, he looked more like a Chicago gangster than a Pentagon spook.

'You like making me work for this, Gerry?' he said. 'This is how you want it?'

'You employed me, Paul,' said Gallen, not getting enough air. 'This has been a wall-to-wall cluster.'

'Let's make it simple, Gerry, 'cos the cops are on their way and I'm not hanging around.'

'Where's Kenny?' said Gallen.

'Here's a better question,' said Mulligan, padding down the steps but keeping the black carbine trained on Gallen's chest. 'Is the Newport report in that bag?'

'You know the answer to that,' said Gallen.

'Throw it here and that's your end, okay, Gerry?'

Gallen smiled. 'Trust me, I'm a spy. Right?'

'Throw it here or I shoot you and pick it up myself.'

Gallen had nothing left, but he had a reputation and that might be worth a bluff. 'Can you shoot me dead before I draw down the SIG in this bag, Paul?'

Mulligan stopped on the steps, his shoes crunching on dry concrete as they looked at one another.

'That's your gamble,' Gallen continued. 'Office guy making a fifteen-yard shot? You might hit me, but if you don't kill me then I draw down and put three slugs into you before I even hit the deck.'

Gallen watched Mulligan's throat bob, then the M4 was rising to Mulligan's eye-line. Gallen started his prayers: there was no SIG in the bag, there'd be no shoot-out, and to take down his opponent he'd have to run up twenty stairs.

The gunshot came quickly and Gallen winced, hoping he got it straight through the heart. He embarrassed himself by shutting his eyes.

But he wasn't hit. Opening his eyes he saw a spray of blood, then

Mulligan's legs folded and he spilled face-first down the remaining stairs in a clatter of rifle and shoes, and came to rest at Gallen's feet. At the top of the stairs, Ern Dale lay on the concrete, collapsed, pistol still in his right hand.

Grabbing the M4, Gallen bounded up the stairs. Rolling Dale onto his back, he saw several gunshot wounds in the man's chest and one in the bowel. Ern was not going to make it.

'Gerry,' said the old warhorse, 'I weren't gonna hurt ya.'

'I guess not, but I still don't know about the money.'

'Two Dales in two days,' said Ern, eyes rolling back as his big voice fell to a whisper. 'I thought I was smarter than that.'

'Hey, Ern?' said Gallen, as Dale went still. 'Thanks for the cover.'

Pushing down Dale's eyelids, Gallen stood and moved to the doorway. Pausing at the threshold, he checked the M4 for load in the breech and quickly examined the clip: he had more than twenty rounds left.

Getting a shoulder on a weapon he knew very well, Gallen controlled his breathing and eased into the empty showroom, covering the room with several sector-arcs of the M4, keeping his shoulders and face lined up with the weapon. It was clear and he jogged lightly across the lino to the other door. Looking around the corner, he saw a corridor with office spaces off it.

Moving along the hallway he checked off the rooms as he jogged from door to door. At the fourth one on the left, he found an old steel-framed bed with leather manacles at each corner. If Winter had been there, he wasn't anymore.

Straining his ears for sound, Gallen moved out into the corridor and had started to his left when he heard it: a vehicle being revved, down in the car park.

Pushing through the door opposite, he got to the window and looked down. In the weed-infested parking apron, he saw the white Oasis van. A dark Crown Vic pulled up beside the van with a squeal. The doors flew open and the muscular, cowboy-legged form of Mike Ford dashed to the corner of the building as a puff of concrete flew up three feet behind him. From the other side of the car, Liam

Tucker ran to the cover of a dumpster as the side windows were shattered.

Racing down the hallway, Gallen took a set of stairs to the ground level, dodging a wounded man who moaned at the foot of the stairs. Kicking the man's rifle away from his feet, Gallen leaned out the door and assessed the ground: the Crown Vic was still running and he thought of making a dash for it. As he moved into the sunlight, more gunfire started from around the corner and then Ford and Tucker appeared, dragging the slumped form of Kenny Winter between them.

Laying down covering fire as he ran, Gallen reached the car, leapt into the driver's seat and gunned the engine. Keeping his door open he lifted the M4 between the car pillar and the doorframe, clattering off the rifle's magazine on full auto at a mound of gravel and weeds that seemed to be the source of the incoming.

Ford reached the car, tore the back door open and climbed in: it was easier to pull an unconscious man into a vehicle than to push him. Gallen kept his fire rate up and Tucker shot too, until Winter was in the back seat.

Flooring the accelerator as Tucker dived into the front passenger seat, Gallen pulled a three-sixty and hit the gas as Ford and Tucker shot at the gravel piles, the windscreen getting a star in the top left-hand corner as Gallen steered them to safety.

Hitting the main road, panting with fear, he saw the police cars coming from the opposite direction, lights flashing. 'He okay?' he yelled.

'He'll live,' said Ford.

Gallen kept the car at a steady, legal pace as the police vehicles flashed past in the opposite direction. When they'd gone, he turned to Ford in the back seat. 'Nice timing. How'd you find us?'

'Thank this feller,' said Ford, lighting a smoke and nodding at Winter's unconscious form. 'He managed to dial his phone while he was being worked over. Went to last number dialled —me.'

'How'd you find the location?' said Gallen.

'Aaron has a cell-tower locator box,' said Ford. 'It told us the call was coming from a tower called East Village, so we drove around a bit.'

'Saw the van?' said Gallen, heading for downtown.

'No mate,' said Ford. 'Heard a gunfight.'

CHAPTER 55

The night air was cold and Gallen caught a look at his watch as he breathed deeply. It was 10.23 pm, Thursday, and the off-the-books doctor that Aaron had provided had declared Winter's gunshot to be a 'flesh wound'—no bones hit, no arteries nicked. Gallen and Winter crossed the dark car park behind the surgery, pausing as they got to a long black car.

As they climbed into the Oasis limo, Dave Joyce, the PR guy, smiled from the rear seat. He nodded at Winter. 'You okay?'

'Yeah, it's nothing,' said Winter, looking down at his leg.

'We clear?' said Florita, who sat beside her PR guy.

Gallen shrugged. 'Mulligan killed Ern; Ern killed Mulligan. I attacked Simon, got a pistol off him, but I didn't kill him.'

'We gotta talk.' Aaron climbed into the limo and pulled the door shut.

'The *Ariadne* launch is tomorrow,' said Florita, crossing her legs. 'You saw the briefing notes?'

'Yep,' said Gallen. 'Still don't get why you want a bunch of greenies down there.'

'It's simple, Gerry,' said Florita, waving a hand at Winter's cigarette smoke. 'The media only cover oil companies when we spill crude or launch one of these monsters. So the media spread is fifty-fifty good and bad—it's our job to ensure we get as much mileage as we can from the good because when the bad news comes around, the media and environmentalists will spin it out for months.'

Gallen and Winter swapped a look.

'So when we have a close relationship with an organisation like ArcticWatch, and the head of that group wants to make a documentary on the *Ariadne*, then we're going to bend over backwards to make it play well for us, okay, Gerry?'

'Just so long as this Du Bois stays away from you,' said Gallen, 'I'm good.'

'Well, they're doing their doco on me, so—'

Gallen stiffened. 'They?'

'Sure,' said Joyce. 'A film crew. This is a doco, Gerry.'

Gallen was too tired for this. 'I thought they were environmentalists. Who are they?'

'Filmmakers, Gerry,' said Florita. 'Martina wants a broadcast-quality documentary. Dave teed it up.'

'*Martina*, is it?' said Gallen. 'You best friends with this woman now?'

Joyce smirked. 'They gave us five Polar Bears, Gerry.'

'I don't care if they gave you a panda's paw for an ashtray. I don't like the idea of an enemy being allowed on this vessel.'

'It's a done deal,' said Florita, grabbing a bottle of water from the centre console. 'Dave's done an amazing job designing all this. His media briefing spells it out.'

Gallen had Joyce's media brief; he'd seen how he and the crew were going to usher Fox News through the *Ariadne* separately to CNN, so both networks felt they were getting access to an area the other hadn't been shown; how the BBC would be given information about the North-West Passage and Northern Sea Route and the *Wall Street Journal* would be given a lecture about how the submersible was going to lift the yield of the entire venture, giving a whole new shareholder-return profile to the site. Newspapers like the *New York Times* and *Guardian* were going to be briefed on how many seals and Inuit could be saved by having the maintenance and pumping side of the rig on the sea bed, not on a semi-submersible rig or a processing ship.

Gallen had already had Mike Ford plan the take-off of Florita, an irritating gap in security but one that the Aussie would handle better than anyone. Gallen simply hated the idea of the enemy coming inside the perimeter; it went against all his training.

'So,' said Aaron, 'you find what you were after?'

Gallen drew the Newport Associates report from the backpack, threw it to him.

'Holy shit,' said Aaron, flipping through the document and handing it to Florita. 'Where was it?'

'Where no one was going to find it,' said Gallen. 'But we wanted it out of play.'

Florita pored through the document. 'Is it all here?'

'It's all there,' said Gallen, reaching for one of Winter's smokes.

Florita hugged the file. 'Well that's one thing less to worry about.'

'Sure,' said Gallen as they sped for the airport. But it still left a list of the other things he'd be losing sleep over.

The flight refuelled at Baker Lake and Gallen awoke and made a quick trip to the head. At the front of the cabin, his three guys slept under blankets.

He washed his face and headed back to his seat, and saw Aaron looking up at him.

'You okay, Gerry?'

'Tired of being shot at.'

Aaron stood, taking care not to wake Joyce in the facing seat, and led Gallen to the kitchenette. 'I caught your tone in the limo,' said Aaron, looking over the seat next to him to check Florita was sleeping. 'You really worried about the ArcticWatch film crew?'

Gallen poured a paper cup of water. 'I'm worried about everything, Aaron. Paranoia can be a life saver.'

Aaron leaned over to his briefcase and pulled out a file. 'Every person aboard the *Ariadne* is profiled.'

'The film crew's okay?' Gallen took the file and flipped through it to the ArcticWatch crew.

'I rang their last references. They check out.'

Gallen saw the intel bio for Martina Du Bois, followed by two French males and one Spanish: the director, sound guy and cameraman. They looked healthy, tanned and sure of themselves. Gallen had no idea what he was looking for. He wouldn't know a film director if one ran up and kicked him on the leg.

Fanning the file, he was about to give it back when the sheaf opened at a page profiling NEGROPONTE, John S, the chief engineer of the *Ariadne*. The name grabbed Gallen's attention because he remembered a Tony Negroponte, a US Navy captain based in Okinawa. The photo showed a round-faced, smiling bald guy—probably not related, thought Gallen, given that Tony Negroponte had thick black hair and a long face.

Handing back the file, Gallen remembered his query on the Newport Associates report. 'You had a look at the Newport file?'

'No. Why?'

Gallen shrugged. 'Harry wrote a few comments in the margins.'

'Like?'

'Like, he underlined a phrase in a section on technology risk, I think it was, and then he wrote, *Star Okay*. Something like that.'

Aaron made a face. 'Want me to ask about it?'

'Just thought you'd know,' said Gallen.

'Well it's too late anyway.' Aaron yawned and stretched. 'She had it pouched from the airport in Calgary. It's been destroyed by now.'

'Thank God for that,' said Gallen, moving back to his seat.

As Gallen sat back in his forward-facing seat, he turned sideways to where Winter was sleeping across the aisle. The Canadian opened an eye and shut it quickly.

'Don't think I've forgotten about you, Kenny,' said Gallen, pulling his blanket up to his neck.

'I didn't steal their money,' said Winter, raising his head to check on Mike Ford, snoring in the opposite seat.

'Well, they don't believe you and they certainly don't believe me.'

'Sorry—about Roy 'n' all,' Winter whispered as the engines raised their revs and the Challenger rolled forward. 'I was laying low, thought Clearmont was perfect.'

'What?' hissed Gallen. 'You *knew* you were being chased? And you didn't tell me?'

321

'It was hard to tell one crew from another there for a while.'

Gallen groaned at the overhead locker. 'I don't believe this. How much?'

'I didn't—'

'How much?' snapped Gallen, wanting to grab Winter by the throat.

The Canadian gulped. 'Twenty-eight mill.'

The Challenger's engines went to full pitch and the aircraft catapulted along the slushy runway and climbed into the night, bound for Kugaaruk. Gallen seethed while Winter chewed his bottom lip.

Calming himself, Gallen looked across at Winter. 'The Pentagon will put an officer under surveillance for fudging a report—but they'll tap the family phones and wire the dog if there's money missing, okay?'

'I see.'

'So, Kenny,' said Gallen, 'for twenty-eight million dollars, they're gonna make us a lifelong project.'

CHAPTER 56

The Sikorsky's loadmaster doled out good coffee and donuts as the helo got to its flight path. Gallen took two chocolate-iced donuts and asked for three sugars in his coffee. It was almost five-thirty am and if he was expected to perform at his peak, he needed to hit his system with a big dose of sugar.

Leaning over Mike Ford—who held the *Ariadne* schematic on his lap—Gallen went through how he wanted things to work and ensured the new guy, Liam, was happy with the approach, since he would be spending three months on the bottom with the crew.

The *Ariadne* was built like a huge steel crucifix, with each of the four arms housing a particular function: lodgings, bathrooms and kitchen in the long wing on the bottom; suit room, dive bell and docking bay in the starboard wing; stores, gas storage, oxygen scrubbers and maintenance workshop in the one opposite; and the control rooms in the forward-facing arm. Each of the shorter wings was a hundred feet long and the size and shape of a 737 fuselage. The dormitory wing was more than one hundred and fifty feet and could house more than a hundred people for months.

On its underside was a mini power station that supplied not only all the power to keep the occupants alive but also enough to run the fourteen pumping stations that would eventually be running under

323

and on the sea floor, pumping crude oil out of the wells, along the sea bed and onto land.

The diving shifts would swim out of the pressure-lock in the suit room and do their maintenance or repair sweeps with the aid of the vast system of floodlights that would illuminate the infrastructure.

It seemed to Gallen's eyes like an expensive venture, but Florita had claimed it was going to halve the typical costs of retrieving crude in the Arctic. Most Arctic drilling projects were in the shallows and were built on gravel islands; the deeper sites relied on drilling ships but they had to shut down for half the year because of the seasonal ice.

The Oasis site was deep, at almost one thousand feet, and by putting the pump function on the bottom there was no seasonal shut-down. Once the well was sunk and cased using a drilling ship during the ice-free summer, the site would be sustained by the *Ariadne* unless more wells needed to be sunk—at which point the ship would be brought back in during the summer months when the ice receded. And the most expensive part of any oceanic oil venture—the rig itself—would not be required. Florita had seemed most proud of that part. That's where she claimed to be saving a hundred million dollars.

'Sorry, Liam,' said Gallen, 'but I need one guy down there for the first three-month rotation. This is an Oasis property and if the captain needs help with these ArcticWatch people, then I need you right there.'

'Got it, boss,' said Tucker.

'You'll take a SIG sidearm,' said Gallen, 'with three clips. I've put a packet of flexi-cuffs in your bag and we have to find you a brig.'

'Brig?'

'Yeah, buddy, you're the buffer,' said Gallen, using Navy slang for the person on a ship who locks up the miscreants.

'What about the suit room?' said Ford, leaning over and putting a sticky finger on the blueprint.

'There's a lot of gear in there,' said Gallen. 'What's in this compartment next door?'

'That's the boilers, is my guess,' said the Aussie.

'Boilers?' said Tucker. 'You mean for hot water? We're not taking that many showers are we?'

Ford laughed. 'In the Arctic, they pump boiling water into the gap between internal and external dive suits. We look like sea lions, but it beats having to piss in your wettie.'

'What's this one?' said Tucker, pointing at another compartment.

'That's an emergency diving lock and dock. If the main one ever gets damaged and you need to take people off, bring supplies on, you can switch to this one. They're usually off-limits. The skipper has the only key.'

'Okay,' said Gallen. 'That's our brig.'

CHAPTER 57

The massive red-hulled vessels loomed out of the fog patches as the pale sun peeked over the horizon. The Sikorsky banked around the Oasis drilling ship—the *Conquistador*—and aimed for the helipad on the front of the *Fanny Blankes-Koen*, a twin-hull Dutch service vessel that had carried the *Ariadne* from the workshops in Rotterdam to its sea trials in Norway, and now to its operational resting place on the sea bed of the Beaufort Sea, in the area between Canada and the North Pole.

Gallen followed the others across the helipad and into the warmth of the guest state rooms. Unpacking in the shared security quarters, he assigned the men different parts of the ship to recce before he joined the executives in Florita's state room.

As he entered the large suite, Gallen saw a group of men in blue woollen naval sweaters.

'Gerry,' said Aaron, jumping up and doing the introductions. 'Meet Captain Wil Armens—captain of the *Fanny Blankes-Koen*.'

Gallen shook a big dry hand.

'Bjorn Hansen, commander of the ship-side operation of the *Ariadne*,' continued Aaron, 'the *Ariadne*'s seabed commander, Captain Sam Menzies, his chief engineer, John Negroponte, and his XO, Ben Letour.'

Gallen shook and smiled, getting a closer look at Negroponte.

'Black gang, right?' said Gallen, referring to the nautical slang for the people who worked in the engine room of ships. He thought it was witty, the way it worked in with Negroponte's name.

Negroponte looked surprised; before he could say anything Gallen felt himself being directed towards the board table where Aaron had charts spread out. The operational aspect of dropping the *Ariadne* to the ocean floor had obviously been canvassed, judging by the checklists and other documents that sat among the schematics.

'Ben,' said Aaron, 'Gerry is probably most concerned with who is on the *Ariadne*, and getting our CEO off her in a timely and safe fashion.'

'Sure, Aaron,' said Letour, who Gallen judged to be a French Canadian in his mid-forties, probably ex-Navy by the way he kept himself in shape. 'We thought we'd use a service submersible.'

'Which is a sub, right?' said Gallen.

'Yes, a mini submarine,' said Letour. 'It will eventually live on the ocean floor with the *Ariadne*, but we can wait for the media to put their cameras away and use it to take Madame Mendes from the dive.'

'So, she doesn't even get wet?' said Gallen, warming to the plan. 'I mean, we can do this without her having to get into a dry suit, swim to the surface?'

Sam Menzies, a younger American, laughed. 'That's what you were worried about? Well, don't.'

The wind gathered strength from the west as Gallen sucked on his cigarette and turned so the icy breeze hit the back of his red arctic suit and his raised hood. Tucker put his hand out for a smoke and Gallen handed the packet and lighter rather than messing around trying to light up for the former Marine.

'That's one hell of a tin can,' said Tucker, getting his smoke lit and nodding.

Above them loomed the bulk of the *Ariadne*, its pale blue paint looking deathly cold in the sunlight. Men crawled over it in their insulated coveralls, checking the massive hoses that were connected to the top and working over every join, bolt and rivet on the huge structure that was going to support a small town on the sea bed for months at a time. Stevedores scale-lifted bagged cargo and pallets of plastic-wrapped boxes into the main lock, which was an open steel hole with a door swung back on its hinges, like a nose door on a cargo plane.

From the main hatch on the top of the vessel, men took readings with black boxes the size of field radios and scribbled on their clipboards. Other men yelled into radios, while high above them the main crane of the *Fanny Blankes-Koen*, which was going to lift the *Ariadne* into the sea and lower it down, was being prepared to swing the dome-like steel door onto the open hole.

The divers would come and go via a pressurised air lock on the underside of the *Ariadne*. This lock entered into the suit room and was large enough to dock two of the service submersibles that would be used on the sea floor.

Gallen had spent the last ninety minutes walking every deck, passageway and companionway on the *Fanny Blankes-Koen*, looking for the source of his discomfort. There was something not right about Negroponte and Gallen had worked himself up about it. What was that look from the chief engineer when Gallen had said 'black gang'? Was it surprise, confusion? Was he hesitating as he worked out the reference to his name? Or didn't he know what a black gang was? It couldn't be that, thought Gallen. Every maritime engineer knew what it was; even long after the steam era, the engine room sailors and officers still referred to their work as if it involved a lot of coal dust and shovels.

Letour walked out of the vessel, giving the go-ahead wave to the crane operators. Beckoning for Gallen and Tucker, Letour ducked back into the vessel as the crane revved up and slowly swung the massive steel bell into place on its hinges.

The inside of the *Ariadne* was warm and Gallen pushed back his hood and unzipped the arctic suit. The tour was fast: Letour's main task was looming in just under an hour, when he took the world's media through the vessel, and Gallen noted that the Canadian XO had shaved and splashed himself with Old Spice.

Standing back, Gallen let Letour brief Tucker, whose concentration and attention to detail made Gallen relax slightly. The back-up air lock was a large internal steel hatchway bolted into the hatch like a bank vault door.

'Shit,' said Tucker, thumping on it. 'No one's getting through that once they're locked up.'

Letour smiled. 'It's designed to stop the ocean entering at three thousand pounds per square inch. It should stop an angry drunk.'

Letour handed Tucker a red plastic swipe card. 'That's yours, but don't lose it. It's the only one.'

Swiping it, Tucker waited for the red light to flash green and then turned the hatch wheel three hundred and sixty degrees. Pushing it open, they looked in at a plain steel chamber with another watertight hatch at the other end and an array of diving equipment, air bottles and suits along the wall.

'Emergency lock,' said Letour, anticipating Gallen's question. 'If the main one is damaged, this is how we hook up with our submersibles.'

Pulling back, Gallen noticed another door in the passageway was opening. As they walked alongside it, the hatchway pulled back and the chief engineer, Negroponte, stepped out, his face flushed. Gallen noticed the hand checking and rechecking the hatchway even as the engineer faced Letour.

Negroponte had changed into pale blue coveralls with his name on the right breast and he hurriedly rolled down his sleeves, covering what Gallen took to be a military tattoo on the inside of his right forearm. The eagle clutching the laurel leaves made the bottom part of it US Army, which surprised Gallen—he'd assumed US Navy. But he spotted something else as Negroponte covered the tatt. It was an insignia on the man's arm. Gallen didn't know it but decided he was going to find out all about it.

They exchanged small talk for a couple of minutes, then Letour broke off as he checked his watch and Negroponte left them.

'Shall we have a look in the engine room?' said Gallen, moving to Negroponte's hatchway. He wanted to have a good recce behind that door.

'Can't do that, Gerry,' said Letour.

'Can't?'

'It's off-limits to me too,' said the XO.

'Off-limits?' said Gallen. 'But you run the joint.'

'Sure I do, but Oasis has some proprietary technology down there and John is the only one with access.'

'And if John gets sick or goes mad?' said Gallen.

'They land another engineer.' Letour shrugged.

'And you're happy with this?' said Gallen.

'Not unhappy,' said Letour. 'Oasis want this guy to run the power, so that's who we have. If he wants to shut himself off, hide away like a hermit, then that's his business, so long as the lights are on, the air's fresh and the water's hot.'

Having looked at Tucker's quarters in the officers' section, Gallen wandered out of the *Ariadne* and rezipped his arctic suit against the blast of sub-zero wind. He was due in the officers' mess room, where the media was going to be briefed in half an hour. Helos were ferrying crews from the airport at Kugaaruk and Gallen watched the reporters running from the Sikorsky to the helipad companionway, stooped over against the shock of the cold.

Making his way back to his state room, Gallen thought about the insignia on Negroponte's arm. A guy at sea, sporting an Army tatt? It gnawed at him, and he had an idea.

Taking off his arctic suit, Gallen took a seat at the fold-down table between two bunks and took a piece of plain foolscap from the writing set. He'd gone through three pieces of paper before he was happy that he'd re-created the insignia. In Force Recon the capacity to commit what you'd seen to a diagram or schema was a skill that had come to some more readily than others. Gallen had taken a while to get it—he'd been a jock at high school, not an arty type, and free-drawing was not his thing. But even with the rise of digital imaging, digital recording and the cut-and-paste age, the US Marines needed its recon operators to be able to demonstrate what they'd seen, and if that meant drawing on the back of a beer coaster with a borrowed ballpoint, then that's what they wanted.

Gallen felt that pressure now, the pressure to use his training to pull from his memory the exact shape of that insignia. He looked down at what he had: it looked like an upside-down crucifix with curved bars attached to the cross-piece of the crucifix. It looked like a lollypop, with a cross inside it.

There were voices at the door and Winter entered, Ford behind him.

'Hey, boss,' said the Aussie. 'That PR guy, Dave, is after you. There's a press conference about to start.'

'Shit,' said Gallen, checking his G-Shock. He'd lost track of the time. Grabbing his arctic suit, he followed the other two along a wood-panelled passage to the companionway that would take them down one flight to the officers' mess.

'By the way,' he said, as Winter grabbed the door handle, 'either of you recognise this?' He handed over the paper with the drawing and watched Winter and Ford take their time looking at it. It was a special forces habit: if someone asked you to look at something, you took it all in because you never knew when a higher-up was going to ask you to remember it.

'It's kinda familiar,' said Ford. 'But I couldn't tell you.'

'Same here,' said Winter, handing back the paper. 'What's it about?'

'The chief engineer on the *Ariadne*. He's got this tattooed on his right forearm. It's part of a US Army tatt.'

'I know who'd know,' said Ford. 'You want me to fax it?'

'Please,' said Gallen. 'Now.'

Following Winter down the stairway, they came out in a passage crowded with milling reporters, photographers and cameramen. Gallen noticed how the media seemed to take up twice the space that their physicality would suggest—what was known in the recon game as a 'big projector': someone who seemed to dominate the area around them and therefore stood out. Most recon operators and spies tried to project the opposite: small, inconspicuous, blending with the human traffic.

Pushing through the scrum towards the mess door, Winter paused and looked down on a man Gallen recognised as being from Fox News. The man decided not to get out of the way until the woman he was talking to suddenly caught a look at Winter and pointed. When the reporter turned, Winter smiled at him like a wolf and the reporter almost fell over getting out of the way.

Dave Joyce the PR guy stood on a small stage talking with Aaron, the Oasis corporate logo on a banner behind them. Joyce saw Gallen and cracked a big smile, sweeping his hand in a chivalrous gesture. 'Mr Gerry Gallen, please meet Dr Martina Du Bois, the president of ArcticWatch.'

Turning to his left, Gallen faced a head of raven hair and waited as the woman turned slowly to greet him.

'Hello, Captain,' she said, a flashing smile and intelligent eyes.

'Gerry will do fine,' said Gallen, shaking her hand and taking her in. She was about five-ten, physically beautiful and very expensively dressed. She gave him that slightly wide-eyed look of expectation that beautiful women give a man when they're waiting to be fawned over.

'So it's your man on the *Ariadne* with us?' she said, her face serious but eyes laughing. 'Thank you so much.'

'Pleasure.' Gallen released her hand and turned to the three men who were with her. Du Bois introduced her crew, whom Gallen knew from their files. He smiled and introduced them to Kenny Winter. But his alarm bells were going off. He wasn't entirely sure what he'd expected from a film crew, but three men built like athletes wasn't it.

As Du Bois and her ArcticWatch crew drifted away to set up their filming, Gallen turned to Winter and Aaron. 'Is it just me?'

'What's the problem now, Gerry?' said Aaron.

'Nothing,' said Gallen, trying to relax.

'Excellent,' said Aaron, 'because the boss is diving with that tin can in exactly forty-five minutes, and if you're good, we're away.'

CHAPTER 58

Gallen walked the sidelines of the press conference as Winter took one side of the Oasis executive team on the stage, and Tucker the other. He noticed how the news crews had different agendas, different tones in their voices when they yelled their questions at the stage. The varied news angles that Joyce had devised in the briefing document now made sense, as did the five-minute one-on-ones that had preceded the press conference: the journalists had what they wanted and now they got to preen in front of one another.

Keeping his eyes on the ArcticWatch film crew, who were camped at the foot of the stage, Gallen caught Du Bois' eye as she looked away from Florita. He didn't like this woman or her crew, but he wasn't going to make it personal. His job was to keep Florita safe and he would focus on that.

'Red Fox, Red Fox, this is Blue Dog,' he said into his radio as a Danish reporter became tangled in his argument against colonising the sea bed. 'Sitrep, over.'

'Blue Dog, this is Red Fox. Situation normal—all fucked up,' came Mike Ford's nasal twang. 'No unfriendlies. The tin can looks ready for Go.'

'Stay in touch, Red Fox,' said Gallen. 'Out.'

A British reporter in a pashmina put her question about degrading the Inuit fishing grounds and the fact that in vast areas of the Arctic Ocean, the Inuit were recognised by the UN and by the Hague as having what she called *native title*; while the current drilling was interesting in a limited sense because of the *Ariadne* experiment, how were Oasis or the other big oil companies going to contend with Inuit control of oil-field leases?

When the woman sat down, Florita swapped looks with her executive team, and then Joyce the PR guy gave a long nod.

Stiffening, Gallen watched the room sit up as Florita cleared her throat. She hadn't said a word but the media sensed something and he watched them come dangerously alive, like a bear waking up as you trod on a stick.

The PR guy stood and opened his palms to the media and sat down when they were silent.

'It's a privilege to launch the *Ariadne* this afternoon,' said Florita, leaning down to the microphone on her table, her helmet of black hair matching the black pant suit. 'I believe it will revolutionise Arctic oil and gas exploration, making it safer for the environment, safer for the drilling crews and more cost effective for the explorers.

'However,' she said, after taking a sip from a glass of water, 'there is another reason we've invited the world's media here today.'

'You're saving the whales, too?' said a shabby-looking Brit, making the whole room laugh.

'No, Mr Beetham,' said Florita, with a confidence that made Gallen realise why she held such a job. 'But we're saving a hundred million dollars by putting our rig on the Arctic floor, does that count at the *Financial Times*?'

The journos laughed again and another Brit ruffled Mr Beetham's hair.

Gallen felt nervous: there was an anarchy about this profession, if you could call it that.

'Before we go to the bottom in the *Ariadne*, I'd like to make an announcement: seven minutes ago, Oasis Energy launched a friendly takeover bid on the London Stock Exchange for the Russian oil and gas company Thor Oil.'

'Takeover?' said one reporter, standing. 'That gives Oasis most of Siberia and Arctic Canada. How's Moscow going to react?'

'It's a friendly takeover,' said Florita. 'An equity swap will see Thor Oil basically absorbed but with an accretive effect—'

'What about the shareholders?' said an American.

'More than eighty-five per cent of the shares are held by two Russian groups,' said Florita, making Gallen's ears prick up, 'and the rest is institutional holdings.'

The media hubbub rose as Gallen recalled the Newport Associates report: the two Russian groups behind Thor Oil were the Bashoff crime family's ProProm oil company and Reggie Kransk's Transarctic Tribal Council. What was Florita doing?

A tall Englishman stood up and raised his hand. 'Excuse me, madam, could you tell us what share price the takeover offer has been made at?'

'Initial offer was nineteen euros,' said Florita, enjoying herself. 'I believe we had our takeover threshold met within three minutes.'

The reporters gawped.

'You mean three days?' said an American, looking up from her shorthand pad.

'No,' said Florita, 'we had our proxies in hand before I announced just now. Guess our advisers read the market perfectly, huh?'

The tall Englishman looked over his colleague's shoulder at her iPad and read from it. 'That's very quick, madam, and very expensive: half an hour before this announcement, Thor Oil was trading at ten euros ninety-one.'

'I believe so,' said Florita, checking her watch.

'That's a premium of ninety per cent,' said the Englishman, looking annoyed. 'Forget about the Russian shareholders, I assume yours are happy with the price?'

'Rather than getting your assistant to fiddle with that computer,' said Florita, signalling for Joyce to start handing out a stack of white folders with the Deutsche Bank logo on the cover, 'I can tell you that the takeover is valued at forty-eight billion US dollars.'

The journos mumbled and a few dialled their sat-phones.

'So what's the projected market capitalisation of the new entity?' asked one.

'Deutsche Bank is projecting ninety-five billion,' said Florita, as Aaron touched her on the arm and gave Gallen the nod. They were heading for the *Ariadne* dive.

'So you've overtaken ConocoPhillips in market cap?' said the tall Englishman. 'You've basically bought out Arctic oil.'

But the comment was lost as Florita stood and the photographers surged forward in a blast of flashes.

They stood on the starboard hull of the *Fanny Blankes-Koen* and formed a guard around Florita as she climbed the ladder and eased into the trapdoor on the top of the *Ariadne*. Tucker followed: he would organise the take-off from the *Ariadne*.

As he made to climb the ladder, Gallen grabbed Tucker. 'Keep an eye on things, okay, Liam?'

'That was the idea, boss.'

'No, I mean it,' said Gallen. 'You see anything you don't like, get her into a safe room and shoot anyone who approaches. Okay?'

'Crystal, boss,' said the former Marine, dancing up the ladder and disappearing inside.

The technicians secured the air lock and radioed up to the control room on the ship; most saturation-diving platforms were run from the ship they were connected to and it was the control room that monitored the temperature, oxygen mix and comms. The *Ariadne* was different, as Aaron had explained: once on the sea bed and set in place on the footings that the Dutch ship had secured ten days earlier, the *Ariadne* had its own power source and could be self-sustaining for months at a time, hence its capacity to keep operating when the sea ice arrived.

'She'll be up in twenty minutes,' said Aaron, stamping warmth into his feet as Bjorn Hansen, the ship-side commander, walked to the outside railing of the service hull and yelled a command into his hand-held radio. Beside him, another man—also in a red exposure suit—trained binoculars on the crane and the lines and murmured updates to the Swede. The crane whirred into motion and the lines on the *Ariadne* went taut.

'Twenty minutes is too long,' said Gallen.

'You worry too much,' said Aaron.

Gallen pulled his arctic suit hood up. 'I worry enough to keep myself alive.'

The submersible pilot was dressed in dark blue *Ariadne* coveralls with thermals beneath and held a helmet in his hands. His yellow mini sub sat on a cradle on the inside of the starboard hull, a smaller crane ready to lower her. He was talking with Mike Ford as Gallen approached.

'Let's do this as fast as possible, okay?' said Gallen, offering Ford and the pilot a cigarette as they watched the *Ariadne* being lifted clear of her derricks, the lines straining and crane groaning as the huge Dutch service vessel laboured under her task, the barked commentary from the big Swede making many of the media contingent stare at him before looking away.

'It is no problem,' said the Dutch submersible pilot, a blond sailor in his late twenties. 'This is easy for her.'

The crane swung away from the starboard hull, carrying the sea-floor drilling rig with it, the media contingent huddling as the Arctic wind bit deep. Gallen saw two reporters patting their cameramen and photographer on the back as they peeled back for the warmth of the ship.

The *Ariadne* swung out over the Arctic Ocean, a slight chop on the cold waters as the crane took her clear of the service ship's starboard hull. The big Swede raised his hand as he yelled into his radio and his sidekick continued to look up and down the lines with his binoculars. When the binoculars man finally spoke, the Swede brought his hand down and said something quickly into the radio, and then the pale blue form of the *Ariadne* was being lowered into the sea, the waves lapping gently at the steel fuselages at first and then slowly engulfing the structure until it seemed tiny. And then it was gone.

Gallen stared at the point where the *Ariadne* used to be and was momentarily struck by how massive the ocean actually was. The sea had swallowed that lump of steel like it was a raindrop, he thought, following Hansen as he charged through the media scrum to the control room.

From the control room—a glass-sided area wrapped around the pylons and gantries of the crane—they watched the cables and lines spill off the decking as the crane lowered the *Ariadne*. European voices barked out of the radio speakers and people responded to Hansen as he demanded answers from the operators at their screens. Gallen had no idea what language they were speaking—they were Dutchies, Swedes and Danes but they seemed to understand just fine when Hansen spoke.

Looking nervously at his watch, Gallen saw they had fifteen minutes until the take-off. The Dutch pilot shrugged into the yellow sub, Ford behind him, and the deck crew screwed down the lid. Gallen's stomach grumbled with stress and he wondered if the ship carried a nice big bottle of Pepto-Bismol. And then the secondary crane lifted the bright submersible clear of the hull and into the sea, and it was gone too.

'We at depth yet?' said Gallen, as the media dispersed. At the rear of the service ship he could hear the sounds of the first Sikorsky being readied to shuttle the reporters back to land.

'Halfway down,' said Hansen, pointing at the main monitoring screen, where a digital read-out on a blue background showed a white 28—the Dutch ship was run in metrics, and at 28 metres, the *Ariadne* was more than halfway to Florita's take-off.

'Can I?' said Gallen, pointing at the comms desk.

'Sure,' said Hansen, ushering him forward with a big paw.

'Yellow Bird, this is Blue Dog,' he said into the mic stalk. 'Are you reading, over?'

There was a pause of a few seconds and then Tucker was on the radio. 'Gotcha, Blue Dog, this is Yellow Bird reading you clear, over.'

'Red Fox is on his way down, repeat Red Fox is five minutes away. You readied for the take-off, over?'

'Ready and—' came the American's voice, and then there was nothing. No static, no squelch, just dead air.

Looking at the mic, Gallen felt Hansen push past and gabble at the comms guy, who shrugged as he played with the settings.

Stepping back as the control room personnel descended on the comms desk, Gallen joined Aaron and Joyce. 'This isn't good.'

'It's not so bad,' said Aaron. 'The radio's just down for a few seconds.'

In special forces, losing comms was usually the starting point for a whole world of wonderful screw-ups, and Gallen wasn't interested in the glass-half-full argument. He wanted the glass fully full.

'We on with the sub?' he said, and the comms guy nodded enthusiastically, hitting a button and pointing to the mic.

Leaning into the stalk mic, Gallen called up Mike Ford.

'We've lost comms to the *Ariadne*. You talking to them?'

'Negative, Blue Dog,' came the Aussie accent. 'We have dead air with the *Ariadne*.'

Gallen felt his pulse bang behind his eyeballs. 'Got visuals, Red Fox?'

'Affirmative, Blue Dog. We have her in our lights and we're continuing to the RV.'

Gallen looked at Hansen and the commander hit a series of switches; the screens that had stopped broadcasting the *Ariadne*'s video footage now leapt to life and showed Mike Ford and the Dutch sailor in the sub itself, while another screen was the submersible's camera view of the *Ariadne*.

The depth counter showed thirty-five metres.

Gallen tapped it. 'Can we stop the *Ariadne*?'

'The descent?' said Hansen.

'Yeah,' said Gallen. 'Just a time-out until we can sort this out?'

'We're on a clock,' said the Swede.

'And I've lost contact with my employer. Let's do the take-off at forty metres,' said Gallen, irritated.

'Sounds fair,' said Aaron, schmoozing between them and giving Hansen the go-ahead. Turning to Gallen, he gave him a look. 'Take it easy, Gerry.'

The cables screeched and the control room shuddered slightly as the descent slowed and then stopped at forty-one metres. The screens on the control console showed the *Ariadne* looming out of the darkness of the killer-cold sea as the submersible closed on her, the flashing red light on the top of the vessel and the lights shining through the portholes a sign that at least the vessel had power.

'Blue Dog, this is Red Fox,' came Mike Ford's voice. 'We're twenty-three metres from the *Ariadne*. Closing.'

'See anything, Red Fox?' said Gallen.

'No, boss. It looks business as usual. You've stopped her, so this is the take-off?'

'Affirmative, Red Fox,' said Gallen, making himself breathe out. 'This is the take-off. Proceed to the diving lock.'

The submersible's camera tracked their path under the massive submerged vessel and the workers in the control room pored over the detail as Ford talked them in. 'Five metres and powering back,' said the Aussie as the submersible moved under the light from the open divers lock beneath the diving section of the vessel.

'And powering up,' said Ford, and the submersible ascended slowly into the *Ariadne*'s belly, the light becoming brighter until the processors had to adjust for flaring light.

'Blue Dog, this is Red Fox. We're docked and ready for take-off,' said Ford.

From the interior shots, Gallen could see the two men doing their pressure checks as the external sensors gave them ATM and psi readings from the diving bell. The outside camera just showed the side of the diving bell with its padded V-docks for submersibles.

'Strange,' said Hansen, as he left a confab with two technicians. 'Power, air and water are up. So are comms.'

'So?' said Gallen.

Hansen frowned. 'So my guys are saying it's ninety per cent the case that comms have been shut down on the sea-side.'

'Someone on the *Ariadne* has shut down comms?' said Gallen. 'There're no faults.'

'Red Fox, this is Blue Dog,' said Gallen, leaning into the mic as the Dutch sailor with Ford indicated the right pressure to leave the submersible.

'Go ahead, Blue Dog,' said Ford as the Dutchie moved out of frame to release the lid.

'Red Fox, present arms and be alert, over.'

'Everything okay?' said Ford, and Gallen watched him pull the black SIG 9mm from his travel pouch and check the slide for load.

'Comms is down, but no faults detected,' said Gallen.

'No contact from Yellow Bird?' said Ford, crouching and turning for the open lid, which allowed fluorescent light into the submersible.

Gallen sighed. 'No.'

Behind him, the fax machine double-beeped and the whir of a received message sounded.

'Talk me through it, Red Fox, you're now out of shot,' said Gallen, as the Aussie moved away.

'Can't, Blue Dog. This headset plugs into the sub. I'm about to unplug.'

'Shit!' Gallen thumped the console. 'Okay, Red Fox, but leave the line open. And you're on the air again in five minutes, okay?'

'Sure, boss,' said Ford.

'I'm serious. I'm running a clock. That's fiver!'

Gallen stood back as the line from the sub hissed, and Aaron nudged him. 'Ford was waiting for something?'

'Sorry?' said Gallen, lost in thought.

Putting a piece of fax paper in Gallen's hand, Aaron pointed at it. 'Got Mike's name on it. Must have requested something. What did he want with the US Army?'

Opening the piece of thermal fax paper, Gallen took it in: the fax was a photocopy from a US Army regulations book, featuring the symbol he'd seen on Negroponte's arm.

'Holy shit,' he mumbled under his breath as he read the description attached to the insignia. 'Pull her up, Hansen.'

The big Swede looked at Aaron, who'd technically been left in charge while Florita was submerged.

'Now look, Gerry—'

'No, Aaron, you look.' Gallen pushed the fax into Aaron's chest. 'You know about that?'

'It's, um . . . ?'

'Read it.'

Aaron looked up from the paper, confused, and Hansen grabbed it.

'It says it's the Nuclear Reactor Operator badge,' said Hansen in his thick accent. 'Who does this refer to?'

'Yeah, Gallen,' said Aaron. 'What's this about?'

'It's the tattoo on Negroponte's arm.'

'Negroponte?' said Aaron. 'The chief engineer?'

'The one who's locked away in his own private engine room,' said Gallen.

'You have a nuclear reactor on the *Ariadne* and you didn't tell me?' said Hansen, blood rushing into his Nordic face as he turned on Aaron and Joyce. 'Are you mad?'

Joyce looked confused. 'Is that a bad thing?'

'Why don't we find out?' said Gallen. 'Master Hansen, can we bring the *Ariadne* to the surface?'

'With pleasure,' said the Swede, as he issued the orders.

342

CHAPTER 59

Winter appeared in the control room, having been paged. Hansen's orders had been acted on and the crane's cables were moving upwards.

'What's happening?' said the Canadian, checking his SIG handgun and replacing it in his arctic suit.

'Lost comms from the *Ariadne*,' said Gallen, watching the cables slowly move. 'And then I found out what that symbol was on Negroponte's tatt.'

Winter squinted through the windows. 'What is it?'

'US Army insignia for Nuclear Reactor Operator,' said Gallen.

Winter twisted to give Aaron a look.

Aaron lifted his hands. 'It might be a mistake.'

'So the power source on the *Ariadne* is nuclear?'

'Looks like it,' said Gallen.

'Is it safe?' said the Canadian. 'I mean, some of these things are really small and really powerful these days.'

Gallen looked at him. 'You know about this?'

'Sure,' said Winter with a shrug. 'They're called STARs—the Russians especially are building them as remote power for, you know, mining sites, oil rigs.'

'You said *star*?' said Gallen, remembering the notation in the margin of the Newport Associates report. That was Durville's scribbled question—was that the information that was being suppressed?

'Stands for Small Sealed Transportable Autonomous Reactor. You can load one on the back of a truck,' said Winter.

'Or the bottom of a submerged oil rig?' said Gallen.

A light flashed on the console and a voice spoke; a French female voice.

'That's far enough, Master Hansen,' said Martina Du Bois in a nasty purr. 'You can stop the crane while we have a chat.'

Looking at Gallen and Aaron, Hansen turned back and issued the command to the technician. The ship seemed to shudder again as the crane stopped and the massive weight on the end of it stretched the cables for a few seconds.

Gallen pushed Aaron forward to the mic.

'That's better, Master Hansen.'

'What do you want, Martina?' said Aaron. 'Is Captain Menzies there? Where's Florita Mendes? Where's her bodyguard?'

'Let's not get ahead of ourselves, Mr Michaels. This is a rare chance to have a proper dialogue, n'est-ce pas?'

Aaron snapped, 'Dialogue about what? Where's our CEO? Who's in charge down there?'

'Everyone is where they have to be, Aaron,' came the superior tone. 'Except the media.'

'The media's halfway to Kugaaruk or Barrow, depending on where they're flying out of,' said Aaron, pushing his hair back on his head. 'What do you want? Is this a hostage situation?'

'I need Fox and CNN back here now, Aaron, or there's going to be consequences,' Du Bois said from the speaker. 'You have thirty minutes, and the Ariadne goes nowhere until I say so.'

'You could always film yourselves, Du Bois,' said Gallen, trying to keep the comms open. 'You could get the lighting and angles just right and do some hari kari—you know, for the environment and the polar bears. I'd make sure Fox News gets the footage.'

'Ha!' said the Frenchwoman, sounding genuinely amused. 'I'm going to take a blind guess and say that this is our suspicious American, the one who's been hit with a baseball bat, hmm?'

'You're a real little Charlie Chan, aintcha, Du Bois?'

'I'm a real little environmental activist who's going to tell the world what Oasis Energy is about to do to one of the few untouched areas left on earth,' said the Frenchwoman. 'It's not yours to rape—it belongs to all of us.'

Gallen laughed. 'Told the Russians this?'

'I'll tell the world this, Mr Gerry,' she said, giving his name a soft 'J' sound. 'And I'll tell them at nine pm Eastern Time, a late news breaker.'

'Coulda done that when the media was all here, Du Bois,' said Gallen, trying to taunt her. 'You'd rather kill people, that it?'

'I'd rather talk to Fox and CNN, and you now have twenty-five minutes.'

The radio died again and the men in the control room looked down at the console as if it might hold clues.

'Master—we got navy or coast guard nearby?' said Gallen.

Hansen instructed an operator to get on it while Aaron moved away and grabbed Joyce.

'You gonna get those news crews back?' said Gallen. 'You think that's a good idea?'

'Only to buy time,' said Aaron. 'Who knows what they have planned?'

Staring at the console, Gallen thought about it and turned to Hansen. 'They're at thirty-five metres.'

'Yes,' said Hansen, distracted as he directed the operators.

Gallen rubbed his face, felt the bruising and cuts that Du Bois had commented on. 'We got dive gear on the ship that goes to thirty-five, forty metres?'

'Of course,' said Hansen. 'This is a rig service vessel. We're equipped to run fifty divers at once if we have to.'

'Can I take one of your guys?' said Gallen, looking to see if Aaron was listening. He wasn't; he was getting pilots to turn their helos around.

'A diver?' said Hansen. 'You sure?'

'I need someone to set us up.'

'Okay. But before you go in the water, you clear it with us, okay?' The Swede pointed to Aaron.

'I'm thinking that if they're focused on media attention, that might be a good time to be stealthing onboard.'

'You hear this?' said Hansen as Aaron got off the phone and walked to the console area.

'Hear what?'

'Mr Gallen wants to dive.'

'Where to?' said Aaron.

'The *Ariadne*,' said Gallen.

Shaking his head, Aaron raised his phone. 'Fox and CNN are on their way back and we might make her deadline. I don't want to risk it—she might just want to make some big point about whales and Inuit and then be led off by the Coast Guard as a martyr.'

'And what if she's not?' said Gallen. 'I say we do it both ways: let her preach to the TV audience and at the same time we storm the fort.'

Aaron frowned. 'How?'

'Use the TV crews as a distraction, stealth onto the *Ariadne* and take these guys down.'

'You've done this before, I take it?' said Aaron, chewing his lip.

'Hell, no,' said Winter, cracking one of his rare smiles. 'That's half the fun.'

Aaron asked Hansen where the nearest navy or coast guard was.

'The Canadian Coast Guard icebreaker *Amundsen* is three hours away and there's a US Navy supplies ship in the western Beaufort,' said Hansen. 'We're on our own till they get here.'

'So,' said Aaron, looking at Gallen, 'you're going to swim down to the *Ariadne* and just climb aboard?'

'The *Ariadne* can see the environment around it with cameras, right?' Gallen said to Hansen.

Hansen nodded. 'There's seventeen external and eight internal cameras.'

Gallen pointed at the control room panel. 'Show me on here the screen for the main diving lock.'

Hansen pointed to the bottom right screen. 'If we had communications then we'd see the diving lock on this one.'

'Same set-up on the *Ariadne*'s control room?'

'Yes,' said Hansen. 'Identical.'

'When Du Bois gets connected again for her address to the TV crews, we'll be connected to the *Ariadne*. Can we mess with the camera systems?'

'Mess?' said Hansen.

'Can we make one of the screens malfunction?' said Gallen.

Hansen looked to his comms guru beside him.

'Sure,' said the Dane with the curly black hair. 'I can do this.'

They wrapped and rewrapped their handguns and placed them in black nylon dive bags that would strap to their belts. The dive technicians suited them in arctic dry suits on top of arctic under suits—padded one-piece systems that sat against the body and under the bulky dry suits. The Arctic water temperature was a typical minus 1.8 degrees Celsius—the coldest you could take salt water before it froze—and they would not be using the suits that pumped boiling water between two layers of wetsuit. Those diving systems required umbilicals connected to a mother ship or diving bell and Gallen didn't want to draw attention to themselves as they approached the *Ariadne*.

'You think they were waiting for Mike?' said Winter, letting the technician from the *Fanny Blankes-Koen* zip him into his silver-blue suit.

'I think they were waiting for all of us,' said Gallen, pulling a Thinsulate bonnet from the undergarment over his head and letting his technician zip the dry suit in place. 'I had a bad feeling about environmentalists going down there with Florita, and I should have stopped it. I'm going soft.'

'Wasn't your call, boss,' said Winter. 'These corporate dudes will do anything to get their photo in the papers.'

'I was a captain in US special forces,' said Gallen. 'My men, my call.'

Winter waved that away. 'Assuming they get their show on prime-time TV, what then?'

'They either give up, or they want to make a bigger point than just talking. I don't want to wait for the decision.'

'I brought something with me; I wasn't going to tell you,' said the Canadian.

'What?'

Winter pointed at his backpack, motioned for the technician to get it. Pulling a grenade from the bag, Winter shrugged. 'Coupla flash-bangs. You never know, right?'

'You gonna throw one of them in a tin can under the sea? You wanna cold bath, Kenny?'

'What do you reckon?' said Winter, smiling at his technician. 'The tin can strong enough for this?'

The technician looked at the grenade and gabbled something in a northern European language.

'He saying,' said the other tech, 'that maybe the *Ariadne* strong enough for a bomb, but better hold your ears, yes, 'cos it will explode the eardrum.'

'Happy now?' said Gallen.

'What's that?' said Winter, eyes set on a long contraption mounted on the wall of the dive room.

'Shark gun,' said the technician. 'Just like a spear gun but it has the explosive tips.'

'Fix me up,' said Winter, squinting at the weapon.

Gallen made himself breathe deeply for thirty seconds as the tech pulled arctic mittens over his hands and restrapped his G-Shock over his suited left wrist: it showed sixteen minutes on the mission clock—fourteen minutes to get to the *Ariadne* and be ready for the camera malfunction that Hansen was going to initiate.

He took a few seconds to compose himself: his last dive in Arctic waters had been terrifying enough. Now he breathed through his nose and envisioned smooth breathing, rhythmic finning and being in that diving lock on the *Ariadne* before the cold properly set in. Then he nodded for the technicians to screw the dive helmets onto the collars of the dry suits.

He gave the thumbs-up and Winter gave him a wink.

'Relax, boss,' said the Canadian as his helmet came down. 'It's what we do.'

CHAPTER 60

The dive platform on the inside of the port hull receded into surrealist shapes as Gallen hit the water and submerged backwards. The cold hit him like a slap as he let himself go a few feet under and normalised his breathing, checking on the regulator and ensuring he had a proper seal on the helmet's collar. He gave a tug on the thin line tied to his weight belt and seconds later there was a burst of bubbles and Winter sank to the same depth, where he did his own checks.

'Okay,' said Gallen into his mouthpiece as he tapped his G-Shock. 'We got twelve minutes to Go. Let's get down there.'

Checking the compass heading he'd been given by the techs, Gallen lined up with the display on his watch and finned downwards, under the starboard hull of the *Fanny Blankes-Koen*.

'Now you'll see what you were missing at that fricking lake,' said Gallen as they descended into the gloom.

'I'd forgotten how bad this was,' said Winter, panting as they left the natural light of the surface. 'I thought Nova Scotia was cold.'

Keeping their flashlights stowed, they finned downwards for three minutes until the orange-faced gauge on Gallen's right wrist showed they were on the same plane as the *Ariadne*: twenty-eight metres.

'See anything?' said Gallen, holding his G-Shock to the face plate in his helmet and rechecking the compass heading as he fumbled to activate the watch's backlight.

'No, boss,' came Winter's rasped voice.

'Blue Dog to Momma Bear, we have zero visuals. About to head out on two-seven-niner. Please confirm, over.'

Hansen's voice scratched through the earpiece in the helmet. 'Affirm that, Blue Dog. We have you on screen. Proceed on your two-seven-niner, over.'

Hitting the backlight again, Gallen lined his shoulder up with the 279 heading on his G-Shock and resumed finning. 'Should be right there.'

They moved slowly through the blackness, their breathing rasping in one another's ears; Gallen kept radio silence and fought against his desire to grab the flashlight on his right leg and illuminate the environment. He felt the beginnings of both claustrophobia and agoraphobia creeping in as surely as the cold was now settling on his chest like a bag of cement.

The safety line tugged at his weight belt, he heard a grunt, and turned in time to see a silver flash disappearing into the murk.

'Okay?' said Gallen.

'Fucking fish,' mumbled Winter.

The lights of the *Ariadne* ebbed in the blackness after another twenty seconds of finning. Letting Winter come alongside, Gallen checked his G-Shock and showed the other man: six minutes to Go.

The set-up wasn't as easy as Gallen had assumed; for a start, no one had told him there was a set of downward-facing lights on the *Ariadne* and that they lit up the deep like a battery of aircraft landing lights.

Pointing down, Gallen waited for the nod from Winter; when it came they descended, remaining a hundred and fifty feet from the vessel, where the lights wouldn't catch them. At any ocean depth greater than sixty-five feet, light couldn't travel as it did above sea level. Gallen was comfortable that they'd be unseen by onboard cameras. His biggest concern was flashes of reflection from the scuba bubbles. Unlike the enclosed rebreather systems they were trained on in Force Recon—that recirculated carbon dioxide through chemical scrubbers—the commercial clearance divers used systems that threw off bubbles like a jet stream.

When he got the 'three click' signal from Hansen, it would indicate that comms had been established with the *Ariadne* and Hansen's people had disrupted the downward-facing cameras.

Finning slowly in the dark to maintain depth, Gallen checked his watch: one minute forty-eight to Go. He raised two fingers directly in front of Winter's face plate and the Canadian gave the thumbs-up.

The cold started to push itself on Gallen's chest and neck and he breathed in regular patterns, making himself think through the steps and the contingencies.

As he thought about how easily the *Ariadne*'s walls could be breached with a 9mm slug, there was a quick series of small explosions and the entire ocean went black.

CHAPTER 61

'Blue Dog,' came Winter's voice, breaking the silence. 'The fuck just happened?'

The shocks from the explosions cracked through the water like whip shots.

'Shit,' said Winter, and Gallen detected panic. Turning, he pulled along the safety line and came up to Winter.

'Cut the dry suit,' said Winter, gasping. 'Got the spear gun in the wrong place.'

'Stay calm,' said Gallen as he switched on his flashlight. Cupping the lens, he found a small tear on the upper leg of Winter's dry suit.

'It's an inch long. You should be okay for two minutes. We're going in.'

Three clicks sounded over the earpiece, and Gallen grabbed Winter. 'That's the signal. You're up.'

'Water's coming in, Gerry,' said Winter, his jaw already setting in reaction to the intense cold. 'Shit!'

'Let's move, keep you warm.'

Kicking out, Gallen led across the inky blackness, briefly looking at the back-lit compass reading on his watch. He had no situational reference point—no up or down, or sense of speed. With his flashlight off again, they slid through the abyss, the silence and cold roaring in like a tropical cyclone. His senses screamed at him, reminding him of the darkness of an Afghan mountain pass at night, where in some of the canyons a man couldn't see his own hand.

'Shit, boss,' came Winter's whisper as they slid through the black. 'It's running down my leg. Man, it's cold.'

As he turned to face Winter, Gallen hit steel, his helmet bouncing off it with a bell-like dong. They'd found the *Ariadne*.

They clung to the side of the huge vessel like a couple of spiders, and Gallen spelled it out. 'We go in like we planned, okay, Kenny?'

'Sure, boss,' said the Canadian, close but invisible. 'Let's get it done.'

Feeling his way down one of the steel hulls, Gallen wondered what had happened for the power to go off in the *Ariadne*. Was it connected to the explosions? Seeing the model of the *Ariadne* in his mind, he felt along the underside of the curved hull and prepared to swim across to the divers lock where there'd usually be light pouring out. He heard a sound, a faint humming. Stopping, he felt Winter run into the back of him.

'Hear that?' he whispered into his mouthpiece.

'Motor,' said Winter, a distinct chatter in his voice. 'There a sub in the water?'

They waited, and as they were about to move again, a strong light came on under the *Ariadne*, making Gallen raise his hand to his face plate. The humming increased and then the light moved downwards, the humming receding once more.

'What was that?' said Gallen.

Winter's speech was now forced. 'Submersible, but I couldn't be sure. I think my retinas are burned out.'

Blinking out the intensity of the sudden light source, Gallen moved across the underbelly of the *Ariadne* by feel again, a big yellow and purple patch now sitting in the middle of his vision. From zero light to an underwater halogen in a split-second was too much for the human eye.

The underbelly of the craft stopped and Gallen felt around the edges of the large divers lock and docking bay for submersibles. They were at their destination but Gallen was confused.

'This is it,' he said, wanting to keep Winter talking. 'Wasn't there a structure under here?'

'The power room,' said Winter. 'Must be on the other side—maybe the tin can swung around with the explosion.'

The original plan had been to send Winter into the light with the shark gun and for Gallen to follow with his SIG. But with Hansen cutting the diving lock cameras and the lights being down, Gallen decided to get Winter out of the water as fast as he could.

'Straight up stealth,' he said over the radio. 'Let's rise up real quiet and see who's around.'

'Suits me,' said Winter.

Running his hands up the side of the divers lock, Gallen moved towards the surface, unable to see where that was. His helmet struck steel, the sound of it echoing in his brain as if someone had set off an alarm. Feeling above him, he grabbed hold of a steel ladder and pulled himself up the wall of the lock, creating cover for their emergence. Breaking the surface, he grabbed a docking buffer and paused, trying to keep movement and breathing to a minimum.

He pulled Winter up by the scuba straps; they remained still for thirty seconds until Gallen gave the all-clear and dragged himself onto the dock that ran around the lock's pool. The room was dark but surprisingly warm and Gallen kicked off his fins then crawled behind large plastic gear boxes.

Spitting out his regulator mouthpiece and unscrewing the helmet, he placed it carefully on the grated steel dock and beckoned to Winter with a tap on the shoulder. Unscrewing the Canadian's helmet, Gallen recalled his guided tour and remembered that the divers lock had lockers along one side and diving equipment hanging alongside. Shrugging out of the scuba rig, Gallen crept through the darkness using his hands, feeling over the dry suits and helmets and then running his hands along the smooth painted steel of the lockers. Opening the first, he felt heavy, padded coveralls on a coat hanger and pulled them out. There was a similar pair in the next locker; grabbing them, he headed back to Winter.

'Shit, I'm sorry about that, boss,' said Winter. He was shivering, and Gallen kneeled in front of him and got him out of the dry suit.

'Get the undergarment off too,' said Gallen. 'Got dry coveralls.'

The sound was very faint but they heard it at the same time, tensing against each other. It was the hatchway opening, a tiny squeak above the lapping of the water.

Ducking further behind the gear boxes, Gallen realised he'd left his fins in the open. As he unwrapped the SIG handgun as quietly as he could, Gallen felt a hand on his forearm and then Winter was holding a Ka-bar combat knife in front of his face.

As the new arrival moved into the divers lock, Gallen remained absolutely still as Winter shifted into a crouch.

The footfalls continued to the other side of the dock and they could hear the person sit on a gear box, the thick plastic groaning slightly. A flashlight beam lit up the area, making Gallen wince again. The flashlight strafed the water and was switched off.

Gripping his SIG, Gallen stayed silent, almost holding his breath. After twenty seconds, there was a small sound beside the intruder—his flashlight came on and, as the man stood to check on the noise, the white flash of a second form moved on him. Standing, Gallen moved around the dock as the gurgling death throes of the man sounded above the lapping water.

'Cameraman?' said Winter in a whisper as Gallen arrived.

Gallen thought he'd been the sound guy from Du Bois' film crew; whoever he was, he lay on the grated floor, a bloody smile inscribed around his upper throat.

'Light,' said Winter, and went to work on the body as Gallen cupped the lens of the flashlight and peered over the Canadian's shoulder. The dead man's build was strong and professionally fit, but not in a gym-bunny way.

Winter checked the man's shirt pockets, then shifted to the jeans. Empty. He took off the boots and socks and then pulled down the man's pants.

'Jox,' said Winter. 'This guy's not standing out in any way.'

'Which means he's standing out.'

'Which means I'm not buying the environmentalist horse shit,' said Winter. 'You ever met a greenie who isn't trying to make a fashion statement?'

Gallen got what he meant: environmentalists weren't this stripped down. They had silly hats and issue T-shirts, and tattoos of Maori symbols. They weren't 'clean' in the intel sense of the word.

'Underwear is basic North American,' said Winter, pulling down the blue Jox, 'but he's circumcised.'

Gallen nodded as Winter pulled them up again. 'Doesn't make him Israeli.'

'Okay,' said Winter, his teeth chattering slightly. 'But I'm going to check his teeth; if there's more than twenty grand's worth of crowns in there, no way this dude's a Frenchie.'

'Israelis ain't the only ones with a thing about their teeth, Kenny,' said Gallen, wanting to get the insulated overalls on.

'Yeah, but the only others I can think of are Americans and Singaporeans, and this dude don't talk like a Yankee and he don't look like no Chinaman.'

'Okay,' said Gallen. 'Check 'em.'

Winter opened the man's mouth, and Gallen shone the flashlight inside. The mouth looked huge and pink contrasted with the dark, and Winter didn't need long.

'This has the same smell as that dude we found in the snow cave. I think we're down here with the Mossad.'

'Great,' said Gallen, standing.

'Ideas?' said Winter.

'Find the hostages, drop the bad guys.'

'Works for me,' said Winter.

The *Ariadne* felt deserted. With the power off there wasn't even the hum Gallen would have expected from such a large submerged vessel. What did worry him was the oxygen supply—with comms shut off to the *Fanny Blankes-Koen*, and the power down, the vessel could get heat and air from emergency back-up batteries, but for how long?

At the main junction, where the control room sat, Gallen and Winter spread out. There was an eerie, abandoned quiet to the place. Looking over the console for clues, Gallen couldn't see a thing. It was shut down.

'I'm lighting up,' he said, and switched on the marine flashlight, cupping the lens as he made a quick search of the computers and screens of the console. It was still warm. Walking around the console, Gallen walked into the back of Winter.

'The captain—what's his name?' said Winter.

Gallen cupped the flashlight and looked down at the focus of Winter's interest.

'His name's Menzies,' said Gallen.

Menzies sat slumped against the legs of the control desk, a third eye in his forehead. His arm extended unnaturally up and over the control modules and Gallen followed it: there was a handcuff on the dead man's wrist to which was secured a security card, jammed in a slot.

They leaned in: above the slot were the words Emergency ejection system.

'What the fuck's an emergency ejection system?' said Winter.

Gallen saw the set-up and he saw someone who'd been lured into the open and forced to put his card into that slot, probably at the end of a gun. When the job was done, Du Bois' team had executed him.

'You hear that?' said Winter, grabbing Gallen by the arm.

They stood in silence, listening to a faint voice coming from somewhere in the vessel.

Holding the SIG in front of him, Gallen led Winter along the hull that held the dorms. At the end of the hull, he could make out a crack of light escaping through an incompletely closed hatch, the voice growing louder, recognisably female.

Pushing into the room with his SIG in front of him, Gallen saw Martina Du Bois, in *Ariadne* coveralls, talking into a camera on a writing desk. There was a light shining on her face and the whole thing was attached to a tractor battery.

'. . . *for the last time has the arrogant West and the hegemony of the big oil companies trodden on the rights of the animals and the indigenous inhabitants in the Arctic Ocean. ArcticWatch has traced the arrogant Oasis Energy as they have lied and deceived their way to the point where they now control most of the Arctic sea floor, and we can now reveal to the world exactly how they were going to make it so profitable: not only were they going to mount an ingenious pumping station on the sea floor, but they were going to power it with a nuclear reactor. Yes, that's right—Oasis Energy has placed a nuclear power plant in the heart of the last untouched wilderness in the northern hemisphere, purely so they can operate year round and prove sustainable profits to Wall Street . . .*'

Gallen stepped forward, checked the room for assailants, and placed the gun against Du Bois' head. 'You're not an environmentalist, you're a murderer. Now get up!'

'Ah, it's our very own John Wayne,' said Du Bois, turning. 'Smile, you're on CNN and Fox, Mr Gerry.'

'Where's the crew, what have you done with the power?' said Gallen, as Winter moved into the room to join him.

'Good question, Mr Gerry,' she sneered. 'You're just in time for my announcement: the STAR nuclear power plant has been ejected from this vessel and now lies on the sea bed.'

'That's useful,' said Gallen.

'No, Mr Gerry,' said Du Bois. 'It's a statement; a statement no oil company will ever forget.'

CHAPTER 62

'Where's the crew?' Gallen asked Du Bois again as he disconnected the camera.

Du Bois smirked. 'They're safe.'

Gallen gave a nod to Winter. The Canadian left and Gallen pushed the terrorist against the wall. 'Where are they?'

'Perhaps not they, Mr Gerry.'

'What are you talking about?'

Sneering, she was no longer so beautiful. 'Your boss has behaved arrogantly, Mr Gerry; now she'll learn some humility.'

'Florita?' said Gallen, wanting to threaten Du Bois but knowing that was what she wanted.

'She your girlfriend, Mr Gerry?' said Du Bois. 'Or doesn't she screw the help?'

'She doesn't drop nuclear reactors on the ocean floor, let's leave it at that.'

A noise echoed through the vessel. Human voices, shouting, confused. Winter appeared at the door again. 'Found Tucker, boss.'

'How is he?'

'Got a hole in him, needs a quack,' said Winter. 'Mike's okay.'

Gallen hated his men being harmed, took it very personally. He wanted Hansen to haul them up, but after too many years of special forces operations in the Ghan he resisted the urge. Gallen's number-one worry was a booby trap and he knew he had to slow himself down.

'Who else?' he said.

Winter shrugged. 'That's it. Menzies is dead, Tucker was shot in the leg. And Florita ain't down here.'

'Where's Letour?'

'Here,' said Winter, letting through Ben Letour, Menzies' second-in-command.

'We need to search this vessel,' said Gallen. 'Who knows what surprises they've left us with?'

'What are we looking for?' said Letour.

Gallen thought about it. 'Anything that will kill us as soon as we ascend. And by the way, is Negroponte here?'

Letour and Winter looked at one another. 'He went down with the power station, when it ejected,' said Letour.

Gallen hissed. 'I'll meet you back at the control room. Let's make sure this place is clean before we move. I need everyone accounted for.' Turning to Du Bois, he felt his guts churning.

'Looking for a bomb?' said Du Bois. 'Why would environmentalists bomb you?'

'Greenies wouldn't,' said Gallen. 'But a bunch of Mossad agents pretending to be environmentalists might.'

Du Bois' eyes darkened in a flash then returned to their normal state. But Gallen caught it.

'Well that's very intriguing, Mr Gerry. Maybe you watch too much the Bruce Willis DVDs, yes?'

'Where are your men, if they're not on the *Ariadne*?'

She shrugged and smiled.

'Where's Florita?'

Du Bois sighed. 'Learning the secrets of the deep.'

'She's down there?' said Gallen, pointing at the floor. 'With the STAR?'

'Do you know how much she stood to gain personally by pushing through this contraption?' said Du Bois, jaw jutting with defiance. 'This *nuclear*-powered contraption?'

'I don't do the books,' said Gallen. 'Wrong guy.'

'Hah!' said the Frenchwoman, seemingly amused. 'You are not like the Americans in the movies, yes? You are the simple ones, the red states? Republican . . . ?'

'Redneck's the word,' said Gallen. 'And I don't vote. You been watching CNN, think every American's wandering around worrying about Tea Parties and having a black president.'

'You're not?'

'The only tea parties I know of happened in Wonderland and Boston,' said Gallen. 'And presidents? If they raise taxes or stop me shooting cougars, they can kiss my ass.'

'Not the racist, Mr Gerry?'

'In Wyoming, all politicians are the same colour, same religion.'

'Four hundred million dollars US!' said Du Bois.

'What?'

'That's what Mendes will make if this project works to budget and yield.'

Gallen could hear approaching footsteps. 'That's a lot of money.'

'Yes, and it only works with the self-contained pumping and maintenance rigs on the sea bed. And now we hear the full picture.'

'Full?'

'That takeover announcement,' said Du Bois, standing. 'It means Oasis controls about eighty per cent of the Arctic Ocean drilling leases. Within a decade, there'll be two hundred nuclear reactors on the sea bed.'

'Where is she?' said Gallen as Winter and Ford walked in.

Martina Du Bois smiled like a snake. 'She's inspecting the site of the world's latest nuclear reactor.'

They crowded around the circular control desk, Gallen allowing the acting commander of the vessel—Ben Letour—to take them through it.

'We've got comms again with the *Fanny Blankes-Koen*,' said the XO. 'But the terrorists have disabled the ship-side air hoses. We're on emergency oxygen bottles, and with the full complement on board we have about ninety minutes of air.'

'And then?' said Gallen.

'We'll slowly start dying, as the carbon dioxide becomes too great.'

'And in ninety minutes we might get thirty people off this tin can with one submersible?' said Gallen.

'Maybe less,' crackled Hansen's voice through the console speaker. 'I've done emergency take-offs before, my friends, and they never work as fast as the crisis manual says.'

'Hansen,' said Letour into the mic, 'given our concerns about a bomb, what would you suggest?'

'Search the vessel,' said Hansen. 'And then ascend. There's no other way, and right now you're using up oxygen.'

Gallen nodded. He already had Winter and Ford searching the vessel and trying to keep the crew out of the way—not an easy task when they were roughnecks and clearance divers, seamen and drilling engineers. People who would not politely sit back and be snow-jobbed.

'Master Hansen,' said Gallen as respectfully as he could, 'the *Ariadne* ain't small and we're going as fast as we can. We also have morale problems with the personnel.'

'I'm sorry, Mr Gallen,' said the big Swede. 'There's no other way.'

Half an hour later, Letour approached Gallen as he gulped at a bottle of water, the heat and muggy atmosphere building despite the *Ariadne*'s climate-control system. Carbon dioxide carried its own heat and Gallen had stripped his coveralls to the waist.

'We're facing a mutiny,' said Letour, flush-faced and now dressed in a white T-shirt and shorts. 'How're your men going?'

Gallen raised the radio handset. 'Tango Team this is Blue Dog—sitrep please, over.'

Winter's voice barked out clearly, 'Situation unchanged since last sitrep eighty seconds ago, Blue Dog. Yellow Bird out.'

Letour rubbed his face. 'What if there's nothing here?'

'What if there is?'

Letour nodded and slumped in the controller's seat. 'I guess you have bigger things to worry about, with your CEO missing?'

'I have to go get her after this,' said Gallen.

'That could be a suicide mission.'

'That's the gig,' said Gallen. He was still waiting on the confirmation of his suspicions. Aaron's bio of the film crew had been checked but Gallen had asked Aaron to email the file to a secure service where it could be picked up and rechecked by Pete Morton. Morton owed him no more than he'd already given, but it might suit him to help.

'Why Menzies?' said Gallen. It had been annoying him: why kill the vessel's commander?

'Why is he dead?' said Letour. 'I don't know.'

'What did he know? You think he knew the terrorists?'

Winter walked up, red-faced, Ford and a limping Liam Tucker behind him.

'How you doin', Liam?' said Gallen, seeing cut-away trousers and a big white bandage on the man's left thigh.

'Only a leg wound,' said the former Marine. 'Worst part was passing out, hitting my head on the bulkhead.'

Gallen turned to Winter and looked at his watch. 'We have nine minutes before people start dropping. Are we clean?'

'There's nothing in the way of an IED on this vessel, boss.'

'Checked the oxygen and nitrogen bottles?' said Gallen. 'They can be detonated.'

'Went over every one—Mike did a tap test on every bottle. Nothing in them or on them.'

'Wiring loops?'

'Did it myself,' said Winter. 'The junction boxes and access points still have their wax seals. The only points accessed were the power and comms boxes, and they're clean of IEDs.'

Gallen tapped his teeth. Everyone was looking sick. 'Okay, Ben,' he said to Letour. 'I'm clearing us from a security point of view. We're okay to ascend if you say so.'

Nodding, Letour leaned on the orange button on the console and asked Hansen to haul them up.

The wary voice of the Swedish master on the ship echoed down the line and a slight jerk shook the *Ariadne*. Then, as they looked at one another, the vessel made imperceptible movements, the shaking stopped and they were moving upwards.

From the various wings of the *Ariadne* a cheer went up as a loud sigh of relief.

Gallen swapped looks with his three men. They still had a CEO to retrieve.

CHAPTER 63

As the *Ariadne* rose to the surface at an agonisingly slow rate, Gallen thought through what had to happen next. He wanted to take Ford in a submersible to look for the vessel that had left the *Ariadne* with Florita apparently on board. But he needed more information on what they might be doing down there.

The technician on the control desk looked up. 'You Gerry Gallen?'

'Sure,' said Gallen, roused from his thoughts.

'Secure email for you, sir.'

Gallen looked at the email on screen. It was from Pete Morton, telling him to go to the Gmail account he'd set up a week earlier.

The tech left him alone and he accessed the account, opening Morton's message. There were two panels and a message from Morton: *You owe me big time.*

The first panel was for the person Gallen knew as Raffa, the documentary director: the panel—a translated file from Syrian intelligence by the look of it—called him Ari Fleischmann, a former IDF Navy commando who had been used by the Mossad in paramilitary work.

The second panel, also looking like a Syrian intel bromide, named a person called Marc Sadinsky—the man Winter had killed. He was a Mossad-trained assassin who had done a lot of work with various navies. There was no bounce for the third of the film crew. But it was confirmed: the crew was Mossad, and they were either dead or gone. But he still had a Frenchwoman who could be useful.

Du Bois was flexi-cuffed to the internal piping of the room he'd left her in. Her lips were white and her face red.

'Can you turn on the air?' she croaked.

'You turned it off, Martina.'

'It was supposed to be for a few minutes.'

Gallen smiled. 'They cut the umbilical for the air and power. You've got one hundred people breathing from a few bottles of oxygen.'

'I'm going to pass out,' she said. 'How close are we to the surface?'

'Let me worry about that,' said Gallen, happy the cocky act had gone. 'We're missing one chief engineer. Where's he?'

'In the power station, I assume,' she said.

'Where's the power station, Martina?'

'On the bottom,' she said. 'Look, I'm an asthmatic. I need air.'

'What's the power station doing on the bottom?'

'A protest,' said Du Bois. 'A publicity event that will shut down Arctic exploitation for the next twenty years.'

'How so?'

'As we speak there's an ArcticWatch statement going to every news desk in the world, and every government in the United Nations.'

'Saying what?'

Du Bois coughed. 'That Oasis Energy's *Ariadne* has lost her illegal nuclear reactor and it's currently sitting on the sea bed waiting to be rescued. The statement also outlines how Oasis planned to incorporate nuclear power into its sea-bed rigs—in total secrecy, of course.'

Gallen thought about Negroponte, the secrecy under which he was deployed. 'How did you know about the nuclear plans?'

'Raffa and Josh approached me,' said Du Bois. 'They came to me through good contacts. They're environmental extremists and they told me about the *Ariadne*.'

'I'm betting this wasn't your plan?'

'It was overseen by me, Mr Gerry,' she said.

'It wasn't your idea, Martina.'

'Maybe not,' she gasped.

'The plan?'

'To drop the power station from the *Ariadne*, and film it on the bottom. Then broadcast it to the world with the CEO of Oasis watching.'

'You think that's all they're doing?'

'What else would they do?' said Du Bois.

'I think your organisation has been infiltrated by Israel's Mossad.'

'How stupid,' said Du Bois. 'You expect me to believe that?'

Someone yelled out for Gallen and he broke away, walked to the control desk, a swinging sensation under his feet: they'd stopped their ascent.

'We have a problem,' said Letour. 'Part of the vessel isn't depressurising—we think it's the emergency lock, from what we're hearing.'

Gallen saw a group of *Ariadne* personnel around the hatchway to the emergency lock.

'What's that mean?'

The vessel groaned, a long, whining sound, like bad plumbing.

'It means that as we ascend the air in the emergency lock expands and blows the thing apart.'

'That why we stopped?'

'Hell, yeah,' said Letour.

Tucker had been jumped by the Israelis, Gallen remembered. 'Liam,' he said, 'you have that card for the emergency lock?'

Checking his pockets, Tucker came up empty. 'They must have taken it.'

'The swipe card has been stolen, and the commander is dead,' said Gallen to Letour. 'Where does that leave us?'

'No manual override to get in there and let the pressure out,' said Letour. 'The power's down so we can't operate the valves manually. We can't go up, we could blow any second.'

Gallen grimaced: that was the IED, that was the trap. A lock filled with air that would expand as they got near sea level and blow its steel constraints apart.

'Do we know our depth, even without full power?'

'Hansen says twenty-two metres.'

'Can we swim from here?'

Letour shook his head. 'One hundred people, Mr Gallen. You'd have to retrieve them from Arctic waters and then stabilise them.'

'If anyone's got the equipment for that, it would be the *Fanny Blankes-Koen*,' said Gallen. Pressing on the mic button, he spoke with Hansen. 'Letour explained the problem?'

'Yes, he did.'

'If we swam off, would you have enough resources on the ship to deal with one hundred exposure cases?'

'We have enough blankets,' said Hansen. 'The transfer of people to the ship is the problem. We'd lose half of you just getting you on board.'

Gallen looked at the emergency lock as it groaned again, this time with a tapping sound.

'Of course, there is another way,' said Hansen, clearing his throat.

'Let's hear it,' said Gallen.

Gallen waited at the console with Letour, their ghostly pallor reflected in the half-light of the battery power. The entire complement of the *Ariadne* was in the staff quarters and the diving rooms. The staff quarters were locked down and the diving room's hatchways hung open, waiting for Letour and Gallen to run.

The emergency lock let out a high-pitched reverberation and Gallen could have sworn he saw the hatch lock shake.

'Hansen, this is Letour. Commence ascent, at full power.'

'Ascent commencing in five seconds,' said Hansen.

Running for the opened hatch of the diving room, Gallen leapt through behind Letour into a room filled with people.

As the *Ariadne* started moving towards the surface again, Gallen heard a loud explosion. Turning, he saw the hatchway's lock being propelled across the control desk at full force into the opposing bulkhead, taking the entire top row of monitoring equipment with it.

Water gushed behind it as Winter got the hatch shut and screwed it down. The vessel lunged as they went to the surface at full speed, feeling like an elevator without its side-tracks. Behind the hatch they could hear the water filling the control room and the sea splashing against the hatch with the force of a thousand punches.

'Stay calm,' said Gallen to the scores of mostly men who stared back from the gloom of the standby lights. 'We're going straight to the surface and we're doing it without getting our feet wet.'

'If we don't suffocate in the meantime,' said an Irish voice. Several had already succumbed to the low-oxygen environment.

It seemed to take forever, but according to Gallen's G-Shock it was only three minutes forty before he felt a swinging sensation, suggesting they were lurching free of the water.

Men surged towards the hatch and Letour stopped them. 'Have to wait,' he gasped. 'Let the water run out.'

Another man collapsed and his friend demanded to be let out. Gallen drew his SIG. 'We do it the way the XO wants it done and maybe we'll live. Okay?' He looked the rig worker in the eye; slowly the man backed away.

There were clanking sounds outside the hatch and then it was being unscrewed. On the other side stood a seaman from the *Fanny Blankes-Koen* in his red suit, as the fresh air flooded in like a wave of life. The men rushed for the exit, Gallen not game to stop them now. Standing back, he and Letour watched them clamber out into the destroyed control area, where they sucked in the air. When they'd left, Gallen noticed a group of men standing around something.

'Over here,' called Winter, beckoning.

Walking to the group, Gallen looked down and saw a dead man: Anglo, balding, with a tattoo on his forearm that Gallen had just recently discovered was for the US Army nuclear reactor officers.

'Negroponte,' said Winter, spitting. 'The fuck's he doin' in the emergency lock?' Kneeling, he checked the dead man's mouth, neck and eyes. 'Strangled,' he said.

'Killed in the power station, dragged to the emergency lock,' said Gallen.

'Yep,' said Winter. 'So who's in the power station now? Who's holding the key to that thing?'

Standing, Gallen gulped at the fresh air sluicing in off the Beaufort like the best drug. 'Let's find out.'

On the deck of the service ship, they found Tucker and Ford keeping Du Bois company. Aaron had his pistol held to Du Bois' kidneys and then he was pushing her along the deck, back to the state rooms.

'Aaron,' said Gallen, seeing a raised eyebrow from Winter as he walked past. 'What's up? I need to talk to her.'

'So do I, Gerry. This is no longer Oasis business.'

'What?' said Gallen, surprised.

Aaron kept walking. 'Join us if you want.'

Two men in *Ariadne* jumpsuits peeled off and joined Aaron, who steered Du Bois through the companionways and passages, into his state room, where he threw her on the bed. From his briefcase he pulled a digital recorder and flicked it on, slamming it on the small writing desk.

'Martina Du Bois, of ArcticWatch, my name is Aaron Michaels, I'm an agent of the US Government. I need to ask you some questions and anything you say will be recorded and used in any way deemed fit by the government.'

'Fuck you,' said the Frenchwoman, struggling against one of Aaron's undercover heavies.

'Who are you working with?' said Aaron, as though she hadn't said a word.

Du Bois spat at Aaron, kicked one of her captors. Grabbing the recorder, she threw it at a mirror, smashing both items.

'This isn't a joke, Martina,' said Aaron, wiping off the spit as the heavies got their hands on her again.

'Who are you, anyway?' said Du Bois.

'It's best if I ask the questions,' said Aaron, and Gallen knew he'd lost the battle.

'Aaron, can we talk?' he said, inclining his head to the door.

Outside, Gallen immediately started in. 'What the fuck, Aaron? I asked if you were Agency.'

'And I said no, which is the truth. You're ruining my interrogation.'

'You ruined it yourself as soon as you went with the Gestapo line.'

Aaron rocked back on his heels, pushing his hair back. 'Shit, Gerry. This has been a long, hard road.'

'Where are you from?'

'An agency that monitors illegal use of nuclear technology.'

'Shit, you're DIA?'

'No,' said Aaron. 'We work with them a lot. But this is separate.'

'That leaves NSA.'

'No comment, Gerry. We've been chasing Mendes for years.'

'Years?' said Gallen, aghast. 'She only made CEO two weeks ago.'

'She was planted at Oasis, groomed up,' said Aaron. 'Shit, I'm saying too much.'

'Say more,' said Gallen, nostrils flaring with annoyance.

'Harry was going to die in a hunting accident in Russia, but another hit team got to his plane first and almost took Florita Mendes and the rest of you with it.'

'Planted?' said Gallen, stunned. 'By whom? Why?'

'Does it matter? Right now we have a team of terrorists on the sea bed with a nuclear device.'

'You tell me why it matters,' said Gallen, 'and I'll work on Martina for you, if you ask me nice.'

Aaron sighed, shook his head. 'Florita Mendes works for the Bashoff crime family in a sleeper capacity. The STARs she's been pushing for in the underwater rigs? They're a Russian design, produced by a Bashoff company. The Oasis takeover of Thor is illusory. It was a reverse takeover orchestrated by the Bashoff bankers and Florita herself.'

'It can go two ways, Martina,' said Gallen, lighting a smoke when he was back in the state room and half recovered from the conversation with Aaron.

'You talk in clichés, you Americans.'

Gallen ignored her, cracked a porthole for his smoke. 'You've killed an American sea captain and a former US Army officer, who happens to have been a nuclear reactor officer.'

'I didn't kill anyone,' snapped the Frenchwoman.

'The CIA might overlook that detail and go straight to the part about nuclear terror. If the Pentagon's spooks get to you first, you'll be rendered to a basement in Egypt where they can have a long chat with you—see who else is planning nuclear attacks against the United States.'

'I'm a French citizen,' she snarled. 'You wouldn't dare.'

'Try me,' said Gallen, exhaling smoke. 'There are few things less humorous to Washington than a bunch of unfriendlies playing rock-paper-scissors with nukes.'

A knock sounded at the stateroom door and Ben Letour entered.

'I know nothing about this,' said Du Bois, 'except what I told you. I didn't know they were Mossad. I still don't know that.'

'Maybe,' said Gallen. 'But there's a whole layer of intelligence bureaucracy devoted to finding people like you and extracting every ounce of information. It's called the Greater Good theory, Martina— you know what that is?'

'I know what civilised Europeans think it is.'

Gallen smiled. 'Let me give you the Pentagon's version of Greater Good: violating the human rights of one Frenchwoman is okay if in doing so you can save an American city from a nuclear strike.'

Du Bois looked away, chewed her lip.

'It won't matter that you're French or that you're charming, Martina,' said Gallen, keeping on the pressure. 'I worked with these people in the Ghan and they don't ever laugh. They'll take one look at you and see someone who values her looks as the core of her very identity, and as soon as—'

'Okay, okay,' she spat. 'I get it.'

Gallen sat in front of her. 'Here's the deal. You talk to me informally, and I can vouch for you later. You get cute and I feed you to Aaron, who's got a Learjet waiting at Kugaaruk.'

Du Bois gulped. 'I don't know what I can tell you.'

'What are they doing down there?'

'Filming,' she said, shrugging.

'The one you call Raffa is actually Ari—former IDF Navy commando and Mossad operator: he's down there with a nuke. The person you know as Josh is a Mossad lifer: his real name's Marc and he's dead.'

She looked at her feet.

'The third one, the slightly older one,' said Gallen.

'Gregor?' said Du Bois.

'What was his relationship with Luc and Raffa?'

'In the background more,' she said. 'What can I say?'

'Well how about this: the two tough guys are Mossad agents who do this sort of thing for a living. What about Gregor? He's not a sound guy. What do you think he is?'

'In real life?'

Gallen nodded, flicking his butt through the porthole.

'Do I get amnesty?'

'This ain't *CSI Arctic Circle*, Martina,' said Gallen, grabbing her by the shoulders. 'Focus. What role does Gregor play in this crew?'

She looked away and Gallen felt her relaxing in his hands. 'Okay, there was one thing.'

'Yes?'

'Before we went under the water, Gregor was talking to one of the senior guys on the *Ariadne* and he came back to the others.'

'He know you were listening?'

'No,' said Du Bois. 'He said to Josh something like, *The well heads are not a problem*, and *The caissons are a good fit*. That make any sense?'

'Letour,' said Gallen, breaking away from Du Bois. 'What's a caisson?'

'It's a big circular hole in the ground.'

'On the bottom?'

'Yes,' said Letour. 'Where else?'

'How big is it?'

Letour made a face. 'About thirty feet across, one hundred deep—we build them to house and stabilise the well head. The well bore isn't anywhere near that size, but the caisson ends up encasing all of the flow-backs and equalisers and emergency valving. On the top of it all sits the BOP.'

'Which is?'

'It's the blow-out preventer. When it malfunctions you get a disaster, like the BP well in the Gulf that blew up in 2010.'

'Some of the well heads aren't finished, right?' said Gallen. 'So the caisson is open?'

'To the sea, yeah,' said Letour, confused. 'But at the bottom of the caisson—about one hundred feet down—the well is capped. It's not running yet. Where is this going?'

'How wide is the power station?' said Gallen, pulse rising.

Letour's eyes widened and when he spoke it was dream-like. 'About twenty-five feet across.'

They stared at each other.

'I'll need that last submersible, and someone who knows oil drilling,' said Gallen.

'You don't think . . . ?' said Letour, then he stopped himself. 'Oh shit.'

CHAPTER 64

The *Fanny Blankes-Koen*'s secondary crane swung the submersible to the inside of the starboard hull, having retrieved it from the holds. It was yellow with black markings—like a school bus—and looked old, maybe 1960s.

Pulling on his thermals and padded coveralls, Gallen looked at it and tried to shake loose any phobias. They were going more than a thousand feet down, where there was no light and no escape if things went wrong. It was like going to the moon.

'What's that?' he said to Master Hansen, pointing at the sign on the side of the sub. 'Sea Otter?'

'It's an old design,' said the Swede. 'But reliable. It's good for four hours.'

'You got nothing modern?' said Gallen, as the technicians did their checks and beckoned him over to the submersible.

'The mechanical arm on the front is the latest design from a team at CalTech—about three times stronger and more articulate than the models it surpasses.'

Aaron walked out of the gear room in his padded coveralls. 'There's really nothing I can do down there, Gerry,' said the spook. 'If it were up to me—'

'Yeah, yeah,' said Gallen. 'Get in the can.'

Aaron shook his head and took the hand of a technician as he stretched his leg onto the submersible.

'We got a skipper?' said Gallen, turning back to Hansen.

The master smiled. 'I'll be your chauffeur, sir,' he said, with a bad Swedish attempt at an English accent.

'You don't have to,' said Gallen. 'I haven't been totally honest with you about what's down there.'

'There's a nuclear reactor loose on the Arctic floor,' said Hansen, his eyebrow rising. 'You saying there's *more?*'

'Like I said,' said Gallen, 'you can sit this one out.'

But Hansen had already taken a technician's hand and was clambering into the yellow tin can.

The sub was cramped and noisy. After ten minutes of their descent, Hansen at the tiller, Gallen had given up panicking at every groan and graunch that emanated from the machine.

'It'll take us about twenty minutes to get down there,' said Hansen, seeing the looks on the faces of his passengers. 'You'll get used to it.'

The ceiling almost touched their heads and their knees came up to their chests. Around them were dials and switches packed tightly, and other than the groans and squeals of the sub, the predominant noise was of the whining electrical motors, the small fans in each corner and the faint hiss of air being released into the coffin-like capsule.

Gallen had once totally freaked out his female neighbour, Daisy Antrim, by locking her in the trunk of his mother's Impala. He hadn't known she was badly claustrophobic until he let her out half an hour later and found she'd gnawed at her own forearms with the panic of it all.

He looked around now and saw an environment that would cause Daisy to tear out her own teeth: they were strapped inside a tiny tin can, dropping to the ocean floor through a sea so black that the massive light beams on the front of the vessel were eaten up in the abyss before reaching more than sixty feet. Everything seemed to press in, the water pressure exerting itself on the rivets and welds.

'So,' said the Swede, as they descended at a forty-five-degree tilt in a series of downward spirals, 'you were going to tell me what else is down there, besides a nuclear reactor.'

Gallen caught a look from Aaron. 'I'm fairly sure the people who hijacked the *Ariadne* and released the emergency bolts on the reactor are Mossad.'

'The Israeli spies?' said Hansen, as if he were asking about flying pigs. 'Here? In the Arctic? But why?'

Gallen realised how silly it sounded. 'I can't tell you why just yet. I know there were three of them—now two: a Mossad officer and someone who I'm assuming is the scientist or the technician.'

'Nuclear technician,' said Aaron, as if Hansen hadn't worked it out.

'Will they make a bomb?' said Hansen, wide-eyed. 'Or just poison the sea?'

Gallen shook his head, craving a smoke. 'Judging by something Du Bois overheard, I think they're going to drop the reactor in one of the caissons.'

'The what?' said Hansen. 'The *caissons*?'

'That's what Du Bois heard the scientist guy saying to the others,' said Gallen. 'But we should ask Mr G-Man here.'

'Don't look at me,' said Aaron, whose forehead shone like that of a man in the middle of an anxiety episode.

'You don't have an opinion on that?' said Gallen, fed up with the secret squirrel act.

'I have an opinion on how easily these STARs can be reversed into meltdown,' said Aaron, squirming as they spiralled downwards. 'These Russian transportable reactors can only be made so small because of their plutonium cores.'

'Plutonium, as in the warhead material?' said Gallen.

Aaron nodded. 'The danger isn't that you can turn it into a bomb in half an hour. You can't.'

'So what then?' said the Swede.

'If you can short-circuit the fail-safes, you can put them into meltdown.'

'Can we use English?' said Gallen.

'Ever see that movie *The China Syndrome*?'

'Sure,' said Gallen, searching Aaron's eyes for clues. 'The reactor's cooling system failed and the thing just melts through the floor.'

'Basically, yes. The plutonium cores feature immense fission activity and so they run at extremely high temperatures unless they're inhibited and cooled,' said Aaron. 'You retard the temperatures with graphite and water and they tick over for a decade at a time before the rods need replacing. They produce steam that drives turbines for power.'

'And if you fail to retard the fission?' said Hansen.

'Like they said in the movie, the rods rise to the temperature of the sun and they simply follow gravity through everything in their path.'

'And we let the Ruskies build these things?' said Gallen.

Aaron shrugged. 'The Russians were using STARs in the Arctic Circle since the 1970s, mainly for remote communities and drilling operations. We had nuclear power in McMurdo, in Antarctica. But those old Russian STARs were uranium-powered; they were stable and were quite large units mounted on barges.'

'Where did the plutonium come in?' said Gallen.

'More energy from a smaller unit,' said Aaron. 'The developers decided there was a large market for a nuclear power station you could carry on the back of a Dodge Ram. Florita had the perfect test bed for them—a sea-bed drilling rig, for Christ's sake.'

'So,' said Hansen, 'these terrorists don't want to blow up the nuclear reactor? They will melt it down?'

'I don't know,' said Aaron. 'We've been keeping an eye on the *Ariadne* project but the hijacking surprised us.'

'We should think about this,' said the Swede, flashing a look at Gallen.

'We should?' said Gallen. 'What should we think about?'

Looking through the bubble windscreen as he manoeuvred the sub with a grip in each hand, Hansen's eyes grew wide. 'It can't be,' he whispered, shaking his head softly.

'Can't be what?' asked Aaron.

Hansen looked as if he'd eaten a bad oyster. 'No one is so evil, surely?'

'Try me,' said Gallen.

Hansen took a calming breath. 'These well heads are on a geological feature called the Gakkel Ridge. You know of this?'

'No,' said Gallen.

'The Gakkel Ridge sits at the confluence of two tectonic plates,' said Hansen. 'Beneath the ridge are vast domes holding down trillions of litres of compressed CO_2.'

'Is that bad?' said Gallen.

'At these depths, it's almost impossible for an undersea volcano to erupt and disperse its plasma.'

'Yes?'

'But the Gakkel Ridge is so volatile, and it develops such incredible gas pressures—maybe twenty times the pressures you see in the St Helens eruptions—that it can explode even under the weight of three kilometres of ocean.'

Gallen felt reflux. 'So a nuclear reactor in meltdown—that would ruin this oil field for Oasis, right?'

'Forget about an oil field,' said Hansen, exasperated. 'If you puncture one of these Gakkel domes in the wrong place, you could tear apart the entire sea floor.'

CHAPTER 65

'Can we hit the lights?' said Gallen as they saw the first signs of the *Ariadne*'s submersible beneath them.

The tiny cockpit was plunged into inky blackness as Hansen killed the lights, Gallen and Aaron gasping slightly at the shock of it. The totality of the light deprivation had a swallowing effect that instantly made human existence seem insignificant.

'Shit,' said Gallen, breathing out. 'That's fricking *dark*.'

'Oh boy,' said Aaron. 'This isn't my thing.'

'You sure they can't see us?' said Gallen as Hansen eased off the throttles and let the Sea Otter sink to the rear of where the other sub's lights were throwing.

'They have good sonar, and they'll be able to sense something behind them,' said the Swede as the Sea Otter hovered fifty feet to the rear of the white sub. 'But their actual vision is forward-facing.'

Gallen leaned towards the glass porthole as he let his eyes adjust to the environment. The white sub's lights illuminated the muddy ground in front of it, and sediment rose in clouds as the props went on and off as it positioned itself. There was a large black 2 painted on the roof of the vessel.

'What are they doing in the mud?' said Gallen.

'Could be the reactor,' said Aaron. 'It may have taken some time to find it on the sea bed.'

'How much air do they have?' said Gallen, watching the sub screw around like a pig with its snout in the mud.

Hansen made a clicking sound. 'About three hours.'

'That means they have about two hours left,' said Gallen.

'There,' said Aaron, as the white sub's pig-rooting ceased and it slowly rose out of the sediment cloud.

They breathed softly as they waited for the white sub to become clearer. Then, as they watched it ascend thirty feet off the muddy bottom, it slowly swivelled on its axis.

'Shit,' said Hansen, pushing one of the hand grips forward as the front glass plate of the white sub turned to ninety degrees. 'She's coming about.'

The Sea Otter lurched to the port side, just avoiding the blinding floodlights of the spinning white sub. As they dipped out of the way, they looked up and saw it: the pale blue reactor room, held between two mechanical arms in front of the white sub's windscreen, and being carried like a garbage dumpster.

As they blended into blackness, the Sea Otter suddenly dropped.

'No,' said the Swede, as he struggled to control the vessel. 'Turbulence.'

He soon had the vessel righted but he couldn't stop it immediately, and the Sea Otter bounced on her side into the sea bottom.

Sitting in blackness and total silence for two seconds, they listened to one another's nervous breathing.

'The sub had a backwash,' said Hansen. 'Should have read that better.'

The silence was total and Gallen felt an important question formulating. Aaron beat him to it. 'We lost power, Hansen?'

'There's a back-up,' said Hansen. 'But that doesn't mean we don't have damage.'

Gallen blinked and still couldn't see a thing. The silence was broken only by the sound of Hansen's fingers moving over a panel. Then he heard a click; and a soft whining hum started up and the instrument panel once again had the red backlight behind it.

'Are we stuck?' said Aaron, his voice slightly too panicky for Gallen's liking. He'd heard that tone in Mindanao, where barracks bullies and cadre course heroes suddenly found they didn't like being in a tropical jungle at night. Especially not when the Abu Sayyaf ambushers were about.

'Let's find out,' said Hansen. The revs climbed and the capsule vibrated slightly.

Backing off the throttles, Hansen sighed. 'We're in mud, but I think we have damage to the rear prop.'

Aaron made a squawking sound. 'Try again. Please.'

'He will, Aaron,' said Gallen. 'Let's do it his way, okay?'

The revs climbed again, this time to an ear-splitting pitch.

Hansen clicked his teeth. 'Perhaps you two can rock, when I say so?'

'Rock?' said Aaron, the fear coming out in a low screech. 'You want us to rock this fucking thing?'

'Sure,' said Hansen. 'I need you both out of the harnesses, and leaning on the starboard side.'

Fumbling at the five-point harness in the dimness of the panel's glow, Gallen got himself free and rose first, grabbing Aaron by the collar and hauling him up. 'We're getting out of here, Aaron, okay?' he whispered. 'I won't let you die.'

Hearing the gulp and the rasped *okay*, Gallen pushed Aaron against the starboard bulkhead and then positioned himself with his hands against the pipes and cables that lined the vessel.

'On my three,' said Hansen, and counted them in.

On three, Gallen and Aaron heaved against the bulkhead; back and forth as the revs rose to a screech. Slowly the sub started rocking and then they were falling in a heap over the backs of their seats as the Sea Otter burst from the mud like a cork and went into a wild spin.

'Okay,' said Hansen as he brought down the revs. 'We're out but the main prop is buckled.'

'That bad?' said Gallen.

Hansen tapped on a small sonar screen. 'It means we're slower than the other sub, and lack power.'

The sonar glowed green, showing a small shape behind them.

'Can we get lights on?' said Aaron. 'Shit, it's dark.'

Gallen peered into the black. 'We need the element of surprise.'

'You think they haven't seen us? I mean, we can see them, can't we?' spat Aaron.

'Only because we know they're there,' said Hansen. 'Unless you're looking for us, we could be a seal or a whale.'

Swinging around, they watched the nose of the Sea Otter line up with the blinking green shape on the screen. 'About seventy metres away,' said Hansen.

After a minute of the whining electric motor pulling them through the dark, Aaron saw the lights. 'There!'

The lights got brighter as they closed, Hansen pulling back on the throttles and positioning the Sea Otter above and behind the white sub.

Hovering in the dark, peering into the other sub's lights, was like looking into an opera stage that you'd run across in the middle of space. It was eerie, isolated and made every nerve in Gallen's body scream.

'They still have the reactor,' said Gallen.

'Not for long—look!'

As the white sub inched forward, the reactor held aloft in the mechanical arms, the lights revealed what they were moving towards. Beyond the sub was the wide lip of a concrete cylinder, its thick sides standing twenty feet high and disappearing into the mud.

'That's the caisson,' said Hansen. 'One of three that were going to be finished in the next month.'

'This is the one that drops a hundred feet?' said Gallen.

'They all do,' said Hansen.

The white sub edged the reactor closer to the lip and Gallen gulped down the fear. He knew Aaron wanted to turn tail and phone it in, and he had no right to put Hansen in the kind of danger he wanted to expose him to. But he couldn't do nothing. It just wasn't an option.

'They can't drop that thing,' said Gallen. 'Let's go.'

'And do what?' said Hansen.

'Yeah, Gerry,' said Aaron, a little too whiny. 'What are we doing here? This is a job for the Navy SEALs or the clearance divers—'

'There might be Navy guys on the surface by now, Aaron. But this won't wait.'

In front of them the reactor was rising to a point where it could slide across the top of the caisson.

'Okay, but what are you going to do, Gerry?'

'Something more than nothing,' said Gallen. 'Take her in, Hansen.'

The nose dropped slightly as they accelerated towards the white sub.

'What do these do?' said Gallen, realising there were hand grips in front of his seat.

'They operate the mechanical arms. Up, down, with a forward movement of the grip,' said Hansen. 'The trigger makes the hands close and open.'

The arms made a loud whirring sound as Gallen tested them. They were responsive and surprisingly articulate.

'Are they strong enough to out-muscle the other sub?' said Gallen.

'Yes,' said Hansen. 'But we have to be careful. These rigs run on two twelve-volt battery sets. You use more power from one minute of using the arms than you do from an hour of normal operation.'

'So how long do we have with the arms?'

'Start with forty-five seconds and I'll let you know,' Hansen said, tapping at the voltage gauge on the dashboard. 'We'll need enough power to make the surface again.'

'Any ideas what I should do with them?' said Gallen.

'Grab the nearest arm and pull?' said Aaron. 'If we can keep the reactor out of that hole we at least have a chance of retrieving it.'

Hansen brought the Sea Otter downwards from the side of the white sub, and at the last second pulled up in a hover over the right arm and turned the Sea Otter to the glass plate of the white sub.

'Hello, friends,' said the Swede with a ridiculous lilt, and he hit the Sea Otter lights, bathing the cockpit of the white sub in a wall of intense light. 'Now,' he said.

The lights illuminated the Mossad agent they knew as Raffa, and Florita, both of whom flung their arms up to protect their retinas. It looked to Gallen like there was just the two of them—so where was the technician?

Pushing the Sea Otter mechanical arms down, Gallen tried to use the grip to secure a hold on the other sub's arms, to wrench the reactor clear. The first attempt failed. He couldn't see very well and asked Hansen to back up slightly. As Hansen pulled the Sea Otter back, the white sub backed up too, trying to retreat from the situation.

'Get me closer,' said Gallen, as the grips of the mechanical arms came up short.

Electrical engines whining, Hansen surged towards the reversing white sub, its pale blue cargo glinting in the floodlights. The white sub went backwards quickly and its hull hit the mud, throwing up silt into the space between the two craft.

'Shit,' said Gallen. 'Can't see a thing.'

'Down there!' Aaron yelled. 'The reactor's underneath us.'

Pushing the arms downwards, Gallen realised he couldn't make them curve back far enough. 'Back up, Hansen. I need room.'

'You've got thirty seconds,' said Hansen, as he reversed enough for Gallen to train the arms on the reactor.

Bringing the arms down to the right arm of the white sub, he depressed the triggers and watched the articulated jaws close on an arm gripping the reactor, like a massive Meccano set. The left jaw missed but the right one found its mark and the motors squealed and protested as the jaw gripped tight and held.

'Okay,' said Gallen. 'Now what?'

The white sub surged forward, taking the Sea Otter with it, thanks to the solid attachment. They moved at speed, and Gallen watched in horror as they bore down on the caisson edge.

'Do something!' he shouted.

'We don't have the power,' said Hansen, trying to use reverse thrust to pull the arm off the reactor. 'Let go.'

'How?' said Gallen as the caisson loomed to their right.

'Take your hand off the trigger.'

Gallen did as he was told, and the jaws released their quarry. But the latent momentum spun the Sea Otter on its axis even as Hansen tried to reverse thrust it out of the way. As inevitable as gravity, the Sea Otter spun sideways into the lip of the concrete caisson, bouncing off it into the mud.

'Christ,' said Aaron, his panting suggesting he was close to full panic.

Above them the other sub shrieked to the edge of the caisson and they watched in horror as the arms pulled sideways and the reactor simply disappeared from view, dropping silently into the hole in the sea bed.

The white sub reversed back again and Hansen got the Sea Otter clear of the mud, but something was wrong.

'We travelling in a circle?' said Aaron as they accelerated into the deep.

'We lost the main prop,' said Hansen. 'We're travelling on bow thruster power only.'

'Where's the other sub gone?' Gallen peered at the sonar screen.

'Behind us,' said Hansen as the Sea Otter swept in a wide arc, the lights illuminating the stunning emptiness of the Arctic depths.

As they came around to face the white sub, Hansen's tone changed. 'My God!'

The cockpit was suddenly filled with light and as the white sub descended on them they raised their forearms to stop the blast of light into their eyeballs. The Sea Otter shook as it was rammed and pushed backwards.

'It's on top of us,' said Hansen. 'Feels like they have a grip.'

'A grip!' yelled Aaron. 'Why? What are they going to do?'

The Sea Otter was pushed back into the mud, where the two vessels became stationary, the whining and whirring of the electric motors sounding ominous in the rising sediment.

A grinding sound came from the roof and then there was a loud tear and the white sub was reversing away into the black, something hanging from between its articulated jaws.

'What's that?' said Gallen, pointing.

'That's our antenna,' said Hansen, sounding defeated.

'For what?' screeched Aaron.

'For the UQC,' said the Swede. 'That's the radio gone.'

'Can we get to the surface?' Aaron asked.

'I don't think we have the thrust,' Hansen replied. 'It could take four hours with just the bow thruster. We have two hours of air, including the emergency tank.'

'Is there any way we can talk to the *Fanny* on this?' said Gallen, holding the radio handpiece.

'The UQC is an underwater system that relies on the antenna,' said Hansen. 'I can try a morse signal.'

'You do that,' said Gallen. 'How long we got?'

'Two hours on emergency air and about fifty minutes each on BIBS.'

'BIBS?'

'It's a face mask and air bottles—one per person, usually used in emergency decompression.'

'It's like a scuba rig?' said Gallen.

'It's not supposed to be. It only reaches as far as the bottles.' Hansen jerked his thumb over his shoulder.

'If you morse the SOS, will they come?' said Gallen.

'They might.'

Gallen nodded. 'Okay, let's start on that then.'

In the Marines they taught the officers to keep the men's minds busy when death was close. If things looked hopeless, only action of some sort created hope; to let people dwell on the inevitable was to invite madness and hysteria.

'Okay, Aaron,' said Gallen, 'while Hansen's sending the message, you and I are going to find a way to get that reactor out of the hole.'

'We're screwed, Gerry,' said Aaron, his eyes glazing over. 'What does it matter now?'

'Bunch of assholes are gonna blow the Arctic apart,' said Gallen. 'That matter enough?'

'Well, yeah, but—'

'So we're gonna stop 'em!'

Aaron shook his head. 'You're crazy.'

'So God made me American.'

CHAPTER 66

Most of the lights were doused to save electrical power and the temperature had plummeted by the time Gallen decided it was safe to explain his next move. They were wrapped in the rustling foil of exposure bags and Aaron's nose was running freely with the cold.

Hansen had tapped out his morse SOS with the handpiece trigger and they'd picked up some crackling return signals. The traffic had gone back and forth for half an hour and the best Hansen had picked up was *No submersible—Coast Guard close.*

Gallen felt the cold leach into his bones and he wondered where the Israelis had gone, what their plan had been.

The window to make a dash for the surface was gone. They wouldn't have made it anyway but at least they would have been heading in the right direction. Now Gallen had to find a way to raise his idea.

'Aaron, you know about these reactors, right?'

'Correct,' said the American, with a sniff.

'So you'd be able to tell what the Israelis did with the thing and maybe fix it?'

Aaron slowly turned to face Gallen. 'Fix it?'

'Let's walk it through,' said Gallen. 'The Israelis pretend to be environmentalist filmmakers for ArcticWatch; they con their way into Martina Du Bois' little media operation with the intention of ejecting the nuclear reactor, sabotaging its cooling system and dumping it into a large oil caisson where, when it finally malfunctions and melts down, it is guaranteed to bore straight down and cause the utmost damage. If this Gakker . . .'

'Gakkel,' said Hansen, his eyes closed. 'Gakkel Ridge.'

'If this Gakkel Ridge is as volatile and as volcanic as Hansen says, then the reactor burning a hole into it is likely to lift the lid on these super-pressurised gases—who knows what happens to an entire sea floor?'

'Okay,' said Aaron. 'So?'

'So they have to be doing something with the reactor and the technician is obviously their saboteur. When we turned the lights on the *Ariadne Two*, who you see in there?'

Hansen interrupted. 'Glad you mentioned that, Gerry. I counted one man and one woman.'

Gallen smiled at Aaron. 'Annoyed me too.'

Aaron sat up slowly. 'What the fuck are you getting at?'

'Tell him, Hansen.'

'He's saying that the Israelis' third man—probably the nuclear technician—is still in the self-contained security capsule around the reactor.'

'Why would he be there?' said Aaron, now fully awake.

'Where else is he?' said Gallen. 'Ain't on the *Ariadne*. Weren't in that submersible. Yet he went down with the film crew.'

'They left him there?' said Aaron, wide-eyed at the idea. 'Inside the reactor?'

'Wanna find out?' said Gallen.

Aaron shrugged and Hansen fired the batteries.

After two rounds of the sea bed, limping along on the power of the bow thruster, they descended slowly on to the caisson, where Hansen allowed the Sea Otter to rest, balancing on the lip.

'Usually the man in your seat controls the winch,' said Hansen to Gallen, flipping a bank of switches which made a small TV monitor in the ceiling in front of Gallen light up as the downward-pointing floodlights went on.

On the TV screen they could see the concrete tube descending into the gloom, the top of the reactor visible at the bottom of the caisson.

'This is the hard part,' said Hansen. 'Drop the winch hook over the U-bolt, which is maybe thirty metres down.'

Using his left hand, Hansen reached sideways and showed Gallen the winch lever. Grabbing it, Gallen focused on the TV monitor as he let out the hook. It shimmied through the white light towards the top of the reactor.

Tweaking the monitor, Hansen gave Gallen a close-up as the hook got closer. As it landed, Gallen slowed it, but the monitor showed it had landed about eight inches to the bolt's two o'clock.

The electric motors whined and Hansen shifted the Sea Otter slightly. The hook dragged back so it was flopping over the U-bolt. Pulling the winch cable up a few inches, the hook lazily slipped over the U-bolt and broke free.

'Fuck,' said Gallen, lowering the hook once more.

'You're almost there,' said Hansen, peering into the TV monitor.

Gallen breathed through his nose and gently eased the hook down through the illuminated water. Letting it flop on the U-bolt, he then raised it slightly. The thin point of the steel hook touched on the side of the U-bolt and he thought it was going to slide off again. But the torsion of the winch cable made the hook twist slightly and it slipped under the U-bolt as Gallen raised the winch.

Breathing out, realising he'd been clenching his jaw, Gallen pulled back on the winch controller. 'Do we have enough power to raise this?' he asked Hansen.

'No point in saving power now, Gerry,' said the master. 'Where do you want it?'

'On the sea bed, standing upright,' said Gallen, and the Sea Otter started squealing with the strain of lifting the nuclear reactor.

Five minutes later, Hansen put the Sea Otter on the sea floor, the pale blue reactor sitting beside it like an outhouse.

'Now what?' said Aaron.

'We gotta talk to Mr Technician,' said Gallen.

'It muggy in here?' said Aaron, rubbing his neck. 'Or is it just me?'

'Oxygen levels are coming down.' Hansen pointed at the emergency tank gauge. 'Another ten minutes and then we go to BIBS.'

'Can we scan all the radio frequencies?' Gallen asked.

'Only the low frequencies work in water,' said Hansen. 'And even then, that technician can receive but not transmit.'

'We can't have a two-way conversation?'

'No,' said Hansen. 'We do all that with umbilicals.'

'Umbilicals?' said Gallen. 'You mean, like a line plugged in?'

Hansen nodded.

Aaron sparked up. 'The reactor had comms when it was on the *Ariadne*. It must have a plug in.'

They looked out to where the reactor sat in the Sea Otter's lights. If someone was inside that capsule, he was the only chance to correct any sabotage.

'We got a comms line that could plug into that reactor?' said Gallen.

Hansen nodded. 'Sure. We have a line that plugs into the junction box on the top of this sub—it would fit in the box on the reactor.'

'But how are we going to connect them?' said Aaron, who'd unzipped his coveralls.

Gallen wondered about the technician; the Israelis' covert operatives—even the pointy-heads—usually had some military background. Some of Israel's best scientists and engineers may have taught in the universities, but they were attached to the IDF.

He looked at Hansen, whose face was glowing red. 'You got a hammer, or a spanner?'

'Sure,' said the Swede.

'Why not bang out one of your morse signals on the hull?'

'Think the technician will understand?'

Gallen smiled. 'He's sitting in a capsule with a malfunctioning nuke at the bottom of the Arctic Ocean, and his friends have split. I think he'll want to talk.'

'What's the message?' said Hansen, folding down a bulkhead-mounted tool box.

'Try something like: *Mission's over—restore reactor to safety.*'

Hansen crawled forward with a large crescent wrench and looked out one of the four portholes at the reactor capsule. Then he started tapping.

'What now?' Aaron rasped.

'We're gonna work out how to get into that thing,' said Gallen.

Aaron's eyes widened. 'Are you mad?'

'Maybe,' said Gallen, the idea forming as he spoke. 'But that thing's not twenty feet away. Can't just let it blow, can we?'

Aaron looked away, a beaten man. 'We're all gonna die, way down here where no one even knows where we are, and you still want to fight? Shit, Gerry!'

Gallen smiled. 'Like my daddy said: never stay down on the ice.'

'Spare me the hockey homilies. What are we gonna do?'

'If I can get into that reactor, can you tell me what I have to do?'

'Depends on what the technician's done,' said Aaron. 'If they took Negroponte's security card, then my guess is they've made a manual override.'

'To stop it cooling itself?'

Aaron shrugged. 'It's what I would do.'

'How do I undo it?'

'You'll need the card.'

'And then?'

'Do another manual override.'

'And if the card isn't there?'

'We'll need manual override codes, which are probably held in one of the security safes on the *Fanny Blankes-Koen*. I'd say Florita's state room.'

'It would be too complicated for me,' said Gallen, giving Aaron a look.

'No way,' said the spook, realising what Gallen was thinking. 'I can't go out there.'

'I'd be with you, Aaron.'

'No, you don't get it,' said Aaron, eyes pleading. 'I'm phobic. Just the sight of all this water and the darkness—I couldn't do that.'

A big Swedish hand swung back and grabbed Gallen's shoulder.

They all froze: in the silence of the deep, the faintest sound of tapping bounced against the steel hull.

For thirty seconds they waited as Hansen pushed his ear to the hull between the forward-facing portholes.

'He's telling us he wants to get out of there. He wants to know where's the take-off?'

'Tell him to revert the reactor to safety,' said Gallen.

Hansen tapped on the hull with the wrench, a mournful rhythm between two vessels of doomed men.

The taps came back, more urgent than before. 'He says he doesn't have the card. He doesn't have codes for a manual override.'

'Well—' started Gallen, but Hansen's hand went up for silence as another, longer message was tapped out.

Hansen sat back, wiped sweat from his glowing face. 'The meltdown has started. He's roasting alive, the equipment is too hot to touch.'

'Okay, I'm going in,' said Gallen. 'Let's brainstorm a bunch of ideas for the manual override codes. What would a dude like John Negroponte use as the security codes?'

'You think it's his?' said Aaron. 'Why not Florita? It was her baby. Negroponte was the help.'

'Okay,' said Gallen. 'How long's the code?'

'Eight digits, typically,' said Aaron.

'Aren't we overlooking something?' said Hansen, who looked like a man on the verge of angina pectoris.

'Like?'

'Like, there's no divers lock on the Sea Otter,' said the old mariner. 'There's no way out there. Even if there was, there's dry suits and helmets, but no scuba rigs. I told you, there's only the BIBS.'

'Well, I wouldn't tell you how this is going to happen,' said Gallen, looking out at the reactor, seeing shimmers of heat coming off the top. 'We'd have to vote. And it would have to be unanimous.'

'Vote on what?' said Hansen.

'On turning this Sea Otter into the divers lock,' said Gallen. 'We flood her slow, equalise the pressure, and then I go over there with as many extensions on the BIBS as we can find, and I shut that sucker down.'

Aaron and Hansen stared at him like men who'd finally seen a pig fly.

'You want to flood this submersible?' said Aaron in disbelief. 'So we all die?'

'Yes, but we stop that reactor melting down.'

'Holy shit, Gerry,' said Aaron. 'You're not in the Marines now.'

'Well, we'll die anyway, right?' Gallen said. 'We can try to do something, or we can slowly peter out, like goldfish on the carpet.'

'I'm in,' said Hansen. 'I'll get the dry suits and the BIBS. You two decide how to shut down the reactor.'

'Excuse me,' said Aaron, as Hansen crawled aft, 'weren't we going to vote?'

'Thanks for thinking of me, but no need for that, son,' said the Swede as he rummaged. 'I've spent all my life on the ocean—I'm not letting these people blow up the sea bed.'

The dry suit fitted okay and the helmet seemed to have a proper seal. The BIBS mouthpiece only just fit inside the helmet and Hansen sealed the join around the hoses with fast-setting silicon gel and strapped it all down with heavy-duty duct tape of the type used on oil rigs.

The BIBS system usually comprised two hoses that ran from the tanks and met at the regulator dangling in front of the mouthpiece. Hansen had rigged three BIBS hose sets to one another, bolted together at the regulators, giving Gallen a theoretical umbilical of seventy-five feet. They figured it would be long enough.

'So that's it?' said Gallen, peering at Aaron. 'Florita's birth date. We got any back-up on that?'

'That's the best guess I can do on an eight-digit code,' said Aaron, who took occasional puffs on his BIBS mouthpiece.

'And once I'm in manual override?' said Gallen, wanting to get out there.

'A number of square buttons on the control panel will light up red,' said Aaron. 'You push the one that says *Safety reset*, okay?'

'What does that do?'

'It triggers every safety protocol. Even if it senses sea-water

394

inundation, it can shut itself down and self-seal. So don't hit any other button, just *Safety reset*.'

'Got it,' said Gallen. 'I would make a speech, but I've already used fifteen minutes of the BIBS air.'

They looked at each other, knowing this was it. Gallen's legs shook slightly and he tried to clear his head. Stay focused.

'It's been fun,' he said, extending a hand to Hansen, who shook it like a Viking.

'See you on the other side, my friend.'

'Save a seat for me,' said Gallen. 'I drink Millers.'

Aaron stepped up, putting put both hands on Gallen's shoulders. 'Shut that sucker down, Marine!'

'Aye, aye, boss,' said Gallen. 'Let's fill this tub.'

Standing under the main hatch, Gallen controlled his breathing as Hansen opened the valves and a sound started that could have been static on TV or a running brook. The foot wells in the cockpit filled first, rising rapidly as they were all left alone with their thoughts.

The air rasped and gurgled inside Gallen's helmet, the BIBS system not designed for what he was about to make it do. The most likely outcome was the BIBS failing, becoming snagged or breaking, and Gallen drowning before he ever got a shot at the reactor.

The water lapped at his knees and it had risen to Aaron's chin as he sat in the cockpit. The spook turned to look at him; Gallen saw the man's terror—but also a man determined to stay calm as they all went to their deaths. He gave Aaron a thumbs-up and a wink but the face remained unchanged: the light had gone out. Aaron was shutting down with the cold.

Gallen turned his attention back to Hansen, who was going to give him the signal when the pressure inside the Sea Otter equalised with the ocean. The engineer's lights left a strange red glow as the water rose, the incredible cold strapping itself around Gallen's legs and then torso, like a python trying to squeeze the life out of him. He gasped as the water level hit his chest, Hansen and Aaron still alive in the hellish frigidity judging by the bubbles rising from their regulators.

The water level hit the Sea Otter's ceiling and Gallen prayed quickly as the BIBS roared with noise inside the helmet. Looking down into the cockpit, through the red glow, he kept his eyes on Hansen. *Come on, you old salt,* he thought. *Stay alive for another five minutes.*

The cold gnawed at his neck and shoulder blades, and he fought to stay calm. Then Hansen turned, looked at Gallen through the red water, and gave him the thumbs-up.

Struggling with the hatch lock, his arms and fingers almost useless in the cold, Gallen grunted to release the lock and pushed upwards as it gave. Easing up into the blackness, Gallen rested on top of the Sea Otter to pull his extended BIBS hoses through: he wanted them coiled on the sea floor, not getting snagged in all the superstructure on the flat roof of the submersible.

He was exhausted by the time he'd coiled the BIBS hoses on the sea bed and pushed off the roof into the mud. The cold was so taxing on his breathing and muscular control that he almost couldn't think straight, let alone move normally.

Making himself take one step at a time—held to the bottom by a weight belt—he struck out through the mud for the fifteen strides to the reactor, moving like a tin soldier with no leg flexibility. He was dying.

Panting by the time he reached the reactor, he could already feel the heat coming off it. It shimmered like bent light and a plume of silvery water rose above the reactor.

Reaching out, he touched it through his dry-suit mitts. It was hot, but not unpleasant, and he put his other palm on the smooth steel until it was too hot to touch.

There was no ladder on the reactor and the hatchway was on top of the structure. Gallen walked around the reactor and saw the caisson rising out of the mud. Putting his hands over the lip, he pulled himself up to the edge, making sure he didn't tangle the BIBS lines in the process.

Sitting on the caisson, he was now at the level of the reactor's roof. Rising to stand on the concrete, he pushed himself away from the structure and stepped out onto the roof. Heaving for breath as he gained his balance, he felt the heat powering up through his dry-suit-booted feet. He hopped slightly, the incredible cold not enough to combat the heat.

Realising he'd have to act quickly, he kneeled by the hatch lock and twisted. But he was too weak; the water pressure and the cold had already drained most of his strength. Then the heat surged through his knees and into his bones.

'Shit,' he said, leaping back from the reactor and onto the caisson lip, where he windmilled his arms, trying to maintain balance. If he fell in that caisson, that would be it: mission over.

Looking at the Sea Otter, he saw the four front portal windows staring back like a big insect; Hansen and Aaron were behind them, lost in their own reveries and fears.

Regaining composure, he thought it through. He'd have to land on the reactor and twist the hatch lock open in one go. And he'd have to do it quickly because the reactor seemed to be progressing into its meltdown state.

Leaping onto the roof again, he leaned over and summoned every ounce of his strength, both hands straining at the lock as the heat burned into the soles of his feet.

'Shee-it!' he yelled to himself and then, slowly at first, the lock moved and he pulled up the hatch.

Steam exploded out, flipping the hatch back hard and throwing Gallen backwards. Sailing through the illuminated sea, he hit the mud back-first and sank into it.

Struggling against the sediment and the sucking sensation, Gallen sat up, checking his BIBS line with his hands. The sediment swirled around him as he stood, the oxygen still making it to his mouthpiece.

As he climbed back to the lip of the caisson, his motor skills had degraded to the point where he even had to think about breathing and how to use his hand. He was shutting down and even on the caisson he could now feel the heat from the reactor. He swooned, blinking hard to focus.

A body floated out of the reactor's hatch as Gallen stood and readied to step across. The Israeli technician drifted out of the hatchway and into the depths, held aloft as if someone was lifting him by his armpits.

Gallen made it across in one step and felt the heat burning into his feet. Finding the internal ladder, he climbed down into a tiny space that was heated like an oven. It was a space big enough for one man to stand, and there was a small seat that folded down from the wall.

Buttons were arrayed across a dashboard that was set into the dark-grey steel structure of the reactor. The light was dim, coming from a single engineer's bulb, and Gallen was quietly amazed that such a small plant could power a drilling rig.

Making himself shut out the sensation of intense heat and cold, he focused. The code, he thought. He had to start with the manual override code.

There was a panel of numbers arranged like a phone pad and above it was a line of buttons, one of which read *Manual override*.

Taking it slowly, even as he felt his feet cooking, Gallen input Florita's birth date: 08211970.

Double checking on the numbers, Gallen danced slightly to ease the pain in his feet, and pressed *Manual override*.

He waited. And nothing happened. Pushing at the buttons, he tried it again, his face screwing up with pain as the heat etched itself into the soles of his feet.

Still nothing.

Turning, he clambered onto the ladder, but the rungs were hot too. His face ran sweaty inside the helmet and his breathing was ragged. Lifting his G-Shock to his face, he checked the mission clock: eight minutes more of air, and then the BIBS system would be empty.

Think! He had to think.

If it wasn't her date of birth, then what? Did she use a fake DOB? Was Florita even her real name?

He breathed slowly and tried to stay calm. The discomfort in his body was overwhelming him, the cold seeping around his throat and the heat burning into his feet. It was too much.

He racked his brain for clues about Florita; what would she use for a code? What did he know about her? She favoured tailored blouses and she wore perfume that he couldn't identify. Her car was a modest BMW but none of the model numbers would run to eight digits.

As the heat rose again and the reactor made a roaring sound,

Gallen had an idea. Florita's house was on a street in Westmount, Calgary. He tried to remember it; he'd spent fifteen years in special forces having to remember every registration, passport number and endless RV times. He'd trained himself to absorb the details that others ignored or could store in a phone or diary. Gallen, like other recon soldiers, had to memorise everything from a train timetable to a helicopter registration decal and he couldn't write it down on a beer coaster. He knew that if he concentrated, Florita's address was in there somewhere.

Mouthing numbers to himself, he felt like a lobster in a pot. He was cooking! And then it came: her house was on a wide block and the street numbers were 1702–1706.

Sliding down the ladder, onto the red-hot steel again, Gallen turned for the keypad. Punching in the eight digits, he hit the manual override button and the full panel lit up, just as Aaron had promised.

Scanning the buttons, his feet on fire, Gallen saw the Safety reset button illuminated, and hit it. It started flashing. Gallen couldn't remember what to do when the button flashed. Looking at the other buttons, he couldn't see an alternative. The heat pressed in on him and then it happened.

The air failed.

Hitting the Safety reset button again, he pushed out of the hatch and into the cool of the Arctic Ocean. He saw the fading lights of the Sea Otter, knew that Hansen and Aaron must be either gone or close to it. A few last tendrils of air wafted through the demand valve into his mouth, but it was over. Gasping, he let himself drift off the reactor, towards the muddy bottom, where his feet hit the softness and he let himself fall into it like he was landing on a goose-down mattress.

He was cold again and as he felt himself drifting off he thought about his mother and his father and wondered if his marriage might have been different if he'd had kids. His head sang and he was drowning—he shut his eyes and thought about Mindanao, about Basilan Island and how he'd do it differently.

He drifted into sleep and lights came down on him, bright lights . . . from heaven?

A monster who looked like the Michelin Man leaned in on him, pulled him by the shoulders, his light flashing in Gallen's eyes. The monster had a human face . . . Mike? Mike Ford?

He was too far gone: was it a dream? And then he was being lifted, carried up, and there was nothing.

CHAPTER 67

Gallen vomited into the face mask as he was lifted and then he was squinting into the lights and hands were dragging him down, putting another mask on him. The oxygen flowed and Gallen heaved with vomit again, sea water pouring out of him as he was pushed onto his side on the steel grating.

He felt like shit, but he was alive. Panting and looking up, he saw crew from the *Ariadne* tearing his dry suit off and a silver blanket hovering over him. As he tried to sit up, an arm grabbed under his armpits as he dry-retched. He sucked at air and a hand put the oxygen face mask on him again.

Across the divers lock of the *Ariadne*, a yellow atmospheric diving suit was being winched out of the water, a man's face visible in the glass dome.

Another diver appeared in the big watery bay, and the personnel ran to take off the body that he held out.

Aaron!

The body was limp. Gallen felt nausea erupt and then he passed out.

* * *

His jeans and shirt had been cleaned and folded. Pulling on clean thermals first, Gallen wrapped up in flannel shirts and a pair of Wranglers as he watched the blizzard outside the window, pounding through the streets of Barrow, Alaska. It felt good to be back in real clothes.

'No need to get dressed up,' came a voice, and Gallen turned to find Mike Ford and Kenny Winter in his room.

Liam Tucker wandered in, sheepish. 'Hey, boss.'

They shook and Gallen sat on the bed as he rolled on his socks. 'Nice timing, guys. I'm assuming that was you two down there?'

'Mike found the damsel lying in the mud,' said Winter, playing with a cigarette but not lighting it. 'I got to Aaron in the tin can.'

'Hansen?' said Gallen, pulling on his boots.

Winter shook his head. 'Didn't make it.'

'What about that reactor?'

Ford helped himself to gum and offered it around. 'You shut it down pretty good, boss,' said the Aussie. 'The US Navy guys retrieved it about half an hour after we found you but they said it was stable and contained.'

Standing, Gallen took it easy. His balance hadn't been good over the past twenty-four hours. Ford packed the rest of Gallen's stuff and carried his overnight bag as they walked out of the hospital.

Gallen wanted answers as they drove to the airport. 'So you took the *Ariadne* down to us?'

'There was no submersible,' said Winter. 'So this Aussie lunatic starts up about how the *Ariadne* is a submersible, and we're going to the bottom and he's not leaving his team down there.'

Gallen smiled, the first time in a long time. 'How'd the Dutchies go with that?'

'Mike only offered to fight the lot of them, and none of them were up for it.'

'Hah!' said Gallen, feeling better. 'Guess that leaves us with one outstanding.'

Winter sneered. 'Two, if you count payback.'

'Let's find Florita first, okay?' said Gallen as they arrived at the northernmost airport in Alaska. 'Then we decide what we do with our filmmakers.'

The private jet landed in Calgary shortly after eight pm. The Oasis chauffeur loaded them into the Escalade and sped them across the city to the Sheraton Suites. When Gallen was unpacked, he phoned Aaron, who called them into his suite.

There was a bottle of champagne in a room-service bucket when the four of them filed in, but Aaron quickly found them some cold beer. Toasting one another, they tried to joke about the mission and the ill-fated *Ariadne*.

'So, you're NSA,' said Gallen, as he took a seat on a white sofa. 'But you're still VP, security?'

'Guess I am,' said Aaron. 'Which reminds me . . .'

Pulling four manila envelopes from his briefcase, he handed them out. Gallen had a peek: a letter of termination and a healthy cheque.

'We sacked?' he said.

'No,' said Aaron, surprised. 'Thought I'd get you guys a nice payout before the new owners start throwing their weight around. The terminations are valid when you sign.'

'We've discussed it,' said Gallen, enjoying the beer. 'And we intend to complete.'

'Complete what?' said Aaron.

Winter cleared his throat. 'Those ArcticWatch dudes still have our employer.'

'Yes, Kenny, but Florita was under surveillance by the NSA. Her links with the Bashoffs and the secret nuke business . . .'

'Don't concern me, Aaron,' said Winter, flat and non-threatening. 'NSA needs information, just ask. But when someone's under my protection, no one just walks in and snatches her. Not how it works.'

Tucker nodded. 'Damn right.'

Aaron looked at his champagne. 'Well, the FBI is on to this and NSA has a watching brief. So how would it work?'

'Keep us on the books for seven days,' said Gallen. 'Then we sign the documents, take our cheques and go home.'

Aaron looked out the window. 'I was going to resign tomorrow. Been recalled to Washington.'

'You'd rather go back with all the loose ends in the bag, right?' said Gallen. 'It would suit your career to have Florita Mendes in tow.'

'Who says Washington is in any hurry to bring her in?'

'She's obviously an embarrassment,' said Gallen. 'But what if we bring her in anyway?'

Aaron looked at him. 'In that case, I'd be the one bringing her in.'

Gallen looked at his team. 'Suits us.'

Standing, Aaron walked to his briefcase and took a device the size of a PalmPilot from the side pocket, handed it to Gallen. 'Then you'd probably want this.'

The screen showed a map with a dark dot pulsating on a grid.

'What's this?'

'That's Florita,' said Aaron, sipping. 'Whatever else they've done with her, they haven't taken her crucifix.'

404

CHAPTER 68

The flight from Calgary to Wiarton in Southern Ontario landed as the sun rose, almost colourless against the slate-grey of pre-dawn. Chase Lang's Toronto representative—a thickly set Lebanese named Arkie—ushered them into the black Chev Suburban which was left running to keep the heat pumping.

'The gear's all there, in the back,' said Arkie, his Zapata moustache jumping up and down with his furious gum-chewing. 'Chase say you might need a crew also, right?'

'We might,' said Gallen. Surveying the ground he noticed that Wiarton Airport was without prying eyes this time of morning. 'You got 'em handy?'

'Close by, and helo capacity too.'

Gallen nodded slowly. He would like the added numbers but for now he wanted a stealth operation. And he didn't want to be indebted to a major mercenary player like Chase Lang.

'Anyhow, you need a crew, call me,' said Arkie, handing over a card with a single cell phone number on it. 'I got five guys ready to go; ex-special forces and no bad backs. Let me know.'

'Thanks, Arkie,' said Gallen. 'We're fine.'

'You sure?' said the mercenary. 'You are not looking so good in the face, Mr Gallen. Maybe you need the help?'

Gallen laughed. 'Tell you what, Arkie—I get in a bind, I'll call. Okay?'

Arkie shook his hand and moved to the other Suburban parked alongside, hopped in and sped across the concrete apron.

'So, boss,' said Ford, 'we got a plan?'

'How about eggs over easy with a big side of bacon and a mug of black coffee?' said Winter.

'When in Canada,' said Gallen, nodding for Ford to drive.

They consulted the maps while they ate, then drove south for an hour, down Highway 6 as the sun peeked over the horizon, shedding reluctant light and no heat. At Mount Forest, they turned left and drove the back country road east through redneck rural country, populated with F-250s and John Deere tractors and endless tracts of pasture and wetlands.

Asking Ford to pull over near a bridge, Gallen sorted through the bags in the cargo area and found the stick-on sign for the sides and back which said Ministry of Natural Resources, with the Ontario government logo printed alongside. Applying the stickers with Tucker's help, they continued east, turning left onto a crossroad and finding Southgate Road 12 after ten minutes.

Parking the SUV in an overgrown farm driveway, they removed the gear bags and checked their stash. It was all there, including each of their preferred weapons.

Ford pulled out the black nylon bag and quickly assembled the Klepper folding kayak, one of the large three-man versions favoured by the British Special Boat Service.

'Guess you don't need a hand,' said Winter, tiger-striping his face.

'In the Navy they'd make us do this in the dark,' said Ford. 'You get it wrong, you get wet.'

'Only get it wrong once,' said Winter.

After covering the Suburban, they dragged the Klepper to the council drain that ran just off the road. According to the Society of Canadian Ornithologists' map of southern Ontario, the drains through the Grey-Bruce counties of Ontario were the size of decent creeks and were navigable for twenty or thirty miles at a time. That was great for bird watching, thought Gallen, and it might even be useful for a snatch.

Doing a last-minute check with Tucker, Gallen showed him the bridge he wanted him to park on.

'This bridge gives you an excuse to monitor the river,' said Gallen, pointing at the map. 'It might even give you an elevation, let you see the farmhouse.' He pointed at their target. 'But we're going silent for this one, okay, Liam? When I need you it'll be three clicks on the radio. Then you come in hot.'

'And if I think they've spotted you in the creek, I give three clicks?'

'Got it.'

The Klepper slipped along the creek, which meandered across wetlands and pastures, under bridges and through culverts. After twelve minutes, Gallen checked the homing device and realised they were close by. Carrying the kayak over a large beaver dam, they paddled for another five minutes and found themselves at the back of a farm.

Stealthing onto the river bank they dragged the Klepper under bushes and checked their weapons. They glassed the ground, which sloped up gently across three paddocks to the farmhouse, set off slightly from an old ramp barn. Each paddock was bordered with cedars and ash, giving them cover as they moved.

Looking at his G-Shock, Gallen yawned: 7.41 am.

'Single file, boys,' he said. 'Kenny, your lead.'

They jogged across the paddocks, uninterested cattle chewing as they closed on the blind side of the barn, hidden from the house. Small patches of snow lay under the trees and Gallen could feel the cold through his jacket.

They crouched behind a pile of old lumber sixty feet short of the barn, heaving for breath as Gallen checked the homing screen. Using the magnify option, he looked closer.

'I don't think she's in the house,' he said.

'Where?' said Winter.

Gallen pointed at the barn.

On the far side of the barn, three horses walked to the top rail of the fence and looked over at them. Lying as flat as they could, the men waited for the nags to lose interest: if any of the kidnappers were farm people, they'd immediately see the horses' attention had been caught.

'Why can you never get a horse focused on any damn thing, until they take an interest in precisely the wrong thing?' said Winter, lying under the lumber. 'Fricking nags got a brain like a pea.'

After five minutes, Gallen raised his head and saw the rail was empty. Getting to their feet, they closed on the barn via the horse yards. Peering through the gap made by the horse door and the upright, Gallen saw an empty line of stalls inside. Gently, he slipped his knife up the gap and slipped off the latch that was holding the door from the inside.

Letting themselves into the cold barn, they moved along the empty stalls, the breeze making a loose piece of ceiling flap slightly. The homing signal said she was close by.

Rounding the corner, Gallen looked down the main lane of the barn, horse stalls leading off it. The smell of burning emanated from somewhere and Gallen stealthed to the first stall. Nothing.

At the second stall, he opened the door and looked in, pistol raised. The smell was coming from a burnt-down brazier. Florita Mendes lay on a bed of straw against the far wall.

Gallen made to move and Florita shook her head, wide-eyed. Gallen froze, and looked down. A few inches from his shin was a filament line that ran across the doorway and up the wall. Gallen saw where it ended: a frag grenade taped to the ceiling.

Gallen mouthed, 'Where are they?' and she responded with a pointed finger. Leaning back, he caught Winter's eye. The Canadian had seen Florita's signal and he and Ford moved softly down the lane of stalls to where an office sat at the end.

Holding his breath, Gallen waited until Ford stuck his head out of the office with the thumbs-up. Winter came out wiping his blade.

Regrouping, Gallen whispered, 'I think we can make the snatch, take her out in the boat.'

'Sounds good,' said Winter.

They cut Florita loose and walked out of the barn the way they'd come. As they crossed the horse yards and made to jog across the fields back to the Klepper, a shot sounded. They turned. The shot had come from the direction of the house, but it sounded further away. More shots sounded.

'Get eyes,' said Gallen, pulling Florita back into the lee of the barn.

Winter got his binoculars free and had a look. 'Shit,' he mumbled. 'Looks like they got Liam pinned down.'

'Okay,' said Gallen, pulse thumping in his head. 'Mike, get Florita to the boat, retrace back to the RV. Can do?'

'Got it,' said Ford, grabbing Florita by the elbow and dragging her into the horse paddock.

Winter and Gallen checked their weapons for load. 'Wanna just rush 'em?' said Winter, screwing a suppressor onto his SIG 9mm.

'Let's finish it,' said Gallen, falling in behind the Canadian as they set off across the lawn that separated the barn from the house.

Gunfire was still coming from the other side of the house. They jogged to the front door and Winter stamped it down. Gallen brought his suppressed handgun up to a cup-and-saucer grip and turned left into the kitchen where the pistol spat twice, the brass hitting the floor louder than the shots. A woman fell to the boards.

Swinging back, Gallen watched Winter stalk into a living room, where a sliding door opened onto decking. They walked through the door and onto the deck where Winter put two shots into a gunman's face before ducking back to join Gallen at the ranch slider door.

'Two shooters, assault rifles,' said Winter as bullets tore into the ranch slider and the wall they were hiding behind.

Gallen brought his rifle to his shoulder, put two bursts of three-shot at one of the shooters and thought he hit a leg as the man dived behind a tree.

Another shooter emerged from the same maple tree and fired at Gallen, the remains of the ranch slider exploding as Gallen hit the floorboards.

Winter leaned against the frame of the destroyed sliding door and slid a grenade into the launcher. He fired at the branches of the maple tree and they watched the leaves scatter and the trunk split as the grenade went off, making the man they knew as Raffa run from his hide for another tree.

Gallen got a bead on the injured man and shot him in the chest as he tried to let more fire go at the house.

Jumping off the deck, they tracked Raffa until they saw the Israeli camped behind the fourth tree in the line. The Mossad man fired at them again and then came an empty click: dead man's hammer.

Gallen watched as Raffa discarded the assault rifle and switched to his handgun. Diving to the cover of trees as the handgun levelled, Gallen was too slow and felt the slap of a 9mm slug in his left shin bone. Gasping with pain as he hit the grass, Gallen sucked air, trying to beat off unconsciousness.

'You okay, boss?' said Winter, joining him behind the tree. More shots came in, ripping the bark off the maple.

'It's a leg wound,' said Gallen, stars at the edges of his vision. 'But it got the bone.'

'I think that's a Glock,' said Winter. 'You counting his shots?'

'I have twelve,' said Gallen. 'If he's got a standard clip, he's got three shots in the can.'

Winter took off his shirt, draped it over his rifle barrel, and pushed it out, making it dance like a puppet. Three shots came in, one of them taking the shirt off Winter's rifle.

Standing, Winter took his time showing himself. Gallen raised himself to one knee, but couldn't put his weight on his left leg.

The Israeli leapt from his hide and aimed-up at Winter. 'So, the famous Kenny Winter finally comes into the open?' he taunted.

'Pity to waste it,' said Winter, pulling a smoke from his jeans pocket and lighting it.

The Israeli fired but all that happened was a loud click. Gallen watched him discard the weapon and fish a military Ka-bar knife from the small of his back. He started circling the big Canadian, his muscular body bulging out of the Levis and black jumper.

'You gotta be careful with those,' said Winter, keeping his chest pointed at the Israeli. 'Those Ka-bars are sharp, dude.'

'You and that redneck Gallen,' said Raffa. 'You really chased us all the way out here? Are you fucking mad?'

'Mad enough to get even,' said Winter, exhaling a plume of smoke into the early morning air.

'Leave it, Kenny,' said Gallen, gasping with pain.

'I don't know why you bothered,' said Raffa as if Gallen didn't exist. 'You know who she is?'

'Who?'

'Mendes, idiot!'

'Oh, her,' said Winter. 'She signs the cheques. Did I pass?'

'You're a smartass, Winter,' snarled the Mossad man. 'Why don't you drop that rifle, see what happens when you're not assassinating lawyers and bankers? Anyone can shoot an office guy.'

'Didn't know the Mossad was using cattiness as a weapon these days,' said Winter. 'Although it suits you, Raffa.'

'Come on!' yelled the Israeli. He was in a crouching stance, knife in his left hand. 'What are you scared of, tough guy?'

'Clowns,' said Winter, 'and grown women with pigtails.'

'Fuck you,' said the Israeli, rushing at Winter, who sidestepped the attack, dropped his rifle and picked up his shirt, wound it over his left hand.

'Leave him, Kenny,' said Gallen, finally getting to his feet and limping towards them with his SIG. 'I'll finish him.'

'No, you carried enough weight, boss. I've got this.'

Raffa lunged again, this time with more caution, clearly realising that although Winter was a big guy he had some athletic balance.

They wheeled and circled, Raffa looking for the opening, but none came. Finally, Raffa lunged and pulled back and Winter stepped forward quickly, kicking the smaller man in the chest and knocking him onto his back. Then Winter pounced, grabbing the knife hand as he came down on the Mossad man and throwing a fast left elbow into the man's teeth, stunning him. As Winter lined up a head-butt, the Israeli leaned away and struck at his attacker's eyes.

Gallen struggled to keep his feet, the SIG now trained on the two men who rolled across the grass, the knife still firmly in the Israeli's grip.

Winter emerged from the melee with a lock on Raffa's knife wrist, which he turned into a quick inside elbow. It knocked Raffa's chin upwards and made the Israeli drop the knife.

Training his SIG, trying to keep his eyes focused, Gallen watched as if in a dream. Grabbing the Israeli by the hair, Winter slapped his massive right paw on Raffa's neck. A cry of anguish echoed around the farm as Winter's grip tightened, his thumb crushing the throat.

Gallen could make out the dying plea from the Israeli as he was choked. 'We're professionals, please.'

Swinging Raffa's head like he was wielding a bowling ball, Winter cracked it into the trunk of a maple tree in one suddent movement. Raffa's body went slack and he collapsed like a sack in the grass, the broken neck finally finishing it for him.

Winter turned. 'Sorry 'bout that, boss,' he said, as Tucker pulled up in the Ford. 'Forgot myself for a minute.'

'Don't matter,' said Gallen, gasping for breath to stay conscious as the pain from his shin pulsed through his body. Letting his legs give out beneath him, Gallen fell to the grass before Winter could make it to him. More than four years of special forces combat gigs, and never taken a bone shot, thought Gallen as Tucker moved towards them. And now here he was, taking lead for some oil executive.

Tucker stumbled. And then Gallen could see why: he'd been pushed. Behind him was a large man in a black field jacket, holding a submachine gun.

'Shit,' said Gallen, recognising the gunman from three weeks earlier, outside a meeting in Kugaaruk.

'Well, well,' said the thug in a strong Russian accent. 'It's the funny man, don't give his name when asked.'

'Fuck me,' muttered Winter, his hands slowly rising.

'Oh, you're fucked alright,' came an American voice.

Turning his head to his left, squinting to focus, Gallen felt the air expel from his lungs and his jaw drop. The man in front of him had his left arm in a sling and a patch over his left eye. But his dark hair was still receding and the Annapolis ring was where it always was.

'Mulligan?'

'The thing I love about Chase Lang?' said the spook, pallid as the sun tried to warm up the morning. 'His vests are genuine Kevlar.'

CHAPTER 69

The farmhouse kitchen was warm and the body left by Gallen's shot had been dragged out, leaving a smear of blood on the timber floor. The Russian tested the coffee pot with his hand and poured. He'd duct-taped Gallen's and Winter's wrists to their ankles.

Wincing at his shoulder injury, Mulligan eased back in a Mennonite chair, waiting for the coffee to be placed in front of him. Through the windows Gallen saw other gunmen roving around the farmhouse.

The coffee steamed and Mulligan turned on a fake smile. 'So, Ace—where's Florita?'

Gallen shrugged. 'What you want with her?'

'Mind your business.'

'You made it my business, Paul,' said Gallen, his leg aching despite the painkillers. 'Remember?'

'I remember bringing you in to run a personal security detail for Harry Durville,' said Mulligan, picking up the coffee. 'Nothing in there about Florita Mendes.'

'I got promoted,' said Gallen.

Mulligan laughed at that. 'Here's my deal, boys. You return that woman to me now, this morning, and I fly away into the sunset, leaving you here with sore wrists.'

'Or?' said Gallen.

413

'I don't make threats,' said Mulligan. 'You know that.'

Gallen thought quickly, avoiding looking at Winter. They had a few seconds to get this right and no margin. No second chances if Mulligan sensed a trick.

'She's with my guys,' said Gallen.

'So tell your guys to bring her,' said Mulligan, smiling like a lizard. 'You're just a soldier, Gerry. No heroes, right?'

'Right, Paul,' said Gallen, wanting to punch the guy. Gallen and Mulligan had once been in a pre-op briefing in the Khost region of the Ghan: Mulligan was the spook from the Pentagon, Gallen was running the men. To end the briefing, Gallen had given his customary sign-off of 'No heroes,' and Mulligan had laughed.

Mulligan opened his hands. 'So get her back. Time is money, Ace.'

His mind spinning, Gallen tried to think through the fog of the Tylenol 3 tablets. The shock of the bullet wound had turned into an all-body pain.

'Gimme a minute, okay,' he said, his eyelids drooping. 'Can I get a glass of water? I'm not feeling well.'

He tracked his brain backwards in time like a computer programmer looking for a piece of data while the big Russian got the okay from Mulligan. He used his old tricks of memory—tricks you used when you carried every piece of information in your head, when RV coordinates and exfil call signs had to be totally accurate, when chopper registrations mattered and secure-burst radio frequencies had to be right first time, because you only got half a second to use them and you didn't want them flying off into space when you had tired and wounded men to lift out.

'Okay,' he said, after the Russian had tipped the glass of water into his mouth. 'How do we do this?'

Mulligan nodded at the Russian. 'Viktor has a phone. Tell him a number and then call your men back. And do it nice, Gerry, like you mean it.'

'Call them back to be killed?' said Gallen, shaking his head. 'You're confused, Paul. No man of mine ever took a bullet for me, and I'm not going out with that said about me.'

'Make that two of us,' said Winter.

Mulligan's shoulders sagged and he looked out the window. 'Does everything have to be so honourable with you people?'

'How it works,' said Gallen. 'How else you gonna get men to go out there, get blown up by Towelie while people like you drink Scotch in the officers' mess?'

Mulligan fixed him with a sarcastic look. 'Okay, *Captain*. Your boys get to live. Now give Viktor the fucking number.'

Gallen watched the Russian walk towards him, cell phone in hand. His mind spun to the recesses of his memory and he was ninety per cent sure he had the number right, having only looked at it for two seconds as he'd pocketed the card.

Looking up, he started the number with 5-1-9 and rattled off the rest, trying to make it sound like a number he'd phoned many times.

Viktor kneeled beside him and put the phone against Gallen's ear. The ring tone was agonising and cold sweat seeped out from beneath his short fringe.

The number connected: a woman called Mae, in the supermarket in Dundalk.

'You're all thumbs, Viktor,' said Gallen, avoiding Winter's eye. 'Get it right this time.'

Viktor looked to his boss, and Mulligan nodded.

Gallen tried the same number with the last two digits swapped. His throat was sandpaper dry as he felt Mulligan's eyes boring into him. This was it—if he couldn't produce Florita, they'd be tortured and fed to the pigs.

The ring tone droned and after four rings it was answered. 'Yep,' came the man's voice.

'Arkie. Gallen here. You got a minute?'

Gallen looked into Mulligan's eyes, trying to ignore the confused pause on the end of the line as Viktor leaned closer to the handset. 'Yeah, so Arkie, turns out I sent you away too quick—I need you after all, and I need the girl back here too.'

Arkie's silence was profound, at least giving Viktor nothing to go on.

'I need you here in half an hour, something's come up.'

Fast Arabic flowed on the other end of the line—Arkie issuing orders.

'Yeah, same place we did the snatch,' said Gallen, nodding at Mulligan. 'Yeah, yeah—I know, buddy. But there's later flights to LA, and you're getting paid, last I heard.'

'You okay, Mr Gallen?' came the Lebanese accent down the line.

'What the fuck's it doin' in the truck?' said Gallen, shrugging for Mulligan's benefit. 'Whole generations of people got by without a GPS, know that, Arkie?'

Gallen rolled his eyes. 'If you're on Highway 6, do a U-turn, come back south through Mount Forest, go left at the lights and down eighty-nine, remember?'

Gallen leaned away from Viktor, who was getting too close. 'Yep, that's it buddy—left at twenty-two, right at twelve, fast as you can.' He nodded at Viktor, who brought the phone up to his own ear while Gallen gulped at a dry throat. Turning to Mulligan, Viktor nodded— the call had seemed legit.

'Arkie left his GPS in the truck,' said Gallen, shaking his head at Winter.

'City boy,' said the Canadian. 'Couldn't find his pecker in his shorts.'

Gallen's leg wound had stopped bleeding by the time Mulligan walked into the kitchen and ostentatiously looked at his watch.

'You told me an hour, Gerry,' he said. 'We had a deal.'

'I said an hour at best,' said Gallen. 'What's your end in this anyway?'

'Just business,' said Mulligan, playing with his BlackBerry.

'You working for the Russians?'

'Just looking after an investment interest, Gerry. Just like you were at Oasis.'

'I don't get it,' said Gallen.

Mulligan smiled. 'A certain Russian family has a big investment in Florita Mendes. They can't have her squealing to the spooks in DC.'

'That was it? You were minding Florita?'

'Until that drunken idiot Durville kicked me out—yeah.'

'Who were you working for? Reggie?' said Gallen, trying to put it together.

'No.' Mulligan shared a laugh with Viktor. 'No, Gerry. The man who pulls Reggie's strings. The man who runs ninety per cent of the liquor imports into Russia—one of the world's biggest oil barons.'

Gallen shook his head but Mulligan stared at him with that inane smile. 'Shit,' said Gallen. 'Ivan Bashoff?' He couldn't help it, he started laughing. 'Holy shit, Paul. The crown prince of Pentagon spooks is working for a Russian gangster?'

'Call him what you like,' said Mulligan, not liking the professional taunt. 'He's going to control the world's largest oil and gas field within the year.'

'And he makes the world's smallest nuclear power plant, is that it, Paul?'

Mulligan gave Gallen a quick look. 'You're one of those soldiers who think too much, Gerry. Coulda had a better war without that to carry round.'

'But I carried it.'

'Like a load in your shorts,' said Mulligan, making Viktor snort with laughter.

'I love all the spooky shit, Paul,' said Gallen, wondering if the phone call had worked. 'Makes you sound important. But chasing down Ern Dale's case? Shit, you just wanted that twenty-eight million.'

Mulligan's face changed, he cleared his throat. 'I never had a problem with Ern Dale, and believe me when I say that I'd never cross the hard-ons he worked with in the Pentagon—it's not in my interests to eat their lunch. You want that twenty-eight, you go ask a certain hockey defenceman from Saskatchewan. What I hear.'

Gallen turned to Winter, who didn't take his eyes off Mulligan.

'Tell him the truth, Mulligan,' said Winter.

Mulligan sniggered and reached for his cigarettes. 'You're hardly in a position to—'

'I said tell him, Mulligan.' Winter's voice was low and mean, like a blizzard howling against the barn boards. The change in tone made Mulligan gulp and Viktor shifted his body weight.

For three seconds the atmosphere was electric and Gallen had an insight into why Kenny Winter had been such a brutal player on the ice, and such a notorious enforcer in Afghanistan. He exuded a power beyond the physical.

'I never lied to you, boss,' said Winter, finally taking his murderous eyes off Mulligan.

'About what?' said Gallen. 'What is this?'

Mulligan lit a smoke. 'It's about a greedy assassin who grabbed twenty-eight million dollars and ran. Didn't think to share with his superiors.'

Winter shook his head, kept his eyes on Gallen. 'I was doing a job. Certain people in the Pentagon think I took the money.'

'What was the job?' said Gallen.

'A Taliban conduit in Pakistan—a trucking dude.'

'Trucking?' said Gallen, old cogs starting to turn.

'The spooks had him turned, promised to bring him out.'

'Yeah?' said Gallen.

'I was supposed to end it for him,' said Winter. 'It was a CIA double-cross—they didn't want his story going to the New York Times. But at the last minute the story changed and the head shed says, He's got twenty-eight million stashed somewhere—let's snatch him, torture the money out of him.'

'That never happened,' spat Mulligan. 'You soldiers gossip too much.'

Gallen ignored him. 'What happened?'

'I wasn't equipped for a snatch, so they sent a Force Recon unit to escort him out of the Taliban zone. But they couldn't steal the money because he was protected by someone in Washington, who'd already been promised a cut of the twenty-eight.'

'His name was Al Meni,' said Gallen softly. 'A trucking millionaire and an al-Qaeda conduit to the Taliban.'

'His name was Youssef Al Meni,' said Winter, nodding slowly.

'He had a much younger wife and three children,' said Gallen. He had never spoken of the night.

'They weren't to be touched—only Youssef,' said Winter.

'They rode with me in the back of a HiAce van, locals driving,' said Gallen. 'I promised them they were safe.'

'They had a safe route into the Marjah compound,' said Winter.

'But the route was changed during the op,' said Gallen. 'We were ambushed. One of my guys—young kid fresh out of Pendleton—was killed before he could lift his rifle. Joe Nyles lost his leg to a homemade grenade. When the shooting was over, the wife was dead, kids in shock and Al Meni gone.'

They looked into one another's eyes, Gallen's nostrils flaring with anger. Was it possible? Was that terrible night engineered by a bunch of spooks for the sake of money?

'You?' said Winter, eyes narrowing. 'It was your unit?'

'Sure,' said Gallen. 'So you're telling me it was our guys pulled that shit? Ern Dale was involved?'

Mulligan sighed. 'Can you girls stop this for three seconds and tell me where Florita is?'

Gallen barely heard him. 'Who made the call, Kenny?'

'Code name Bellbird—never met him but apparently he called everyone Ace.'

'Okay, okay,' said Mulligan, holding his hands down for calm. 'Gerry knows the answers to this. I called it, okay? End of the Vincent Price mystery hour.'

'You fucker, Mulligan,' said Gallen, straining at the duct tape. 'You don't pull that crap on the US Marine Corps.'

'I was executing an order, Gerry,' said Mulligan, looking at his watch. 'You think the Ghan was all about you? Think it's all about Silver Stars and homecomings in Shitsville, Wyoming?'

'It was about duty,' yelled Gallen, tears welling up from God knew where. 'What is it about you pen-pushers that you don't get that?'

'Shit, Gerry, you're breaking my heart,' said Mulligan. 'Point is, here we are talking about twenty-eight million dollars, and I don't have it. Ern Dale's people thought Kenny had it, and I have no reason to doubt that.'

'That's bullshit, Mulligan,' said Winter.

'Really?' said Mulligan. 'Only other guy close enough was Gerry.'

They looked at each other, Gallen heaving with anger.

'You're wrong, Paul,' said Gallen, as he calmed down.

'About you having the money?'

'No,' said Gallen. 'The point isn't money—the point is duty.'

'Can't live on duty,' said Mulligan.

'Tell that to a soldier who's seen action,' said Gallen, 'and he'll know you were never there.'

The first shot cracked the window with a small tinkle and hit Viktor in the forehead. As the big man collapsed on the floor, Mulligan stood and flattened himself against the wall, pulling a black 9mm pistol from a hip holster.

Gallen struggled with the ties around his wrists as automatic gunfire sounded around the farmhouse. Windows smashed, a man yelled out in pain and voices barked at one another. Lebanese voices. Gallen's call had worked—Arkie's crew had arrived.

Mulligan took a quick look through the shattered window and swore. 'On your feet, Gallen. We're going for a walk.'

'Not going anywhere with Viktor's gift-wrapping,' said Gallen.

Duck-walking to a briefcase, Mulligan pulled out a set of flexi-cuffs and crouched to Gallen's position. Locking Gallen's wrists in place with the flexi-cuffs, Mulligan used a small pocket knife to slice the duct tape from where it was wrapped around his wrists and ankles.

'Up,' said Mulligan, gesturing with the pistol in Gallen's face.

Another bullet hit the kitchen wall above the sink and Gallen groaned in pain as he got to his feet, his shin now throbbing and not wanting to take any weight.

'Keep down, Kenny,' he said, as Mulligan pushed him out of the kitchen and into an internal passageway. Opening what looked like a broom cupboard, Mulligan revealed a set of narrow stairs into the cellar.

Hobbling down the stairs into the musty basement, starbursts of pain in his eyes, Gallen looked around at a blue-grey furnace and a stack of beer crates. At the far end was a concrete ramp that rose to a trapdoor.

'Move,' said Mulligan, slapping Gallen over the head with his pistol. 'You disappoint me, Gerry—we had a deal.'

Gallen climbed the ramp and waited for Mulligan. He wanted the spook to climb the ramp and put himself in range of a kick—maybe he could knock him on his ass, take the weapon and turn the tables. But Mulligan gestured to Gallen to slide the bolt himself.

Reaching above his head Gallen slid the internal bolt with both hands as the gunfire abated.

'Now push it open,' said Mulligan, and Gallen pushed up with his manacled hands, forcing the left-side trapdoor over. Light flooded onto them and Gallen stepped up further: the entrance came out behind a water tank and a wood pile.

Mulligan joined him in the cold air as Gallen saw a man he didn't recognise run towards the farmhouse. Mulligan shoved him in the back and Gallen limped towards the barn, his left foot now virtually dragging along the gravel, the agony roaring throughout his body.

They got to the barn without being seen and Mulligan forced him upstairs to the hay mow. As Gallen looked around, Mulligan shoved him again and his leg wouldn't take the weight. He collapsed against an old square hay bale, which looked tiny compared to the large round bales stacked along the back of the mow.

'I don't have Florita,' he gasped, reaching for his shin but too scared to touch it.

'No kidding,' said Mulligan. 'So who's out there?'

'My guys,' said Gallen, his voice a thin rasp.

Mulligan peered through a gap in the boards. 'Two F-250s and at least five operators. You don't have those numbers, Ace. So who'd you call?'

Gallen gasped. 'I called God, you asshole.'

'Fuck you, Gallen,' said Mulligan, pressing the barrel of the pistol against Gallen's forehead. 'I gave you a deal for Florita and you pull an ambush? On *me*?!'

Gallen's eyes rolled as the pain overwhelmed his senses. He could barely think. Above him he saw the workings of a barn like the one he grew up with, stacks of round bales along the barn wall and the old hay gantry running the length of the pitched ceiling, a hundred feet in the air. Looking around he realised he was sitting on the loading platform of the mow, and in the corner of his eye was a loop of hemp rope tied to a cleat in a basic horseman's hitch. If this barn worked the same way as Sweet Clover's, that rope was the hay gantry tie-off.

Mulligan cocked the action on his pistol. 'I go down, you go down, Gerry. You got that, you fucking redneck hillbilly?'

Smiling, Gallen looked his killer in the eyes. 'Us hillbillies, we got one thing going for us.'

'Last words, Gerry.'

'We know how a hay mow works.'

The spook squinted in confusion as Gallen reached behind his right shoulder and slipped the pulley rope from its tie-off. The pulley block hanging just below the ceiling held a six-hundred-pound round bale aloft; released from the tie-off, it descended a hundred feet with a whir of rope, slowing only as it crushed a man who didn't know how a hay mow worked.

As the bale bounced in front of Gallen and rolled away, a thickset Lebanese man scoped the hay mow with his assault rifle and turned back to Gallen.

'Arkie,' said Gallen, weak. 'My instructions worked?'

'No, you can thank Chase for that,' said the smiling mercenary. 'He tracks all his vehicles with RFDs.'

CHAPTER 70

The blonde woman who smiled too much put the coffee on the desk in front of Gallen and left the observation room. He picked it up and sipped as Aaron Michaels adjusted the sound volume in the room. Behind the one-way glass in front of them, Florita Mendes spoke in relaxed but articulate sentences with two NSA spooks who'd been interviewing her for the past hour and ten minutes.

'Like I said, Aaron,' said Gallen, feeling his shin itch beneath the cast. 'I'm not hearing many discrepancies here.'

'Yeah, she's pretty clean,' said Aaron. 'But I don't want to cut an immunity deal and be embarrassed by it.'

'I guess not,' said Gallen. He'd been in Washington for a week and had spent his own day with the National Security Agency's WMD team, of which Aaron Michaels seemed to be one. He'd been asked to sit in on the Florita sessions and pick the lies or the half-truths in her story and they were now into the third day of the interview. But he wanted to be back on the farm helping Roy, and he didn't like sitting behind one-way glass. He felt like a pervert.

'And by the way, Gerry,' said Aaron, as Florita rolled her eyes and told the investigators she'd already answered the question four times about her commercial relationship with ProProm, the Russian company making the nuclear power plants. 'I'm sorry about those questions concerning Harbour Light Inc.'

'Harbour Light?' Gallen couldn't recall the name.

'You know: Chase Lang's company? It was your good fortune being rescued by those special forces guys.'

'Oh, that,' said Gallen. 'I have nothing to hide. I don't know Arkie's full name and I don't know why Chase is operating an Arab crew in North America.'

'They were out of line,' said Aaron of the investigators. 'They know Ahmed Masri—they just wanted to see how you knew him.'

'Why don't they haul Chase Lang in here?' said Gallen with a smile.

Aaron smiled back. The CIA and the Pentagon used people like Chase Lang for off-the-books weapons and deniable crews. Washington investigating Chase Lang and Harbour Light was as likely as a real inquiry into Halliburton's military base pricing or the actions of Big Oil in west Africa. It wasn't going to happen.

'So, I'm out of here?' said Gallen, trying to stand but wincing at the pain in his leg.

'Sure,' said Aaron. 'Anything I can do for you?'

Gallen thought about it. 'You can tell me.'

'Tell you what?'

'What was Oasis Energy about? I mean, really?'

Aaron laughed and put his hands on his hips. 'In simple terms?'

'Sure.'

'Okay. An aggressive Canadian oil explorer with one truck and three employees makes a find in Alberta when he's nineteen years old. He sells the lease to Chevron and soon realises that if he'd kept the lease and drilled it himself, he'd have made twenty or thirty times what he made by selling the lease.'

'Harry?'

'That's him,' said Aaron. 'So this young Harry's in a hurry. He attracts a secret source of capital and with his next find, builds his own drilling and pumping infrastructure and gets real big, real fast. After decades of doing this, the Berlin Wall comes down and suddenly the race is on for Arctic oil—the race to control the sea floor of what could be the source of our hydrocarbons well into the twenty-second century.'

'So where does Ivan Bashoff come into this?'

'Bashoff is a gangster who has bought into Russian oil and gas but he knows that the Russian government won't ever let him get too big. So he helps Reggie Kransk set up the Transarctic Tribal Council, basically incorporates it and waits for a big North American fish to bite—a big, greedy fish that thinks it can control Arctic oil by controlling indigenous territorial interests.'

'They made Florita their agent?'

'They made her an offer,' said Aaron. 'You heard her interviews— we'll help you become the CEO of Oasis, and if you do, you can have three per cent of the stock.'

'They honoured that?'

'Sure did,' said Aaron. 'It was sitting in escrow before Harry was killed. Florita's a lawyer, remember.'

'Why blow up Florita, if she's your agent?'

'The Bashoff clan didn't, and neither did Reggie's council,' said Aaron. 'We think it was the Israeli crew. They don't want that oil field opened up, especially not with US interests in it.'

'Which is the part I don't follow,' said Gallen.

'Harry Durville's secret financiers, way back in his early twenties? Probably our friends in Langley, arranged through all sorts of nominee funds, controlled by lawyers and accountants all over the world. The Bashoffs thought their merger with Oasis gave them control, but the Israelis knew better. They knew that merger put Washington right in the middle of Arctic oil.'

Gallen nodded. 'And if we're up there, why would we bother with the Middle East?'

'If you see it from Tel Aviv's perspective, it makes sense.'

Behind the glass, Florita stood up and left the room.

Aaron offered Gallen a handshake. 'One final thing, Gerry.'

'Yep?'

'Would you mind dropping in to the cafeteria on your way out, buy a Sprite or something?'

'I got nothing to say to her.'

'So, let her do the talking.'

Gallen smiled, shook the hand. 'I'll see what I can do.'

Florita was sitting on her own at a Formica-top table, chewing on a sandwich and reading the *Washington Post*, when Gallen started feeding coins into the drink machine. She waved him over and he collected the can, took a seat.

'Hi, Gerry,' she said. Gallen noticed a few extra lines around the dark eyes, and a paler face than he remembered. She was still good-looking, but tired.

'What they got you for?'

'Oh, nothing,' she said. 'What about you?'

'Interviews about the *Ariadne*, the nuclear power plant, the Israelis, Harry Durville, Reggie,' said Gallen, ripping the tab on his Sprite. 'Basically nothing.'

Florita laughed, her teeth flashing briefly. 'Actually, me too.'

'They told me you were working for the Bashoffs, the Russian crime family. That ain't true, is it?'

She looked at him, begging for understanding. 'I did nothing wrong, Gerry. They wanted me in the CEO's chair because they liked my ideas and I wanted to push the nuclear power angle—it's the way of the future. In ten years they'll be amazed that someone could have been arrested for it, called a terrorist.'

'I see . . .'

'And I had no idea Harry would be killed. Harry was going to hand over to me anyway. And besides, I was on the same plane that got bombed. Remember?'

'I remember.' Gallen didn't have the heart for intrigue. The fact that Aaron and his friends were listening made him feel creepy and he decided to end it. 'Anyway, it was nice meeting you, Florita,' he said, standing with pain. 'I hope it works out for you.'

Florita looked down at her hands. 'You're not going to tell me off?'

'For what?'

'Doing it for the money.'

Gallen grinned. 'I did it for the money too, Florita.'

'You know what I mean.'

'I wanted to stop the bank foreclosing on my family's farm. So I took the gig.'

A tear ran down her cheek. 'You did all this to make up a few mortgage payments?'

'That's about it.'

She sniffled as she shook her head. 'That's so . . . so . . .'

'We all have our reasons,' he said, not hating her. 'We all need a creed.'

'I did it for the money, Gerry. I'm talking about four hundred million dollars.'

'Must be nice.'

'You're walking around with a bullet hole in your leg; your guys risked their lives to save me in that snow. You're not angry about that?'

'No, Florita,' said Gallen, turning away. 'It's what we do.'

CHAPTER 71

Colorado's spring sunshine poured out of clear skies. Gallen sipped on a cup of beer as he watched a man on a black stallion stumble through a jumping round, already with too many penalties. The program for the Douglas County No More Snow event listed the next rider as Yvonne McKenzie, on Peaches.

'She's up,' said Gallen to Yvonne's daughter, Lyndall. 'Next rider.'

'She's going to be so good, I just know it,' said the child.

Sitting on the other side of Lyndall, Kenny Winter leaned forward on his seat. 'I'm liking our mare, boss,' said the Canadian, jiggling his legs as the struggling rider made more mistakes. 'There's nothing out there Peaches can't do with her eyes closed.'

Roy arrived with a tray of beers and a lemonade for Lyndall. The announcer gave the score to the previous rider as the rails were replaced, and then he announced Yvonne McKenzie.

When Peaches stalked into the arena, all plaited and dandied up, Winter stood and made a long shepherd's whistle, making some of the champagne picnickers turn and stare. Gallen stayed seated, feeling something he hadn't experienced in a number of years. His chest relaxed, the anger evaporated and he smiled.

He was feeling pride.

* * *

Yvonne sipped on her third beer, her second-place cup sitting on the picnic table in front of her, her hair loose now that she'd taken the pins out. The giant beer tent was filled with horse lovers and the barbecues were churning out steak and potatoes.

'And you, Mr Gerry,' said Yvonne, smiling at him like she used to at high school. 'Old Roy's just given me the lecture about you and me.'

Gallen blushed. 'Tell him to shut up. Whatever he told you is wrong or a lie.'

'He had a theory, that an old dog's better than a young wife.'

'Shit, Dad!' Gallen called across the tent to where Roy was in the middle of a conversation. 'I'm sorry about that—he knows better than to talk that way.'

Yvonne pushed her hair back. 'So old dogs and young wives, huh?'

'Yeah, well,' said Gallen, not wanting to get into it, especially knowing that Lyndall was nearby.

'Well?' said Yvonne. 'What's the difference?'

Gallen could sense Winter turning away, abandoning him. 'It's nothing, just Marines humour.'

'Gerry Gallen isn't scared of a little joke is he?' she teased, sipping at the beer.

'Okay, but it depends on who you ask.'

Yvonne frowned. 'So it's not a joke?'

'No, I've seen thousands of answers in latrines all over the world,' Gallen said, before clearing his throat. 'Sorry, ma'am.'

'Tell me one.'

He hesitated. 'It's more a male thing, you know?'

'Don't be shy,' she said, resting her chin on her hand.

'Okay,' he said carefully. 'An old dog never asks for more than you got.'

Yvonne spurted beer and laughed. 'You men!'

Winter turned and joined in. 'When an old dog shits on you, he don't need no lawyer.'

Gallen leapt in again. 'An old dog will let a sleeping man lie.'

'An old dog don't cost you more than you earn,' said Winter.

Yvonne laughed so hard she cried, and when she recovered she had her hand inside Gallen's arm. 'It's good to be back, Gerry,' she said.

'I'm starting to get that,' said Gallen, smiling. 'Just starting to get it.'

They were interrupted by a commotion at the bar. Looking over, Gallen saw Roy in the centre of it. Hobbling across the trampled turf on his busted leg, Gallen forced his way through the throng and finally got to his father, who was handing out trays of beer and whisky to the bar.

'What are you doing, Dad?' said Gallen, trying to keep his voice down.

'Shouting the bar, son,' said his father, smiling ear to ear. 'Everyone! This is my son, Gerry. Fought for this great country!'

The freeloaders raised their drinks and the roar went up.

'Dad, stop it—we can't afford this,' Gallen said, turning to the bar manager and gesturing a throat-slit with his finger.

'Yes we can,' said Roy, fishing something from his pocket and handing it over.

Opening it, Gallen saw a Wells Fargo Bank receipt from an ATM located on the back of a truck outside the tent.

'So what?' he said, trying to get his father moving away from the bar.

'Read it,' said Roy, pointing at a group of people and nodding at the barman for more drinks.

Looking again, Gallen saw the farm account and then the balance. 'There must be a mistake,' he said, heart speeding up. 'We're not fifty thousand in the black; we're seven hundred thousand dollars behind. You been messing with the line of credit?'

'There's no mistake, son,' said Roy Gallen, the booze making him smile for the first time in a long while. 'I just called the bank—it was deposited yesterday. There's no mistake.'

Backing away from the growing crowd of free drinkers, Gallen wandered back to Yvonne's table, stunned as he read and reread the ATM receipt. And then something occurred to him.

'Yvonne,' he said, eyes darting around the beer tent, 'you seen Kenny?'

'I saw Mr Kenny ten minutes ago,' said Lyndall. 'He said goodbye to me over there.'

Gallen followed her finger to the tent entrance. 'Goodbye? What did he say?'

'He said stay in school, go to college.'

Limping on his aluminium crutch to the entrance, Gallen exited into the warm dusk, searching for his friend. Dust hung in the air as Chevs and Fords hauled horse trailers out of the Colorado Horse Park. There were too many people, but Gallen moved as fast as he could with the procession.

After three minutes he stopped, the pain too much to keep walking. Sweat poured down his back as he heaved for breath. There was no chance of finding Winter—the man had simply disappeared.

As Gallen turned around for the beer tent, he saw something on the other side of the road: a white straw Stetson and an old Carhartt jacket with worn elbows. Kenny Winter was leaning into the passenger side of an old Chev Silverado, and then he was opening the door.

'Kenny,' yelled Gallen. The Canadian didn't hear him, so he tried again, feeling weak and hoarse.

The white Stetson bobbed up and then that impassive cowboy face was staring at him across the traffic on the South Pinery Parkway, chewing slowly on gum.

They stared at one another for three seconds. There was too much to say and not enough time. So Gallen just lifted the ATM receipt and yelled, 'Thank you.'

The Canadian stared and then saluted. The Silverado's door slammed and the old truck found a gap in the traffic and headed east.

An old man disturbed his thoughts. 'Looked to me like you got yourself a first-class salute there, Mister,' said the old fellow. 'Officer are you?'

'No, sir,' said Gallen, the dust making his eyes water as he watched the truck disappear. 'I'm a farmer.'